HUNTED

Quantum Twins Series

RIPPED APART
HUNTED
BETRAYED
REBELLION

HUNTED

QUANTUM TWINS

ADVENTURES ON TWO WORLDS

GEOFFREY ARNOLD

Copyright © 2016 Geoffrey Arnold
The moral right of the author has been asserted.

Apart from any fair dealing for the purposes of research or private study, or criticism or review, as permitted under the Copyright, Designs and Patents Act 1988, this publication may only be reproduced, stored or transmitted, in any form or by any means, with the prior permission in writing of the publishers, or in the case of reprographic reproduction in accordance with the terms of licences issued by the Copyright Licensing Agency. Enquiries concerning reproduction outside those terms should be sent to the publishers.

This is a work of fiction. Names, characters, businesses, places, events and incidents are either the products of the author's imagination or used in a fictitious manner. Any resemblance to actual persons, living or dead, or actual events is purely coincidental.

Matador
9 Priory Business Park,
Wistow Road, Kibworth Beauchamp,
Leicestershire. LE8 0RX
Tel: 0116 279 2299
Email: books@troubador.co.uk
Web: www.troubador.co.uk/matador
Twitter: @matadorbooks

ISBN 978 1785891 854

British Library Cataloguing in Publication Data.
A catalogue record for this book is available from the British Library.

Printed and bound by CPI Group (UK) Ltd, Croydon, CR0 4YY
Typeset in 11pt Goudy Old Style by Troubador Publishing Ltd, Leicester, UK

Matador is an imprint of Troubador Publishing Ltd

ACKNOWLEDGEMENTS

My continuing thanks go to my supporting team. Cecily Wheeler who types the stories the Twins tell my whilst we're on holiday, my editor Judith Henstra, Caroline Swain who proof reads and copy edits, and although this is 'self-published' I have a publisher - a great team at Matador. Anna Langa who built the framework for the Twins new website and steers me through all that techy work. Stephen Ling and Pegggy Driscoll who read the books and give me invaluable reader advice and suggestions. Through it all there is my wife who gives me the space and the time it takes on holiday and then at home, and the interest and support of friends and family.

HUNTED

Welcome to The Story the Twins have told me. They do not consider this to be a work of fiction.

PRINCIPAL CHARACTERS

VERTAZIA
Qwelby & Tullia (15) their father: Shandur, mother: Mizena
Tamina (girl 16) & Wrenden (boy 13) sister & brother
Pelnak & Shimara (boy & girl 15) the not-twins
Shandur's Great Uncle Mandara (Gumma), Great Aunt Lellia (Gallia)

Ceegren, the Arch Custodian
Xaala (girl 16), his acolyte
Rulcas (boy 16) Xaala's side-kick
Dryddnaa, a Chief Readjuster (Psych or Psi Doctor)

FINLAND
Hannu Rahkamo (15), father: Paavo, mother: Seija
his girl-friend:
Anita Keskinen (15) father: Dr Viljo, mother: Taimi

Miska Metsälä, Suojelupoliisi (SUPO) Finnish Intelligence Service
Chief Inspector Penti Harju
Sergeant Piia Sjöström

KALAHARI
The Meera Tribe
Tsetsana (11) father: Milake, mother: Deena
Xashee, her 16 year old brother
Tomku, their 4 year old sister

Nthabe, their 7 year old sister
H'ani (boy 17)
Kou-'ke and Nlai, 16 year old girls
Mandingwe & N!Obile, 12 year old girls
Ghadi, tribal chief
Kotuma, his wife
Xameb, the Shaman
Xara, senior hunter
Tu, a healer

Police
Inspector Modisakgosi
Constable Ditau

RAIATEA
Professor David Romain
Drs Miki & Tyler Tamagusuku-Jefferson

PRONUNCIATION

The various San languages all use a variety of what are termed 'click' sounds. There are a lot. Wikipedia says forty-eight for Khoisan – which is a group of languages. When I was with the San I was told that the various tribes in Botswana use about twenty, but an individual tribe may use only eight or ten.

The sounds are indicated in several ways. Some by ordinary letters or combinations such as X, Q and Ts, ordinary symbols such as "˙" and "!" and special symbols such as ☉ and ǂ which would look odd in the story. There is no universal agreement on usage, so I have been able to keep to ordinary symbols for people's names.

Tullia learnt these in Ripped Apart.

X Imagine the way the English say 'Gee up' to a horse, a click at one side of the mouth, usually the noise is made twice. The X is pronounced with that sort of click made at both sides of the mouth at the same time.
Ts A normal Ts movement but with the tongue pressed hard against the back of the top teeth and pulled sharply away. The sort of 'tsk' sound someone makes in a 'tut tut' expression.
! An explosive sound made with the tip of the tongue pulled from the top of the palate. A sort of 'tok' sound – without the 'k'.
' A glottal stop – made by closing and reopening the back of the throat quickly.

ꞌ A single 'gee up' click.
ǁ Half way between ǃ and Ts

MAKGADIKGADI Pans National Park, is easy to say if you use the letters as normal. I'm not going to try and translate the letters k, d and g into "clicks". I lost a lot of bottles of beer betting that I would – eventually – get the pronunciation correct!

BACKGROUND

The Twins' ancestors left their homeworld of Auriga a very long time ago as their sun was turning into a white dwarf. Not wishing to interfere with the lives of other sentients, they sought an uninhabited planet.

Although Aurigan life started in the solidity of the third dimension, they needed to find a world close to a Galactic centre in order to provide the high energies necessary to support life in the higher dimensions through which Auriganii progressed during their long lives.

The Space Ship they used to search for a new homeworld was a massive sphere. The centre of that existed in the third dimension and contained the Seed Generation, with the inhabitants of the higher dimensions through to the eighth surrounding that in successive layers.

Those Auriganii who existed as pure energy beings in the ninth dimension, often well over two thousand turns old, provided a vibrational cloak that enabled the entire HomeSphere to travel faster than light.

After a long period of unsuccessful searching close to Galactic centres, they were surprised to meet extreme hostility as they explored several successive planetary systems. The fighting forced them well away from the Galactic centre and left the Auriganii so weak that they took refuge in the first solar system they entered without opposition.

A brief stopover on one planet showed it had insufficient resources to support a growing Seed Generation. Reluctantly, because of a small and varied population of sentient inhabitants, they finally settled on the third planet from the sun, which they named Azura Yezi, the Blue Planet.

There, they settled in many places. Around an enormous lake in a fertile valley that lay between two continents, on islands and mountains, and always keeping a distance from the several tribes of hominids. They intended to resume their search for an unpopulated planet when they had restored their strength. That was seventy-five thousand years ago.

Then, fifty-two thousand years ago, some of them started to mix with members of one particular tribe and several of the Aurigan bases effectively became the ends of transdimensional bridges between the third and higher dimensions.

As with all youngsters, the Twins had been taught that there had been a terrible war amongst the inhabitants of the third dimension twelve and a half thousand years ago which caused the planet's crust to shift, an ice age to end and the seas to rise. Several of the Auriganii's bases sank below the seas, one big island became covered with ice and eventually they had to leave their last mountain base.

The tragedy, which became known as The Great Schism, was a vibrational energy separation whereby two parallel worlds came into existence, with the Seed Generation becoming trapped in the third dimension. Following the separation, the Auriganii gave their part of the two parallel worlds a typical name in the complexity of their three dimensional language.

The one word meant: 'A temporary home on half of the Blue Planet, carrying with it the implication that in the future we will rejoin what are now two separate races back into one.' As use of the original language was lost over time, that word became Vertazia and the inhabitants Vertazianii, which they shortened to Tazii.

Similarly, the original Aurigan name for the parallel world on which the Seed Generation was trapped became Azura – or Earth as it is called by its inhabitants.

Originally, those Auriganii inhabiting the ninth dimension had all one hundred percent of their DNA active. Following the separation, the whole pattern of Auriganii progression was disrupted and their DNA degraded rapidly. As a consequence they lost their ability to exist in the eighth and ninth dimensions.

What are now the Tazii have managed to retain three active segments out of their original twelve and are thus restricted to living in the fifth dimension, although they can leave their bodies and travel in the seventh. The active DNA of the mixed race – homo sapiens sapiens – has reduced to less than half of one segment.

Extremely limited communication is still possible between the two worlds through the shared fourth dimension of consciousness, that is via dreams and trance states.

Cave Art in France, Spain and South Africa shows that such communication via trance states has been going on for at least thirty-seven thousand years.

Since the inhabitants of Earth started transmitting pictures and sounds by satellite, the Tazii have learnt a little of current life on Earth. A very confusing little as, so far, the Tazian experts say that they are unable to translate any of the Earth languages because what slips across dimensions through unpredictable space-time rifts is an incomprehensible muddle.

The Twins were hurled away from Vertazia when they interfered with an experiment being conducted by their Great-Great Uncle Mandara, the Arch Discoverer.

CHAPTER 1

ALARUM

FINLAND

Qwelby fought the sharp vibration that was bringing his mind to the edge of consciousness. Every fibre of his being craved rest – and sleep.

The vibration increased in intensity.

Alarum!

With a mental groan he focussed his awareness into drawing his Self together, slowing his vibrations and morphing into his fifth dimensional Form.

Impossible images were being beamed into his receptors. Spaceships of the attacking Solids had materialised just outside the third dimensional core of the HomeSphere. Three hundred kilometres in diameter, that inner sphere housed the Aurigan Seed Generation, Seeders as they were called. Space-suited bipeds were storming through what should have been an impenetrable barrier.

Even as Qwelby forced himself into the skinergy suit that would help him slow his vibrations right down to the level of the third dimension, a hole was blasted in the core's perimeter. Several space-suited figures were blasted away into space before the secondary force fields shut off the outflow of atmosphere.

A small spaceship swept through the breach. Rocket motors fired. Before it had completed touchdown on the wide expanse of grass and killed its jets, humanoid figures leapt out, all clad in camouflage combat suits. The bright lights shining from their space helmets made them look like every child's image of bug-eyed aliens.

They ran forward, opening fire on the few Aurigan warriors who had already positioned themselves behind a ridge in the ground just beyond the edge of the village. The attack faltered amidst confusion as the leading invaders fell to the ground without any indication of weapons having been fired, or any signs of injury.

Several of Qwelby's wing of DragonRiders were still with the healers, recovering from their injuries sustained in what they had considered to be the successful defeat of the latest attack from the nearby planet. As those fit for duty linked mentally, he ordered them into three groups. Eight warriors with himself to take positions at the edge of the village, another eight on the right flank where the country was wide open and the remaining four to the left, behind a bend in the meandering river.

It was with hearts in their mouths that the warriors translocated into the core. What use would spears, swords, bows and arrows and short-range stunguns be against the invaders' long range, projectile-firing weapons?

Qwelby's senses were flooded as he landed. The small spaceship had gone but another was sliding in through the breach, where a lot of movement was taking place. To his front was the thin line of warriors using the slight ridge for cover. Beyond them was the small group of invaders. Apart from some movement as the enemy dragged back several unconscious bodies, all was still. He saw his Riders taking up their positions, and sensed the fear and panic behind him amongst the Seeders who were sheltering in the village.

Unnoticed by the Riders, two of the attackers rolled over the far left end of the ridge and continued rolling down until they were on a level with the defenders. Rising up, they levelled their weapons at the unsuspecting Auriganii.

Shrieking a mental blast at the attackers, followed by a wide cast warning to the Riders, Qwelby leapt forward. Over three metres tall and with his seventh dimension energies flowing through his third dimension form, he was upon the enemy before they had recovered from the shock to their brains. Hissing through the air, his long sword swept around and a bug-eyed helmet was flung into the air, leaving a headless body standing, seemingly waiting for the next blow.

Qwelby's back swing severed the head of the kneeling soldier as he swung around. The gun chattered and Qwelby was knocked over by hard blows to his side and shoulder. Grimacing with pain, he thanked the multiverse for the good misfortune that had knocked him over as a hail of bullets hammered into the crest of the ridge and others flew over his head.

Images reached his mind. He was to run back as his men covered his retreat with flights of arrows. Keeping low, he dashed back and flung himself to the ground at the corner of a building. Wincing with pain he turned to assess the battle.

A bright flash of light alongside the newly arrived spaceship caught his eye. He just had time to shout a warning before the solid projectile landed on the front line. A split second later it exploded, flinging an Aurigan warrior into the air along with the dismembered parts of another.

As his eyes cleared from the sting of the dust, he saw a figure run forward and kneel by the wounded man. She! Firing a barrage of bullets, a group of invaders leapt to their feet and rushed the forward defensive line.

Calling for a covering volley of arrows and once again keeping low, Qwelby leapt to his feet and sprinted towards her. She, the preeminent healer of all, his people could not afford to lose her. His angry thoughts at her stupidity burst forth as bullets hammered on his raised shield. Rescuing a wounded warrior was a warrior's duty, not hers.

Her reply of a swift image: he doing his job of fighting and she her job of healing, stung him with its tartness.

With gritted teeth he held back the thought that one day when there was peace, he was going to tell her how much he loved her, in spite of her stupidity. He denied that really meant "because of her unquenchable spirit."

As he reached healer and warrior, his mind took in the absence of enemy fire. Peering around his shield and over the ridge, he saw the cause. Not only was the ground littered with bodies from which protruded long arrows, several soldiers were reeling around, screaming and trying to cover with their hands the places where arrows had pieced their suits, letting in what had to be the core's deadly atmosphere. He smiled grimly as he acknowledged how battle effective were the Seeders' simple hunting weapons.

Picking up the wounded man, Qwelby threw him over his shoulder and ordered the healer to take her place in front of him. They got up and raced back to the shelter of the village as more arrows whispered overhead.

Reaching shelter, Qwelby put the man down with a grunt and shook his head as the healer looked at him, her purple orbs framed by pale blue ovals.

Leaning his uninjured shoulder against the building's wall, he swept all his senses across the battlefield, noting with dismay the number of enemy spreading across the terrain, the equipment they were setting up and the arrival of a larger spaceship alongside the smaller one.

There was another bright flash. Monitoring the trajectory, he realised it was going to hit the top of the building where they were sheltering. He stepped back and lifted his shield up to cover the healer and her patient and, in a vain attempt to protect himself, raised his sword over his head.

A stone struck his shoulder with a thud, followed by a second thud as another struck his head and he pitched forward into darkness.

That noise came again. Two thuds. Qwelby jerked awake. Where was he? A healing room? Why this thick cover made of a strange material? There was light to one side. A bright patch of light. A figure was standing in it. A doorway. The figure was short and wide. Not an Aurigan. Attacking solids!

Qwelby tried to roll off what he assumed was a medcouch as he reached for his stungun. With his feet tangled in the heavy covering and his hand sending objects crashing off the side table, he fell to the floor and threw off the covering. The figure in the doorway turned towards him. In stark silhouette, Qwelby was unable to see any detail, but knew the Solid had to be holding a weapon in the hand he sensed moving in his direction.

Thank the stars these solids are so slow, he thought, as no laser beam pierced the darkness. He launched himself at his attacker, grabbed the Solid's outstretched hand and the two of them crashed to the floor. Light fell on a face. The thought that he knew that face stopped Qwelby from wrenching the Solid's shoulder out of joint.

'Yeow!'

'Uhnk?'

'Shit! That hurt.'

'Hannu?' Qwelby asked, as he sat up and let go of the hand.

'Yeah. Too damn right,' Hannu said as he sat up. 'What the hell's going on?'

Qwelby heaved a sigh of relief as he got up and offered his friend a hand. 'I was on the HomeSphere. I thought you were a Solid. Attacking.'

'Solid?'

'People like you who live in the third dimension. Huh. And now me.'

'Bad dream?'

'No,' he replied in a tone of wonder. 'Timeslipping through past .... memories. When we lived in higher dimensions and our... bodies were... flexible.' Qwelby's shoulders slumped. There was so much to explain. 'Effects from last night.'

'Yeah. Last night. You promised.'

'Later. All together.'

'Aw, come on Qwelby,' Hannu wheedled as he sat on the bed and put an arm around his alien friend. 'At least tell me what your twin's like, how she got here and why... well...' Hannu had seen a tall, naked and beautiful young woman in his alien friend's arms, impossibly bathed in sunlight in the pitch black night of the snow filled woods. Then she had simply disappeared.

'Irritatingly bossy. Wants to be a healer. Seventh dimension. I was there with her at the same time. On Mars in a hollow on a bare mountaintop in bright sun. She'd been absorbing the sunlight and the mountain's strong energy.'

'But what's she like,' Hannu insisted.

Qwelby's shoulders slumped. 'When we restore our full mental connection I'll take you to meet her,' he said in a sad voice.

'Yeah. That'll be good,' Hannu said, knowing how real the experience was when his alien friend thoughtwrapped them, as he termed his vivid descriptions. 'Come on, let's get dressed and go to Anita's,' he added as he got off the bed and switched on the light as he left the room.

Missing the warmth of Hannu's arm around his shoulders and thinking of his twin, Qwelby was swamped by a flood of emotions. Sadness that they were still apart. Anger as he blamed himself for not having ensured they were reunited. Pride that he had fought well against heavy odds and saved his twin's life. And determination.

His homeworld had always been full of peace and harmony and totally non-violent.

Until last night.......

If he had to fight his way to his twin, and then back home..... he would. To succeed he needed her support – their twinergy.

CHAPTER 2

LITTLE SISTER

KALAHARI

Tullia awoke feeling comfortable and warmly snuggled, arms wrapped around her.... not her Comfort Doll but Tsetsana! Horrified, yesterday's feelings ripped through her. The fear of the vicious fight in the seventh dimension and the heart-rending pain as her beloved twin was wrenched from her arms. Even now the inner pain was far worse than the cuts and bruises all over her body.

Pouring all her emotions into a Comfort Doll was fine. That was what it was for. But not another human being! It would have been bad enough had it been Tamina with all her Tazian energy skills. But this lovely, eleven-year-old girl! How much damage had she done?

Tsetsana stirred. Her lips curled into a smile as her soft brown eyes gazed adoringly up at Tullia. 'You all right?' she asked.

'Me? Err.... yes. But are you all right?' Tullia asked, slipping inside her friend's mind to look for signs of disturbance.

'Mmh,' Tsetsana murmured as she frowned in concentration. 'I'm still sleepy but feel more awake than ever. Inside, I mean.' She blinked her eyes several times. 'You hurting last night. Give me lots of energy. I feel.... different. Nice.' She grinned. 'Like Little-Sister,' she added, savouring both what her Sun Goddess friend had called her yesterday and that she had intuitively understood the three words spoken in Tazian.

Tullia sighed with relief, more at what she had mentally detected than the words. Thanks be to the Seven Sisters, she thought to herself. She has not absorbed my negative emotions but received the power. And what a powerful outpouring that was! She has more than just "The Sight".

Tullia lowered her head and kissed Tsetsana on the lips, just as she would her BestFriend Tamina. Then gave a little gasp as she remembered the reaction when she had briefly kissed Xashee, Tsetsana's sixteen-year-old brother.

Tsetsana giggled. She had come to accept the strangeness of being a guide and teacher to the tall and beautiful young woman who the whole tribe considered to be the daughter of the Sun Goddess. Happy to reassure Tullia, she reached her hand up and placed her small fingers on Tullia's lips. 'Okay for girls to kiss,' she said with a smile.

Why not girls and boys? Tullia thought. That made her think of her twin, and that took her back to earlier the previous evening when she had lain with him wrapped in her arms and blood from his many wounds trickling over her. Her heart had gone out to him. Never before had she felt like that. It was more than confusing, the depth of her feelings for her twin puzzled and worried her.

And there was the violence - from her own world! She was a healer and able to channel far more power than ever before. Yet to return home it appeared they would have to fight against their own people. She could not face that prospect. It was a betrayal of all she believed in. She would rather remain living with the Meera, as long as the two of them were together.

CHAPTER 3

BRUISES

FINLAND

The twins had grown up on a parallel world that was a haven of peace where the people were extremely reluctant at any thought of contact with Earth, which they saw as riddled with appalling violence. Yet the previous night, New Year's Eve, when Qwelby had been captured and had called out to his twin in his desperation, the result of their meeting had been a vicious attack from their own world. His mind was still buzzing with all that had happened.

He relived the joy at having held her in his arms and then the pain when they were ripped apart. Knowing that he loved his twin more than anything in the world – two worlds – was a revelation. He wished Tamina was there. She was nineteen months older than them and loved Tullia. She might help him understand some of the new feelings he was having. Those for his twin were especially confusing. It was as though they had been bound together forever. Identical genes, identical inheritance, yet they were a boy and a girl.

'*QeïchâKaïgiï*,' a voice whispered in his head and took him back to his memory of the healer's face. On unsteady feet he got up and stood in front of the mirror. The twins were just over fifteen years old and one metre eighty-five tall, with broad shoulders and slim hips. He looked into his eyes – the slanted ovals of pale blue and large, purple orbs. Their eyes. The healer's eyes. A colouration that was unique on Vertazia except for the one previous pair of Quantum Twins centuries ago.

His twin was set on becoming a healer, but he had no idea of what he wanted to do with his life. Becoming a Dragon Rider, even though nowadays only for peaceful purposes, would mean being ostracized by most of Tazian society.

An image flashed into his mind. He and Tullia had been visiting family who worked with the Shakazii in their principal homeland they called Tembakatii. In the far distance the twins had seen three dragons lift above a hill, circle around and dive down in an arrowhead formation. There had been something chilling about the screeches of the dragons faintly carried to them on the breeze. Their aunt and uncle had explained the incident as a practice for an event, leading the twins to infer a future Shakazii festival. Hearing the dragons' cries again, Qwelby was certain that was not the complete truth and that dragons and riders had been hunting.

The cuts on his body were healing well, but now it was a mass of ugly bruises, the pattern of dark yellows and greens on his reddish brown skin looking like some out-of-the-world body camouflage.

A soft knock on the door went unnoticed.

'You're not ready!' fifteen-year-old Hannu exclaimed as he opened the door. 'Shit, man! You're one big bruise!'

'Tell me!'

'You've grown,' Hannu said, giving his friend an appraising look. 'You're a bit taller than you were, and... well... more muscular. And somehow, I don't know, bigger, older. You could easily be eighteen.'

'Last night...'

'Yeah! Right!' Hannu exclaimed. 'Get dressed. We're all going round to Anita's for brunch.' He smiled at the puzzled look on his friend's face. 'That's breakfast-cum-lunch.'

CHAPTER 4

BRAIDS

KALAHARI

Once again feeling relief, Tullia cuddled the smaller girl to her. So much was happening, so many new feelings flooding through her, she wanted at least to thoughtshare with Tamina. Nearly seventeen, Tamina was her elderest. Shortly before the twins had left Vertazia, she had achieved her Awakening. Tullia had been aware of her elderest having been unusually moody and preoccupied for a while and a distance had sprung up between them.

After the actual Awakening had happened, Tamina had not wanted to talk about it. Tullia had not been concerned as her own Awakening was not likely to happen for another eighteen months, so she had plenty of time to find out what happened.

Now, with Tsetsana's head nestled against her breasts, Tullia recalled the previous night. Seated around the family's small fire, four-year-old Tomku had said, 'You sad, Tully,' and had climbed onto her lap to comfort the bigger girl. Discovering that she enjoyed the role of big sister, Tullia had chuckled. Compared with the much smaller Meera she was indeed a "big" sister.

Tullia knew that Awakening was the first step for both girls and boys in the process of the body preparing itself for the creation of children. For girls, internal physical changes similar to those producing an Azuran girl's first period, but without the actual period itself. For boys, the emergence of their reproductive organs. And for both, the first stirrings of sexual feelings.

She also knew that it would be several years after that before her body would be able to produce an egg when she wanted a child. That was so far in the future it was irrelevant, yet with Tomku on her lap, new feelings had stirred. Deep within, they were warm and nice. In her body, they were unsettling. Yet at one level they were not new. All very disconcerting.

Her thoughts were interrupted by the sound of scratching on the edge of the entrance. Although much larger than the huts used by the Meera, the guest hut she occupied was constructed in the traditional manner of dried grasses with a low, arched entry that could be closed by a blanket.

Although the nights were cold, Tullia never bothered to close the entry. She liked to see the morning sun shining into the hut and the position of the sunlight on the earthen floor of the hut was important. It helped her to keep a check on the recalibration of her own internal clock to the shorter Azuran diurnal rhythm.

Looking up, Tullia saw seven-year-old Nthabe, another of Tsetsana's sisters who had come to check on them. She nudged the girl in her arms, who groaned and tried to bury herself in Tullia's embrace.

'Stomach hurt,' Tsetsana mumbled. 'Happy. But hurts.' Lifting her head to look at Tullia she tensed for a moment, screwed up her face, gave a wan smile and added: 'Soon gone.'

Apart from giving Tsetsana a sympathetic squeeze, Tullia made no comment. She naturally assumed that her friend's discomfort was due to her body adjusting to the changes brought on by Tullia's outpouring of energy during the night. Just as she assumed that her own discomfort in that region of her own body was due to the battering she had taken from the vicious fighting the previous evening.

Washed and dressed, they joined the family for a breakfast of milimili, which Xashee said tourists called African Porridge. When they finished eating, Deena, the children's mother, said that several of the older girls had asked her to ask Tullia if she would allow them to braid her hair.

'Oh, yes please,' Tullia replied, excited at a sign of being accepted as a girl and not an untouchable goddess. 'But I think I want to keep it long,' she added, as all the Meera women wore their braids tight to their heads.

'Oh, yes, Tullia. You'll look like a Himba. They're big and red,' Tsetsana said. 'But that's from using ochre,' she added dismissively.

CHAPTER 5

CLUES

FINLAND

It was late on the morning of New Year's Day by the time that Qwelby and the Rahkamos joined the Keskinens at their big kitchen table and were tucking into generous helpings of porridge, whilst the sight of lingonberries on the table and the smell of eggs and black sausage cooking promised the delights to come.

The two sets of parents were a contrast. Hannu's father, Paavo Rahkamo was tall, big and solidly built. The senior engineer at the Muurame ski centre, he was a practical, placid man, his skin tanned from all the exposure to the elements. Shorter than average, his wife Seija, was a homely woman with a build best described as motherly. Anita was Hannu's girl-friend. Tall and slim, her parents, Viljo and Taimi Keskinen, looked like the typical image for Scandinavians. All six Finns shared the same blonde hair and had the inevitable rosy cheeks from the cold.

When they had finished eating, Qwelby kept his promise. Once again his almost musical, rich baritone carried his listeners into his experiences as he told the full story of what had happened the previous night when he had been held at knife-point by Arttu, the leader of the thieves, and Hannu and Anita had seen Tullia in his arms, impossibly bathed in sunlight in the dark, snowfilled woods of Finland.

Hannu was swept into the action. He was there, not alongside Qwelby, but he was Qwelby. He was a magnificent dragon, fighting fierce inhuman beasts and slavering wild-eyed dogs. He flew. From high up he saw a beautiful winged, silver and gold unicorn about to be carried away by an evil beast. He dived down and grabbed the monstrosity in his massive talons as he swept past. He heard Tullia's screams and felt her pain as the beast's claws were ripped from their hold on her back. Landing, he turned back into a boy and held a beautiful girl in his arms, pressing her naked body against his bare, sweat soaked torso.

Pain ripped through Hannu as a great landquake split him away from Tullia.

Anita was terrified. Attacked from all sides by an evil that had no shape or form, she was imprisoned in the body of a winged unicorn. Yet she fought and with hooves and horn she beat back all the attackers until a great evil beast settled on her back and she felt its many claws digging into her flesh. She heard the beating of mighty wings as a dragon swooped down and screamed as the beast's claws were wrenched from her skin and blood ran down her body.

The dragon landed and Qwelby was there, wrapping his arms around her and pressing her naked body against him. Her cuts no longer hurt now that her beloved twin was in her arms.

Pain ripped through Anita as a great landquake split her away from Qwelby.

There was a long silence when Qwelby finished talking, broken only by the sound of heavy breathing.

'She loves you so much,' Anita whispered to Qwelby.

Hannu wanted to strike the alien for having held a naked Anita. Trembling, he calmed himself as Qwelby turned to face him with a startled look on his face. A picture shot through Hannu's mind of himself having held a naked Tullia. He felt Qwelby's anger so strongly that it made him rock back in his chair and stare at his grimfaced friend who was breathing heavily.

'That was so real,' Taimi Keskinen said. 'I felt I was there, watching, both here in Finland and wherever Tullia is.'

The other adults started commenting and the tension eased.

Hannu was two people. His normal self was confused, hurting and jealous. Another self felt a strong bonding with the alien and understood how much he loved the beautiful woman that Hannu had held in his arms. He had not been listening to a story. He had been there, so real that he was checking his body for the mass of wounds that he and Anita had seen on Qwelby last night. He had to show the adults how real was the Otherworld, as Qwelby called it, and how his alien friend had suffered. He persuaded Qwelby to strip to the waist and show the heavy bruising and cuts all over his body.

In spite of his insides churning because of the extensive violence he had just re-experienced, Qwelby had to agree with Hannu that it had also been the most exciting experience of his life.

'Qwelby. Looking at you, I see a young man,' Taimi said. 'As you were telling the story I saw a beautiful and very obvious young woman. How? When you say you have identical genes.'

'Boys have a boy gene sequence,' Qwelby said. 'Girls have a girl gene sequence. Tullia and I have a mixture. Gumma, our Great-Great Uncle Mandara, thinks it's some sort of effect from a higher dimension where we used to live in Aurigan times. It's unique. We're unique. It's called a quantum gene, so we're called Quantum Twins.'

Taimi looked at her husband and raised an eyebrow. He shook his head and gestured to her. He knew where her interests lay. Having found what he believed to be Qwelby's first and big mistake in his story he was happy to discuss X and Y chromosomes with the boy when they were by themselves.

Taimi questioned Qwelby closely about Out-Of-Body travel, the seventh dimension and the healing he had done for Arttu.

'Sorry, must stop,' Qwelby said after a while, putting his hands to his head. 'Bad energies from last night. Need be outside.' He turned to Hannu and Anita with a hopeful look on his face and a thoughtsent, *Please.*

With not much daylight left, the ski centre at Muurame was out of the question, so the three youngsters contented themselves with the easy skiing on the slope on the edge of the village. The hill where Qwelby had arrived five days before.

Dinner that evening at the Keskinens was a quiet affair. Anita was thinking about Tullia, what it must be like for the twins to be separated, how much she felt Qwelby was looking to her to be a temporary substitute and how amazing that felt.

Her parents were recalling their discussion as they went to bed in the early hours of the morning. Having agreed that someone in authority had to be notified of Qwelby's presence, Taimi had persuaded her husband to let the children have their adventure over the weekend and they would talk to the Rahkamos after work on Monday.

After dinner, Anita went round to the Rahkamos and joined the boys in Hannu's room for an evening introducing Qwelby to Azuran games consoles and some markedly different games from those played on his homeworld of Vertazia.

As Qwelby settled down to sleep that night, for the first time since arriving on Earth he felt unreservedly happy. He was able to sense Tullia's presence strongly. As he had explained to his friends several days ago, without Tullia in his mind he was only half a person. With all the differences between Vertazia and Earth, that half was only half functioning.

Last night he had known that Tullia was there in the room in his mind that was hers. There had been no mental communication. None of the almost perfect telepathy of being quantum twins. But she was there. A warm presence. Now, there was more than that. He knew the door was not locked, yet he was unable to open it, but it had become opaque and her warmth was shining through more powerfully than last night.

He had seen the change from last night's ordinary door as he finished his story-telling. He had not said anything. It was too precious. And he had been afraid the change might not last.

He remembered with embarrassment his anger when his friends' minds had been so open that he had known what Hannu was thinking and feeling about Tullia. Yet that puzzled him. Tullia was Kaigii. The word 'twin' did not convey anything like the full complexity of the Tazian word. She was not his girl-friend. He had no interest in girls. Not for another eighteen months or so would those hormones activate. So why his anger?

If his BestFriend Wrenden had those thoughts, Qwelby would laugh at the idea of anyone feeling like that about Kaigii. So why? Why now? Was this another sign that he was growing up faster than at home? And again. Why feel like that about Kaigii – his identical twin?

'Tomorrow,' he muttered. 'Tonight, we are a little closer. I will enjoy that.' He fell asleep with a smile on his face.

CHAPTER 6

AN OMEN

KALAHARI

The midday meal finished, still playing with her new braids, Tullia asked if she could talk with the men.

'My twin will never forgive me if I cannot tell him about their lives,' she explained with a smile. What she said was true. Beginning to realise that men and women had different roles in a way that was markedly different compared to life on Vertazia, and uncertain of what they were, she thought it better not to say that she also wanted to know for herself.

San tradition accepted the Goddess Nananana, and more specifically the Daughters of the Goddess. Tullia looked like a Siska, a well-known extraterrestrial in Africa, and was automatically assumed to be one of the Daughters of Nananana. Yet from the very first time they had seen her with her highly excited energy field, the pattern of flames on her skin-tight body suit, and then the same pattern all over her body and limbs caused by the radiation burns from travelling through dimensions, she had appeared to be on fire.

With misunderstandings of language as her compiler built a

dictionary and syntax, they had understood her explanation of where she came from and how she had arrived amongst them as being from the sun and travelling on a ray of sunlight. Xameb had hypothesised that as she had a mother and father for parents and a male twin, then the Sun God and Goddess were a pair. Naturally they had children, twins who in their turn would become the Sun God and Goddess. The Meera had happily accepted that.

The Tazii had no tradition of Gods and Goddesses. In creating its dictionary, Tullia's compiler translated "Goddess" as "KosiKosuu", the honorific for a Venerable of at least one hundred and forty years of age, and the Meera "sun" into Tazian as "planet." Tullia thought she was being referred to and addressed as "Planetary KosiKosuu," a sort of exalted Ambassador, and wanted the Meera to accept her as what she was, an ordinary teenager.

When Testsana took her to meet a group of men, they explained that, as the San were no longer allowed to hunt, they were happy to relive their past by talking with her. Xara, the tribe's leading hunter, said that there was only one way to explain. Soon, accompanoed by Tsetasan, she was out in the bush and learning their skills.

Earlier, she had admired his red headband made from hundreds of tiny beads, with a white edge and black beads making a central pattern of interlocking diamonds. From that moment on, of all the men he had proved to be most at ease with her.

'Oh, those beautiful ponies,' she said as a small herd of animals passed.

'Zzzebra,' Xara said as he led the group over to examine their spoor.

Tullia thought it all very logical. The footprint itself told what animal it was. The depth gave an indication of weight and age.

'Here the adults. Here the young one,' Xara said, pointing out how the spacing and the way the marks dug into the sand, showed speed and direction of travel, and again an indication of size and age.

One of the other hunters found the spoor of an ostrich that was many days old. Tullia learnt to compare them, and see how the amount of tiny grains of sand that had flowed into the depression, together with a knowledge of the winds and weather, told how long ago the animal had passed that way.

'In my mind I store the pictures together with what you are telling me. Sort of like the way you use knots in the string you make from those plants to record complex numbers.'

'And that is similar to how we learn to recognise one tree from thousands of others,' Xara commented.

Time passed as they moved further into the bush.

'Kudu,' Xara whispered, pointing.

Tullia looked up to see what looked like two beautiful, large stags silhouetted against the dark blue sky, each with a pair of long twisting horns and the funniest large, round ears she had ever seen. Suddenly they bounded off. Something must have alarmed them...

'Are you all right, Tullia?'

Hearing Tsetsana's voice jerked Tullia back to the present.

'Did you not feel it?' Tullia asked, looking around the Meera.

They shook their heads.

'Like a breath of cold air. And the sun went dark,' she explained.

They looked up to the sky. No clouds to be seen.

Tullia shivered.

'We return?' Xara said, looking at Tullia.

She looked around, searching for a clue. There were lots of places where they could walk between bushes and trees, but nothing looked like a clear track leading anywhere. All the trees looked so similar and she had not been cataloguing them. She was lost.

'Xzarze!' she exclaimed. 'That way,' she said, pointing. Then turned to Xara and explained the angle and position of the sun when they had left the village. 'I was looking for an actual path through the bush. I had forgotten the sun,' she added, blushing and feeling stupid. In the wide open spaces on Vertazia, navigating by the sun and her internal clock was second nature.

Xara smiled. The Daughter of the Sun Goddess, forgetting the sun! It was the sort of mistake any very young San child might make.

Tullia liked Xara. She was loving learning from him with his gentle energy and, although she sensed respect, there was no hint of fear. Embarrassed, she was unconsciously flooding him with energy, asking him not to think of her as foolish.

Xara warmed to the tall young woman, momentarily perceiving her as little different to a young Meera girl, anxious to please her teacher.

He gestured, and they started to walk back to the village, Tullia following. As the gap between bushes narrowed, she motioned Tsetsana to proceed her. In spite of being lost in introspection, Tullia was noting the differences between the footprints left by her young friend and those of the heavier men with their longer strides. She smiled as she connected facts. That narrow track between her favourite Mongongo trees was a path made by the cute little deer that they called Oryx.

Reaching her hut, she was brought out of her inner space as Tsetsana spoke. 'Xara says you are to tell him when you wish to go tracking. Then he will speak with Ghadi.'

Tullia nodded and went inside, feeling unsettled by the odd experience of cold and dark.

More and more often Tullia was finding herself in two moods, almost as though she was becoming two people. One Self was loving her time with the Meera and all that she was learning. And learning in such a traditional Tazian manner of exploring and practising. The other Self was unhappy that in spite of their mental reconnection she was still not able to thoughtshare with her twin. And she had so much she wanted and needed to share with him.

She wanted him there with her, living with the Meera. They would build their own hut just like young Meera couples did. But they were not married and they should sleep separately with the unmarried girls and boys. She smiled. She had the answer to that. For once being considered a Venerable would be useful. Then she had a little laugh at the thought that the Meera would also think of her irresponsible and younger-by-twelve-minits twin as a Venerable!

That then plunged her into her unhappy Self. She tried to struggle out of that and into a deep meditation as she attempted to reach through to more than just a feel of his presence.

Later that night she awoke feeling disturbed. It had not been a mere dream but a dreamstate. There had been one of those beautiful kudu. It was surrounded by a group of almost naked men, wary of its slashing horns. There was a flash of red and one of the men was on the ground. It was Xara with his red headband, and he was not moving. She knew he was dead. She shivered and pulled the blankets close around her.

It was an omen, frightening and disturbing. What did it have to do with her? She felt that sharing it now, even with Xameb, would only distance her from the very people she wanted to accept her for who she was. She would see how she felt in the morning.

CHAPTER 7

STRIVING

VERTAZIA

In the twelve days since the twins had disappeared from Vertazia, their family and four BestFriends had been trying everything possible to establish the normal, Tazian, telepathic contact, but without success. Eventually, the youngsters' parents had reluctantly agreed to an attempt by the four to make contact through the XzylCavern.

There was an exceptionally strong bond between the twins and their friends created out of the mixture of being BestFriends, the esting relationships and the sixth dimensional Talisman all six had created. As yet, even Mandara did not know what the Talisman might be used for or how the twins had been able to access the lost Aurigan knowledge necessary for its creation. All any of them knew was that it was imbued with the little understood energy of the sixth dimension.

Lungunu was home to the most important of the six XzylStroems that maintained the link with Azura, or Earth as the inhabitants called it. Four days ago the youngsters had been sucked out of their bodies through the Stroems and into the seventh dimension where they had been launched onto a perilous journey through dimensions that had nearly cost them their lives. Bleeding from countless wounds, they had returned with the certain knowledge that Tullia was all right and that Qwelby had to be.

They had made a clear colour contact with Tullia and were convinced the healing energies they had experienced during their fighting had come from Qwelby. Wrenden was more than convinced. With the close esting relationship, where Qwelby was like an older, caring brother and guide, Wrenden just knew that the red and green energies that had bathed all their wounds whilst travelling Out-Of-Body had come from his elderest.

Although Tazian knowledge of life on Azura was confused and full of inaccuracies, the youngsters were certain that the images they had seen on reaching Tullia's location were of Azuran objects. Having feared that even if alive the twins were lost in the NoWhenWhere, to discover they were on Azura was a great relief.

Whilst all the attempts were being made to locate the twins, Mandara had been working furiously on the basis that they were on Azura. Since being elected the youngest ever Arch Discoverer of the Academy of Discoverers decades before, he had been consumed with efforts to unearth the long lost arts of Aurigan science. Now, he was desperately seeking to discover a way to cross the dimensional barrier and rescue his great great niece and nephew.

When Shandur, the twins' father, had looked in on his great uncle a few days previously, he had found him facing a series of multi-layered, transparent display screens which were crawling with mathematical formulae interacting with one another.

'For a long time I have thought that all the unknown universe, what we call Shadow and Azuran scientists call Dark Matter, must be the same,' Mandara explained in a tired voice. 'If we proceed on the theory that the visible universe is a hologram, it must be possible to construct a Shadow hologram which will reveal the whole of the Shadow universe.'

Shandur nodded slowly. Logical but....

'Combining matter and anti-matter together is straightforward,' Mandara continued speaking with obvious difficulty. 'We use that enough for physical energy creation, propulsion....' He made a dismissive gesture with his hand. 'The challenge is doing it in such a way that the anti-matter is not contained here in the fifth dimension, but in effect to reverse the process and have the Shadow world enfold our world.' He took a deep breath. 'And return.'

As he finished speaking he slumped back in his chair, looking old and tired. He managed a faint gesture towards the display. 'You can see my computations working themselves out. I should have the result soon.' His head dropped onto his chest.

Lellia had taken her husband to their one of the five wings of Lungunu to rest. Knowing that his great uncle would not remain inactive for long, Shandur had gone to the laboratory and made a wheel chair. Providing it with a simple Personality Module as for any HouseCarl, he had created WheelChair.

When the twins were very young they had been inseparable and games were always played with them pitted against everyone else. To counter the fact that they were referred to just as "Twins", Wrenden, the youngest of them all, had come up with the name of "The Fearless Four" for what had become a group of four BestFriends. Tazii would have many best friends during their lives, usually in specific areas of study, sport or work. BestFriends were very special and invariably life-long companions.

The name had been dropped as they grew up. After their recent terrifying journey through the seventh dimension, and with the increased depth of bonding that had occurred as a result, Wrenden had declared them once again to be "The Fearless Four".

When Mandara had heard of that he had been heartened. It was what he needed. What the twins needed. In a world where using energy was second nature, the very particular, adventurous and penetrating wavelengths generated by teenagers were an essential ingredient. The more so because it was a pair of teenagers that had to be brought back home.

Following the separation of the two worlds the Auriganii had named their planet Vertazia and renamed themselves Vertazianii, usually shortening that to Tazii. As their DNA degraded and they lost their original sixth finger they changed their number system from base twelve to base ten. Biological development of course continued in its cycles of twelve phases. That produced the odd result that the second, or twiy, Era, from oneteen to nineteen, became in Tazian base ten, thirteen to twenty-three. The attempt to rename teenage to twiyera failed, and that period was still referred to as teenage, which was correct, biologically speaking.

Although still in need of rest, Mandara had soon moved into his laboratory. There he had gathered everyone together and announced that his computations had provided a suggestion as to how the twins might be recovered. Since then, he and his wife, the twins' parents and all four friends had spent most of their time there.

A hoped for transdimensional recovery vehicle had been finished and was ready for testing by the evening of the twelfth day. To the youngsters' disappointment, Mandara said that everyone's energies were too low for tests to be run safely that night. Mizena said she had spoken with the youngsters' parents. 'And, surprisingly,' she added with a smile. 'They all want to see you for a few minutes.' Mandara confirmed that testing would begin the following morning.

CHAPTER 8

LIGHTNING

VERTAZIA

Having said hullo to her parents, Tamina headed for her room looking forward to a long soak in Bath before dinner. She would ask it for a relaxing, swirly effect, softly coloured music and, after several days pinned under a safety helmet, a complete hair detangle. At one metre ninety-five she was taller than the twins and her slim figure made her seem even taller. When she let it out, her auburn hair with its natural golden highlights fell in wavelets to mid thigh.

Just short of seventeen, Tamina was nineteen months older than Tullia and enjoyed her role as a guide and caring big sister to the younger girl. No-one knew how Life chose the esting relationships. They just happened. Qwelby was sixteen months older than Tamina's brother, Wrenden, and his elderest. A source of annoyance to Tullia who considered she was far more suited to being an elderest, which she was not, than her irresponsible twin.

As well as the Esting relationships, the brother and sister were the twins' BestFriends, making a bonding so strong that Tamina and Wrenden had unhesitatingly risked their lives in attempting to save Qwelby from leaving Vertazia.

The atmosphere at home for the brother and sister was bad. Yarannah, their mother, was making it very clear that she did not want her two children searching for the twins and saying incorrectly that she had been forced against her will into accepting the decision made by the other parents that, along with Pelnak and Shimara, the four children were the best hope for the twins' rescue.

Yarannah's aura was in a horrible, swirling mess. Anger, jealousy, resentment, denial, fear and untruth were clearly on display. She was "boiling angry". On Vertazia where a person's energy field was almost tangible, that was very dangerous.

Tamina and Wrenden had been only too happy when the twins' mother had produced her study plans and permission had been given for them to stay at Lungunu for several days to work in the laboratory and keep up with their college work.

Tamina was just about to undress when a faint thought reached her.

'Yes, Eeky?' she almost growled, but quickly thought better of it.

The door opened. Her brother's shoulders were slumped, a glum look on his face. A slim one metre seventy-five, he also was tall for his age and had the same rich coffee-cream skin with a coppery tinge as his sister. His wavy hair was dark brown with the top cut 'en brosse'.

Irritating younger brother or not, she understood. She sat on the bed and gestured for him to sit by her.

'I miss them, him, us...' he stopped, unsure what he meant.

'Yeah. I do too.'

'Qwelby's not just my elderest, he's also my BestFriend. And, you know, through him I link with Tullia a lot.' He grimaced. 'And even my bossy-boots sister.'

She grunted. 'Yeah, and through our estings I link with my irritating little squirt of a brother.'

Obligatory insults had been traded but without any feeling.

'Oh, Sis, will we get them back?'

'I don't know Eeky.'

'But Aunt Gallia said it's up to us. Just the four of us?'

'Not just the four of us, but with our Talisman we are the key element.'

'The Fearless Four. We've resuscitated our nick-name. But I didn't feel fearless in the XzylStroem. Just the opposite. I felt full of fear.'

Tamina had been going through exactly the same thoughts herself. After all their good working time together and without him having played any practical jokes on her since the twins had gone, it struck her that without Qwelby around, her little brother was looking to her to be his elderest! Wow. Scary. Was that part of her having become Awakened, her first stage of womanhood?

Wrenden tilted his head to one side. There was such a mix of colours swirling through his sister's aura that he was unable to read all of it.

'I think that's what that name really means, Eeky. We have fear, lots of it, but we don't let it have us. That way we act as though we haven't got it. If you see what I mean?'

'But all those years ago, you, me, Pelnak and Shimara, we needed a sort of identity for ourselves to help bind us together when we were playing games against the twins as they were, are, so strong. It's different now.'

'Well, we're playing another game now. To rescue the twins, Ngé'zânâ,' she said, using his middle name to remind him of his genetic inheritance from Ngélûzhra, who had been known variously as the Great Adventurer or Great Explorer. And also as the Great Trickster, Tamina's mind added. She squashed that before it was projected as a thought for Wrenden to hear.

At just under fourteen, Wrenden was the youngest of the six. Normally impulsive and exuberant he looked lost and uncertain.

'I miss Tullia an awful lot,' Tamina said. 'And Qwelby.'

They felt a dismal silence growing around them.

'We'll do it,' Tamina said. 'We've been XOÑOX for well over two years now. We can make the connections,' she said with assuredness, because she needed to believe what she was saying.

'We had a good wrist grip,' her brother said, looking down at his hand. 'He let go. Slipped through my hand.' The sadness and bewilderment in his voice was painful to hear.

'If you had saved him, Tullia would be all alone, wherever she is. Remember Qwelby's healing energy when we were searching for Tullia. We have to assume they are together,' Tamina said gently, taking his hands in hers. She completely dropped her Privacy Shield and let their energies flow together.

He saw how the pranks that he and Qwelby played upon her were annoying, yet also a part of her life and their relationship. He felt he had glimpsed how awful it would be for the twins if they were not together.

Satisfied more with the feelings than her words, and the unprecedented openness she had offered him, Wrenden nodded and left the room. *I trust Sis.*

Needing reassurance, he had relaxed his Privacy Shield and forgotten to reset it. Sensing his thought, Tamina grimaced. *I'm not yet seventeen and Aunt G said even grownups don't do this! But it was Eeky's faith that saved me, saved us, on that terrifying journey. Oh Eeky, I don't think you're my "Little Squirt" any longer. You really are a vital member of the Fearless Four.*

She turned to look at herself in the mirror. She knew that one day she would be a Fire Lady, and since her Awakening was beginning to experience the strength of those energies.

Her reflection said: 'Dancer!'

She gave a little twirl and smiled at the memory of when Qwelby had given her the nickname of Lightning when she was dancing at the twins' fifteenth rebirthday celebration. When she had asked him why, he had blushed and mumbled something about the silver streaks on her black bodysuit looking just like lightning strikes as she danced.

Tamina had laughed with pleasure as that had been her intention when she had designed it. Her mind opened the door to the memory and she recalled the strange look that had appeared on Tullia's face. Something was waiting to be explored. It could wait. It was late, she was tired and there were far more important matters to be dealt with.

CHAPTER 9

QUESTIONS

FINLAND

Starting with Einstein and his theory of General Relativity, mathematics had conclusively proved the existence of other dimensions. Professor Romain was one of the world's leading quantum scientists. He had left CERN when he had been refused permission to carry out a series of what he hoped would be ground-breaking experiments. He was determined to prove the physical existence of other dimensions and had invested a fortune in creating a laboratory-cum-home on the South Pacific island of Raiatea. There, he had developed the only equipment in the world capable of detecting fluctuations in the Earth's quantum field.

Together with his two doctoral assistants they had carried out an experiment using the energies generated by what was fondly termed the Big Doughnut at CERN, situated under the Franco-Swiss border. As a result of detecting on the twenty-seventh of December the first ever, and major, disturbance located on the edge of Kotomäki, Romain had arrived in nearby Jyväskylä on New Year's Eve.

He had felt frustrated when enquiries at the police station that evening produced no information about what he believed must have been a major event. At least very observable lights and noise, even if not an explosion. That left him with having to go around the small town and ask questions. Careful questions that would not reveal what he hoped had happened: that some form of data package from another dimension had arrived at the very specific location indicated by his equipment.

Being New Year's Day, Romain waited until the afternoon before leaving his hotel in Jyväskylä to start his search in Kotomäki. Thus it was with the perfect irony that Life reserves for such situations that the "event" he was seeking was in Dr Keskinen's laboratory whilst Romain was knocking on the doors of the houses on the road opposite the ski slope. Then, by the time that Qwelby and friends were skiing on that slope, Romain had moved into the village and away from the road with its clear view of the hillside.

Mrs Rahkamo was taken aback when she answered the door to find a man standing there in a three-quarter length camel overcoat with a black collar, tan gloves and a dark brown fedora. Romain asked about any strange event she may have witnessed. By the time she had recovered from her surprise at such an unusually dressed caller in their small town, Romain had moved on from his opening comments to explain the sort of weather-oriented event he was looking for. Seija relaxed and answered truthfully. She was not aware of any of the weird effects of the sort that he was describing.

All afternoon, Romain continued knocking on doors and stopping those he met in the streets. He heard about the capture of the thieves the previous night, but nothing else. Feeling defeated and in need of somewhere to rest he was heading towards a bar when he was stopped by a tall, well built youth who looked to be in his late teens.

There was something about the Finn Romain did not like. He had the typical blonde hair and blue eyes. In fact the handful of youths Roman had encountered looked as though they were all sisters and brothers. It was like looking at the negatives of photos taken on his island of Raiatea where everyone had black hair and a reddish cast to their dark skins.

Although dressed in a style similar to everyone he had seen in a padded black jacket, dark trousers and a dark blue cap with "CCM" embroidered in light blue, this youth was different. Romain could not put his finger on it. After exchanging a few words he was about to walk on when he was stopped by the words: 'A boy and a find.'

A few minutes later they sat facing one another at a table in the corner of the bar. On the table were a coffee and a pastry for Erki and a Kukko for Romain. Faced with a choice of lagers he had selected the Kukko with a touch of amusement because of its emblem of a black rooster, reminding him of his favourite Chiantis from the region of Italy known as Gallo Nero, the Black Rooster.

Erki told his story. A strange looking boy, who had not been seen around the village until late on the afternoon of the Monday that Romain was asking about, was seen wearing only a skin-tight tank top and shorts. Finnish was a difficult language to master. This boy spoke it. What was particularly strange was that his accent was very good. He sounded Finnish.

He claimed he came from the Czech Republic, but certainly did not look Czech. It was said that his father was Dr Jadrovic. Erki had seen the scientist around Jyväskylä. No way was that black boy his son. And what about his name: Kwelby. That was no Czech name. He was staying with a local family. Where were the people who had brought him? There were no more black faces to be seen, not that they were wanted. And why here?

Erki was quite worked up by the time he finished, saying: 'He's hanging around with that bunch of losers from school. That prissy girl. All stuck-up because she comes from Helsinki and her father works at the Research Institute. Won't give me the time of day! What do they see in him? Black as the ace of spades!'

'What about the find?' Romain pulled Erki back to his story and away from what he sensed was a racist diatribe in the making.

'You've come a long way,' Erki said. 'What's it worth to you?'

Romain was also a businessman and had made a lot of money through a variety of inventions, manufactured and marketed by his father's companies. What he was now pursuing was not a moneymaking idea but the possibility that his dream had come true: a breakthrough in science that would elevate his name to stand alongside people like Einstein and Newton.

You have no idea! Romain thought as money changed hands. This time asking questions as Erki talked, Romain heard the rest of the youth's story. How he had seen the family make their way into the woods, not using torches until the last moment. How he himself had searched after that, and then again the next morning. He had found nothing. If they had found something it must have been small enough to conceal in a pocket. Erki was careful not to say anything about his two mates and the deserved beating they had given the black boy.

A few more Euronotes were passed across as Erki provided the names and locations of the two families and agreed to find out whatever more he could.

'You have a mobile?' Romain asked. He smiled as Erki produced a RonaldSon, one of Romain's own designs.

Taking his own mobile from his pocket, Romain thumbed a dial and a virtual tablet hovered in the air between them. Erki whistled as almost immediately it displayed his number.

Roman touched an icon. 'Please open the message and follow the instructions,' he said as Erki's phone rang.

When Erki had done as requested, including quietly speaking a password which he saw displayed on the tablet, then restarted his phone, Romain explained.

'A call on that number will be relayed to me anywhere in the world. But only you and only with that mobile. All communications are secure.'

'Impressive,' Erki said.

'One of my hobbies.' With his "hobbies" making him a lot of money, Romain allowed himself a slight smile as he stood up and carefully slid his chair back under the table. He had reached an understanding with Erki, that was all. An old fashioned Englishman, it was not a deal on which he wished to shake. With the youth lounging against the back of the bench that was set against the wall, Romain was able to leave without making it obvious that he was not offering his hand.

Erki remained seated, watching Romain through narrowed eyes. He reckoned that whatever it was the Professor was looking for was worth a lot of money. Although only sixteen years old, his deep voice, height and the time he spent in the gym made him look older, easily passing for twenty at night. He worked part-time for Lokir, a small time crook based in Jyväskylä. He would have to be careful how he handled this or he would be in trouble. That sort of trouble with Lokir he did not want.

As he walked to his car, Romain turned over in his mind what appeared to be the facts. Everything was too much of a coincidence. Had the boy gone up the hill to hide something, found his contact in the village and then a group had gone and fetched whatever it was. Leaving the boy.... what? Under guard? By the girl's parents? Until his story proved to be true? But why would anyone drop him off without winter clothing?

Romain shook his head. That was all too much like a spy story. Much more likely it was all innocent. The boy had just arrived to stay with this family. Upstairs changing, looking out of the window, he had seen something. Something so exciting that he had rushed out wearing only his underclothes. But so minor – a bright flash of light? That only he saw it?

Then why was the reason given for his being in Kotomäki a lie? That was according to Erki. But Erki was adamant the boy was not returning to where he was staying. Why had he spoken to him in a language that clearly was not Finnish, yet was now speaking it with an accent like a Finn?

Romain got into his car, started the engine and waited for the heater to warm up. Just like a problem in the laboratory, he would start where he could and follow the trails. Plenty of dead ends, and eventually a route to the answer. He sat staring through the windscreen for a few moments, watching the snow flakes slowly drifting down, settling on the bonnet and on the screen. Faster and faster, bigger and thicker.

He shook himself out of his reverie. Time to go. As he drove back to the hotel his next move became clear. Erki was a racist and also held a grudge where the children were concerned. Yet some of his facts were definitely true. The story concerning Dr Jadrovitch? That might be the youth's racist bias, wanting to create trouble. A visit to the Research Institute was an obvious first step. Setting that up would have to wait until Monday morning, which gave him time to get his assistants to research the Czech scientist.

Back in his room in the hotel he powered up his GlobeSync, took a bottle of Velamo water from the fridge and sat down to compose his message. After briefly advising that, as yet, he had found nothing of significance except a possible connection with the Doctor, he added: 'I need to get close to him.' He nodded, that would do. 'Command: End. Command: Location RaiLabTwo: send.'

His message was encoded and sent in a brief burst to the main communications room on the second floor of the laboratory complex. A few seconds later a green light appeared in the corner of the screen, an automatic confirmation that the message had been received.

He showered and returned to the main room where he checked the GlobeSync. He was pleased to note that although it was early morning on Raiatea a second green light had appeared indicating that the message had been opened. He went down to the restaurant to enjoy a well-earned dinner.

CHAPTER 10

MONGONGOS

KALAHARI

Tullia awoke in the pitch dark. 'This is my seventh day here,' she said in a soft voice as she sat up. 'Every day I am more accepted by these people, the younger ones treat me like a big sister, and yesterday with the men I felt like a Bushman. Yet every day I feel more out of sorts. My inner world is breaking apart and my body is full of irritation and unaccustomed aches and pains.'

As she got out of bed she was struck by the cold. The bowl of water by the open doorway had a thin film of ice over the surface. Breaking that and splashing the freezing water on her face helped calm her for a moment. Shivering, she slipped into khaki shorts and a white t-shirt, stepped into dark blue tracksuit bottoms, pulled on a thick, dark green sweater, thick socks and a pair of brown, men's shoes, finally adding the colourful blanket she used as clothing.

Today, she wanted to speak with Xameb, the tribe's Shaman, about trying to find her twin. But right now, she had to do something.

As she left her hut she looked up at the Milky Way with its

billions of stars illuminating the whole scene so clearly that she had no difficulty in walking through the village and out into the bush to a special copse of Mongongo trees that towered over all the acacias. She smiled with pleasure at the thought that a visitor would not know they were there. She felt a deep sense of pride that, having found them by accident, she had then used the sun and the terrain to work out a path back to the village. Now, like a Bushman, she was able to find her way by starlight without using any of her energy sensing Tazian skills.

Stepping carefully with the blanket wrapped around her shoulders to avoid catching on the spiky thornbushes, she arrived at her group of three trees. They were old, soaring to several times her own height, their grey trunks no longer smooth and round, if they ever had been. The trunk of her favourite, 'Mother Tree' she called it, was as wide as her outstretched arms. It had cracked open, forming an archway like the entrance to a cave as if it could be the mouth to other dimensions.

Sweeping back her hair, she smiled at the memory of being surrounded by a group of girls as they spent ages plaiting her long, thick, luxurious hair into scores of tiny, tight braids. She dropped the blanket to the ground and backed into the mouth-like opening in Mother Tree. She could just stand inside with her palms resting on the rough, gnarled bark. She relaxed and let its energies engulf her.

She felt her chest swell with pride. She had been here for over a hundred years, sun and rain, freezing cold and boiling hot. She had grown, leaved, produced her fruits, watched the animals and humans collect and eat her gifts. She felt her roots going down, down, so deep, deeper than anyone could imagine. Far below at the very tips was the life giving moisture she needed.

From the tip of the topmost branches she saw the sky start to lighten as the sun prepared to climb over the rim of the world and bring a new day. Silently, she acknowledged her place in the cosmos. A home for countless insects and grubs, a nesting place for birds, shelter for animals and humans, provider of food for all of them.

Sunlight tickled the twigs, ran down the branches, reached the trunk, warmed the face of the girl far below. The heart of the mother was warmed at the realisation that yet another life was enjoying her gifts.

Then it felt the sadness that emanated from the life that ached for the half of its life that was missing. An aching love that spread through the trunk and up past the tree's crown, and out, out into the multiverse, seeking, seeking.

CHAPTER 11

REVENGE

FINLAND

Early Sunday morning Qwelby came half awake as a faint thought reached him from his twin. She wanted..... reassurance? He imaged himself holding her hand. It felt nice. As he relaxed into the sensation he fell back asleep.

Eventually, a human need awoke him and sent him into the bathroom. Washing, he pulled away the bandage that Anita had applied to his neck and nodded with pleasure. The nasty gash was now only a long, thin, faint line. The many cuts had almost disappeared and the vivid colours of the bruises were fading nicely.

His self-healing abilities were almost as strong as at home. He nodded with satisfaction. Almost better than the healing was the proof that the energies of the subatomic world were a cosmic constant. And, as theory stated, they were just as accessible here in the third dimension as at home in the fifth, but a lot harder to reach and slower in acting.

He dressed in a red t-shirt, a pair of black shorts and flip-flops. Both the Rahkamos and Keskinens had got used to him finding their houses a lot warmer than he was used to on Vertazia.

Paavo Rahkamo was at work as Qwelby shared a late breakfast with Hannu. When Seija joined them for coffee and commented about the speed of his healing, Qwelby was happy to explain.

'It's a matter of tuning in to the underlying quantum energies and directing them to the affected parts. The difficult aspect is balancing the desire for healing, and for that to happen quickly, along with accepting that Life might have different ideas.'

'Yes.' Hannu's mother nodded. 'Different words, but the same principle that Taimi Keskinen teaches us in her Yoga classes.'

'You mean if I hurt myself and wasn't able to ski for a long time, I'd have to, well, look at other bits of my life. What else I can do. That sort of thing?' Hannu asked.

'Exactly,' Qwelby confirmed.

'Hannu,' Qwelby said as he got up and stretched. 'Yesterday, so much talk and going over the events on New Year's Eve. I need to be outside. Not enough energy to go to Muurame. A little time on the ski slope here?'

'Good idea,' Hannu replied, wanting to spend some time with "his alien" without Anita around.

Arttu was released from hospital late on Sunday morning, with strict instructions to be very careful of his lightly bandaged right hand. The police had taken him there in the early hours of Saturday morning, with his knife still stuck to his skin. One of his mates had brought a change of clothing and then given him a lift to the edge of Kotomäki.

Arttu had two thoughts in his mind. The first was to find the black boy who had totally ruined the jewellery heist on New Year's Eve and had landed him in hospital. Kotomäki was a small town, really little more than a village, so finding him would be easy. The second was to disappear down to Helsinki for a few days. The police would want to question him, but that could wait, he wanted time to think. His mates would not dare give him away. They knew how vicious his retribution would be.

The previous Friday night, after tackling two members of his gang and recovering the sacks of jewellery they had been carrying, the person he was calling JuJu Boy had walked into him whilst he was successfully hiding in the woods. Then, with Arttu's knife cutting into his throat, the boy had set off some explosion that had not just given away his position to the police, but had welded Arttu's knife to his hand.

He was sure that when the boy kicked him, he had badly damaged Arttu's knee, but something he had done later meant that Arttu only had a slight limp. That was all well and good, because in spite of his hurting hand he was ready to pay JuJu Boy back for crossing him, Arttu, The Bear Man.

As Arttu walked along the pavement he glanced over to the ski slope. It was a reflex, he knew that no darkie was going to be skiing. JuJu Boy had to be freezing away from his jungle home. Something caught his eye. A dark face? Zigzagging down the slope. It had to be him! Arttu knew the timing was right, Skadi was on his side. Not only was she the Goddess of Snow and Ice, she was also the Goddess of Justice – and Revenge.

As Qwelby reached the bottom of the slope, Hannu tapped his watch. Qwelby looked at his Tazian wrister and showed it to his friend with the word "Hungry" displayed on its face. The boys laughed and shared a high five.

A few minutes later they were crossing the road, aiming for the gap in the high wall of packed and frozen snow that lined both sides of the road. Hannu had his skis over his left shoulder, Qwelby over his right. As Qwelby followed Hannu he became aware of a sharp, hard energy, and realised that it had been there for a while. He saw Hannu step across the pavement and start to turn to his right, waiting for him to come though the gap.

Belatedly, he realised he knew the energy. It was the man who had attacked him on New Year's Eve. He saw the man's hand grab the back end of Hannu's skis and swing them around – the front ends were going to smash into Qwelby's face. He ducked hard and fast to his left, dropping his skis and sticks and butted his head into Arttu's stomach.

Arttu was sent crashing into the wall of ice and, off balance, Qwelby fell to his knees. As Qwelby got up he saw a knife appear in Arttu's left hand and come slashing towards him. He jumped back, and again as the knife swung back. Qwelby was shocked. His attacker's whole energy field was displaying such hatred and determination to harm him.

The knife came swinging again, this time on an upward curve heading straight for Qwelby's face. Qwelby swung his head back and grabbed Arttu's arm with both of his as he felt the knife slice across the underneath of his chin. Stepping back, off balance, trampling on skis or sticks, Qwelby rolled to the left, taking Arttu with him, and heard a yelp as he wrenched Arttu's arm backwards as the two of them collapsed on the ground.

Letting go of Arttu's now knifeless hand, Qwelby scrambled to his feet and stood breathing heavily, totally puzzled by what his compiler had translated of Arttu's shouted diatribe.

Arttu scanned the ground and then launched himself to his right, knocking a ski to the side and revealing the knife.

'Dragon's Breath!' Qwelby roared as he pulled his foot back.

Arttu yelped with pain as his damaged right hand took his weight as he grabbed the knife.

Qwelby froze as his instinct to finish the movement with his foot by kicking Arttu in the head was stayed by awareness of the heavy ski boot he was wearing.

Arttu flicked the knife across the pavement to his left hand. And yelled with pain as Qwelby's ski boot smashed on top of it.

Qwelby slid his boot back, dragging the knife with it. The two boys watched as Arttu slowly got to his feet, his eyes burning with hatred. With his bandaged right hand holding his now damaged left hand, Arttu limped off into Kotomäki to meet his mate and a lift back to the hospital, where the police were to find him later that afternoon.

'How the hell did you do that?' a shaken Hannu asked.

'His intention. So focussed. Easy to read. Even for an Azuran,' Qwelby replied. 'I didn't want to hurt him. But I had to stop him.' He kept to himself the feeling of satisfaction at his fighting skills, whilst puzzling over the sensation that he was recalling hard learnt lessons from long, long ago.

The boys collected their skis and sticks, and Hannu picked up the knife that Qwelby refused to handle. They headed for home with a corner of Qwelby's mind concentrating on his healing energies.

CHAPTER 12

HOSTAGE

VERTAZIA   KALAHARI

Xaala half opened her eyes, puzzled at the faint sound of a bell. As she watched the first glimmers of dawn streak the sky she came fully awake as she realised there were no bells in Ceegren's mansion. No external sound. Internal. Ah! The slightest feeling of.... Tullia?

At two metres five, Xaala was taller than average for her nearly seventeen years, with a slender, boyish figure. With a mouth smaller and eyes less slanted than usual, her face looked more Azuran than Tazian. Her one compensation was her rich, chestnut coloured hair which she wore in her own design. The sides of her head were shaven, and from a spiky centre the rest hung down almost to her waist, styled to look like a horse's mane. To her surprise, her HorseMane style had become a fashion amongst youngsters and known as FillysMane or ColtsMane.

Moving slowly so as to hold onto the faint impression, Xaala slid out of bed, padded across the floor to the bathroom and splashed cold water on her face. Returning to her room she put on her electric blue meditation robe, sat on her bed in the lotus position and breathed into her power centres, activating the rainbow of colours. Cautiously, she let her mind follow the impression through the dimensions and found herself enfolded in peace and harmony. She sighed as fine tendrils surrounded her and she sank into..... a bed of love?

No! This cannot be. She pulled herself away. That abomination of a twin cannot be sending forth love like this. She's evil! Calming herself, she searched around the energy field and sensed a darkness. Fear and despair. She knew those emotions. And there was more. Death! She shivered as she sensed an opportunity. Guide the darkness to the abomination and let happen what may. All safely far away on Earth.

Attaching a thread to the darkness was easy but linking it to the brightness was not. She gritted her teeth against the burning sensation and forced her mind on, carrying the end of her fine thread as she sank ever deeper, finally attaching it to the bright core. Love like that could NOT come from an abomination!

The strength of her denial sent her crashing back against the headboard. On unsteady feet she made her way to the bathroom, shedding her robe as she went, stepped into the shower and turned it full on. The cold water hammered on her, bringing her back to her senses as she ran her hands across her well toned Form. She let the pounding water beat out of her the treacherous thought that it might be nice to experience again that feeling of..... pathetic, sloppy, cloying, weak girlishness.

Tullia became aware that she was feeling stiff and her neck ached. She collected her thoughts, slowly withdrawing them from Mother Tree, thanking her as she did so. Why had she come back now? She could have remained like that forever. There was something else. Something different. There. Movement, out in the bush.

Twenty minutes later she was sitting on the ground and trembling as a sad looking Bushman wearing faded grey trousers, a brown jacket and a black head covering, ate several maramas, put a few in his pockets and shared the water with Tullia. He had threatened her with what he said was a gun and that he would kill her if she did not do as he said. Then sent her to get food and water and not say anything about him. She had gone to her hut where Tsetsana had just arrived and taken from her friend the jug of water and a bowl of maramas. Unable to speak, she had shaken her head and reinforced the gesture with a mental "stay" command.

'Who are you?' the Bushman asked. 'Where do you come from?'

'I am Tullia !Gei-!Ku'ma. I come from the planet Vertazia.' Except that with the errors in learning their language she had said "sun", not "planet."

There was a long pause. He put the gun away. 'Tullia, Red Goddess of the Original People,' was how he translated her name into Afrikaans, as the San believed they were the first humans to live on Earth. 'Daughter of Nananana. And a very young one to be so frightened of me.' He gave a mirthless laugh. 'You'll be worth a lot of money. To someone.'

He questioned her about the times and routes the tourist trips took and when and where the women would go foraging. Answering him slowly steadied her and she was pleased at how much detail she had absorbed, showing that some of her Tazian skills were working normally.

'We go now,' he said.

Tullia swallowed nervously and carefully set the bowl and jug to the side and rolled up the blanket as her captor walked a few paces away and stood there, searching the land. He beckoned to her, and when she reached him, swung her to face the open bush. 'That way,' he said, pointing south east with the gun. 'Remember. You live as long as you are useful.' Then thrust her forward.

Movement steadying her racing mind, she thoughtsent to her twin, and almost staggered as that bounced back from a dark covering that had appeared over the door to his room in her mind.

CHAPTER 13

ELDEREST

VERTAZIA

Tamina awoke from a good night's sleep. Returning from the bathroom, she sensed her mirror beckoning. Turning to face it she immediately noticed that the crystal of Bula'kabilii in her necklace was gently pulsing, the flecks of red, orange and blue flickering like miniature flames. She held it in her fingers and felt the heat. She had been surprised and delighted when on her fourteenth rebirthday the Arkaana had presented her with a small tray of those crystals from which she was to make her choice. It was one of the few crystals with a dual energy. A difficult to handle mixture of Fire and Water, emphasising her creative nature.

Reluctantly, she allowed herself to recall the jealousy and resentment that had been in her mother's aura at the time. How they had argued about it as her mother considered it blatant and unladylike, but would not explain herself. Dad had been proud of "his little girl", but worried for the future in view of the inherent power in her choice emphasising her genetic inheritance. An inheritance his wife refused to acknowledge and wanted to deny to her daughter. Trying to seek a compromise in true Tazian manner, the Arkaana had suggested she should offer alternatives. Tamina had refused and deliberately chosen not merely the most powerful piece, but one that bore signs of hidden energies. She shivered as a presentiment ran down her spine and watched as a tingling rainbow of colours swept through her energy field. That brought her attention to her reflection.

She had recently Awakened. The two day retreat with only her mother for company had been an uncomfortable experience emotionally, and a much more painful one than was usual. Her mother had continued to refuse to speak about the heroine Léshmîrâ Kûsheÿnÿ, known as "Reconciler", from whom they had inherited genes. Yet annoyingly hinted that it was Tamina's fault her time was so painful because she had acknowledged her inheritance. She had done that in the traditional manner by taking the middle name of Lésh'zânâ. Her mother had not done that and had strongly advised her daughter against doing so. The Uddîšû's entry in the Archives was small. There had to be more, but even with all six BestFriends working together they had not been able to find it.

Once Tamina had got over her embarrassment at having developed larger breasts than she wanted, and stopped rounding her shoulders to try and hide them, she had gone back to wearing the close fitting clothes that emphasised her tall, dancer's figure. Now, the expected physical changes following Awakening were taking place. She liked the way her hips were rounding out and reluctantly accepted that her bust was even larger.

There was a subtle shift in what she was seeing and she realised she was now looking at Mirror. A pair of purple-orbed eyes appeared in the background. Tullia? She focussed and saw they had violet rims – Qwelby.

Tamina was in the final third of the fifth phase of her second era, exploring creativity. She had been moody since her Awakening and was still not interested in boys. At nineteen months her junior, Qwelby certainly was not interested in her as a girl. They were just friends. So why now his eyes? And why had he blushed and what was it about Tullia's look?

Stunned, she stared as Image raised an eyebrow. He liked her – as a girl!

Stirred by a gentle wind, her golden-highlighted, thigh length hair caressed her Form. 'One day I will be a Fire Lady and will need my Power of Creation to nurture. Since I developed all those years ago I've always assumed that my generous bust meant that would be for children. But right now.... for Qwelby? Not like that, but as an elderest?' She laughed. The thought of Tullia's irresponsible brother looking to her as a guide was too silly to contemplate.

Her memory replayed a recent occasion when he'd asked her a question. He'd been acting overly casual as though embarrassed. She now saw he'd been seeking her advice in his role as elderest to her brother! She shook her head in disbelief whilst Image smiled and nodded.

Wrenden. His heart was aching at the loss of his BestFriend and elderest. 'I am Tullia's elderest,' she said, and saw Image nod encouragingly. However uncomfortable it felt, when Image represented a person's true Self, it was impossible to deny that. She was looking at a tall and attractive young woman. Powerful. Awakened. Responsible. A woman who loved her irritating young brother, and who, with their mother's current attitude, needed his elderest more than ever. She studied Image. 'Energetically I am a little softer. Can I be a caring big sister?'

Image nodded confirmation.

'Tamuchly,' she said, as she prepared her Self for a new phase in her life.

CHAPTER 14

SIBLING DREAMS

VERTAZIA

A thought reached her from her young brother. She felt his sadness and responded. He entered and sat on her bed as she dressed. 'I was awake a long time last night,' he said. 'I finally accepted what you said. That Qwelby needs to be on Azura so the two of them can be together. I then went into a dreamstate....You know someone can receive a crystal before their fourteenth rebirthday?'

Tamina nodded.

'I would be a lot stronger if I had mine now. And I guess a lot more protected. What do you think, Sis?'

'Tell me about your dream.'

'You and I were two pairs of hands. No bodies or anything, just our whole Selves were the hands. We were holding the twins between us. Your hands were on top, mine on the bottom. There was another pair of hands, smaller than ours and on long arms. They were moving up and down between our hands and around the twins. Had to be Pelnak and Shimara. But it was all shaky.' He paused and Tamina gave him an encouraging nod.

'There was a hollow feel here.' He put his hand to his EraBand. 'I understood the message to be that I don't have the strength because I don't yet have my crystal.... but I need it for us to save Qwelby.'

Tamina took his hands in hers and they shared energies. 'I had a similar dreamstate, with a difference. Instead of hands I saw crystals. Four.'

'I had one?'

'Yeah. A green one, Eeky. You deserve it.'

'Ah, gee, Sis. You're being nice to me.'

'Yeah. Sad girl.'

He grinned. He had missed playing practical jokes with Qwelby, but this new relationship with his sister was, well, yes, he had to admit, quite nice. 'Shall we tell Dad?' he asked, knowing their father would at least listen.

'Yes. And I'll ask him,' Tamina replied, ruffling the short hair on the top of his head. He did not like her doing that and, in the past she had done it to annoy him. She thoughtsent a feeling of big-sisterly fondness.

'Gee, Sis, you've changed. Your sharpness has gone. Your bossy energy. It's softer.' He smiled and nodded. 'Now I can see why Qwelby looks on you as a big sister.' He gave her a cheeky grin. 'I never could understand it.'

Grinning, but unable to explain why she felt happy, Tamina said 'Sorry!' to a pillow as she picked it up and threw it at her brother as he ran from the room.

Downstairs, they explained their dreamstates to their father and Tamina asked if Wrenden could have a crystal now. Jailandur agreed to speak with their Arkaana, the family's spiritual advisor, counsellor and exemplar of the True Aurigan Teachings. The Arkaana had been kept in constant touch by Yarannah, Jailandur's wife, with what had been happening. She was happy to accept the offer of using the family's energy credits to transweave so as to speak personally with the whole family without delay. Everyone was surprised when Yarannah readily agreed to Wrenden having a crystal.

'I hope the change from being a child into a youngster will bring him to his senses,' she said with a strong censorious tone to her voice. 'Perhaps it will knock some sense into his sister as well. But,' she added in a very firm tone of voice. 'We will maintain tradition. There will still be the formal Transition ceremony on his fourteenth rebirthday.'

'A wise decision, Yarannah,' the Arkaana said. 'The real inheritance of power is in the full ceremony itself.'

The Arkaana knew the family well and had brought with her a selection of Lazabatanzii, a rich green stone that was a twin power, linked to both the elements of Air and Earth. Wrenden was delighted. It was what he had hoped for. Unable to make a final choice between two of them, and as it was not part of the formal ceremony, he was allowed to keep both to discover which spoke to him the clearest.

CHAPTER 15

COMA

FINLAND

Hannu almost dragged Anita up to his room as soon as she arrived after lunch and promptly told her the story of Arttu's attack. To Qwelby it had all been so fast that it was only hearing Hannu speak that made him realise just how skilfully he had fought. As he basked in Anita's admiration he puzzled as to how he had been able to react so instinctively, then....

'I don't like it,' he said. 'There's never any violence on Vertazia. Yet it's almost as though I'm being trained fight to get to Tullia.' He pulled his torc out from inside his t-shirt.

'My EraBand was throbbing. Every Tazian receives one on our twelfth rebirthday. They're all different. There were two that had been handed down in our families from generations ago, each made of gold and platinum, and one of them had a little Xzyliment. That's a very rare, black metal, believed to originate in the Shadow World.

'Because Quantum Twins are so special, those two bands were completely reworked, so both Tullia and I have exactly half the metals from each in ours. The designs are very different. Hers is a beautiful, triple necklace, looking like the very fine scales of a snake. Mine.' He lifted the collar of heavy looking, hexagonal links with its rich red crystal, and smiled as he ran his fingers over Othrys, as his EraBand had named itself. 'Each Tazian is given a crystal on their fourteenth rebirthday. Tullia's is purple.'

Hannu did not really understand. He thought that Qwelby should have been feeling pride both at what he had done and that he would be able to fight his way to his twin.

Anita thought she understood and wanted to lighten the atmosphere. Thinking of how they had celebrated New Year's Eve after the fighting, she asked Qwelby about festivities on Vertazia.

Qwelby talking about how the Tazii celebrated the four KeyPoint days, what on Earth were termed solstices and equinoxes, led on to what the Finns had done at Christmas.

Qwelby was told that the celebration was based around a man who had lived two thousand years ago and who said he was the Son of God. To Qwelby "God" translated as the "Multiverse". That left him puzzled. Surely everybody was the son or daughter of the multiverse?

He learnt about religion. The idea of worshipping somebody who had created everything seemed very strange. Especially when the somebodies, sometimes were or had been human beings. As more and more was explained to him, he began to understand that people who did not see the whole universe from a scientific point of view could look at it in different ways.

Then came the shock that there were other religions. Other people worshipping different Gods.

'So there are different Gods, who've all created everything?' Qwelby asked.

'They must think that because there are lots of wars between people who believe in different Gods. Killing each other just because of that,' Hannu said.

'But surely if they believe in a God who created absolutely

everything, it has to be the same God, doesn't it?' Qwelby shook his head. It was getting all too much for him to cope with. 'It's like people going to war and killing each other because they believe in eating eggs from different ends!' he said, thinking of the times he and Wrenden glued the big end of Tamina's egg into her eggcup.

'It's not just that,' Anita added. 'Our history is full of wars between people who believe in the same God, but fight each other because they have different ways of showing that belief.'

'Those wars are still going on,' Hannu said, more to Anita than Qwelby.

'But. What. Why. It makes no sense, they can't, I mean...' Qwelby stopped as he felt an oppressive atmosphere pressing down on him. It was as though he was sinking into a morass of hurt and pain, a mixture of helplessness and bewilderment laced through with anger and righteousness. The MentaNet was airy, light and easily searchable. This was like an emotional equivalent yet it was horrible, cloying. It made him think of a spider's sticky web.

'There are some differences,' Anita said. 'There are religions where they believe that women are not the equals of men. And that we women have been put on Earth to serve men.' Her words pierced through Qwelby's darkness like arrows.

'That's not just religions,' Hannu retorted.

'True,' Anita agreed.

Qwelby stared at them, incredulity written all over his face. No matter how irritatingly bossy Tullia had become in recent years, always siding with Tamina against him and Wrenden, she was not just his equal as were Tamina and Shimara, she was Kaigii! The thought that someone might believe that she was inferior to him because she was a woman...

Getting to his feet, he lurched out of the room, clutching his stomach. A few moments later his friends heard the door to his bedroom slam shut.

Bent over and clutching at his midriff, Hannu started to rise.

Anita put her hand on his arm. 'No. He's learning that in our world there is hatred, distrust, fear. Unlike anything he has ever experienced before.'

'Help me.' It was Hannu's mouth that had moved, but the faint voice was not his.

Anita pulled Hannu down, wrapped her arms around him, pulled his head onto her chest and stroked his hair. She had two boys to look after. One was in her arms. The other..... was in her heart.

No. Not her heart. Tullia's.

Anita felt so much love for her two boys flowing through what seemed like her two hearts that tears trickled from her eyes.

A lot later Anita and Hannu were to tell Qwelby how frightening that moment when he had walked out of the room had been. The ovals of Qwelby's eyes had turned completely black. When he spoke and lurched out of the room it was as though they were in the presence of one of the undead from a horror film.

Qwelby was in a terrible state, struggling to find a way to rationalise what he had been told. All Tazii knew that Azurii were always having wars. It was why there were very mixed feelings about Tazii having any connections with Earth. To his people, who always managed to find compromises, the whole concept of fighting to steal something that somebody else possessed was incomprehensible. Now to discover that they killed each other simply because of different ideas, that was just too extreme a concept to grasp.

And then for someone to say that Tullia was not as good as him, the most important person in his life...

That last thought stabbed him through both hearts. It was all his fault! After all they had achieved over more than one hundred thousand years, his actions had turned what had been the beautiful Azura Yezi into the terror that was Earth today. He tried to shout and scream and deny everything his friends had said. He was only a fifteen-year-old boy! The apparent memories of space wars and Dragon Riding were only dreams, compelling and totally real, but fantasies of his mind.

All the energy centres in his body were flooding him with emotions he was unable to control. Underneath everything was awareness of the thrill he had felt each time he had been in a fight and the pride at being victorious. He felt that his body was about to explode and be plastered all over the room. The doors in his mind closed in rapid succession. He put his hand to his throat to feel his torc. His fingers had no sensitivity.

The room started to dim. A black hole opened in front of him and its mouth grew larger and larger. With its series of curved striations it looked like the funnel web of the twelve legged lycosan. He heard the seductive music as she strummed on the strands. He was being drawn into the tunnel. She would devour him. He would be at peace and free from any more experience of the disaster that he had caused. Free from the monumental feeling of guilt at his betrayal of all that the Auriganii held dear. Free from his guilt over the war that had separated the two worlds, and free from his betrayal of his beloved twin.

With the last of his awareness, he threw himself into the lycosan's embrace, tripped over the rug and cracked his head on a frame post of the wooden headboard.

A little while later his two friends crept into the room. Where he had fallen it was easy to roll him to one side, roll the duvet back towards him, then roll him back and pull the duvet over him. Anita saw Hannu hurting as he felt Qwelby's pain and incomprehension. She knew that Tullia didn't love Qwelby like she loved Hannu. The alien's love was a beautiful mixture of loving, caring, sharing and timelessness. And Anita had felt it.

Relaxing as a sense of caring spread through her, looking at the pain in Hannu's eyes and the tears glistening in the corners,

Anita took his hand and led him down to the kitchen. There, she made them both hot chocolate and took him into the living room to sit by the fire. Just as on New Year's Eve, Anita-Tullia knew she had two boys to look after.

Seija, Hannu's mother, noted their silence as they sat down on the settee. She slipped upstairs and checked on their guest. As she came back down into the kitchen, she stopped and thought. Decision made, she took the handset from its rest, dialled the Keskinen's number and had a long, mother to mother chat with Taimi.

The next time Seija checked on Qwelby she was alarmed. He had gone very cold, his pulse rate had dropped unbelievably low and she had to listen carefully before she was able to say that he was just breathing, very shallow and very slow. She dug out an old book of medical conditions while Hannu and Anita explored the Internet. A coma was the best conclusion they could draw.

They went back into the bedroom and Hannu sat on the side of the bed.

'He's still here,' he said eventually, in almost a whisper, looking at the others with tears in his eyes. 'I've got used to feeling what he's feeling, a bit.' He wiped his eyes. 'He's terribly sad and lost. I've never felt anything like that. It's terrible. And I know I'm only picking up a little of what he's feeling.'

CHAPTER 16

PLOTTERS ALL

VERTAZIA

On becoming Arch Custodian, Ceegren had immediately set about establishing the two pillars of his plans for eventually taking control of Vertazia and restoring to the full the race's Aurigan heritage.

Now, twelve years later, there were a small but significant number of young adults who would be his fervent supporters, when he activated the hidden programming he had set in their minds whilst officiating at their adulthood ceremonies.

The issue with the twins had proved the effectiveness of the other element: what he thought of as his parliamentary base. One of his earliest suggestions to the Convocation of all Custodians had been that in order to reach out more effectively to the Tazii, every Custodian also needed to belong to another Guild, meaning they were also working in another profession. He himself continued to be an Educationer and Arkaana, and prior to becoming Arch Custodian, had been a Readjuster.

As many Tazii followed multiple life paths and thus belonged to more than one of the twelve basic groups into which society was divided, that was a small change which had been readily accepted.

Individual Tazii neither liked nor were accustomed to making far-reaching decisions, so the Convocation had been content to leave it to Ceegren, in consultation with the Arch Custodian's personal Inner Council, to carefully select members of other Guilds to become Custodians. Following their training and initiation he had invited several of the new members into his Inner Council. 'To bring a breath of fresh air,' he had explained.

Added to the several Custodians he had selected over the years, his Inner Council now included a senior member of each of the other eleven Guilds. Those Custodians had kept the other eleven Guilds fully appraised of current events, whilst he had done the same with the Arbiter of the Spiral Assembly.

Within the Assembly there was a lot of dissension about his acting so precipitously. He smiled. It would take the Assembly a long time to decide how to react to what he had created, effectively a mini-parliament capable of acting quickly and decisively, let alone consider the decisions being made. By the time they did reach a consensus, it would be irrelevant. He would have established himself as the leader the Tazii needed.

The twins had presented him with an unparalleled opportunity. The problem was that it was several years earlier than he had been planning. How to take advantage of it? He needed to relax and would think while his acolyte massaged him.

At one hundred and sixty-two years old, Ceegren's face belied his age. Smooth, wrinkle-free, looking as though it had been carved from a solid, shining block of walnut, he scarcely looked a hundred. The chestnut colour of his hair was a consequence of the genes he had inherited from his hero, the Uddîšû Insûmâne Haa-Zeyló. The only age revealing feature was his eyes. Typical of all Venerables, there was no white to be seen. They were two complete ovals of deep, rich, sea green, giving him the cognomen of Ceegren.

As he lay on the Relax Couch, Xaala's hands moved through

his energy field, a few centimetres above his robe, relaxing his tensions, physical, emotional and mental.

'You work too hard, Kosuu,' Xaala said. 'You should have summoned me before.' "KosiKosuu" was the respectful address for a Venerable. He had not wanted that formality with what was at the time a recently orphaned ten-year-old child. They had settled on "Kosuu" as a neat diminutive. Now, nearly seven years later, the familiar form of address softened their disciplined relationship.

Lying face down, Ceegren smiled. None of the other acolytes he had trained would have dared to tell him off. He knew it was because she was devoted to him. 'Ahah!'

'Kosuu. Have I hurt you?' she asked in a tone of concern.

'No, my child. You have brought me an idea.' He paused, choosing his words carefully. 'Those Quantum Twins that have gone to Azura. What do you think should be done?'

'They must never return. The energies of the third dimension on what the inhabitants call Earth will not support all the active DNA we Tazii have. We know the Azurii are very violent. Those genes reside in the first segment. Logic dictates that the twins' third segment will deactivate first, leaving them unable to control their own violence,' she replied in an assured tone, almost as if she was reprimanding him for having asked the question.

Ceegren shielded the wave of sadness that swept through him. All by herself she had intuited that the real cause of what was termed the Violence Disease was not a virus, but the Azurii's limited DNA with its lack of the violence controlling genes and also the possibility of degradation. Mentally and intellectually she was perfect. Even with her Form of a tall, lanky boy, she was perfect for his plans – if only she had charisma!

Even he as Arch Custodian, who was privy to a range of matters unknown to any other living Tazian, was not certain of what would happen to the twin's DNA whilst they were on Azura. As well as fearing exactly what Xaala had said, he also feared the opposite. The possibility that away from the strict controls imposed through the Tazian belief structure that mentally linked all Tazii together, more of the twins' DNA might become active. It was impossible to decode the language of many of the ancient Aurigan records. What he could decipher merely hinted at the exceptional abilities inherent in Quantum Twins.

He was not really concerned about the two children returning with violent tendencies. That was why Vertazia had Readjusters. And Chief Readjuster Dryddnaa was a powerful ally. He had two concerns. The first was their developing more power and then using that to inflame the natural questioning nature of the uninhibited teenagers, especially those in their fifth and six phases of creativity and integration.

Normally any such energy surges were easily controlled through the influences of the MentaNet, with little need for Readjusters to become personally involved. But if the majority of teenagers was strongly influenced, the situation would be difficult to control. Unusually repressive means would be necessary and there would be opposition to that.

His second and much more worrying concern was the possibility of greatly increased mental strength allowing the twins to reach deep into the Archives and uncover his secrets. An area where he could not ask anyone for help without taking that person into a dangerous partnership.

So far his basic plan was working. Small teams of Junior Custodians were monitoring the interdimensional divide and keeping in place a thick mist. As soon as an attempt was made to penetrate it that carried any part of the twins' or their family's signature, the mist was reinforced and communication prevented. Or that had been the situation until very recently when he had been advised of a brief penetration. Fortunately, there was no indication of communication having been established.

The Senior Custodian who had selected a team of Juniors unequal to the task had been disciplined. That may have been unfair as the youngsters who had sought the twins had demonstrated far more power than before. Yet, if Ceegren's plans were to succeed, he had to maintain absolute control, however contrary to Tazian norms and values that was.

'Would you like to help me.... help them?' he asked.

'Oh, yes please, Kosuu,' she said with undisguised enthusiasm. 'Now please turn over. When I have finished the body massage, I will massage your head. Your mind needs to relax just as much as your body.'

'Yes, Xaala,' he said meekly, hiding another smile. He relaxed under her ministrations, letting his thoughts settle into place until it was time to move to a low-backed chair.

Whilst Xaala rested her hands gently on her teacher's head and let the subtle energies do their work, she thought back to the time when she had been instrumental in preventing the twins from re-establishing their telepathic communication. Identical DNA of a boy-girl pairing was inexplicable and created a pair of abominations. Yet for a time their energies had flowed through her as a powerful and beautiful rainbow, in spite of the viciousness of the energies that Ceegren and others had unleashed to keep them apart. A corner of her mind hinted at possible, personal benefits if they were kept apart.

Xaala knew that love was what she felt for Ceegren. That it could never be reciprocated made it pure love. The twins' energies had not been like that. Yet, there had been a warmth that had bathed her so much that she had almost been sucked into the rainbow. A part of her ached to experience that warmth again.

When she had finished with her healing energies, she rested her hands gently on her teacher's shoulders. 'Please, Kosuu, share your burden with others.' She wanted to say more but was afraid that she had already presumed too much.

'Thank you, my child. You are right,' he said in a soft voice, letting one of his hands momentarily rest on hers.

Xaala felt her face heat and the blush spread all down her body. She knew he loved her like a father, yet was unable to show it, as nothing must interfere with her strict training regime. Except for brief moments like this which she treasured.

'Kosuu,' she almost whispered as she bowed her head and silently glided from the room.

Ceegren reminded himself that although outwardly shy, his acolyte had an inner core of steel. After all, she did have the same genetic inheritance as himself, from the great proponent of the True Aurigan Teachings. She was correct. He could not risk the twins returning. He needed to find a way to get her close to the twins' friends so that she could report back to him without their knowledge.

If their return could not be prevented. If they were to unlock the powers that the ancient records only hinted at...... drastic measures. Once again he blocked the thought that was arising.

CHAPTER 17

WRESTLING

FINLAND

Qwelby opened his eyes and saw his friends struggling to get him into a tracksuit. He didn't even think about trying to help. He had no energy or thoughts, except that he was looking down at them.... and his Form along with the fine silvery white cord that attached him to it. He was in his InForming Matrix, but the colours around his Form were not normal for Out-Of-Body travel. Meditation, deepstate, dreamstate, dreams: nothing fitted what was happening and he had no experience to draw on. Lost, he watched as Mrs Rahkamo put a glass of water at the bedside and left a soft light on as all three left the room.

Outside the house it was dark. A lot of time had passed since he'd run into the bedroom. He had to do something. What? Tullia! Of course. She'd have no experience but, together, surely they could help his somnolent Form? He sent out a searching thought, a gentle rainbow arcing its way across the planet.

A few moments later the rainbow curled back on itself as Tullia appeared, wearing a hooded ski suit and goggles. No! Much too tall and slender, it was a boy with a coffee coloured face. His mouth not wide enough for a Tazian, but too wide for a Finn.

Hovering in the air with his head almost touching the ceiling, the new arrival took in Qwelby's Form under the duvet then Qwelby himself, a grin slowly spreading across his face.

Busana, Qwelby thoughtsent, only to have the boy dive across the room and make a slashing gesture at the curling rainbow, which quickly pulled back out of the way.

NO! Qwelby launched himself in a counter attack, wondering why the rainbow and his potential connection with Tullia were being attacked. He gripped an arm and swung the boy around. Instead of crashing into the bed his attacker leapt on top of it, twisting out of the grip. A foot came swinging towards Qwelby's head. Taken aback by an attack that was nothing like any of his practice fights with Wrenden, Qwelby still managed to get a hand under the foot and sweep it to the side. His attacker flipped over backwards, landing on the far side of the bed.

Half minded to leap on the bed and then on to his attacker, Qwelby paused at the thought of injuring his Form lying on the bed. With no such restraint, his opponent leapt up, stepped across the inert body and threw himself at Qwelby, who grabbed the boy by the waist as they met, swivelled and bashed him against the wall.

'Enough!' Qwelby shouted. Then grunted with pain as a knee slammed up between his legs. 'Enough!' he said to himself as he threw the boy along the wall, belatedly switching from his expectation of a properly regulated physical exchange as on Vertazia, to what to him was a typical Azuran fight without rules.

He turned to the side, grabbed a chair and swung back. *Xzarze!* The lanky boy was fast. Long legs pushed him off the bed high into the air and he came crashing down on Qwelby, taking them both to the floor. A tangle of arms and legs and precious seconds wasted for Qwelby as he extricated himself from between the chair's legs. On his feet already, his opponent swung a leg, aiming his foot at Qwelby's head. Qwelby ducked to the side and launched himself off the ground, head-butting the boy's backside and sending him smacking into the wall.

Stepping up behind his attacker, Qwelby threw his arms around the boy's chest, pinning his arms to his sides, then halted in confusion. He was holding a girl! Qwelby had no problem fighting with a girl. Not only was Vertazia a world of total equality, evenly matched, he and Tullia occasionally wrestled for fun. The momentary pause was enough for Xaala to thrust her arms out, break free and swing around, aiming a punch at his head.

Ducking, Qwelby grabbed the girl around the waist and they crashed to the floor where they struggled until Qwelby eventually succeeded in pinning her arms above her head. He was puzzled by the colours flowing through her aura. With his Form in a strange limbo he was unable to read the girl's mind. He needed to look into and read her eyes.

Pinning both wrists with one hand, Qwelby used the other to reach for the goggles, but she wrenched one hand free and tried to claw his eyes. She was strong, but it was a wiry strength, Qwelby on top had the advantage of weight and more solid muscle. As he again pinned down both her hands he firmly planted a knee on her stomach. As she gasped and sagged, Qwelby leant towards her face. Momentarily fearing being kissed, she jerked her head away, just as Qwelby's teeth caught the goggles and pulled them down to reveal soft brown eyes blazing with intensity and..... excitement?

Understanding flashed through Qwelby's mind. The out of kilter colours were due to the strong male energies wrapped in the softer female shading of her aura. Warrior genes?

Why? Qwelby thoughtsent forcefully.

Abominations. Too strong together. Xaala, the perfect acolyte, had to answer truthfully.

But... Qwelby was jerked backwards. Dragons Breath!

Helplessly, he looked out of his Form's eyes as he was raised up on one arm whilst the other reached for the glass of water on the bedside cabinet and started drinking. Qwelby struggled to get free, but there was just sufficient consciousness in his body's actions to keep him in place. He groaned as his Form finished drinking and lay back down, trapping Qwelby back into the Coma.

CHAPTER 18

XAALA SHOPS

VERTAZIA

Xaala returned to her Form with mixed feelings. As she had returned to her suite of rooms after massaging Ceegren she had felt a vibration in her mind. It had to be one of the abominations seeking, but the signature was incomplete. It seemed to be the boy. She had changed into her electric blue meditation robe, lain down and slipped Out-Of-Body. As she had followed a gentle rainbow into a room she had seen what had to be an Azuran ski suit and goggles hanging on a door, and mentaformed the same for herself.

It had been a good match, her speed and agility against his brute strength. And she had won. There had been a momentary thrill when he had pinned her down and was staring at her. Those purple eyes! But she had recovered and thrust her body up with all her strength, sending him back into his Form. She had prevented him travelling to his twin. Mission accomplished.

Realising she was enjoying the replay – of violence and with an abomination, she went into the bathroom and let the neutron shower clean her completely: robe, aura and body, whilst the feeling of excitement slipped into Deep Memory.

Now, settled in her suite of rooms, Xaala thought over what

Teacher had said. It was clear what Ceegren wanted, in fact needed, for the benefit of the whole Tazian race. Beautiful as it was, her robe, which had been a gift from Ceegren, shielded only the six major power centres in her torso. It was not enough for what she was now having to do, had just done. For that, she wanted coverage for all bar her crown chakra.

She decided that a BodySuit such as BodyDancers wore would be good. A complete, skin-tight covering with its millions of tiny holes allowing energies to flow unhindered. The right one would have to be black pseudoleather with an electric blue threading for extra protection. That she might not choose to imagine wearing it when travelling Out-Of-Body in the seventh dimension was irrelevant. It was there to protect her power centres and ensure safe return to her Form in the fifth dimension.

She successfully thoughtsearched the MentaNet and flew her twistor to the only boutique advertising one with the blue threading.

Although the Tazii did not normally practice any form of gender discrimination, part of their Aurigan legacy was that the particularly strong genes of the ten great hero/ines were almost exclusively passed along either the male or female line. Her parents had made it very clear that they had wanted another boy to add to what they saw as the family's honour of continuing to pass on the genes of the great proponent of the True Aurigan Teachings. A very traditionalist family, they had considered it an affront both to his memory and their honour, that a girl had inherited his strong genes.

She had tried hard to please them, acting and dressing like a boy and seeking to emulate her older brother. No matter how hard she had tried, and in her own mind had succeeded, she had never gained her parent's approval, and her brother had gone out of his way to disparage her.

She didn't want the girl's body fate had given her. She had worked hard at exercise but had failed to produce the bulky muscles of a male. Yet she was proud of a Form that was lean and toned and honoured her mind and spirit. All but for those annoying breasts. They betrayed her and she hated them.

It was with disappointment that she accepted the bodysuit the boutique owner proffered. Not only was it a drab black, but as she held it up it was clear that it had been designed for someone shorter and with a bigger build.

A few minutes later she left the changing room in a daze. Not only was she wearing the most expensive clothing of her life, she was luxuriating in the sensation. The suit felt like a living second skin, gently massaging her whole Form as it continued to adjust to her slender height.

With complimentary words, the boutique owner gestured to the mirror.

Xaala watched as her reflection turned all the way round and came to a standstill.

She turned to the woman, frowning. Instead of a shy, boyish acolyte, she was looking at a composed and attractive young woman. Xaala's thoughts were clear to read. She wanted a true reflection, not a sales gimmick.

The woman smiled and gently nodded her understanding. From Xaala's strong aura showing maturity and a very high degree of prowess at both mental and psychic levels, the boutique owner read the youngster as several years older than she was. The lack of signs of her being Awakened – she had seen that before in acolytes who were intensely dedicated to their studies of the inner worlds and subsumed their sexuality.

'Please, Kulaa,' she said, 'switch vision and observe.'

Puzzled, and somewhat taken aback at being addressed as Kulaa, "Young Mistress", Xaala switched vision and looked again. It was Mirror and displaying a true reflection. She gawped. That wasn't her!

The now softly glowing suit hugging her Form showed a tall, slender and self-possessed young woman. The hints of electric blue threads emphasised the curves of her long legs and her flat stomach. No longer hidden under the soft drapes of her working tunic or the baggy tops she wore when relaxing, those annoying round protuberances....... looked all right.

And her face. Her mouth smaller than average, her eyes not as slanted as customary. No longer ugly.

She smiled in amazement.

'Tall, slender and neat, my dear Kulaa,' the woman said. 'Ignore those puerile boys who say that all they want on girls are big breasts and a big bottom.'

Feeling dizzy, Xaala ran her tongue around the lips of her mouth as she accepted the impressions she was receiving. She had to admit she looked good. More than that, she looked like the person she needed to be to work on the DarkSide. Running her hands down her body they dangled by her hips with an empty feel. Where was the belt that should have held..... what?

'Aurigan women were also warriors,' a voice whispered inside her head.

A little later, a still dazed Xaala left the shop with a parcel tucked securely underneath her arm. The suit had been ridiculously expensive, but in her heart she knew it was going to be worth every energy credit it had cost. She was both excited and afraid of the turn her life had taken. If she was right, she was going to need as much protection as possible. And what was that missing belt all about?

Back in her suite, she dropped the suit on the floor and stripped. A quick twist with one hand piled her long mane of hair on top of her head as she stepped into the suit, and savoured the sensation as it slid up her legs, up her arms and around her body, followed by the comforting feeling of security as the szeame swiftly closed all the way up the front and the suit moulded to her figure.

She could have consulted Ceegren about her plans, but had felt impelled to act for herself. Besides which, if she understood the situation correctly, and she was never in any doubt about her wide range of skills, there could not be anything explicit between them. At all costs he had to be protected.

She loved him and would shield him.

Once again she ran her hands over her body and was reassured by the protection provided to all her power centres by her..... DarkSuit. Looking at the mirror, she was surprisingly proud of her reflection as she saw it turn completely around. She nodded. She would accept her female Form. After all, it only existed to host her powerful, male Kore. A fleeting smile crossed her lips as she sensed the potential for deception that might be useful in the future.

CHAPTER 19

CREATION

VERTAZIA

With his great uncle masterminding the work in his laboratory, Shandur stood in for Mandara at a meeting of the Council of the Academy of Discoverers. His agitated thoughts having brought his great aunt to the front door, she opened it as he dismounted and left his twistor happily rotating in a cradle on the patio.

With all the tensions and worries, the tall woman had stopped wearing her Gelele Silk as she did not have the energy to infuse it with her normal seasonal range of colours. Instead, she was wearing a simple calf length dress in varying shades of blue with white highlights. Her hair was more midnight blue than black, with an unusual streak of white that fell to one side. 'In sympathy with my husband,' she would say with a laugh when asked.

Seated a few moments later in her Homely Room, still in his two-tone orange flying suit, Shandur came straight to the point. 'The meeting was a disaster. The Academicians were unable to agree on whether what we are developing may be used to recover the twins now, or only after all other, unnamed and unspecified options have been explored, or whether to forbid its use. They adjourned to another meeting to make that decision but, because I pressed the urgency of the situation, our plans will be referred to the Spiral Assembly. Without even a recommendation from the Council!'

Lellia groaned, thinking of the impossible delay. Tazian society divided itself into twelve groups, the numbers in each varying from large numbers of Artists and Maintainers to small numbers of Custodians and Readjusters. Each Guild contained two Councils of thirteen members. A Professional Council of senior members, a Collector Council representing adults of all ages who gathered the thoughts and opinions of all the members on anything and everything that affected Tazian life, apart from professional matters.

Those twenty-four Councils formed the basic membership of the Spiral Assembly. In addition there were the Focalisers for the fundamental energy basis of Tazian life: generation, consolidation and distribution. Always Venerables, there was one pair of each for the Professionals and one pair of each for the Collectors. With the addition of the final pinnacle of the pyramid, always a Venerable and known as the Arbiter, that made a total of three hundred and twenty five adults.

As the Tazii did not believe in excluding minority views by way of majority voting, there had to be a consensus for the Assembly to float a suggestion to the whole population. There then had to be a consensus throughout the MentaNet. For several millennia that form of government had suited the leisurely process of Tazian life.

'Impossible delay,' Lellia said.

'Agreed. We have to act. And now.' Angry reds and blacks flared though Shandur's energy field.

'A MentaShield will give us away,' Lellia said, colours of despair tingeing her aura.

'Not if the disruption seems to come from the XzylStroem,' her great nephew said, firmly.

She looked aghast. 'That kind of deception is unheard of...'

'Outside of the Shadowlands.'

Shandur reacted as if stung. He had not heard his wife arrive. 'Mizena! I didn't want you to know...'

'They are my children! I have a right to know,' she reprimanded her husband. 'You need not protect me!' she added, sounding almost ferocious. In place of her usual harassed look, solely due she said to her children's antics, was a look of fierce determination. Although only of average height, she was strongly built from all the work on the families' gardens and farms. That and the colours flaring in her aura made her seem to tower over her husband.

Lellia took in the colours strongly flowing through her great niece's aura. Steeling herself against what they were going to do, setting themselves against the traditions that had maintained the peace and harmony amongst the Tazii since time immemorial, she took a deep breath and got to her feet. 'Let's go do it!' she said, and summoned Lift.

Delivered at the door to Mandara's main laboratory, they opened it, stepped inside, and stopped. 'What? How? Who?' they chorused. Looking past the youngsters' broad grins, their stained bodysuits and smudged faces were proof that they had thrown themselves into the work, a little too literally for Mizena's liking.

All the adults and youngsters had been working for several days on the construction of a transdimensional recovery vehicle. Tangled in a complex of interacting algorithms, Mandara had spent most of his time conducting the transdimensional symphony, whilst Shandur had been blending matter and energy with the Shadow World and Lellia melding the esoteric into the whole framework.

Mizena was not a scientist, engineer or psychic. 'Just a homemaker,' she would say, referring to all she did in running Siyataka, the family home, which felt so empty without the twins. As well as caring for all the family semi-sentients, she ran the garden and the farm so that every meal she prepared came from what she had cultivated, and had made sure that everyone took short breaks for food and drink. In addition, she had applied balm to burns, plasters to cuts, eased tired minds and occasionally rubbed ointment onto bruised pride.

The youngsters had never worked so hard in all their lives, nor had so much fun. Fetching, carrying, holding, pushing, pulling, lifting, dropping and thoughtcatching so nothing was broken, and constantly thoughtweaving.

Whilst Shandur had been at the meeting of the Academy, Lellia and Mizena had decided to take a break, leaving the others at work in the laboratory. Mizena had planned a solid programme of study for the youngsters so that whilst they helped with finding the twins they were also able to continue their college work. As she had persuaded their parents to agree to them staying at Lungunu for a few days, she had taken the opportunity of the break to check on how they were progressing with their studies.

When the three adults had left the laboratory, the intended recovery vehicle had been an almost translucent, gently shimmering, rectangular block. Now they were looking at the sort of shop you could find on any Tazian street corner. A domed, oval building with an arched, central door, large round windows on either side and another window "around the corner". Each window was awkwardly displaying all sorts of inexplicable objects, just demanding that passers-by enter and ask: 'What on 'Tazia is that?'

CHAPTER 20

CUCKOO CLOCKS

VERTAZIA

Recovering from their surprise, they looked to Mandara for an explanation. With a smile, he pointed to his apprentices as he thoughtsent with a chuckle: *'Youngsters' idea. A mega-thinking session.'*

'It's an Auto-Locating, Self-Defining, Twins-Come-Home, Corner Shop,' the four chanted, grinning all the time. They had empowered themselves with the energy of the sixth dimension by using the twelve-sided symbol called Óweppâ that all six had created some time ago under the twins' direction, and then mindmelded on a scale they had never previously attempted.

'X.O.N.N.O.X. XOÑOX!' they chanted. A drum roll, flashing lights and over the doorway, resplendent in its rainbow of ten colours of shimmering music, was the finishing touch to all the scientific and esoteric work that had gone into its creation: the name.

THE CORNER SHOP

Between them, the youngsters managed to explain that wherever the shop appeared it would automatically transform its appearance to be that of a Corner Shop fitting in to the locality, plus a back room that remained Tazian.

'Right. Let's test it,' Mandara said. 'Lellia. Will you and Shandur activate the Stroems. Mizena will monitor the Sending.' He held up a hand to still the youngsters' protests. 'You will link hands in a circle around her to give her the strength she will need. We cannot risk your being sucked into the Sending.' He acknowledged their glum looks. 'We promised your parents.'

'For this first test I will send it to Azura, not very far but a mountainous area of little population.' WheelChair took Mandara to the control console.

As Mizena settled herself comfortably and slipped into a deepstate, the youngsters put cushions on the floor, settled into the lotus position and held hands.

House trembled. They could hear a Moan knocking to be let in. Door slid Bolts across and Frame gripped Lock's tongue tightly. Claws scraped across Window, which tightened the Catches. Room shivered as Stroems wailed and Xzyled. Drawing on Shadow energy they bypassed all restraint, coruscating through the central dome and slithering all over the outside of the building.

Lungunu withdrew behind the transdimensional shielding, colourscoped its walls and merged into the landscape. All five wings drew themselves in, like the five pairs of legs of an arakan preparing to defend itself against an attacking ichnedae.

A soft hum emanated from the machines set all around the room. It rose to a whine. Ribbons of coloured music reached out from the very walls themselves, twisting and turning, feeding quantum energy from other dimensions into the shop. The algorithms broke down into their constituent equations and merged with the ribbons.

Mandara saw the heads of all five people fall forward onto their chests and felt panic rising as they seemed to shimmer in and out of his vision.

In all its vibrant, crystalline, double-holographic lattice-work, The Corner Shop quivered and revolved on its axis. The name blurred, stretched, became illegible, returned. The whole construction was spinning at the speed of light so it looked as though it was standing still. The whine grew louder. The shop flickered in and out of view. Mandara glanced around. All appeared well.

Then.

With a rumble, a flash and a smell of seaside ozone, the shop disappeared. Mizena slumped as though unconscious. Her face lost all its colour and veins of ice started to form across her arms. The heads of the four youngsters returned to being upright. Mandara could see their eyes were open. Four pairs of bright rainbow coloured ovals. Twirling.

TIME stood still

All were frozen in suspended animation

TIME became TIMELESSNESS

There was an almighty, reverberating crash as though the stars had fallen from the sky and plunged into the sea.

TIME returned

Not trusting his voice to command the audio controls, Mandara's hands darted rapidly across the touchpads. There was a sound like a space rocket taking off. The whole room rocked. The air was sucked into the centre of the room. As Mandara fought for breath, the air exploded back into his face, choking him and blowing the youngsters onto their backs. As he hacked and coughed, the shop reappeared a few microns away from its original position.

The friends sat up with the end of a scream. As Mizena looked around her, they seized their heads between their hands and the beginnings of four screams arrived.

'Lift,' called Mizena. 'Six to the Homely Room. House. Cook. Special Restorative Chay, strong and hot!'

Hearing the message and having watched the Stroems pour back into the cavern like a class of liquid children jostling to be first into the school canteen, Shandur and Lellia sealed the dome to the Cavern and joined the family just as Cook arrived with a trolley bearing healthy cakes and a large jug of steaming Jungle Juice. It was her pride. The jug bore the legend: "Internal Consumption Only". There was a legend that the words had been etched on by using the Juice itself.

The jug of Jungle Juice empty and the last cake eaten, all eyes focussed on Mizena.

'The instruments show the shop was gone for six minits, yet had been on Azura for about twenty-one,' Shandur reported as he put an arm around his wife.

'What's even more curious,' said Mandara, 'was that instead of one of the holographic, lattice-arrays remaining on Vertazia as we expected, the whole shop completely disappeared from the Laboratory.'

'Sixth dimension travel,' Pelnak muttered thoughtfully, earning a surprised look from the two scientists.

'It was the opposite to what I'd expected,' Mizena said as she looked around. 'You four were drawing on my energy, rather than me on yours.'

Not intentional, all four thoughtsent.

'The shop didn't look anything like it did in the laboratory,' Tamina said. 'Where it had arrived on a snowy hillside, there were several other buildings. They were log cabins with verandas and porches, gently sloping roofs covered in thick snow. The shop looked almost identical, right down to having a log pile outside and smoke coming from a chimney. The only difference was that it looked like a shop and not a house, with its shop door, a round window either side of that and one round the corner.'

Mizena sighed with relief and rested against her husband.

Tamina took another sip from her mug and cradled it in both hands. 'I walked up to the window and looked inside. It's worked just as we planned. I think. Because what was inside was very curious. Definitely not Tazian. It was filled with what I guess were miniature houses. Some had toy people going round the fronts, others had birds popping out and making cheeping sounds.'

'We didn't see much,' Shimara said.

'No. It was like we were feeding Tamina with our energy,' Pelnak added.

Acting more like indivisible twins then Qwelby and Tullia, Pelnak and Shimara were known as the not-twins. Although a few months older than the twins, the boy and girl were markedly shorter than them, rounder in build and had a stronger red cast to their skins, emphasised by their red hair which each wore in an unusual unisex, page-boy cut, falling just below their ears.

'I couldn't get close,' Wrenden added. 'But I think the name was changing. I couldn't make it out as it was all blurry.'

Lellia nodded. 'It is working and better than we'd hoped, I'm sure.' She smiled as she sent a thought to the laboratory. A few moments later everyone heard the music as the ten colours of the rainbow hanging in mid air spelt out:

CURIOUS SHOP

'Welcome, Curious Shop,' Mandara said, addressing the airwaves, knowing that House would spread throughout Lungunu the knowledge of the arrival of another Semi-Sentient.

'Let them try to stop us now!' exclaimed Mizena with a steely glare, daring anyone to contradict her. Then she blushed deeply with a mixture of surprise at herself and a most un-Tazian feeling of determination to fight anyone who dared to oppose her.

Lellia looked around at the tired faces. 'Bedtime,' she announced, looking at the youngsters. 'Lift will take you. You deserve it after all you've done. Sleep well. Meet at breakfast. A late meal?' Nods and grunts were all the confirmation she needed.

Deep inside a mountain on Raiatea, Professor Romain's unique equipment continued searching for a signal that would make their creator's dream a reality.

Sensors quivered. Gigabytes of data splurged along pathways, thundered through connections. The hum of the air-conditioning rose to a whine as it fought the waves of rising heat.

On the backs of millions of excited photons, terabytes of data pulsed along fibre optic cables until they reached a break. Without the protection of the conduit, they splurged forth, their message swept away by the electro-magnetic field created by all the machinery in the room.

A few hardy photons leapt the gap and reached the switch. Too few, too weak a current. The switch quivered, then fell back, unable to close the gap. Unable to sound the alarm.

The scientists slept on, their dreams of fame undisturbed.

On a bench in the corner of the room, the tail of Romain's ruptured logic analyser, which he had named Purple Python after its coiled shape and colour, twitched, then fell still.

Had the dream died along with the Python?

CHAPTER 21

SURROUNDED

KALAHARI

In the middle of the morning a now very hot Tullia was granted a short rest break. Whilst she ate one of the water filled maramas her captor had saved, she removed her tracksuit bottoms and thick sweater. To her surprise and discomfort she was ordered to remove her white t-shirt. She wilted under his sneering explanation of how it stood out against the brown landscape. That was obvious. She'd been so focussed on trying to establish a good relationship by navigating through the bush that she hadn't stopped to think that they were hiding.

She felt her face being gripped and was unable to turn her head from his foul breath. 'Remember. You live only as long as you are useful to me,' her captor repeated. His grasp was so firm that she was unable to speak. She made the slightest of nods and trembled with shame as she felt warm liquid run down her thighs.

They walked on, Tullia leading as before.

Midday and another short break. A brief conversation and she learnt that he'd killed a woman. He grimaced. 'I was drunk. We argued. Once too often. A knife. She was my wife.' He paused.

'This gun I took from a man. He didn't even know I was taking it.'

Tullia was stunned. Beyond anything she'd ever seen at the Elmits, where Tazii were able to see what they called flikkers, essentially a mixed bag of heavily censored television programmes beamed around Earth via satellite. This was real. Horribly, frighteningly real.

'What will happen to you if you are captured?' She was surprised at how calm she sounded.

'If they catch me, they will put me in prison. I will die. No Bushman can live in a metal box, locked away from the sky, the ground, our homeland.'

He has said that I live as long as I am useful. If he is captured, then I will be no use to him. He will kill me.

He grunted. 'Move. That way.' He indicated a new direction.

In spite of feeling numb, 'Due east,' Tullia automatically said as she got to her feet and picked up her bundle of clothes.

By the late afternoon Tullia and her captor had moved into an area where the bushes were much thinner on the ground and there was hardly a tree in sight. Beating into her nearly naked body the sun had more than filled her solar energy quotient. Sweat was trickling from every pore, the weight of her bundle of clothes was a drag, and she was beginning to feel lightheaded. She desperately needed to rest, but the sun was getting close to the horizon and she decided it best to wait until it was dark, when it would be cool.

Her thoughts were cut short as she heard the sound of yet another engine and dived to the ground. She was about to crawl to the nearest bush when she felt the gun being pressed into her side.

'Stay still, face down,' he commanded in a harsh whisper.

The noise was coming from behind. As it got closer, it divided and she realised that there were two vehicles. From the sound as they passed on either side, smaller than the open lorries she'd seen carrying tourists around. She recognised a new sound. 'Whirlybird,' she said as she glanced out of the corner of her eyes. She had learnt that from Xashee and much preferred it to "helicopter". "Whirlybird" was what it looked like, its rotating wings reminding her of a BorerBird. Although that was bright orange and emerald green, not the white and blue she was looking at.

A harsh wind beat down on her as the whirlybird hovered right above them. Moments later it pulled away and the awful wind ceased. She heard shouted commands in Afrikaans to surrender.

There was movement behind her, a rustling of material. She risked turning her head. He was pulling her t-shirt from the bundle. Holding it in his left hand, he stretched his arm and waved it.

'Stand up. Slowly,' came the clear command.

He captor stood up, the gun concealed behind his right thigh.

'Get up,' he said.

As Tullia complied, he stepped behind her and grasped her left bicep, her white t-shirt dangling at her side, clear for all to see. From the corner of her eye she could see he was holding the gun by the side of her head.

She saw two vehicles facing her. On the left was a small blue truck with men in grey-blue uniforms standing in the back. On the right was a small sand-coloured truck. Standing in the back were men in khaki uniforms, carrying strangely shaped sticks.

'Can you drive?' he hissed at her.

'No.'

He grunted. She sensed his anger and frustration and guessed he could not drive.

'Put your guns down and get out of the trucks. All of you,' her captor commanded. 'Not that driver.' He pointed his gun towards the men in khaki.

No-one moved. 'Do it. You want me to shoot a Siska. Worth a lot of money. Alive.'

Tullia felt the barrel of the gun pressed hard into her right breast. With everyone else fully dressed, she suddenly became embarrassed at her lack of clothing. Her self assuredness fled and panic flooded through her.

They had seen many different animals during the day. Most times they had crouched down to merge with the bush, and several times the animals had come so close she could almost have stroked them. On one occasion a bull elephant had made a mock charge and display – flapping its massive ears and trumpeting through its raised trunk. Then moved on with the rest of the small herd, including a baby elephant with its trunk holding its mother's tail. Each time she had sensed her captor's connection with the land and the animals. And he had been impressed by her reactions, and how she had not been frightened of the elephant because she knew it was a young male showing off.

Navigating by the sun, sinking into the energy of the land and its inhabitants and forgetting the gun, she had allowed herself to think of him as just another bushman with whom she had become friends. Jerked out of her complacency, angry at her stupidity and fearing death, she was trembling uncontrollably and once again felt warm liquid run down her thighs.

'Remember you have warrior genes,' a voice inside her head whispered.

Looking around, Tullia saw that all the men had moved far to the left, except for one man in the driver's seat of the sandy-coloured truck.

CHAPTER 22

FREEDOM

KALAHARI

'Move,' her captor ordered. They crabbed sideways towards the sand coloured vehicle facing them, on the opposite side to the driver, with Tullia being used as a shield from the men in uniform, the gun now digging hard into her side.

The movement had broken that terrible moment of sheer terror and she started thinking. Although she had not been in a vehicle, she had seen the tourists go past and had learnt that there were no thought controls, the driver having to control it manually. Her captor's plan had to be that they would get in and he would make the man drive just as he had made her walk. But. If the driver got out the other side as they got in? The computation was simple. Capture plus Gun equals my Death.

She studied the little truck. Focussing on calculating the distances to the last twelfth of an ynchi helped stop her from trembling. The risk factor? She was sure from the way he handled the gun that there were no thought controls. She hoped that would give her enough time.

'Get in,' her captor ordered, as Tullia reached the side of the Land Rover.

All sound ceased. There was no whisper of the evening breeze. She was calm. She had no need of any weapon. Certainly not the two-handed sword she'd fought with during the Great Schism.

The step was a long way off the ground, perfect for her plan. She put her hands on both sides of the doorway, lifting up her left leg she put her foot on the step, took a little hop and launched herself forward, her right leg lashing out with all her strength.

With her memories taking her back to Aurigan times, her mind failed to fully compensate for the over three metre Form she no longer inhabited and her foot missed the gun. The heavy, man's shoe she was wearing crunched into her captor's face. She heard his shout and the sound of him falling to the ground, followed by the sound of heavy boots running, a thud and a cry, a crashing sound followed by an awful scream.

'I missed!' she exclaimed in disgust as, losing her grip on the doorway and falling flat on her face on the seat, she saw a look of surprise on a young man's face. His hand reached for hers, they touched, grasped fingers, but sticky with sweat she slipped through her would-be rescuer's grip and slid down, crashing her face against the bottom of the doorway and then the step. She rolled over and ended up half sitting against the front wheel, blood pouring from her nose and cut lips.

She was in a dream. Hearing the piercing call of the Hoopoo: uip, uip, uioooo, took her back to her fall on the Tsodilo Hills several days ago.

Tullia saw a man in khaki stop in front of her, looking alarmed. Barked commands from another stirred him into life. He picked up the T-shirt and tried to staunch her bleeding. She saw him wrinkle his nose and realised how disgusting she smelt.

A call from further off, someone had found a parcel of clothes. The same strong voice ordered them to be brought and for her to be helped into the sweater. There was blood everywhere. A box was produced with a big red cross on the side. Clean dressings were applied to her battered face and she was offered a metal bottle. She drank warm but beautiful water.

'How are you feeling?'

In front of her she saw a grizzled face with a kindly look. 'Better. Lucky. Hurting.' She managed a wan smile. She understood the muscle pains. It was the occasional sharp stab in her belly that puzzled her.

'That was very brave,' the man said

'Is he hurt?' she asked, registering three white marks forming a big letter V on his shirt sleeve.

'He'll be alright,' was the gruff answer.

Just as well, she thought to herself. I'm in too much shock to heal him.

A man in blue knelt down, the setting sun glinting off silver and blue badges on his shoulders. 'Did you set the plates, jug and blanket that way?' he asked as he wrinkled his nose.

'Yes.'

'You are a clever young woman. It was your sign that told us in which direction to look. I doubt we'd ever have found you without that.'

Xara would have found me... or my body. She shivered. 'Can I go home now?'

The men heard the voice of a little girl. 'How old are you?' the man in blue asked.

'Fifteen.'

As the two men got to their feet and stepped away, the army sergeant turned to the police Inspector who'd asked the question. 'They're both yours. But we'll take the murderer to the station for you?'

'Thanks. We'll take her home. Talk with her uncle.' The Inspector looked around the two groups of men with their handcuffed prisoner on the ground. 'Meet you back at the station? Keep her out of this.' He gestured to Tullia.

'She's San?' the sergeant asked.

'Must be. Some strange mix. Her uncle is a mix himself.'

'Only seventy thousand years apart,' Tullia mumbled as she smiled faintly and nodded. She shivered again, feeling the cold as the sun started to dip below the horizon. Tears welled up in her eyes.

'Let's get some more clothes on you,' the sergeant's kindly voice said as he passed her the track suit bottoms, assuming that the odd-looking girl who said she was younger than his oldest child, yet a lot larger, had to be some mix of Himba and San.

Tullia quickly stripped. Steadying herself against the Land Rover she got up and held out her hand. 'Water please,' she said to the man holding the bottle. Unaware of the stunned silence, she splashed water around her loins and down her legs.

'Turn your backs,' the sergeant barked.

She put the water bottle on the seat of the Land Rover and, avoiding the bloody patches, used the t-shirt to wash and dry herself, puzzling at the men's energy fields and strong thoughts reaching her. She sensed they considered her little more than a savage, yet V-Man as she named him, was treating her with what had to be a courtesy of his own people.

Bare feet on the thick sand. She wriggled her toes, digging deep into the land. Happy memories of the day flooded in. The soft whispers of the animals' thoughts of food, awareness and... Of course those lovely animals saw us and smelled us but were not afraid as we were no threat to them because... we're Bushmen. The mock charge of the young bull elephant. He was showing off... to me! Oh, Kaigii, come to me. If we can't get back home, we can live here. Living is very different but life is not that dissimilar.

Her thoughts were interrupted by a cough. She recognised V-Man's kind energy. Embarrassed that she had been lost in thought, she picked up the bottle and held it out to him saying: 'Thank you.' Then pulled on her jumper and tracksuit bottoms.

The sergeant wrapped a blanket around her. She felt his warm and caring energies and, happy that she no longer stank, lent against him as he led her to the blue Land Rover, sighing with the pleasure of her feet sinking into the warm sand.

'Are you all right?' he asked.

'I can feel the planet.'

As they reached the vehicle she felt the man in blue put an arm around her waist. The two men lifted her up as the young driver successfully reached for her hands.

'Put her in the middle seat,' the Inspector said.

'Yes, sah,' the driver replied, keeping hold of her hands and gently pulling her next to him. He reached across and pulled a strap around her, clicking into place by her side.

She was angry with her twin for not being there when she needed him, and angry at herself for needing him. The young driver was cute. Out of spite and knowing that when they were together she and Qwelby would share memories, she gave the policeman a big smile, made her purple orbs shine and fluttered her eyelashes. No big, round eyes, this was not her "Little Girly Act", but a genuine "Thank you". Qwelby would still hate it.

Colours flared through the policeman's aura as he smiled. Colours she had noticed in her captor's energy field. But his had been dark and dirty. The young man's were bright and clean and she felt a nice, warm energy coming from him.

She leant back against the seat. The strap was uncomfortable, nothing like the gentle form-fitting safety fields on Vertazia. She moved it to a more comfortable position, noting how it made her breasts jut out, and was only vaguely aware of an increase in the warm energy from the driver.

A brown arm reached in and put her shoes and soiled clothes on the floor of the cab.

'Where's the pistol?' the Inspector asked.

'One of my men has it,' growled the Sergeant. 'The young officer is in the doghouse.'

The Inspector nodded. Everyone knew of the unrivalled abilities of the San in the bush. Slipping up behind a soldier and removing his holstered gun was no challenge. 'See you at the station,' he said. The two men shook hands. The Inspector climbed into the cab alongside Tullia as the sergeant walked back to his men.

CHAPTER 23

THE GREAT SCHISM

FINLAND & EARTH

Qwelby's eyes opened as he reached for another glass of water and an Inner Self slipped out. How to stay free? Not in this room. New Year's Eve, the fight in the woods. As he thought that, Qwelby's InForming Matrix appeared in the dark forest. In his mind he flicked back to that evening, imaging the moment when he had been clutching onto Hannu like a drowning sailor to a lifebelt. There was a slight tug, a soft breath and..... he was free! His Form had slipped back into what Qwelby decided must be a DarkState, although he'd never heard of one.

What to do?

Reaching out to Tullia – another attack.

Trying to get back to Vertazia – impossible. He knew from Great-Great Aunt Lellia's teaching during his and Tullia's early experiments with travelling OOB, that it was impossible to move from the solidity of the third dimension into the fifth. Besides which, he was aware that without having been consciously released from his Form he was in a strange half-way energy state. A sub-set of his full Self.

Whilst the fighting he had experienced when he and his twin

had tried to connect had been in the seventh dimension, sadly, travel to Vertazia that way was not possible as long as his body was firmly anchored in the third dimension.

He had learnt one important item from the girl who had attacked him – the power that he and Kaigii must possess when together. When his Form regained consciousness, he would try and insert that into a dream.

'Strike one,' he said to himself, thinking of StickBall. Why the DarkState? Can I find the answer? Dare I slip into his memory and not get trapped?

In the room all is third dimension. Out here there's a great interplay of seventh dimension energies. I will concentrate on those. Use them to anchor me here. Okay Form, here I come. Please don't wake up.

Qwelby was on a very large island in the middle of an ocean. As if in a dream, he knew that the planet was in the grip of an ice age with only a narrow band around the equator inhabitable. A long way ahead across rolling fields of many coloured crops, a city rose out of the hill as though it was an extension of the ground. As he approached, he realised it was. It was all made from living stone, shaped over centuries by Aurigan architects into the most beautiful array of buildings he'd ever seen. Several towers rose high into the air and columns of light reached out of sight behind the softest of white clouds. Shining colours travelled up and down the columns. Auriganii travelling between the different dimensions of the two planets.

On Vertazia he had seen many images of what the Tazii thought Aurigan buildings looked like. None had ever approached the indescribable perfection of what he was seeing. With the many colours producing their own music, the birds flying around seemed to be part of an orchestra of movement and sound. Yet. He sensed a disturbing darkness.

Over a few moments the sun set and rose many times before he reached the city. The beauty was diminishing, the colours leaching out of the stone, fewer birds flying. Thunder rolled around the ground but there was no lightning.

He was in a very large circular room high up in a tower. In the centre was the largest and purest crystal he had ever seen. It was vibrating but the music was not harmonious. Several Auriganii were working around it. He understood they were seeking to bring it into balance for....

He was outside the city, an Aurigan warrior, a youthful nine hundred years old. The governor of the city. But more than that, the leader of.... a scrambling of words that reduced to something like The Undivided Party.

He was in the midst of a battle, fighting men and.... Auriganii. This was impossible. This had never happened. An arrow flew towards him. He ducked and let it clang off his helmet. He was over three metres tall with a sword to match. He swept it to the side and decapitated a.... human!

Total incomprehension filled him, yet the warrior was in command. The attacking humans carried simple weapons. He understood that Aurigan rules of fairness were being applied and the Auriganii on both sides were using the same, simple weapons, otherwise there would have been a total slaughter of the humans - the offspring of Aurigan-hominid mating and the future inhabitants of Earth. And Qwelby was in his Self of thirteen thousand years ago.

A hail of arrows fell all around, many glancing off his armour and forcing his own human fighters to retreat. The attackers had drawn back under cover of the arrows. As they ceased falling Qwelby expected his warrior to stride forward, yet he did not move but watched as what looked like a rectangular tortoise crept towards him. A large group of humans were pressing forward, long shields locked together in front, on the sides and over their heads, with a row of much longer shields rising out of the centre. The tortoise began to look more like a porcupine as a barrage of arrows thudded into the wooden shields.

'That's a new one, Kaigii,' he murmured.

Kaigii? His twin? On the opposite side? NEVER! He shouted as his warrior raised his sword above his head and twirled it around before plunging into the ground. Slowly, the sounds of battle ceased as a wave of silence spread out from where he stood.

The tortoise parted down the centre and from within a central group of shield-carrying Auriganii – she emerged. Kaigii! 'Zeyusa,' a memory said. Like himself, she well over three metres tall and magnificent in her armour. She looked like a warrior queen from a forbidden flikker he and Tullia had seen in the ShadowMarket. Now, he understood why both of them had felt uncomfortable at the time and never talked about it.

He assumed that there must have been a brief communication as the forces on both sides drew back. On each side an Aurigan wearing white robes and holding a shining staff stood facing, not the enemy, but their own troops.

Qwelby gulped as he saw he was trapped and about to face his twin in single combat.

The clash of swords echoed across the battle field. Birds in the city rose up squawking. Swords hammered on shields as the twins circled, feinted, swung and thrust. Zeyusa was fast and light of foot, too often slipping out of the way of his blows. Her strikes on his shield were strong, but as she staggered backwards from his own blows, he realised he was the stronger.

His strength and her agility made them an even match.

His fear forgotten in the excitement and still not really believing what was happening, Qwelby felt a thrill each time their swords clashed. When they locked swords and for a moment stared into each other's eyes – it was his Tullia he was seeing. Large purple orbs in ovals of blue, each limned in silver. Labirden Xzarze, she is magnificent!

They thrust each other apart and a blow sent him stepping back apace. For a split second he thought of getting back to his Form as he had so much to dreamfeed him. Then swords clashed and Qwelby exalted as he forced his twin back a pace. This was better than any mock battle on Vertazia. Playing dragons and unicorns had nothing on this. And they were as evenly matched as at home. And they weren't going to hurt each other.

Swords locked again and she was staring into his eyes. This wasn't the first battle they'd fought. It was never supposed to have come to this. Arguments between opposing views had grown out of control, humans had become involved on both sides. Somehow a fight had started, escalated and grown into a protracted war. With the Auriganii seeing their children dying, each battle had ended as individual combat between the twins. And a tie.

The faintest of smiles crossed her lips. His own mouth curved into his lop-sided smile.

A thought exchange took place. Qwelby discovered that the full Aurigan heritage was fast being lost. There was a window of opportunity when the essential stars were in the correct alignment for an attempt to be made to restore that heritage. There were two opposed views. His Self of thirteen thousand years ago and his supporters believed the only way was to use the power of the massive crystal.

Zeyusa and her supporters considered that the crystal would shatter under the stress and that would destroy the planet. The alternative was to carefully separate the crystal into twelve segments, but that was going to take time.

The fear of all was that if separating the crystal took too long, the Auriganii would not have the strength to try again when the next stellar alignment occurred, several thousand years in the future.

Convinced that his actions were going to destroy the world, Zeyusa was determined to seize the city and try the separation. He,

Ananki, was equally convinced that his plan would not destroy the world and was the only way to restore their heritage.

There was a resounding clash as Ananki and Zeyusa locked swords again. Each feeling the slight prick of a dagger in the gap between breastplate and backplate, they stared into each others' eyes, thoughtshared and stepped apart until well out of sword reach. Saluting, each asked the other to concede – and refused.

Qwelby was parched. *I need..... ah, no.....*

Too late. He watched through his Form's eyes as the glass was picked up and did his best to encourage his Form to take little sips while he focussed on creating a dream sequence. All that Qwelby had was genetically implanted memories. He was not his own ancestor of thirteen thousand years ago. His murmured 'Strike two,' as he was once again enfolded by the DarkState prevented him from sensing the question mark that had arrived in his mind.

CHAPTER 24

HOME

KALAHARI

The jolting ride roused Tullia. She noticed Sah, as she thought he was called, leaning forward and concentrating. Frustrated that she was unable to see anything in particular in the headlights apart from the rough, winding track through the bush, she asked what he was looking for.

When he explained that he was watching for places where the sand was so deep they might sink into it, Tullia immediately showed her interest and started talking in her limited Afrikaans about tracking animals. Soon the Inspector was teaching her what to look for.

The depth of the tyre marks at the sides of the track that indicated the depth of the sand. The difference between the heavier lorries that the Meera drove when taking tourists sightseeing and what they were in. Then explaining about the shifting nature of the underlying rock that could turn what had been and continued to look like a safe and shallow layer of sand into a trap, and how a vehicle was rescued.

The constable was happy to tell her what he had to do to drive the Land Rover, as she learnt it was called. She thought it all very complicated as in answer to her question as to why it was not all automatic, he explained about gears and relating them to the driving conditions.

By that time they had reached a wide strip of black road. The Inspector had been out before sunrise and still had a lot to do. His prisoner was injured and he had to ensure he was being given proper attention. The man might be a Bushman and a murderer, but the policeman was proud to be a Motswanan. There were standards, and although the injuries had been caused by the soldiers who had been nearer to the San than his own constables, he was the senior officer and would have to justify the action taken.

He leant back, relaxed and dozed, half aware a little while later of a head resting on his shoulder. It felt like past times, being with his children, all of them tired after a long day out.

Shaken about as the Land Rover turned off the main road, the Inspector woke up and once again concentrated on watching for deep sand. Tullia tried to help but her eyes kept on closing. Eventually, they arrived at the village to find the whole tribe waiting.

Getting down, the Inspector turned back and reached up for Tullia. Warm in the cab, she had pushed the sleeves of her sweater up her arms. As she leant down, he reached for her arms and swung her round as he would do with any of his children, aware of the surprising velvet-like feel of her skin.

'Thank you, Sah,' she said in her musical voice.

The purple eyes of an innocent child smiling at him registered in his brain. She was not being cheeky. The uneducated girl thought that was his name.

As Tullia stepped back, stiff legs gave way and she staggered. H'ani was immediately at her side to stop her from falling. 'Oh H'ani, you are sweet,' she said as she clung on, then snuggled up to him as he supported her back to her hut.

Reaching the entrance, Tullia turned to H'ani, but just in time her Intuition stopped her from giving him a quick "thank you" kiss.

Deena and Tsetsana arrived and helped Tullia out of her clothes and into bed. As she lay there, soaking up the comforting smells and noises of her Haven home, mentally she pouted at her Intuition. It wasn't fair. H'ani was a lovely young man and she had felt his warm, caring energies and she really wanted to kiss him.

Kissing girls was normal. She had even kissed Kaigii when they were very young. But a young man? Slender he might be, but she had felt his strength as he had helped her back to her hut. She drifted into sleep wondering what it would be like with his strong arms around her as she had her first real kiss with a boy.

Meanwhile, Inspector Modisakgosi was talking with Ghadi, the tribe's chief and Xameb, the Shaman. Her unusual looks was explained by the Shaman saying, 'I am part Meera and part Dogon. My niece is..... different.' He shrugged his shoulders with a smile. The Inspector didn't really care what the girl's antecedents were. It had been an idle question. He just wanted to be able to keep her out of his report. Like the rest of his countrymen, he did not like the San. In his opinion they were a waste of space. Yet the girl had been useful and brave. She could have sided with a fellow Bushman and made life difficult. Respect was due for that.

Ghadi made it clear that the story was not going to be told outside the tribe, and they did not want the interference of journalists and such like.

That was exactly what Modisakgosi wanted to hear. He took out the three packets of cigarettes that he'd liberated from his constables and handed them over. Smiles wreathed the faces of the Meera. Even as he shook hands with Ghadi and Xameb the packets were being opened and the cigarettes passed around the tribe. A bargain had been struck, not with two people but the whole tribe. It would be kept.

The police had gone by the time that Xara and six others loped back into the village. The men went to their huts to get warm and eat whilst Xara reported to Ghadi.

When Tsetsana had returned to the village at midday and discovered that no-one knew where Tullia was, she had gone to see Kotuma, the head woman, and spoken with her and Ghadi. She said that when Tullia had taken her breakfast and so clearly indicated that she was not to be followed, she had assumed she was meeting someone. She had not been surprised. Tullia was an attractive and desirable young woman of marriageable age and with a strong energy clearly inviting people to be friends. Aside from the fact that she was a Goddess, and therefore unreachable, there were many young men and women who harboured thoughts of being alone with her. Now she thought about it, Tullia's gesture and the light touch Tsetsana had felt in her mind had not conveyed the excitement of a "walk in the bush".

The news of the murder and that a member of another San tribe had escaped and stolen a soldier's gun had reached the tribe that morning. Ghadi was alarmed and had called for Xara. The tribe's leading hunter had soon discovered the two sets of tracks leaving from the Mongongos, and had selected several men to accompany him. He was ashamed to say that the presence of the helicopter had forced them to slow their pace. They had only just got close enough to act when he had seen her knock down her captor. He had made the call of the hoopoo to signal the hunters to return.

CHAPTER 25

DANCE OF DISCOVERY

VERTAZIA

Seated under the cupola of her rooftop study with its view across a broad swathe of grassland to where the river tumbled over a waterfall, Dryddnaa was thinking very carefully. In spite of her comparative youth she was recognised as one of the most powerful Readjusters, Psych or PsiDoctor as her profession was often called, and had been elevated to the rank of Chief Readjuster at an unusually early age.

She was not a hard-line Traditionalist and had been surprised at being asked to become a member of the Senate of Custodians shortly after her one hundred and thirteenth rebirthday, in the partnership phase of her ninth era of philosophy. She saw it as an indication that it was expected that eventually she would become the Arch Readjuster and the Traditionalists wanted to ensure that she was sympathetic to their views.

Not only had she become a member of the exclusive Inner Council four years ago, now she had been invited by Ceegren to join him and just two other Venerables in their fight against the twins' family and friends. She wondered why not another Venerable. Was Ceegren testing her in some way? Perhaps her commitment. But again, commitment to what? The Kumelanii cause in general or himself personally?

She had at least one clear reason. It seemed that he needed her power. She had been surprised by the extent of his violence when preventing the twins from reconnecting. She had contributed willingly because at present that suited her own plans. She recognised that he had seen more in her than she had in herself. Which is why he was not a mere titular Arch Custodian like his predecessor, but the most powerful member of the Senate. And why she needed to be so careful.

Dryddnaa was a statuesque woman, well over two metres tall. Higher than normal cheekbones gave her an Aurigan appearance. A natural bloom to her smooth, coffee-cream skin and bright red hair, all belied her age. Soft, dove grey eyes made for a sympathetic listener, turning to steel when opposed. She did not like the thought that as a Venerable she might be known as 'Steel', or worse, 'Grey', and was contemplating a simple alteration to her genes.

Needing to clear her mind, she changed into her figure-hugging flying suit in shades of apricot. It was an affectation, but a conscious one that her good looks and youthful face enabled her to carry off. It also served a useful purpose in that its casual nature had a disarming effect when arriving at the homes of what she referred to as "The Unsettled".

Flying her twistor high above the ground she was free of the slower vibrations of the soil, crops and buildings. Her mind liked the freedom, and an idea presented itself. Releasing personal control, she asked her twistor to fly them back home while she meditated.

She had already set in motion a discreet attempt to find out what the family was planning. Amongst their many members and friends there would be a concerned adult who would welcome a sympathetic listener who had the twins' best interests at heart. To that end she had made personal visits to several carefully chosen Readjusters.

She had seen Ceegren's weakness. It was typical not just of the Kumelanii but also most Tazii. The fear of what they called The Azuran Violence Disease. She had sensed excessive fear in Ceegren. She was unaware of the cause. But it was strong and he had made it very clear how much he wanted the twins to remain on Earth. She wondered how far he would go if and when they returned. Was he contemplating the unthinkable?

If she was right about his plans, and her own were to succeed, she needed to be carried along by him as he seized power. Then she would be ready and waiting in his shadow for the right moment to supplant him. What she considered his irrational fear was handing her the very means to destroy him. Or cause her own demise if she was not very careful.

This was the Dance of Discovery at its most intense. One false step and she would be isolated and demonized. She might even be cast into the NoWhenWhere and lose all hope of redemption and the recovery of the full majesty and power of the Aurigan life.

If she was interpreting Ceegren's plans correctly and executed her own at the right moment, he would be disgraced, the Tazii shattered by his actions and the MentaNet in total disarray. She would be in the perfect position to step forward, calm the situation and restore order. She would do that with assistance from a carefully selected team of people who would appreciate her future patronage when they ensured her election as Arch Custodian. As the effective ruler of Vertazia she would return the Tazii to their Aurigan heritage and be seen forever as The Saviour. And doubtless be granted the title of Uddîšû. The first since the Space Wars eighty thousand years ago.

Her gaze was drawn to the waterfall where the sun was creating a faint rainbow from the spray as the water crashed onto the rocks at the bottom.

As long as I am very, very careful.

CHAPTER 26

SEEKING

VERTAZIA

Following the successful test run of Curious Shop, the four friends gathered in their suite in Lungunu to hold a Council Of Action. They had taken time every day to try and reach the twins via their Talisman but, just as with the two women who had been using Lellia's crystal, all they had found had been a thick mist that got darker and more solid the further they had penetrated, until their searching was halted.

When they didn't respond to Cook's call to breakfast, Lift appeared muttering about a 'waste of energy coefficients' and deposited them in the dining room where the adults were waiting.

'We have to know where to send Curious Shop,' quiet Pelnak said, uncomfortable at having been chosen as spokesman. 'We need to try a MentaSynch.' He took a deep breath. 'And we think that one of Wrenden's crystals should be attuned to his EraBand. I am Qwelby's elderest and Wrenden is his youngerest, so...'

'You are acknowledging the energy link, esting,' Lellia said, encouragingly.

'Yes.' Pelnak sat back in his chair, relieved that was all over.

The adults thoughtshared.

'Yes, to Seeking,' Lellia announced. 'I will think about Wrenden's crystal. Now eat, before Cook comes in wanting to know why you haven't asked for seconds. And thirds,' she added, smiling at Wrenden.

After they had finished eating, Lellia took the youngsters to her Homely Room and listened to their dreamstates. Between them, Pelnak and Shimara shared their identical experiences, similar to Wrenden's but from the perspective of the moving pair of hands.

'Thank you, my dears. That's all very clear,' Lellia said, relaxing back in her armchair. 'Wrenden, your parents have agreed to your making a final choice of crystal and allowing me to attune it to your EraBand.' She carefully concealed the memory of the thought exchange. It was only the increased level of protection that he would have that had finally persuaded Yarannah to agree.

Wrenden's mouth dropped open in surprise. He did not know that Aunt Gallia was a spiritual advisor, counsellor and exemplar of the True Aurigan Teachings.

'It is not only Arkaanai who can attune,' Lellia said. 'Your father fully supports this. Like all of us, he has seen the change in you. And in you, Tamina. You are both growing up earlier than normal. Tazian hormonal development cycles are not so rigidly fixed they cannot ever vary. There are occasions when events prompt, even force, the pace of development. That is happening for all of you.' She looked at Pelnak and Shimara. 'We can only guess at what is happening with the twins.

'Your dreamstates have again confirmed that through your relationships you are our best hope for reaching the twins. The esting relationships, the vitality of your second Era energies, the Talisman, and above all the love you all share.'

'With its twelve sides all carefully engraved in a very strong ritualistic manner binding all six of you together in pairs and triads, and imbued, Multiverse knows how, with sixth dimensional energy, I had expected that to be the energetic key to success,'

Mandara said. 'That you have not succeeded in tuning into them via Ôweppâ indicates the great power that is opposing us. The shop must be the right way. If one of the twins has both the Globe and the Backwards Clock there is a good chance that that twin will know when and where the shop will arrive.'

As he was speaking he had been thinking. There were too many coincidences. The twins disobeying strict rules not to try to enter the attic. A XzylStroem eruption at the very moment that made House override its programmed security in order to save them. Their finding the room supposedly securely hidden in a different time and space. Opening the trunk he thought was secured far beyond their capability, and then taking exactly what was necessary to allow them to detect a transdimensional vehicle that he had not even thought of designing.

Aurigan energies reaching from the past? From the time of the Great Schism thirteen thousand years ago? Mandara tightbeamed to his wife. *But why?*

Lellia raised her eyebrows, echoing his question, and then continued speaking.

'Tamina, you are not only the strongest and oldest but as a Fire Lady, the most powerful. Your natural affinity is to work with your brother, who will provide the solid base of Earth and the balancing Air to add to your Fire and Water. The insights and mental connectedness that Pelnak and Shimara provide through their element of Air are invaluable.'

'Fearless Four,' Pelnak said. And they linked hands to wrists in a double quaternion.

'Has Life planned all this, Aunt Gallia?' Wrenden asked as the dropped hands.

'You know Wrenden, that is a very good question,' she replied, leaning forward in her chair. 'It seems too perfect to be otherwise.' Shielding the uncomfortable sensation that her husband was correct when he said that what was happening seemed to be deeply rooted in Aurigan times, she asked Wrenden for his EraBand and chosen crystal and left the room.

She returned after a few minits and led them to the Seliya Chamber, watching their eyes boggle as they met the Isuna of the Night, bathed in her moonlight.

They entered a room of the blackest black, softly lit by lights shielded in the seven alcoves. They made their way to a sunken circle in the middle with comfortable cushions. On the floor in the centre of the circle Lellia placed a black crystal bowl filled with water. She dared not risk Sianarrah, her crystal ball, sucking them into NoWhenWhere.

'Please stand up Wrenden,' she said. She stepped into the circle holding his EraBand in her hand. His eyes lit up and whirled when he saw his crystal mounted in the centre.

'Wrenden Ngé'zânâ Jailandurkul, Child, with your father's blessings and the Power I have through my own birthright as Lellia Kûll'zânâ Xzendarshanytyr, seventeenth Warden of the Crystal Sianarrah, Orchestrator of the First XzylStroem of Vertazia, Keeper of the Esoteric Traditions of Auriga, I pronounce you no longer to be Child. From this moment in Time you are Youngster. May your journey to full manhood be true and strong.'

She brought the palms of her hands together in front of her heart and bowed, raised her head as she swept her arms to the sides, palms facing towards Wrenden. 'May the Multiverse be with you and guide you, Wrenden Ngé'zânâ Jailandurkul. Youngster.'

The others let out big sighs. Something special had happened. Each of them had received their own crystals from an Arkaana at the celebrations held on their fourteenth rebirthdays. None of those traditional Tazian ceremonies had evinced the power of the simple gifting they had just shared.

Lellia walked to the door. 'Seek. Let your love for the twins guide you. When you have finished, come to my Homely Room.'

It was some time before Lellia responded to a thought, asked Door to open to be greeted by four very serious looking faces. Tamina looked pale, and Lellia beckoned her to sit alongside her on the settee, taking the girl's hand in her own. The others sat together on another settee.

'Qwelby's in a terrible state,' Wrenden said with tears in his eyes. 'All we got was a Nothing, a great, big, black Nothing. He was enveloped in it.' He broke down and Pelnak wrapped an arm around him.

'It was difficult,' Pelnak explained. Just as we thought it was going to be the same as using Óweppâ, the mist gave way. Although he is on Azura, we sensed that he is not very far away. There was a feeling of cold and we are sure we sensed snow.'

Shimara nodded her agreement. 'We succeeded because of the extra power coming from Wrenden's crystal.'

'The contact with Tullia was faint, but somehow strong underneath,' Tamina said. 'And it was like she was in two moods. I felt a sense of contentment, but then a part of her was shielded as though she was guarding, I don't know what, a secret, a problem?'

Shimara nodded. 'My sense was that she was far away. I guess she is round the other side of the world and contact through the third dimension is different from here on Vertazia where distance makes no difference.'

'Whenever I meld with Tullia there's always a feel of Qwelby as well,' Tamina said. Sadly, she shook her head. 'That was only just there, extremely faint.'

'It's getting late. You've done well. And I can see you're all tired. You know where the Enjoy Suite is. Go there, have fun, but not for too long! You need to recharge your energies,' Lellia said.

A few minits later as they were choosing the games to play, Wrenden left the suite saying he needed a walk in Garden.

Keeping his thoughts carefully under control, he made his way to the main laboratory. Everything had been left on energy conserving mode, so he opened the door manually. Holding his breath, he peered around the edge. All was dark. He checked for the light switches. They were where he remembered. He closed the door and turned the lights on. The Curious Shop was gently humming to itself.

'Welcome, Wrenden, Youngster,' Wrenden heard to his surprise. '"Curious Shop," please,' the Curious Shop said, picking up Wrenden's thought of "it." 'I am more than a semi-sentient, in fact I am a Trans-Sentient, and entitled to be referred to by my name.'

Wrenden gulped. 'Sssorry,' he stammered.

'You are forgiven,' Curious Shop replied. 'However, should you wish, a diminutive of CuSho, note the capitalisation you hear, will be satisfactory. When referring to me in the third person "It" is just tolerable. "Shop" is appropriate for ordinary shops, corner or otherwise.'

'Yes, CuSho,' he answered, standing on one foot and rubbing the other behind his leg in consummate indecision.

'You have a crystal to be attuned?' CuSho asked.

'Gulp,' was all Wrenden could manage at having his thoughts read in spite of his careful shielding.

'Well?'

'Do you know where I should put it?' Wrenden asked, not believing what was happening. Is this because I've got my crystal. I'm now a youngster?

'The answer to your spoken question is yes. Here.' A soft light appeared in the central column.

Wrenden walked into Curious Shop, took the second crystal of Lazabatanzii out of his pocket and carefully set it in a shallow dip where the light was glowing. The light pulsed and golden threads weaved around it. When the light disappeared, he saw the crystal was set in a silver cradle and held in place by a cocoon of golden threads. And it seemed to be illuminated from inside.

'Thank you, Keeper,' CuSho said in a solemn voice.

'Gulp,' again, was all Wrenden could manage in response.

There was a noise outside. Wrenden swung around, his eyes quickly searching the laboratory. He ran to a corner and squeezed himself in behind one of the many mobile machines. Xzarze! He had left the lights on. Crossing his fingers and toes, he put his mind into Hide-N-Seek mode, shutting down his thoughts but not so strongly for his MentaShield to be detected, he hoped.

He heard the door open. Nothing happened. Then he heard soft footsteps.

Wrenden smiled as he heard CuSho welcome Tamina as a Fire Lady and their conversation then proceed as his had done. He turned up his hearing as he heard CuSho ask about a crystal to be attuned

'Yes, CuSho,' his sister replied. 'It is only a small piece of Bula'kabilii. Wrenden, my young brother, gave it to me years ago. I used to wear it until I received the one for my EraBand. I'm sorry it's not very powerful. I was just hoping...'

'What?'

'That it would be good enough to help me be with you when you go to find the twins. Ever since he's been old enough he's been a thoroughgoing pest, he and Qwelby embarrassing me whenever they can.' Looking down, she stroked the unusually shaped, vibrant and colourful piece of crystal, recalling her surprise when he had given it to her one rebirthday. "Just found it," he had said. She had never believed that. He had to have made an energy exchange. And he was so young at the time.

She raised her head. With the two round windows either side of the arched doorway, she felt she was looking at Curious Shop's face.

'It is special,' she said in a reflective tone of voice.

'Then it is Perfect,' CuSho said.

'Thank you,' she said, as the slightest of smiles seemed to tickle her mind for the briefest of moments.

Carefully peeking around a machine, Wrenden watched as Tamina went into CuSho then returned.

'Thank you, Keeper,' CuSho said in a solemn voice.

'Thank you, CuSho,' Tamina replied, then brought her palms together in front of her heart and bowed her head, turned and ran from the room.

Wrenden walked up to CuSho and bowed in the same way as he had seen his sister give thanks. 'Thank you, CuSho,' he said in a steady voice. He was about to ask CuSho what would happen when they travelled and so be one-up on his sister. Then thought. No. I am a youngster now. We are partners. In this together.

He could swear that CuSho smiled.

CHAPTER 27

A HAPPY STUDENT

KALAHARI

At the end of her day held captive, Tullia had been tucked into bed as soon as she had been brought back to the village. Awakening after a long sleep, she lay as a series of thoughts and images cascaded through her mind. Overlaying them all was anger at her twin shutting her out when she had really needed him. For the first twelve years of their lives they had done everything together. Even since then they were together most of the time. They were one. Yesterday she had managed by herself, blending together a mixture of Tazian and newly learnt skills.

She sat up. Has Life planned our separation so that we develop independently? Learning new skills? Make a stronger pairing when reunited?

Why?? Mentally adding a second question mark for her twin she got out of bed and splashed cold water on her face. Late morning and with the day already warm, she pulled on a pair of shorts and a tank top that left her shoulders bare. Stepping out of her hut she found Deena sitting on a blanket making jewellery, items to be taken to the Tourist Village for sale. She exchanged morning greetings with the mother of what she had come to think of as her Haven family and sat silently as the woman prepared a simple breakfast of milimili.

'I need to go back to my hut,' Tullia said when she had finished eating. 'My body has recovered from yesterday, but...' She shrugged her shoulders. It was too complicated to explain.

'Xara wishes to speak with you,' Deena said. 'It will be good to do that now.'

Puzzled, Tullia walked across to the hunter's hut and squatted down by his family.

With a few words he outlined how Tsetsana had alerted him, and then what he and the other hunters had done.

As Tullia opened her mouth to thank him, she was stopped as he started to question her. As she answered his questions about what she had seen and done, then how she had navigated and finally what she had discovered, Tullia smiled to herself. He was not showing concern for her but, like one of her Educationers at home, checking on what his student had learnt. A corner of her mind felt disappointed, but mostly she was awash with the sense that he was treating her as he would any other Bushman.

She was overcome with the feeling that at least Xara no longer looked at her with awe as a Venerable, or Goddess which was their word for her, but accepted her as a young girl and eager to learn. She had to say something. What?

Needing to control her emotions, she stood up and reached into her Kore with a deep breath.

Xara had risen as Tullia stood up, so she stepped forward, hugged him, then stepped back. 'It was your lessons that saved me, my Teacher,' she said. Towering over the slightly stocky man she lowered her gaze and inclined her head, hoping that indicated humility and a genuine appreciation of what he had taught her that day in the bush.

That gesture that Tullia made when embarrassed and did not know what to say was always misinterpreted as her acknowledgement of her due. This time it was seen as an acknowledgment of Xara's status as being worthy to instruct, an albeit young, Goddess.

As Tullia lifted her head and looked at Xara she saw his face go deep red as embarrassment and pride flowed through his aura. She was only talking to a man standing outside his hut and was completely unaware that, by reaching into her Kore, her energy was pouring out as if she was performing in the centre circle of a Tazian amphitheatre. Reaching the whole tribe, her words carried much more meaning than she had intended.

By acknowledging Xara as her teacher, it was seen as a sign that Tullia was making a powerful statement of her place amongst the Meera. The dreams of many young men and a few young women were inflamed by the possibility that she might become as approachable as any young Meera woman. Many other women were disquieted by that possibility. And jealousy and resentment inflamed one young women who believed she was much more fitted to act as companions to a Goddess than Tsetsana, who was still a child.

As she walked back to her hut, Tullia called at the family hut to thank Tsetsana. Tomku, Tsetsana's four-year-old sister, came running up. 'She is collecting food,' she said, before running back to a group of young children clustered around two of the tribe's oldest women.

Tullia went into her hut and lay on the pile of blankets that served as her bed. Once again she needed to reflect on all that had happened since her arrival on Haven.

CHAPTER 28

SOFTLY, SOFTLY

FINLAND

Monday morning, the first working day of the New Year, Professor Romain telephoned the Institute at Jyväskylä and learnt that the Director was flying to the United States the following day. The Director's PA was surprised at Romain's interest, saying that he thought it had been decided that the temporary loss of communications the previous Monday afternoon had nothing to do with the restarting of the LHC. Grateful for the gratuitous information, using all his charm and his connections with CERN, Romain wrung a short appointment with the Director from a grudging PA.

It was a little after eleven o'clock when Romain was shown into the Director's spacious office, its walls adorned with photographs of the Director with famous visitors. The Director's portly build was enhanced by his lack of height. A florid complexion seemed to indicate that the man's days as a scientist had long ago been replaced by his enjoyment of the conference circuit, along with the associated good dining.

In contrast with Romain's dark grey, bespoke, tailored suit with fine stripes of red and blue, coordinated with a paisley tie and matching handkerchief in his breast pocket, the style of the Director's plain, dark grey suit clearly hinted at Swiss tailoring.

Whilst the Director enquired, then ordered coffee for two, Romain sat admiring the view over endless miles of snow covered Christmas trees and congratulated himself on his foresight. CERN did not like bad publicity. When he had left, it had been by mutual agreement. The story, which was completely true, was that he was leaving to pursue other parallel researches.

In the scientific world that code covered a disagreement in ideas and approach. It happened from time to time. The code also indicated that it had been amicable. That was far from the truth. One day he would have his revenge. Until that time, he would play the game to his advantage.

Another part of his plan had involved negotiations with a minor University in America. Coupled with his reputation as one of the leading scientists in the field of quantum physics, the provision of a not insubstantial donation had resulted in his appointment as Visiting Professor of Quantum Mechanics.

He honoured that appointment by visiting the university each semester to partake in the usual dinners and provide lectures. Those, he had to admit to himself, were always well received by the students who liked to have conventional theories challenged.

The initial pleasantries having been exchanged, including Romain's carefully crafted apology as to why it had not been possible to give advance notice of his request for a meeting, he got down to the purpose of the visit: unusual events around Kotomäki.

The discussion was brief as the Director had nothing to add to the facts that there had been a brief breakdown in communications and some other electro-magnetic disturbances, all of which had been dismissed as the consequences of an unusually large flare-up of the Aurora Borealis so far south.

Disappointed but not entirely surprised, Romain enquired about Dr Drahomir Jadrovitch, his supposed old colleague with whom he had lost contact. The Director had a lot to do before leaving for the USA and was glad of a reason to terminate the meeting quickly. Perhaps influenced by a feeling of pity, he offered Romain a short tour of the Institute, saying there was a faint possibility that one of his colleagues might be able to help with Romain's enquiries. The PA was summoned and asked to take care of the Professor.

The tour was a good opportunity for Romain to update himself on developments in research that were not likely to be published for a long time. In the process, he discovered the very limited facts about the restart of the LHC. Towards the end of his tour he asked after his old friend, saying they had lost contact and he had hoped to be able to speak with him.

The PA was being careful with what he said. When Romain mentioned his surprise that Drahomir had returned to Czech, yet his young son Kwelby was in Kotomäki; equally surprised, the PA exclaimed, 'Surely you remember that his two sons, Radoslav and Otokar, are both at University now?'

Covering up the confusion by playing the absent-minded scientist role, Romain took his leave, expressing his appreciation for the visit. Containing the excitement that was building within him, he managed to walk calmly back to his car and drove out of the facility.

Crossing the bridge in Jyväskylä, he turned down the road along the lakeside. He got out and stood looking across the expanse of crisp, white snow and the sun-sparkled water. In the distance, under their snow covered branches, the trees formed a dark and almost menacing backdrop. The contrast reflected his inner world as he walked back and forth along the road, struggling with ideas of action. Eventually the cold brought him back to the reality of the moment. He pulled himself together.

He smoothed his neat moustache and flicked the errant lock of hair back into place. Yet he could not totally suppress the excitement within him. He swung around, his arms wide open and cried: 'Thank you, Finland, thank you.'

Calmer, he looked out over lake Jyväsjrävi. A faint breeze ruffled the surface, diamond points of brilliance hurting his eyes. Jetting up from the lake was a magnificent fountain. He had been impressed the first time he had seen it, feeling it was an omen. He saw himself as an exceptional man, standing out from the common herd just like the fountain. One day my work will stand out like that.

He knew the fountain was giving him a message.

He thought of the billions of molecules of water. Each identical to every other, wherever they were in the universe. And equally so for their constituents, the atoms of oxygen, hydrogen and right down to the quarks.

He walked along the road, his thoughts merging with his surroundings. The living, breathing trees. The tarmac, 'dead' yet alive in its own way with all the vibrating energy of its millions of molecules.

Romain mused. What is a human being? Ultimately, we are the same as everything else. Energy. Trillions of cells, minuscule packets of data, each with its own 'signature' piece of DNA. That DNA unique to the individual, thus allowing for the recreation of the original. And our consciousness, what Miki calls our soul. If energy equals life and life equals soul: does that mean a tree has a soul? Can a quark have a soul?

He shook his head. Too much metaphysics.

He stopped and turned towards the fountain, eyes unfocussed. If that fountain was switched off, it would collapse back into the lake. Was that merely what had happened to all the data that he had been transmitting as a waveform, intending to piggy-back it on one of the latest experimental runs involving CERN. It had fallen off in Finland? Taking a whole week? Or had it reached into another dimension as hoped for and, subjected to a different level of consciousness, the superpositioning had collapsed, bringing onto Earth an object from that other dimension?

He took a deep breath and coughed as the cold air hit his lungs. With a little chuckle to himself, he got back in the car, switched on the engine and turned up the heating. He needed a place where he could think clearly. Away from the fountain sucking him past his dream and into pure fantasy. Not his room at the hotel. A wide open space. Of course! Where the event had happened. He went into the centre of the town and bought a pair of boots.

CHAPTER 29

A BIG GIRL

KALAHARI

Lying on her bed, trying to make sense of all that had happened over the eight days since her arrival, Tullia was pulled out of her semi meditative state by the sound of talking and the soft susurration of several footsteps on the sand. Opening her eyes, she noticed from the shape of the shadow of the open doorway on the ground that it was early afternoon.

Tsetsana's face appeared in the opening. 'Would you like to watch the Melon Dance?' she asked.

'Oh, yes please,' Tullia replied as she rolled off her bed. Stepping outside, she was puzzled to see a group of girls with blankets draped around their shoulders, yet with bare legs. Two were standing in front of her looking shy. Tsetsana nudged one of them who opened the blanket to reveal what she was wearing.

Tullia's eyes were drawn to a narrow band around the girl's slender hips from which hung a triangular shape made from animal skin. The girl was also wearing a long necklace made from varying mixtures of dark seeds and small pieces of white ostrich shell.

'This is what we wear for celebrations,' twelve-year-old Mandingwe explained.

'We thought you'd like to see our traditional wear,' added N!Obile, another twelve-year-old. Handing her blanket to her friend she turned around revealing that what they were wearing also had an almost square piece of the same animal skin hanging down at the back.

Tullia looked down on the top of the two girls' heads, not even level with her bust, as the happy, chatting group walked out of the village. 'Why are the skirtlets so small?' she asked. 'Why do you not make them like, well, the ordinary skirts you wear?'

'I like your name for them,' Mandingwe said. 'We call them loinskins.'

'Here, in this village, we still live our traditional way of life,' N!Obile explained.

'In part,' Mandingwe added as the girls held hands.

'We've always lived off the land, taking the minimum we need for survival.'

'Animal skins are very precious and have many uses. We use only the minimum that is essential.'

You can say that again! Tullia said to herself. And once again thought of her elderest and BestFriend, Tamina, and how gorgeous she would look wearing the same when she danced.

'We used to be nomadic. Never staying in one place for long.'

'Now that's changed and we live here all the time.'

'There are good parts to that.'

'We have mugs to drink from, pots to cook with.'

'And a whole tribe together, lots of friends, girls....... and boys.' The girls rolled their eyes and giggled.

Tulia was shocked. She would be almost seventeen before her hormones would give her any interest in boys. With the time differences between the two worlds that equated to almost twenty here on Haven, yet these two.... 'How old are you?'

'Twelve,' N!Obile replied.

'Just waiting for warm weather,' Mandingwe said as she nudged her friend and the two giggled and rolled their eyes.

Twelve. And they're interested in boys! What a different world, Tullia thought.

'The Himba wear something similar to us,' N!Obile said.

'You are so big, Tullia,' Mandingwe said. 'You could be a Himba. And they are very red. They cover themselves with ochre.'

Tullia was nonplussed. Tall, all right, but big? She'd never been called "big" before. Her thoughts came to a stop as they reached an area of rich, thick, red sand. A rough oval shape about ten metres long had been cleared of the lumps of limestone that covered much of the ground.

The girls grouped together at one end, Tsetsana steering Tullia to stand in the middle of them. From either side of her, a girl holding a melon handed her blanket to a friend and started down the oval. The dance was really only a series of skipping steps, each girl moving as she wanted. Before they reached the far end, two more girls, one on each side, started to follow. On reaching the end, the leading girls crossed over and continued skipping back to the beginning. All four girls occasionally glancing over their shoulders.

As the girls who were following neared the far end, so the girls with the melons stopped looking over their shoulders and threw the melons backwards, aiming for the girl on the opposite side of the oval. Those girls turned, hopefully catching the melons and, when they did, trying to kick up a shower of sand behind them. Tullia was surprised at how easy the slightly built women made it look: throwing a heavy melon that far, backwards and quite accurately. It will be easy for me "being big!" she thought wryly.

'The traditional dance is performed only one way round. Now, we dance both ways. It's more difficult and more fun,' Tsetsana explained.

'Fun. Yes..." Tullia said.

Tsetsana had grown to understand her big friend's feelings, they were so strong. 'Would you like to dance?' she asked.

'Yes. But...' It was only seeing them out of their thick clothing that made Tullia realise how slender they all were and that what she had thought of from their height as young girls, really were mature young women. And how very big she was in comparison.

'You don't have a loinskin?' Kou-'ke asked, having completed her turn and hearing the conversation.

'No....'

'I'll find you one,' Kou-'ke said with obvious enthusiasm as she threw her blanket around he shoulders.

Tullia hesitated. With the lithe way in which the girls moved, she'd look clumsy and stupid. Yet to join in and have fun. Be accepted as one of them....

'I'll bring it to your hut,' Kou-'ke said, seizing the initiative.

'Thank you,' Tullia replied, as Kou-'ke grabbed the hand of the girl standing at her side and the two ran back to the village.

Tullia made her way to her hut, puzzling over the tone of voice Kou-'ke had used and the brief energy swirl in her aura.

'Why you do that?' Nlai asked her best friend as she ran alongside.

'You remember my first loinskin?' Kou-'ke replied. 'I tried a different style. Didn't look right. Longer but too narrow. Wearing that it will be obvious just how big she is. And clumsy. When Xashee sees her amongst us, all so much smaller and slimmer and with her ugly face. And trying to dance like us. Well...' There was venom in Kou-'ke's voice.

'That'll never go round her hips,' Nlai said.

'Thought of that. I'll add a narrow strip to the waistband,' Kou-'ke replied.

Nlai grunted. She understood what her friend was feeling, and like many of the other women was worried about the effect Tullia was having on the young men. Part of her feared that what her friend was proposing might have the opposite effect. Thinking of K'dae who had been in the party sent to rescue Tullia, another part of her hoped it would work.

At Tullia's hut, Kou-'ke handed over a costume, saying the woman who made it no longer wore it. Having quickly shown how she wore her own, she and Nlai returned to the others.

As Tullia put the skirtlet on she smiled wryly at the extension to the waistband which just enabled her to tie it securely in front of her body. The front piece that hung down over the tie was different from what the girls were wearing. Long and narrow, once again she thought how it would suit her elderest, the tall and slim Tamina. Thinking she had been given two necklaces, adorned with dark seeds and pieces of white shell, she found that one was attached to the skirtlet. She felt the love and care that had gone into the creation of the whole costume.

Adding the necklace, she looked down at her body, really pleased that all the red patches from her strange journey to Haven had finally gone and she had become her usual rich, red, honey-brown, summer colour, along with a very high solar energy quotient.

When she returned to the oval area she saw that several older boys and young men were watching. She smiled as they called out and encouraged various girls. Some of the more daring got very close to where the girls turned at the far end. There was a lot of laughter when any one of them got hit with a shower of sand. Then it was her turn.

Although she had quickly got used to walking in the uneven depth of sand when outside the village, now, her co-ordination was badly thrown when she tried to turn, catch and kick. She stumbled. The shiny surface of the melon slipped through her outstretched fingers and she crashed to the ground. There were restrained laughs. Feeling silly, she got to her feet.

'Not as easy as it looks!' she said to the men as she brushed sand from her body.

CHAPTER 30

HUBRIS

FINLAND

Back in Kotomäki, Romain pulled into the side of the road opposite what had to be the correct location. He changed into his boots and made his way alongside the ski slope and through the strip of trees where, at last, he allowed himself to explore the idea that would not go away.

Protons, psien, the data being carried, all that could not simply disappear. When protons collided in an atom-smasher, their components were there to be seen, no matter for how short a period of time. And the energy released was measured. The event around those ski slopes had to have been a massive one, yet all anyone at the Institute knew of was the momentary interruption to communications.

Apparently at the exact same time a black boy had appeared. A boy who clearly was not Finnish. A boy who was the wrong age, name and appearance to be one of the two sons of Dr Drahomir Jadrovic. With what his equipment had detected of a surge in the Earth's quantum field so massive that it had ruptured his Python, he saw only one logical explanation. Quantum entanglement. Matter transportation. But from where?

To prove the existence of other dimensions and to prove the

possibility of travel between them was his one, all-consuming dream. More than just a Nobel Prize for science would be the result. His name would resound through the centuries to come. He grunted. A nice prospect, but first he had to find the boy.

A corner of his mind said 'Hubris' and reminded him of the story of Icarus who had flown too close to the sun, whose wings had melted and he had plummeted to his death on Earth.

Romain's thoughts came back to the strange coincidence of the boy's arrival and the search that Erki had seen being made. No matter. He was here. He would follow the lead he had. That was the scientific approach. It was his only approach.

He steadied himself, took out his binoculars and explored the landscape. Whatever had happened had been close to where he was standing. From the back of his mind came the memory of the ghost image. With it came the suggestion of another, exciting explanation.

Erki had said that several people had been searching the ground for a long time. What if the ghost image was not a ghost at all, but something else had arrived on Earth. Something much smaller so less energy involved. What if it was part of the equipment used in teleportation. Unlike science fiction where objects could simply be beamed down, the experiments on Earth required equipment at both ends, a sender and a receiver. A shiver ran through him as an idea blazoned itself across his mind.

What if teleportation was uncertain and the boy had been carrying a portable device as a safeguard. Like an emergency beacon, so he could be recovered if he failed to reach the receiver at his destination. The device would be some form of miniaturised sender. The boy would be desperate to find that. And. Romain shivered again. There would have to be communication. As a minimum, a 'beam' of some sort sent from that 'sender' back to a detector. Or was it a reflector and a 'beam' would be sent out like a radar pulse seeking a reflection?

All theoretically possible. His legs went weak with all the

implications. There was a fallen tree close by. He brushed the snow from it and sat down, little realising that exactly one week ago Qwelby had done the very same.

ET is NOT going home!

He covered his mouth with his gloved hand and took a few deep breaths to calm himself. First he had to get the boy safely stowed away in his laboratory. Access his secret data storage and narrow down the second location. Then to Africa. He was now sure that what he had initially assumed to be a ghost image, had actually shown the arrival of the boy's 'lifebelt'.

'And how will you do that?' Asked a voice in his head, jolting Romain out of his reverie. For a moment his mind went blank. My musical friends. He chuckled. Franz Shosta and Pierre Kovich. He had known Franz for years, but had never been able to penetrate his cloak of mystery.

During the months that Franz had spent on his island, working together to install a lot of very specialised equipment that Romain had designed, he had opened up. Although Romain suspected he had only been told part of the story.

In his previous life, as Franz called it, he and Pierre had run black market operations in East Germany. For a price, they provided the sort of products that were normally available only to a highly select group of top officials. And delivering packages. When Franz had said that, he had stopped talking and looked grim, as if recalling bad times. The discussion had ended and Romain had never raised the subject again.

'I'm sure they could deliver a package to the island,' the voice in his head added, as icy fingers ran down his spine.

Getting up from the fallen tree, he walked back through the strip of forest to the path alongside the ski slope that would take him back to his car. His eyes were drawn to the houses on the opposite side of the road. It was in one of those that Erki had told him the boy was staying.

Assuming that the boy's arrival was the event his equipment had detected, that would have happened close to four o'clock. It would have been getting dark. He remembered from his visit the previous night that the upstairs curtains had not been drawn in several of the houses that backed onto the ski slope. It matched his earlier thought that someone could have been looking out of a bedroom window with a clear view over the slope. Then, he had thought that the dark-skinned boy had seen something so exciting that he had rushed out in his underwear. But if the event was his arrival, had someone else seen that?

The police were not involved. Someone had prepared a cover story. A very poor one. Romain smiled to himself. He knew about preparing cover stories. So, somebody had found the boy and taken him in and then decided to conceal that from the authorities. Why they should do that was an intriguing question. An alien with unknown powers? The thought of mind control made him decide to be very careful.

As he looked at the houses, two boys came along the path at the side of the road. One with blonde hair and fair skin, the other with dark skin and jet black hair and wearing ski goggles. Wherever he was from, that boy was not Finnish. Erki was right.

Roman lifted his binoculars which whirred softly as the built-in camera continued to take a series of pictures as the dark-skinned boy stopped, looked up and pointed to the opposite side of the trees where Romain had been sitting.

'What more confirmation do I need?' Romain said to himself. 'This IS where he arrived!'

In spite of the cold air, a bead of sweat trickled into his eye. Annoyed, he lowered the binoculars and wiped his eye with the back of his gloved hand. His mind went into overdrive, thinking of what he would do with the boy once he had him in his laboratory.

'Whoa!' a corner of his mind said. 'You are a scientist. Is that boy really who or what you think he is? First establish that!'

'Come on Reginsen,' the voice said. 'Time for action! Did your forefathers hold back and explore the English coasts? No. They stormed ashore from their longboats AND TOOK WHAT THEY WANTED!'

Franz and Pierre: interesting but unusual companions for a scientist. He gave a grim smile as he nodded to himself. He was sure they could arrange a kidnapping. But they would need more information, papers would have to be prepared, and he would need to give them a photograph without ski goggles.

He needed to think. He looked at his watch. Time for a late lunch. He smiled to himself as he thought of Hercule Poirot. The Belgian detective always said fish was good for 'Ze little grey cells'. The Finns liked seafood and a little later he was tucking into blackened Alaskan cod served with shrimps sautéed in garlic, capers, tomatoes and fresh basil.

The cold bite of a Chilean Sauvignon cleared his mind. It was entirely possible that the boy's arrival in Kotomäki was a coincidence of timing and that he had seen whatever had arrived. There was one, very simple way to find out. Ask the boy. But. What if he was an alien and was exercising mind control? What if the feeble cover story was because of an urgent escape? And what would that mean as to who he was escaping from and having had to leave his family?

As Romain was sipping his double espresso a memory came back to him of an airplane trip he had taken whilst working at CERN. There had been a talkative passenger in the adjacent seat. It turned out the man had worked for the Stasi in the former East Germany. Following unification he had established a small business in Berlin as a private investigator and was looking to extend to Switzerland.

Romain left the restaurant in deep contemplation.

CHAPTER 31

TRACKING

FINLAND KALAHARI

As his Form's eyes opened, Qwelby's subSelf slipped out and again put his InForming Matrix in the forest where he had caught the thieves on New Year's Eve. This time it was full daylight. He grinned. He was becoming a dab hand at the sip-and-leave routine.

His trip into his Form's memory had been a startling eye-opener. He well understood why he had dived into the Black Hole when he was confronted with what he thought was his fault – the Tazii's loss of their Aurigan heritage and the millennia of pointless violence on Earth.

What Qwelby did not know was what had finally happened. Had the twins eventually reached an agreement or had one defeated the other? Had it been the one crystal that had failed or had they tried to divide it and run out of time? He was not in the mood for exploring that any further, not without Tullia. Genetically implanted memories or not, that was a terrible rift that lay deep within their psyches and had to be healed. And that could not happen whilst his Form remained in deep unconsciousness.

Tullia. A rainbow thread. That fighting bitch. She'll come and.... I'll trap her.

A few practices and he was content that he was able to produce images almost as normal. They did not form as quickly, nor were they as convincing. But he decided that didn't matter. She would know what he was doing and would see the poor results as showing weakness. She had been a dirty fighter, but he had detected a core Tazian quality of innocence. She was not going to be expecting his Azuran honed duplicity.

Checking that Zhólérrân would co-operate, he ran through his plan as he moved to the very spot where on New Year's Eve he had summoned his dragon Attribute and called on Tullia for help. From there he sent out a very gentle twin-seeking rainbow. If the girl did not sense it, all the better.

He nodded to himself as it arced away though the trees. As he'd expected, there was a residual energy signature from that night's events and the thread was heading to wherever Tullia had been at that time.

A tall and slender figure clad all in black dropped through the trees and he recognized the mixture of soft feminine and strong masculine energies. As they circled each other in wrestling poses he noted the electric blue threading running through what had to be a powerful suit and experienced a moment of trepidation. He was facing a determined opponent. Had he overreached himself?

She leapt high and fast and he threw a lion at her as he ran back, then he had an eagle swoop down on her as he dodged to the side. Neither slowed her down. Panicking, he mentaformed a massive werebeast right in front of her, its slavering jaws spewing saliva. Still she did not hesitate. She was not bothering to counter attack the images but lanced her thoughts straight into his mind, knocking out the projections at source. His head ringing from the blows, Qwelby realised how very much more skilled she was than his subset Self. His strength had overcome her physically, but here the power of his images was useless against her speed and skill.

He had one chance. She had actually glanced momentarily at

each of his projections. He imaged the ground opening beneath her into a deep pit. She glanced down and jumped across the opening even as she lanced the image from his mind, then looked back up at him as he looked high into the trees, thoughtcalling 'Zhólérrân'. He was right, it was logical that she needed to see the projection and know its energy signature before removing his sending. He felt a fast search of his mind, then saw the look of fear on her face as she realised the massive, brightly coloured dragon was not a thought projection.

A gentle puff of "fire" issued from the dragon's jaws and Xaala fell to the ground, unable to move as all strength had gone from her limbs.

'Do not try to thoughtsend,' Qwelby said. 'Zhólérrân will not like that.' Her eyes flared with rage. 'I will return and release you.'

He walked back to where the events of the night had started and lifted into the air, flowing along the rainbow thread. He was puzzled by the increasing layers of darkness as he travelled. He'd expected to see the planet rolling by underneath him. Yet it was only a few moments before the darkness changed back into day-time and he was looking down on Tullia, standing head and shoulders above a group of boys and girls.

He mindsearched. Xzarze! With my Form in its DarkState I cannot reach her mind.

CHAPTER 32

CHALLENGED

KALAHARI

For her next two turns, unaware of her twin's encouragement, Tullia concentrated on turning and catching the melon and ignored trying to kick sand. By her fourth turn she was relaxed into her sensing. Without looking behind, she made a steady and accurate throw back and across the oval and grinned as she heard murmurs of appreciation.

As she returned to the group of girls, her whole body covered in a sheen of sweat that appeared to be shimmering due to her excited aura, she realised just how economical with their movements they were. *And I think I'm athletic. Goddess be Xzarzed!*

By now Tullia had come to realise a silly mistake she'd been making. Having previously only seen them fully clothed, without thinking she'd equated their small stature with both age and the culture on Vertazia. In fact they were all a lot older then she'd assumed and also much more mature than youngsters of the equivalent ages on her world.

Expecting a nice rest before her next turn she was surprised when Kou-'ke grabbed her arm and swung her round to face down the oval. 'You follow Ungka,' Kou-'ke said as she took hold of Tullia's arm and indicated the attractive and unusually tall seventeen-year-old.

Tullia knew when she wanted to start her skipping, but was happy to wait until Kou-'ke let go her arm, revelling in the naturalness of the familiarity.

Part way along the side, Tullia glanced over her shoulder and noticed Tsetsana on the opposite side. Being treated as just another girl, feeling the sun's energy invigorating her skin cells and converting that into her own inner energy, Tullia was the happiest she had been since leaving Vertazia. She grinned and gave her friend a little wave.

Seeing the gesture, assuming that Tullia's attention was distracted, Ungka quickly turned round to face the group of girls and deliberately threw the melon almost directly behind her instead of across the oval for Tullia to catch.

Tullia spotted the melon out of the corner of her eye. As she turned to focus on it her brain fed the trajectory into her mind. The melon was going to smash into Tsetsana's head. With her friend glancing over her shoulder towards the girl who was following Tullia, who in due course would throw her melon across the oval to Tsetsana, there was no way her friend would see the melon heading for her. Tullia immediately thoughtsent to alter its flight path.

Nothing happened.

Khuy! Idiot! This isn't Vertazia! Tullia reprimanded herself.

Flexing her knees, digging her toes into the sand and calling on all the available energy she launched herself into the air with her arms outstretched.

'Dabultuu!' Knowing how slow everything was, and with no previous experience of working with group energy on Haven, Tullia had drawn in too much and was going to pass over the melon. She had taken off as she was turning and was already revolving in the air. Her brain flashed a potential solution down her optic nerves, seeming to sketch three trajectories in the air.

She dipped her head and shoulders, starting a somersault and lowered her right arm. Her open fingers met the melon and scooped it up. As her body continued to roll and her arm swung upright, the melon was sent high into the sky on its new trajectory.

Rolling and somersaulting she flung out her arms to steady herself. As she landed on both feet, facing the men, she did what she would do at home: flexed her knees, bounced up, flung her arms above her head and landed back down, forming a perfect letter Y.

'Yay-ho!' she exalted, pleased at recovering from her initial error and having saved her friend from a serious head injury.

Yay-ho! Kaigii, Qwelby thoughtsent, albeit unheard by his twin.

Silence.

A silence that was all the more pronounced because of the call of a bird. Uip, uip, uiooo.

Does that Hoopoo follow me around for times like this? Tullia wondered.

Slowly, the men turned and looked behind them.

'Sorry!' Tullia exclaimed as she saw the tallest youth walking away towards the bright yellow melon, a long way off.

A happy young girl sprinted over the sand. Full of exuberance and solar energy, Tullia sprang into a somersault, picked up the melon, twisted in the air and landed facing H'ani. Brimming over with excitement and energy, she threw the melon the thirty or so metres to where he was standing, staring at her. Catching the melon with both hands, he staggered backwards at the force of the impact.

Tullia giggled at the look of surprise on his face. As she bounced up to apologise she deciphered the reds and oranges flaring through his aura as saying he was enjoying the fun, yet was puzzled by his deep blush and a look on his face she could not decipher.

Qwelby had dropped down to stand behind the tall boy,

looking over his head. He had laughed at his twin's exuberance. He was happy she was all right and was having fun. The longing to be together again was stronger than ever.

Silently, H'ani held out the melon.

He's only a hand's-breadth shorter than me, and he is cute, Tullia said to herself. She leant forward, took the melon, and at the last moment with her lips only centimetres from his, remembered not to give him a kiss. Surprised that she wanted to do more than give him a "thank you" kiss, as she would to any of her girl-friends, she grinned and fluttered her long eyelashes at him, only half aware that her eyes were twirling.

As Wrenden would laugh, Pelnak would grin and Qwelby would growl – he hated her doing that, it was so little-girly – she was totally unaware of the effect it had on H'ani.

'Yetch! Kaigii. That's gross,' Qwelby said aloud, uselessly, and drifted over to the village he noticed as he'd arrived. He had a good look around until he was certain that he'd seen and felt enough about where Tullia was living that his Form must sense clues when he regained consciousness. He was sad that what he assumed were true descendants of the Auriganii had changed so much.

Unsettled by the hot flush spreading through her body, Tullia covered that up by chatting animatedly as they walked back to the oval.

For a moment she was puzzled by the flickers of yellow through the men's auras, but that was rapidly swept aside by her feelings of joy. She was exulted. She had prevented a nasty accident, had corrected her initial error and, best of all, had discovered that, just as at home, she was able to draw on both the planet's energies and those of the Meera. She was even more convinced that the Meera, and presumably the other San, were descendants of the original Auriganii, sadly now with only two active segments of DNA.

With so many people gathered together she was aware of strong energies of freedom, fun, happiness and friendship. She was also aware of an under layer of darker, disturbed and disturbing feelings that she could not clearly identify, including fear and jealousy, and was puzzled by the look on Ungka's face.

Tullia found Mandingwe at her side as everyone started walking back to the village. 'You miss your twin brother?' the girl asked, puzzled, as no-one had ever heard of the Sons of the Goddess.

'Oh yes, terribly. He's the most important person in my life.'

'And when you find him?'

'We must find a way home.' She took a deep breath and let it out. 'If we cannot do that, we'll stay here.'

In the silence that followed, Tullia again detected tension in the air. Amongst the flashes of fear other colours flickered: reds, oranges, greens and even hints of violet. She knew the colours but was not able to interpret their meaning in this situation

Later that night as the older girls and young women talked amongst themselves, they wondered what Tullia really meant by "Twin". Someone suggested that as it was a Goddess and a God, they would always be together, like a married couple, but different.

'I wish I had not offered her that outfit. Nor helped Ungka with that trick with the melon,' Kou-'ke confided to her best friend, not liking the way that Xashee had looked at Tullia during the Melon Dance.

Both had backfired. The men had definitely approved of Tullia dressing like the girls, and her actions in saving Tsetsana from a nasty accident had enhanced her desirability.

'If Ungka's plan had worked and she'd taken Tsetsana's place, even for a short time....' Nlai said, raising her eyebrows. She'd not liked the way K'dae had being looking at Tullia. 'She's too tall and much too big to be pretty. That face with those weird eyes and big mouth, almost ugly. But, that display. It's not what she did. She's a

Goddess. There's something about her... an energy... it's like she's pulling people towards her.'

They were not the only women to hope that "Twin" meant something other than a brother, however special.

Back in the woods in Finland Qwelby knelt by the girl as he asked the dragon to ease back on the restraint. 'You said, "Too strong together." For what?'

'Together you will return and bring violence with you,' Xaala replied, carefully choosing her words.

Qwelby was stunned at what she'd said and told her that he and Tullia were going to be reunited whatever she or anyone else wanted. She left as soon as Zhólérrân released her and the dragon disappeared.

'Strike three,' he said to the forest, and stood there wondering how to proceed. His inability to reach his twin's mind confirmed what he had suspected: that as a subset he would not be able to communicate directly with his whole Self when out of the Darkstate and back to normal. 'I will have to dreamfeed my Form with clues as to where Tullia is. Next time he half wakes to drink water, I will stay there and try that.'

That evening after a meal of nuts, tubers and some delicious sweet !kerri berries, Tullia was content when four-year-old Tomku climbed onto her lap for a cuddle. Several people came by and squatted down to talk with various members of the family, including a number of young children who stood looking at Tullia. For a reason she could not fathom, she spoke to them in Tazian and discovered how that sounded to the Meera when Tomku said: 'You sing nice, Tully.'

Tired, Tullia was soon in bed. Reflecting on the day, feeling warm at how she had felt accepted and puzzling over the look on H'ani's face and how shy he had been as they had walked together, she sat upright with a jerk. She could not have seen him blush bright red, nor Xara. Their skins were much too dark. At last her energy-sensing was working properly. It had just taken time to become accustomed to the slow vibrations of the third dimension.

She fell asleep, comforted by the thought that soon she'd be able to understand the colours in people's auras that she was finding difficult to interpret.

CHAPTER 33

KEEPERS

VERTAZIA

Lungunu was full of happy, nervous tension as everyone gathered for breakfast on the morning after the successful test of Curious Shop. Breakfast for eight people did not need Cook, FAC, SAC and TAC, as her First, Second and Third assistants were called but, as Cook said unashamedly, the atmosphere had been so bad since the twins had gone that House and the other semisentients had been full of doom and gloom, and she and her team of youngsters needed to share in the happy feelings.

Breakfast finished, all bar the Cooks made their way to the laboratory. By midday, everything had been checked and tested and Curious Shop was ready to go. To the youngsters' disappointment, Cook and her team arrived at that moment with food and drink.

'You all need food in your bellies to help anchor your energies here on Vertazia,' Lellia said.

'Sorry. Went down the wrong way,' Tamina and Wrenden said in unison as they choked and spluttered over their drinks. Tamina's thoughtsent question bounced back from her brother's Privacy Shielding.

Lunch finished, Mandara ran his eyes over the mass of data banks and monitors. 'Initiate,' he said. And a few moments later announced, 'Okay, it's working.'

'CuSho,' Wrenden and Tamina said together, correcting Gumma's use of 'it'.

'I am a genius,' Mandara said with a smile. 'But I'm not so good that I can create a TransSentient!'

'Come on you two,' Pelnak called to Wrenden and Tamina, interrupting their Privacy Shield struggle as Mizena checked all four were settled comfortably. The two longest weeks of her life and the fate of her children was out of her hands and into those of four, very young Tazii. She carefully clamped down on that thought. The youngsters were nervous enough as it was. She nodded to Mandara.

When the monitors showed the psidelta waves were stable for all four youngsters, Mandara flicked through a bank of switches, setting the alarms for each and every monitor. Mizena joined him. She would watch the youngsters' console whilst he watched those for the Shop and the Stroems.

CuSho shimmered, the room quivered and there was a sudden whoosh as the air was sucked from the room. As Mandara and Mizena gasped for air it flowed back in and all was silent. CuSho had disappeared.

Mizena looked over the youngsters. They were all steady in deepstate.

After a while, a warning light on Shop's console started flashing.

'Shop is using more power than is available,' Mandara said, startled, and swung to the bank of Stroem monitors. 'It's taking it direct from the Stroems. In between dimensions!'

'Is that safe?' a worried Mizena asked.

'All the other monitors are well within the safety limits,' he replied. 'See for yourself.'

'The youngsters are all fine,' Mizena confirmed after a few moments.

'The Stroems are stable,' Mandara said. 'You know what this means? Shop is drawing on the Shadow World, what Azurii call Dark Energy, through the Stroems.' He sat back in WheelChair and ran his fingers through his hair. 'I never programmed it to do that!'

He looked at Mizena. 'Everything is stable and operating well within the limits we set. Now, we wait.'

Everything was shimmering and quivering, nothing was clear. It was like looking through a waterfall. As CuSho stopped moving and her vision cleared, Tamina was stunned to see her young brother. 'What have you done?' she asked angrily as they stood up.

'Same as you,' he replied as he pointed to where their two crystals nestled side by side in what she now saw was the bifurcated central column.

'Why didn't you tell me?' Tamina asked plaintively.

''Cos you'd have tried to stop me,' he replied with a shrug.

There was a long silence.

'I'm glad you're here,' she said, and spread her arms wide.

They hugged.

'I was hiding in the laboratory and saw you.' Wrenden pulled back and looked his sister in the face. 'I've never been so happy in all my life to know that we would be together.'

'Now you're being nice to me.'

'Yeah. Sad boy.'

She ruffled his hair, once again sending fond thoughts.

'Hey, Boots, Partners?'

'Yeah, Squirt, Partners.'

They gave one another a quick squeeze and stepped back.

'Now we mentaform some clothes,' Wrenden said.

'Not advisable,' CuSho said. 'Extra physiological travelling in me is very different from travelling by yourselves in the seventh dimension. With your crystals constituting an essential ingredient in my construction, through those in your EraBands, you, personally, are attuned to me. In future, place whatever you wish to wear in the Tazian room.'

'Yes, CuSho,' they said, solemnly.

'Now, if you step through Door into the Azuran side, you will be clothed. But do not try to leave me. Remember my fundamental construction. I am two holograms oscillating in and out of SigmaSpace and TauSpace.'

'Err??'

'SigmaSpace is what you perceive as your normal existence, where three dimensional Space is the basis and Time flows through that. TauSpace is where Time is the three dimensional basis and Space flows through that. It is by slipping into TauSpace that I may travel through what you call the Shadow Worlds. Your pairs of attuned crystals are what enable you both to travel with me and be safe within this oscillating field. If you step out of me anywhere other than on Vertazia, my time in TauSpace will sever the energy link between your InForming matrix and your body on Vertazia. Your current existence will be terminated.'

'Gulp,' they swallowed together.

Tamina opened Door and they stood, amazed at the sight. They were standing behind a typical shop counter, looking at a scene similar to the one Tamina had seen through the windows when CuSho had made its first trip to Azura. There were shelves on the walls full of jars and boxes. Several of the odd little houses were hanging on the walls. Skis and ski sticks and boots and a plethora of other items were scattered all about. Those that were recognisable could almost be Tazian, but only 'almost'.

Tamina took a deep breath and walked into the Azuran shop. Wrenden watched as she seemed to be covered in a thick, translucent, liquid coating. Colours slowly formed and took shape. Her blonde hair hung in two, long bunches. She was wearing a white blouse, a short dark blue skirt, white knee socks and sensible, dark blue shoes.

'Err, Sis. Look at your hands.'

'They're white!' She pulled her bunches in front of her face. 'And my hair's blonde! What...'

'This is correct,' CuSho interjected. 'Remember, you are not in your physical body but in your In-Forming Matrix. It has a similarity to what the Azurii term the Etheric Body. Just as I and everything inside me adapts to blend in with the locality, so must your energy forms.'

'Oh, all right.' Tamina sighed with relief. 'Now, what about these clothes?' she asked.

'According to my databanks, correct clothing for a schoolgirl of your age.'

'Can't I have proper Tazian clothes?'

'Please remember that your programming requires me to blend in harmoniously with the relevant environment. And you are attuned to me.'

Wrenden stepped into the shop, Door closing behind him. He felt as though warm water momentarily bubbled around him and every cell in his body tingled.

'It looks as though we go to the same school,' Tamina commented dryly.

He was wearing a white shirt and striped tie, grey shorts, knee length grey socks and black, lace-up shoes. His skin was white and his hair blonde.

'Aw, CuSho, I'm nearly fourteen years old,' he complained.

'Again, according to my databanks, correct clothing for a schoolboy of your age and in this culture.'

'You said we could bring our own clothes,' Wrenden objected.

'As long as you remain in the Tazian part of me, your InForming Matrix will remain constant and you may clothe it how you choose. Once you step into the Azuran part through the transmogrifying bubble, you replicate an appropriate Azuran.'

'Transmogrify?' they asked together.

'As well as providing external assimilation into the required culture, the bubble also operates on your genetic structure. In essence it is a molecular computer, operating within your individual cells.'

'Oh, all right. As long as no-one sees me,' he said.

'Us,' his sister added.

'Oh I don't know,' Wrenden said with a grin. 'You do look kind of cute.'

'And I thought we were being nice to one another!'

'Come on let's explore,' he said, still grinning.

They looked through the three round windows, two either side of the door and one in the side wall. From what they had seen at the Elmits, they guessed they were in a typical, small, Azuran town. And what was exciting was that they were on the corner of a road.

'Hey, CuSho, how did you manage that?' Wrenden asked.

'How did you describe me?'

'Err...'

'Auto-Locating, Self-Defining, Twins-Come-Home, Corner Shop,' CuSho said.

'But...'

'You forget the power of Imagination. The thoughts and ideas of four of you Creators were very strong, clear and coherent and extended well past what you considered I should look like merely to be inconspicuous. As they were appropriate and relevant and completely in alignment with the fundamental purpose for which I was being created, it was axiomatic that I incorporated them into the Arch-Discoverer's interacting algorithms. You completed the process when you brought your crystals for atunement. Your energy forms are subject to my... our programming, Keepers.'

Brother and sister were looking at each other in awe.

'He addressed us as "Keepers", again. Not just "ShopKeepers". What's that mean, Sis?' Wrenden asked.

'I don't know, Eeky.' She felt helpless and frightened. 'What have we got ourselves into? I thought it would be all so simple.'

A movement caught their attention. A man had stopped to look in one of the windows. He was tall and slim with a neat moustache. A lock of hair fell over his forehead as he peered into the shop.

'What do we do?' exclaimed Wrenden.

'You are ShopKeepers,' CuSho replied. 'Act as such.'

'But we don't speak their language,' Tamina objected.

'That does not matter. I will impress on his mind what you are saying. He will think you are speaking his language,' CuSho reassured them. 'I will do the reverse when he speaks. Impressing his thoughts onto your minds.'

They ran behind the counter and stood staring at the visitor. A few moments later they heaved big sighs of relief as he walked away.

'I suggest you lock the door and turn the sign hanging on it around the other way. It will read "closed", in the local language. Pull all the blinds down. Then try to MentaSynch with Qwelby.'

'Where are we?' Tamina asked.

'The conscious intent of you and those supporting you on Vertazia directed me to the locus of Qwelby's consciousness, subject to my overall programming. This is the nearest place to where he is that I am able to materialise as a Corner Shop.'

'Here, or in our Tazian room?' Wrenden asked.

'Here, where the Azuran vibrations are strong,' CuSho replied.

Having locked up, sister and brother settled into their accustomed lotus positions and went into a deep MentaSynch. It was not long before they returned, opened their eyes and with sorrowful looks agreed: Qwelby was fully in the grip of an impenetrable Darkness. And what was really serious, it was steadily shrinking and crushing him.

'We made that contact quickly and it was so very strong, slow and solid that we must be very near,' Tamina said. 'CuSho has brought us to the right place.'

'If Uncle Gumma was right when he said that the Globe should light up when CuSho arrives, Qwelby can't see it whilst he's in that state,' Wrenden pointed out. 'We must help him.'

'Help? Rescue, you mean. Even then I expect Mother will summon the Readjusters.'

Wrenden's already pale face blanched at the thought of the psychomental probings and realignments that they carried out on people considered to be deviants. 'I think I'd prefer to live with the Shakazii.'

'Me too. But. We're here. Come on, Eeky, let's focus on Qwelby.'

'I regret to inform you that will not be possible,' CuSho announced. 'Elder Mandara set a time return. You must return to the Tazian room now.'

CHAPTER 34

HEARTENING NEWS

FINLAND

Walking back to his car after lunch, still musing over his sighting of the dark-skinned boy, Romain stopped at a ski shop. He was puzzled. He didn't remember seeing it before. He looked up. Over the unusually arched doorway was the name: Utelias Kauppa. Faint music was coming from what he assumed were speakers hidden behind the letters.

He knew the Finnish for "ski" was "hiitää", but especially in tourist areas they normally used the word "ski" itself. With the letters picked out in the seven colours of the rainbow as opposed to the usual six, and combined with the music, he assumed it was the name of an idiosyncratic owner.

He browsed the window display where he caught a glimpse of two people behind the counter. The window was cluttered. He removed his hat to get closer to the window. Even so, the old-fashioned glass distorted his vision making it difficult to discern their faces. Both had blonde hair, with that of the tall girl's falling in bunches out of sight below the counter top.

His mind provided a convenient set of assumptions. A schoolgirl, her shorter companion probably her younger brother, the two of them minding the shop for their parents. It was good to see them learning the business at an early age. That was what had made him rich. He hoped their initiation would come without the same sense of betrayal that he had experienced with his father whilst he was still in his teens.

'Made a man of you, Reginsen,' his inner voice said.

He straightened up and looked at the glass. Bull's-eye panes were interspersed with plain glass. But no. The whole round window was seamless and slightly convex. The bull's-eye effect was there all right, but there were no individual panes.

Although his inventions were mainly in the fields of electronics and communications, he appreciated the genius of people working in other areas. And thus, as he continued on his way back to the car, he allowed himself to put his problems to one side and relax with the pleasant exercise of thinking how he would set about creating such an effect.

The puzzle about the existence of the shop itself was quickly forgotten. After all, it did not have the slightest relevance to his search.

When Romain reached his hotel room there was a light on his GlobeSync indicating a voice message. His paranoia naturally extended to communication. From where it was placed on a table the machine projected an ovoid shaped area that covered a large part of the room and made it impenetrable to any listening device.

Communication with his assistants was conducted by ultra-short-burst, encrypted transmissions. If he ever required sensitive data, that was retrieved from the computers in the laboratory on Raiatea in the same way. Romain sat down and listened to the expanded message

Taking turns in speaking, his assistants said that they had made progress with their investigations. There were limited reports of electro-magnetic disturbances much further north and all of the sort that were experienced in connection with the Aurora Borealis. The only unusual fact, which was already known, was that the Aurora had been seen from much further south than normal.

Raiatea being a French Overseas Territory, both of them also spoke French. They had decided to make phone calls as if they were Americans working for French or Belgian news media, satellite broadcasters or energy suppliers. From that they had discovered a significant number of very temporary EM interferences across a fairly widespread area late on December twenty-seven. A few people had been specific about the time, and even those who were not precise confirmed that it had happened just as it was getting dark - around four o'clock. Looking at the map being displayed, Romain saw that Kotomäki and Jyväskylä were well towards the centre of the area delineated.

Tyler said that through an old friend who worked at Princeton for the Institute of Noetic Sciences he had been able to discover that Random Number Generators had been affected. As yet the data had not been fully analysed but was already showing up a greater divergence than either of those that had occurred at the times of the funeral of Princess Diana or the terrorist attacks on nine eleven. He did not need to say that little if any notice was taken of such data by the mainstream scientific community.

Miki added that there had been reports of more meteor showers at that time, again much further north around the impact structures of Lakes Lappajärvi and Karikkoselkä.

Romain easily dismissed the meteor showers as being too far north to cause the EM disturbances around Kotomäki. Although there had undoubtedly been an enhanced display of the Northern Lights, he considered that this far south they would not have caused the extensive effects his assistants were now reporting.

Their conclusions were that clearly there had been widespread EM interference at or about the time of the event that had been detected, and that as it was so short-lived and there had been no reports of any accidents as a result, it had not been newsworthy. There was a caveat. Where local newspapers had websites they appeared only to upload the main news items. That applied to Jyväskylä's Keskisuomalainen. The puzzle was that the effects seemed to be so minor compared with the major disruption they had been expecting.

'Command: Reply,' Romain said to the GlobeSynch. 'Thank you. Very helpful. Will refine my questions. Will check local paper. Will advise later. Command: End. Command: Location RaiLabTwo: send.'

With raised spirits he went down to Reception. His luck was in. A few moments later he was talking with the Assistant Manager who had a copy of Saturday's newspaper. Asking how she could help, she provided a translation of a brief article she had read and confirmed that the hotel had experienced a brief interruption of both telephones and internet. Back in his room a few minutes later, Remain sent another message to Raiatea.

'Keskisuomalainen. Small article Saturday about the interference, including a quote from the Public Relations Officer at the Institute in Jyväskylä denying that they had done anything to cause it. Apparently, someone had noticed that there had been more life around the Institute that day when it was supposed to be closed through to the New Year. The reason given was that an automatic alarm had sounded and a small maintenance team had attended.' He sent the message, forbearing to say that he wished he had known that before his visit that morning.

CHAPTER 35

REKKR REGINSEN

FINLAND

Romain sat back and sorted through what he had learnt. The meteor information was irrelevant but useful. Anyone questioning his research would consider that was what he should be concentrating on and that his equipment was faulty. Unpleasant in one way, but anything that could help to make others ignore what he was doing had to be good.

So far the "evidence" was circumstantial. Yet in his mind it did point to something having gone into another dimension and then returned. And both occurrences were connected to CERN and now Jyväskylä. So. Where was his data that had been on the neutrinos and, or, what had returned? An artefact that was so tiny it could be hidden in a pocket yet cause such widespread EM disturbances? Or the boy himself?

He sat there taking deep breaths. The boy fitted the scenario and the window that must have opened between the two dimensions had caused the EM interference. He questioned himself. Was he becoming delusional, was his obsession, he allowed the word momentarily to enter his thoughts, driving him over the edge?

As he sat there thinking of how to proceed he broke out into a cold sweat as a nightmare scenario crossed his mind. A policeman spotting an unaccustomed black face. Curious, asking to see the boy's identity card, then taking him to the station for questioning. The answers to those questions causing heavens knew who to descend on Kotomäki.

Romain gritted his teeth at the thought that scientists would be well back in the queue after the military, intelligence agencies and such like. And himself, out of favour with "The Establishment" and not even at the back of the queue! He had to act fast.

Then his scientific training asserted itself. This was not a situation in which he was going to publish a paper reporting the results of an experiment, effectively asking others to see if they could reproduce it. He had to be sure of his grounds before approaching the boy and even more so if there was denial, refusal to cooperate and "Plan B" came into operation. Not only his own career and reputation were at stake, but Franz and Pierre were unlikely to be forgiving if they kidnapped a boy who had family and friends.

A scenario presented itself. The boy's father was a scientist who had supported, been part of, his country's leadership. A revolution and a violent change at the top. The father knew Dr Keskinen who had agreed to help. Getting the boy to safety and needing to conceal his identity had all been in such a rush there had been no time to prepare a proper cover story.

What if he stirred up a hornet's nest by approaching the boy directly, and whoever was really protecting him thought that he, Romain, was acting for their enemy? The possibilities were endless. He had to be sure of the facts, or their lack! And that had to be done discreetly to ensure he did not make the biggest mistake of his life.

Taking a bottle of Velamo from the fridge, he poured the water into a glass and sat down at the desk to prepare a plausible reason for wanting a young boy investigated. In the process, he discovered that Helsinki was not like big cities in novels. Finding a private investigator was not going to be easy.

When he had decided to change his name and obtain a second passport, it had not taken long for Pierre to have the necessary papers prepared. He could not see why preparing papers for the boy should take any longer. Even so, how long could he wait before acting? Where could he hide him if there was a delay? Could Pierre and Franz arrange that? And how could he get the boy out of the country?

One of Romain's developments had been to extend the power of subliminal messaging by improving on a technique known as 'functional magnetic resonance imaging'. He had built that into his GlobeSynch but had no idea how long it could hold someone against their will.

Hands unpleasantly sticky with sweat, he went into the bathroom to wash in cold water. As he looked at himself in the mirror, he wondered: if the boy was an alien, was his mind even sufficiently like a human's for the GlobeSynch to work at all? So many questions, so many uncertainties. His mouth was dry.

'I left CERN convinced I was right to pursue my researches. I have staked everything on my faith in myself. I cannot, I WILL NOT falter now,' he said to his refection.

A picture came into his mind of the boy agreeing to accompany him and happily installed in his laboratory. The vision shattered as he thought of an unwilling experimental subject, not a rat but a human child. Tyler? 'No problem.' he said to himself. 'At his age, his career is tied to mine, to our work.' But Miki? She was an excellent and dedicated scientist but not what he would term 'hard nosed'. It was clear that she had a soft spot and her philosophy would definitely not condone holding the boy against his will. And then back to Tyler. He was devoted to his wife.

A feeling of panic, of being overwhelmed, was rising in him.

'Miki gets close to the boy,' his alter ego said. 'The boy is away from home. She mothers him. Think of it. She is just old enough to be his mother. Tyler becomes his father figure. You are remote, the probing scientist. What do you know about children?'

'Very little,' Romain acknowledged.

'They become family. You cannot use your Globe Synch to control him when he is on Raiatea as you will need his mind free for all your experiments. You will have no hold over him. They see a way of achieving fame. Even the Nobel Prize for themselves. And take him away from you.' His alter ego's comments pierced the core of Romain's vulnerability.

As Romain sat staring blankly out of the hotel window, a memory came back to him of a comment made during one of the faculty dinners when he had announced who he had recruited as his assistants. Just at that moment an interesting conversation had started on the opposite side of the table. Romain had switched his attention to that and had not really been listening to what the Professor sitting at his side was saying. He recalled that it was something about Miki having been ill whilst preparing her doctoral dissertation and her tutor having been exceptionally supportive.

Hearing a name he knew, Romain's attention had been pulled back to the man at his side. He distinctly remembered his colleague's final words. "Tyler must have been particularly interested as her thesis was very much in the area of his speciality. Of course they were not married at that time."

Having already checked Miki's excellent references, assuring himself they were genuine and not overstated in order to get rid of an unwanted colleague, Romain had taken the facts commented upon as further evidence of their dedication to each other and her desire to succeed.

He now saw there could be a different interpretation. Was there a suggestion that Miki had not written all of it, that what was stated as having been her research, might not have been. And what if Tyler had contributed directly? If that were to be known she would be stripped of her doctorate and it would destroy both their careers.

He sat back in his chair and savoured the possibility. If those suppositions were true, then proof of that would give him the hold over them he needed. He would break the return journey to Raiatea with a short stay in California where he could explore the situation at the University where he lectured. There was another benefit. The medical facilities at the University were far superior to anything he had ever needed to establish in his laboratory complex. If he was careful, he could have the boy physically examined.

As Romain settled back down to work, a deep-seated energy pulsed from within, once again bringing the image of a Viking longship ploughing through storm-tossed waves. As before, he was both manning the steering board and standing in the prow, peering into the mists. Pulled into the image standing in the prow he raised the horn to his lips and drained it to the last, once again renewing the blood oath he had taken so many months ago.

As his consciousness returned he discovered that he was standing up, looking out into the night sky. Any doubts he may have harboured about taking the alien by force had fled. His alter ego had given him the courage to act on his conviction. Better than nothing, he raised his glass of water to Rekkr Reginsen, as he had named his alter ego. Reginsen being the old family name and Rekkr the Norse for both 'man' and 'warrior'. If the boy was unwilling, he would have him kidnapped. But before that....

He telephoned Reception and asked to be transferred to the Duty Manager. He explained that he wanted to visit Helsinki for two nights and agreed that the Scandic Grand Marina would be perfect.

'Right, David Beauregard Romain,' he said softly, as he put the telephone down. 'Now. Think and plan. A lot more precision is required than for a Viking raid!'

CHAPTER 36

CURIOUS SHOP RETURNS

VERTAZIA

As Curious Shop returned safely to the laboratory from its trip to find Qwelby, Wrenden's words as they left Azura reached the ears of his older sister. 'Don't say anything Sis. I'll explain.'

'I feel too sick to talk right now,' Tamina replied in a shaky voice.

'We've got to rescue Qwelby,' Wrenden said in a slurred voice. 'He's in a terrible state...... It's getting worse. He....'

'Lift,' Mizena called. 'Five to the XOÑOX Suite. Tamuchly.'

Lungunu, the home of Mandara and Lellia, was constructed of five wings centred around the massive, circular, domed StroemCavern. Each wing was divided into two halves. The central family wing at the rear of the house was the largest. The youngster's parents had given permission for them to stay at Lungunu whilst the search for the twins continued. House had reorganised the left half of the family wing by adding on to the twins' suite, which already had its own Enjoy Suite, a Lounging Room and several bedrooms.

The name "XOÑOX" had been scribed over the entry to the complex. It was the name they had chosen based on their mantra:

"xátuyé osiy nola nola osiy xátuyé". A lot later they were to discover that they could make xonnox from several of the Azuran languages, but that it didn't quite work in the most common one: six all one one all six.

Lift deposited Mizena and the youngsters in the Lounging Room, where the furniture was rearranging itself to provide a pair of double Relax Couches. The youngsters slipped out of their clothes and, in their inevitable pairs, the not-twins Pelnak and Shimara, Wrenden and Tamina, they snuggled into the Couches which enwrapped them and started to gently massage their bodies and minds.

Meanwhile, Lellia and Shandur who had been monitoring the Stroems, closed down the Cavern and joined Mandara in the laboratory. He summoned Lift to take them to the Lounging Room where they were greeted by four happy but tired faces.

'They are low in energy,' Mizena said, as she tightbanded her thoughts to her husband that their son was in a bad way. 'But otherwise they are well.'

'That's good to hear, because there is a puzzle,' Mandara said, looking at Tamina and Wrenden.

He glanced at Mizena who had been monitoring the youngsters' console. 'Nothing you could have detected. I do not understand it. The recordings are showing different situations from what the monitors were displaying.'

'How can that be?' Shandur asked.

'Have you ever watched an Azuran flikker where they record, say, an empty corridor and play that through the link to the monitors. The watching security guards see an empty corridor whilst people are actually walking along it?' his uncle asked.

'No,' Shandur replied, wondering just what sort of flikkers his uncle watched with his children in Lungunu's Elmit room.

Mandara turned his attention back to brother and sister. 'You know what I'm talking about,' he said slowly and deliberately.

Wrenden's crystal, linked to the one in CuSho, was pulsing. He understood. CuSho had modified the real-time techinfo being sent back to the monitors, but could not alter the facts being recorded.

Although his crystal had only been attuned to his EraBand the previous day, Wrenden confidently took on his new status as Youngster. Concealed by the coverspread of their Couch, he reached for his sister's hand and squeezed it. If there was one thing he knew about his elderest, it was that Qwelby had to look out for Tullia because she was a girl. Qwelby was Wrenden's hero. He would follow him anywhere – and often did – into no end of trouble.

'It's my fault,' he said. 'I had two pieces of Lazabatanzii. I placed one inside CuSho so I had to travel with It.' Into the stunned silence he added: 'Tamina had to follow me because.... she has to boss me about.' He squeezed his sister's hand again, thoughtsending: *Stay with my story.*

Uproar broke out with everyone talking at once. 'Stop!' Lellia commanded. 'We mustn't continue talking here. The energies are so strong they'll spread throughout the MentaNet. Lift. Everyone except me to my Spherical Room. Tamuchly.'

CHAPTER 37

ALARM!

FINLAND

The day after Qwelby had fallen into a coma, Seija, Hannu's mother, continued to look in on him on a regular basis. He always seemed the same: his breathing shallow but steady and his temperature a little below normal, for a human. Although she never saw him awake, when the glass was empty she refilled it. That made her decide to leave it until the following morning before calling the doctor.

Hannu had become accustomed to slightly sensing his friend's moods through their energy connection. He missed that, but he was still not sure how much he was comfortable with Qwelby sensing his own feelings clearly. Not wanting to explain that to Anita because he was uncomfortable with how close she was to Qwelby, he went round to see Timo, his best friend, feeling guilty because he had hardly seen him since Qwelby's arrival as Timo had been unable to ski following an injury to his ankle.

After some time with Timo, Hannu felt as though he was being drawn back to his Alien friend. He had read that talking to a person in a coma could help bring them back to consciousness.

Back home, he found Anita dozing in a chair beside Qwelby's bed, her hand resting on the side of the bed and a book on the floor that he assumed had fallen from her lap.

There was a strained atmosphere as Anita woke up. Explaining that she thought reading was what Tullia would do, did not make Hannu feel any better.

With a cry, Qwelby half sat up, waving his arms and legs about and knocking the contents of the bedside cabinet onto the floor before crashing back down, all tangled in the duvet.

Hearing the noise, Seija came upstairs. As Hannu helped his mother ease the inert boy back into a comfortable position, Anita knelt down to collect all the things from the floor. 'The carpet's dry. He must have drunk all the water,' she said.

Seija wiped spittle from Qwelby's lips. 'We must call the doctor,' she said, resting a sympathetic hand on her son's shoulder.

'But, Mum!' Hannu wailed. 'You said you'd wait until tomorrow morning.'

'Better he's alive than dead,' his mother replied.

'Please, Mum, can't we wait until tomorrow? Please!' Hannu begged.

There was silence as, with his feelings for the alien overcoming his jealousy, Hannu put an arm around Anita as they watched Seija taking Qwelby's temperature, then checking his pulse and his breathing. Finally, she held his hand for a few moments before tucking his arm under the duvet.

'He's not really any different from before,' she said as she looked at her son. 'We'll see what your father says when he comes home tonight.'

'Thanks Mum,' Hannu said, crossing his fingers and hoping his alien friend would be better by then.

CHAPTER 38

POLE POSITION

VERTAZIA

They were all still arguing as Lift deposited them in a room that was totally thought and energy shielded. Today, the floor was an intricate mosaic pattern and the walls appeared to be made of fluted marble columns, the tops of which spread out to join part way up the sphere, leaving an open circle representing the afternoon sky. The peaceful nature of the surroundings calmed the energies and, as the several armchairs that ringed the wall morphed into curved sofas, the youngsters sat on the long one and the husband and wife pairs on the two shorter ones. Still feeling sick, Tamina's feeble protestations had gone unnoticed by all except her brother.

'I left you to go and speak with Curious Shop,' Lellia said as she arrived, and went on to explain exactly what Wrenden and Tamina had done with their crystals. Leaning forward with a hand raised, she halted the horrified exclamations of the twins' parents.

'I said I spoke with CuSho. House, please replay what happened.' She sat back in her chair as a virtual HoloViewer started to play.

'Greetings, Keeper of the Ancient and Sublime Esoteric Traditions of the Auriganii,' CuSho said as Lellia entered the Laboratory.

'You can see I was taken aback,' Lellia commented. 'How could It know my full title? I had not used that even when I attuned Wrenden's crystal. You will see how my thought was answered.'

'I am created out of the Arch-Discoverer's beautiful, asymmetric algorithms. Imbued with your dreams of Conscious Awareness. Melded with the Stroems. And empowered by myriad thoughts, the strongest of which was that the four youngsters are the only ones who can rescue the twins.'

'How could you allow those two chi...youngsters to place their crystals within you? You must have known what would result!' Lellia said.

Everyone felt the surprise that emanated from CuSho.

'I could not refuse two of my Creators!'

'Taking them with you was not included in your programming,' Lellia countered.

'Over the several days of my creation, amongst everything that was happening, two, strong, clear and coherent directives were constantly impressed upon me. Maximise my capabilities to the full in order to recover the twins and those two Creators were to journey with me. The Consciousness Programming with which you imbued me requires me to act on those directives.'

'You mean it's my fault!' Lellia buried her face in her hands.

'That does not compute.'

'They are so young,' Lellia almost wailed in her despair.

'Essential. Unlike adults, their Imaginations are clear and focussed. Their thoughts are free from extraneous concerns. Their energies as yet unfettered by adult-age programming.'

'But...'

'It was the Imaginations of the four younger Creators that made me in the form of a Corner Shop, able to blend unobtrusively with any Azuran environment. If I am to succeed in my purpose, my abilities are obviously enhanced by the presence of fully sentient input. Those two Creators chose to provide that.'

'I will insert a crystal of my own and become another Keeper,' Lellia declared, her tone grim with defeat.

'Impossible. That thought is not included in my programming. With the addition of the crystals enabling the InForming Matrices of those two Creators to journey with me, my programming was finalised. I am Complete.'

'Then I will remove the crystals.'

There were gasps of surprise as everyone saw Lellia step forward and then almost bounce back from what had to be a soft, gently sprung barrier.

'I am sorry, Elder Lellia,' CuSho said. 'You have triggered an automatic defence. Until my purpose has been served the crystals cannot be removed without considerable harm to my Keepers.' CuSho harrumphed, sounding like Mandara. 'And myself.'

As the virtual HoloViewer disappeared the adults thoughtshared behind strong privacy shielding. Eventually, they all nodded.

'Why?' Mizena asked.

Tamina reached out a hand and her young brother took it. They turned back to the adults. 'We wanted to go to Azura to rescue the twins,' they said together.

'It's our role to support the mission,' the not-twins said together.

'It suits us,' Shimara added, turning to look at Pelnak.

'We're not as adventurous as SisBro,' Pelnak said, revealing a name new to the adults.

'Of course!' Mandara exclaimed. 'Twins, Not-Twins, SisBro. 'Tri-Unity. Massively increased because each one of the three is a mixed gender pairing reflecting the uniqueness of the basic building block of the whole Multiverse, the Kwozakubezeninii, half matter and half anti-matter, half SigmaSpace and half TauSpace.'

He sat back, letting out a big sigh. 'Tamina is Tullia's elderest. Wrenden is Qwelby's youngerest. Top and bottom as your dream showed. Not only a right balancing of energies, but.....' He gave a heavy sigh as he looked at the twins' parents. 'These two and your children carry the genes of the four most powerful of all ten Uddîšû. This will work.'

'Yes. And, SisBro,' Lellia said with a grim look on her face. 'The strength of those genes in you is why your parents are so concerned for your future.'

'Tazian life is changing,' Mizena almost whispered as she squeezed her husband's hand, acknowledging a shared and very reluctant feeling that there was a rightness about the whole situation.

'Aurigan,' Pelnak muttered, causing everyone to sink into deep reflection.

'We must go back,' Wrenden said.

'I know you want to reach my son before he is totally engulfed by the Darkness,' Mizena said. 'Believe me, I want that more than you do. But you need to restore.....'

'We have to go back now,' Tamina interrupted in a tone so firm and assured that it shocked the adults. She was still smarting from having her young brother try to take all the blame. She would correct that later. Right now she agreed with him. Qwelby was in such a bad state that rescuing him could not wait. And Mandara had just said how strong she and Wrenden were.

'Midnight,' Lellia announced in a tone that brooked no contradiction. 'It is a powerful time for the ebb and flow of natural forces between our two worlds.'

'Agreed,' Tamina said, taking one of her brother's hands in hers and looking at Shimara and Pelnak.

'We agree,' the not-twins said together, holding hands and each raising the other to shoulder height.

Tamina and Wrenden followed suit with their free hands, and all four made their XOÑOX sign. Thumb and little finger bent in to touch the palm, the other three fingers pointing to the sky and spread apart, then coming together and bending over to touch the centre of the palm.

'Midnight,' all four said together.

There was something so definite about the energies surrounding the commitment that the adults openly thoughtshared: *The future belongs to the young.*

'Right, you four,' Lellia said, bringing their attention to her. 'It's important your thoughts do not leak out to your parents. They need to be told, carefully, and hopefully at the right time.'

Looking serious, the youngsters nodded.

'Will you all accept me entering and gently sealing within the framework of House, that set of memories each of you has concerning this. I will cover the Seal so that as your thoughts travel outside Lungunu, they will be cloaked by a period in the Enjoy Suite.'

Again they nodded.

When that had been done, Lellia summoned Lift to take the four to their suite, asked Cook to take them a selection of light refreshments and then take some more for the adults to her Homely Room.

Lift arrived.

Lellia nudged her husband.

'I know the twins refer to us as Gallia and Gumma and you call my wife Aunt Gallia,' Mandara said in a gruff voice. 'I require the same courtesy... of being addressed as Uncle Gumma... Right!'

'Yes, sir, Uncle Gumma, sir!' they chorused as they stepped into Lift.

CHAPTER 39

FRIENDS TO THE RESCUE

VERTAZIA

Mizena awakened the youngsters a short while before midnight. When they had freshened themselves and slipped on their relax robes, she led them to the Homely Room where Lellia was waiting. After a light snack, Lellia took them along the corridor. Once again the Isuna of the Night was waiting for them. She opened the door to the Seliya Chamber.

As they entered, Mizena gasped with surprise. It was so different. This time the walls were a deep, rich, burgundy colour, as was most of the floor. In the centre everything was the blackest black. There the floor was sunken to form a circular seating area. In the centre of that was a circular table. On it sat a jet black cube. Lellia seated the youngsters, equally spaced around the table, with the not-twins opposite each other.

'What you've told us shows that something terrible has happened to hurt Qwelby so much that he has shut down,' Lellia said. 'What I need you to do. What he needs you to do. Is to get him to open up and allow that awful negative energy to drain out.'

She looked around the people much too young to be asked to undertake something as important as this. Their faces reflected back the seriousness as they nodded with a calmness that surprised her. *Seliya's Phases! They are growing up fast. I hope not too fast.*

'Pelnak and Shimara. I know you've not made the same strong connections with Qwelby that Tamina and Wrenden have, because your connection is so much with the twins as a couple. Nevertheless, your love for the twins is vitally important to the success of what will happen tonight.'

They nodded.

'Tamina, my dear. You must lead the journey tonight, reach Qwelby and persuade him that whatever that awful secret he is keeping locked within, he cannot deal with it by himself and must let the energy flow out.'

'Eeky.' Wrenden looked up, surprised. That was Tamina's special nickname for him. He thought it rather nice coming from Aunt Gallia. 'Qwelby is your elderest. That he wants to be there for you he showed by his shout of "Never apart" as he let go your hand and fell back into the Stroems. You must be the bridge between your sister and Pelnak and Shimara. Do not be concerned about draining the energy. That will happen as Tamina persuades Qwelby to open.'

Lellia moved to the table and lifted up the black cube. The others gasped with amazement. In front of them was a most beautiful array of jet black Melanite crystals.

'Pelnak and Shimara, you must focus on this array and hold it in your minds as firmly as possible. Tamina, you must send that image to Qwelby. It is into this that his Darkness can be drained with complete safety. Qwelby's conscious mind does not know about this. But his inner Self will recognise it and respond.'

Mizena took four, black, hooded cloaks from The Isuna. 'These are made of Night itself,' she said as she handed them out. 'They will shield you completely from the Darkness as it drains into the crystal array.'

The women stepped up out of the sunken circle.

'Remember what I said to each of you,' Lellia said as she turned back to face the youngsters. 'You are BestFriends and it is your love for the twins that will give you the strength for what you must do tonight and the protection to keep you safe.' She made eye contact with each of them and nodded when satisfied that each was as composed as could be.

'You know where to find us when you are finished.'

As the two women left the room, The Isuna closed the door. This time she remained on the inside, on guard.

Tamina closed her eyes and steadied her own breathing. Slowly the colourlessness of deepstate deepened until she sensed the energies. Deep and rich with a feel like velvet, Wrenden's green colour snaked forth. *Eeky being cautions. That's a first!* Tamina thought to herself as, taking a deep breath, she eased out of her body. *I might not have wings but this must be like what a Wenkosi butterfly feels when it drops from its chrysalis, with its sort of umbilical cord still attached to its home.*

She headed down into an ever darkening gloom, slowing as the syrupy consistency thickened. As she followed her brother's thread she became aware of a rainbow mix of vibrant colours from her own crystal of Bula'kabilii extending ahead of her through the gloom to what had to be Qwelby's Darkness.

As she neared the black sphere, although still large, it was smaller than when they had last seen it. She was almost repulsed by a smell and a taste so vile she gagged. Ahead, she saw her brother's cord hesitate. With a great effort she managed to drop down and wrap it in the rainbow from her crystal.

After a few seconds he energised alongside. His hand flew to his face as he tried to block the awful, emotional stench. It was overpowering. This was no longer, if it ever had been, merely Darkness. This was Depression and Despair, full-on and heavy.

Dropping his hand he turned to his sister. They smiled at one another. Not only had they remembered to be clothed, they had both successfully imaged tight fitting skinergysuits. A sort of spacesuit that the Auriganii had worn but the Tazii were no longer able to make. Tamina had chosen reds and flame oranges, Wrenden a grounding mix of browns and greens.

Wrenden stepped forward, searching all around the ball. 'I can't see any sign of an opening,' he said. 'All I can feel is his guilt.'

'Because he's not being your elderest,' Tamina explained.

'That's stupid,' Wrenden expostulated. 'It's not his fault.'

'I know. But that's how he's feeling,' she replied.

They stood there at a loss what to do.

'Surely he must want to be with Tullia,' Wrenden said eventually.

'Of course.'

'She's a girl. You're a girl. He's always liked you, which is why he joins with me to tease you... and now you're softer.'

'Mmm.' Having a private conversation with Image in Mirror was one thing, but to actualise it...

'Sis. Is there anything he's ever said to you that you can reflect back to him?'

'He called me "Lightning" that time I danced for their fifteenth rebirthday,' she reluctantly acknowledged.

'That's great. Wear that suit now.'

'Eeky?'

'Oh come on Sis, Imagination! We're Out-Of-Body. It's got to be easy. Please, we've got to save him.'

Tamina imaged herself in figure-hugging black with iridescent lightning-shaped silver streaks down arms and legs. Long, glittering, silvered fibres twined themselves through her golden-flecked, thigh length hair. Feeling self-conscious, she twirled, thoughtsending *Lightning*.

An image came to her of the look on Qwelby's face just three months ago. Forever playing her up along with her young brother, she was unable to resist the temptation, and added an image of herself cuddling him and stroking his hair as if he were a little boy.

'That's going to help him come out?' an annoyed Wrenden asked. For the last few months his sister had been moody and short tempered. Now she was going all mushy. And all because of her Awakening. Thank the stars he was a boy. Images crossed his mind of some much older boys at college, mooning over girls. Yetch....

CHAPTER 40

QWELBY RESISTS

BETWEEN WORLDS

Retreating from a shocking reality, Qwelby withdrew so deep inside that he reached the collective unconscious of his race.

I am Aurigan. There are no Tazii. Aurigan life starts in the third dimension – the Seed Generation. Deep inside its third dimensional core, my HomeSphere carried that life. We wanted to find a planet without sentient life. After forty thousand years searching and the Space Wars, the numbers of us in the ninth dimensions who provided the shielding to allow the HomeSphere to travel faster than light had sunk too low to continue. We had to settle on Azura Yezi. Temporarily.

The Great Schism. The rupture of the whole Aurigan life cycle. The Seed Generation no longer able to progress beyond the fourth dimension. With Azura Yezi split into two realms we renamed them Azura and Vertazia, ran and hid from what I had brought about. By banishing that terrible time from our collective psyche by calling ourselves Tazii we denied our true Aurigan nature. Our active DNA decreased and we became almost completely confined to the fifth dimension. Even today most of my people deny that we share the fourth dimension of consciousness with the Azurii.

AIYEE! he screamed his pain. *Ruining the beautiful planet that you, Ngélûzhrâ Khèrñîszón, found for us. The violence all over Earth. It's all my fault. Thirteen thousand years ago. I didn't listen to my twin. Life is an infinite, eternity of energy cycling – in balance. I destroyed that balance. What was the point in saving my people for me to do that!?*

I deserve to be punished. I need to be punished. But Auriganii or Tazii, we have no such concept. Only the rebalancing of the energy cycle. Retribution.

And redemption.

How can I ever redeem what I did?

Eyes danced before him. Straw yellow ovals with central orbs that looked to be made of green amazonite. *Léshmîrâ Kûsheÿnÿ! You came a thousand years after the Space Wars, grew up with the Auriganii divided into dissenting groups, and in your inimical way restored harmony. What a time that was!*

But my inherited genes come from the Dragon Lord. Both of you were after that. Ngélûzhrâ a full five thousand years after......

Qwelby's head was spinning as a kaleidoscope of people from different millennia assailed him. Faces of people he'd known and couldn't have known appeared and slipped away as he tried to talk to them. A maelstrom of emotions ripping through his mind and body. It was like being trapped in a timeslipping, HoloWrapper Adventure. *Léshmîrâ.... Ngélûzhrâ....*

Ngé'zânâ. Lésh'zânâ. The middle names for Wrenden and Tamina, recognising their inherited Uddîšû genes.

Tamina? You? Thoughtsending? You mustn't come in here, my Despair will crush you.

Wrenden? NO! He's my youngerest. My duty to look after him. Protect him.

Qwelby reeled back as tender caring swept all around him. He was a tiny baby, being...... Dark images cascaded through his mind, bringing feelings of terror, horror and self-loathing. NO! *No-one can love me after what I did!*

A multitude of images assailed him as if he was Wrapped in several different Adventures all at once. 'Leave me alone!' he screamed at Léshmîrâ and Ngélûzhrâ. 'Don't you understand? I deserve this! '

'GO AWAY!' he yelled at Tamina and Wrenden as he tried to hurl them away and safely back into their physical bodies.

A crack appeared right down at the bottom of the ball. It looked like a mouth opening.

'It's working,' an amazed Wrenden said to his blushing sister, who was trying to shield her embarrassment at having felt her first stirrings for a boy, her confusion that it was for Qwelby who was too young to understand, and what did it say about her feelings for Tullia?

A jet of repellent goo shot through the opening, throwing brother and sister to the ground.

Wiping her eyes as she got to her feet, Tamina saw the mouth closing. 'Eeky!' she yelled as she threw herself forward and forced her way through the flow of gunk.

Like a mouth sucking on a lemon, the opening drew back, widening into a grimace. Desperate to save his friends, Qwelby was striving to prevent the opening from snapping shut and trapping Tamina inside his doom.

'How do I send "Elderest Guidance" to Qwelby?' Tamina thought to herself. 'No. That's "Bossy Boots." That won't work. She remembered Mirror, and the discovery that Qwelby liked her as a female. She felt her power. And she felt silly. Was that really how he saw her? A tall, attractive, powerful, young woman – who he teased so as to hide his feelings? Impossible! Tullia would know. She would have said. But..... identical, Quantum Twins......

Surrounded by strong pinks and greens, an image reached her

from her brother of the day the twins had disappeared when he had thrown himself into the Stroems, risking death in his attempt to rescue Qwelby, and she had thrown herself onto Eeky's legs to save him from being swept away.

Love.

She liked Qwelby, most of the time, but knew she did not have a love that was strong enough for this.

Another image arrived. The Uddîšû Léshmîrâ Kûsheÿnÿ, whose genes she carried. Tamina bit her lip. Léshmîrâ's usually used sobriquet was Hîaûlettâ, Reconciler. But Tamina knew that for her mother to refuse to acknowledge that heritage, there had to be a lot more to discover about that heroine.

An energy reached her that was so different she could not believe it came from Qwelby, yet it contained his signature. With it flowed a voice that was and was not Qwelby's: 'Ÿenlûmâ na Kûÿ-maó-lâš'tûn.'

Tamina did not understand the words. She sensed they were more sobriquets for her Uddîšû. The surrounding heavy energy made her uncomfortable, yet deep down inside she sensed an acknowledgment – from her own, deep seated power.

Tamina had only recently achieved her Awakening. Yarannah, her mother, had made it very clear that she did not want her daughter to formally adopt Lésh'zânâ as her middle name. At that time Tamina had felt a power rise within that both compelled her to acknowledge her genetic inheritance and enabled her to do so behind the most powerful Privacy Shield she had ever erected.

That same energy was now arising inside her. She would use that to reach Qwelby.

With both hands gripping the top lip of the opening, feet streaming out behind her in the continuous flow of revolting putrefaction, she opened herself fully to her genetic inheritance and poured all her energy into sending love to Qwelby. As she wrapped it in the rainbow coloured energy of her crystal, she saw it cleaving a path deep inside the ball. Intuition called to her and she was nudged by the memory of a previous and terrifying journey, when the four friends had been searching in the seventh dimension for the twins.

She let go her grip on the opening and dropped her head between her arms, imaging herself diving from her favourite hill top into the lake far below.

Qwelby fought against the love reaching him. No-one could love what he had done, especially not Tamina who so loved his twin. As the pinks and greens flowed around him he thought he sensed a big, plump bird and felt like a baby cuddled against his mother's breast. Where was Kaigii?

Every cell in Qwelby's body was on fire, trillions of bright points empowering him. He had to send his friends back to the safety of their Forms in the fifth dimension. He strained with all his might to break free of the massive weight of the Despair. He was not strong enough. Out of all the images still assailing him, one became clear. Had it been days ago or countless lifetimes? It was all the same.

Tamina was operating on two levels. She opened herself fully to Tullia's twin, asking him to accept her also as his elderest, and to share his Disillusionment with her. At the same time she was living another life. It was all hazy as she felt an energy she knew well drawing her towards him, yet hurtling her backwards in time.

Her heart told her that she loved him as much as she did his twin and even her annoying young brother. Thinking of Wrenden reminded her of what she had to do. She called up an image of the Melanite Array and thoughtsent that to Qwelby, showing him that it needed all his negative energy to be what it was.

Qwelby was in a Black Hole. He needed the strength to turn it on itself and drain back into the other universe that had spawned it. He called to Léshmîrâ Kûsheÿnÿ.

Again Tamina imaged that suit. She drew the silver lightning up her legs, along her three spinal canals and down into her heart. She had intended to hurl it from her fingertips yet she felt her eyes blaze as an inner voice cried in triumph: '¡Šâlâmañder Kèhša!'

Qwelby saw Aurigan eyes appear, the ovals of straw yellow with their large green orbs this time limned in silver. They flared and hurled bolts of lightning at him, tinged with pale pinks and greens.

He had never studied Old Aurigan yet understood the accompanying symbols. '¡Fight! ¡Lord Of Dragons! ¡Fight!' they demanded.

Watching his sister, Wrenden had read her aura and the thoughts that had struck her so fast and hard that the effort of adjusting to them had left her no energy to even try to conceal them. Even though only half comprehending, he was held immobile with surprise. As she moved, he shook himself out of his stasis. 'Go! Ngé'zânâ,' he said aloud and leapt for the mouth-like opening in the black sphere.

Grasping the top of it with his hands, he found a purchase with his feet on the bottom lip and braced himself against the flow, holding the mouth open as he sensed Tamina struggling slowly towards the centre of the sphere.

Qwelby was fighting with all his strength to cleave a passage through the ocean of gunk to reach his friends. He had to save them.

Tamina was desperately swimming against the flow of putrefaction, not making any progress, but holding on to the image of the connection with the Melanite Array

It was all taking so long……

With his arms aching, Wrenden knew he was reaching the end of his endurance and could not hold on much longer. As a thin black cord snaked from behind and caught the fast disappearing end of his sister's rainbow of energy, he made a mighty effort.

The flood of gunk striking him lessened as more and more of it was sucked into a widening black tube and the pressure on him steadily eased. *The Melanite Array! Thank you Pelnak and Shimara*, he thoughtsent with relief.

Accepting Tamina's request to be his elderest and strengthened by.... a love they had once shared? Qwelby made a determined effort to reduce the barrier between them. He knew if he reached her, he could hurl her out of his Despair and back to safety.

A loud belch stunned Wrenden and the mouth opened wider. Horrors! A great ooze of revolting green gunk surged out. He lost his grip. Covered in unbelievable slime, he struggled as if in a sea of mouldy, green syrup. Gasping for air, fighting for his life, what could he do? No good calling on Tamina. She was deep inside the ball and had to remain in contact with Qwelby so the darkness could drain through the black tube into the crystal array. The slime was forcing its way into his mouth, choking him. His energy field was collapsing. He couldn't breathe.

Wildly, he thrashed about. His head broke through to the surface. He was in a stream of slime. To one side he saw a narrow strip of soft pastel colours. Shades of aquas, pale blues, turquoises, jades. The not-twins' colours. Lungs bursting, he struggled to swim to it but was being forced downstream, further away from the opening.

A thick lump of Depression struck him and knocked him to the side. He grasped for what seemed to be the river bank, got a grip on a piece of aqua and was pushed against the bank by the sluggish flow. He dragged himself out of the river of slime onto a narrow strip of what felt like firm ground. Looking around, he saw the mouth slowly closing.

Sis! There was only one way to reach the opening. He ran along the not-twins' strip of colour. It was thinning. He sensed their energies would not keep it in existence for much longer as they concentrated on sucking all the gunk into the Melanite Array.

He lost his footing, felt himself falling and turned it into a dive into the river. Now a putrid brown froth, it was easier to swim through. He was getting closer to the opening. But it was all taking too long. His energy field was being drained with the effort.

A thick lump of coagulated Despondency rolled along in the river. He pulled himself onto it. More clumps were following. They were not moving fast. He jumped from one to another, then another, arms flailing as he sought to keep his balance, slowly getting nearer to the almost closed mouth.

Legs aching, pain in his thighs, still too far away, he saw the mouth about to shut. No! At the last moment a clump of Dejection got wedged in the centre. He leapt for it, lost his footing and fell, sliding into the river of bubbling froth.

His hands grasped the bottom of the mouth. He heaved himself out of the river, brown slime treacling down his body as he stood on the lower lip.

Recovering his breath, he considered the situation. He needed props to keep the mouth open. There was nothing he could use. The thin strip of the not-twins' colours was now below him, edging against the bottom lip of the mouth. Must be the not-twins? Can they help?

He stepped onto it. The surface was uneven. There, an edge. He got his fingers under a strip of turquoise and lifted. It came away like a narrow floorboard. Carefully, he reached out and stuck it in between the lips in the middle of the mouth. Bracing himself, he pulled it along the line of the lips. It was working. The end of the mouth had been forced wider open. It groaned under the strain.

Moving quickly, he went back to the floor and to his joy was able to pull up two pieces of pale blue. Now all I need is some way to carry them whilst leaving my hands free. Remember. OOB Imagination works. He tore a thin strip of aqua from the floor. It became a long and flexible cord. Wrapping it around his waist, he stuck the two props between it and his body and pulled the cord tight.

Gripping the upper lip with one hand, precariously balancing both feet on the lower lip, ochre slime washing over them, he crabbed along to the centre of the mouth, planted the second prop, and dragged it towards the opposite end of the mouth. Again success. The mouth opened further and the lump of Disillusionment rolled past him.

With both hands on the upper lip, he edged his feet back towards the centre. With one hand, he pulled the third prop from his belt. Reaching out to plant it, he looked into the ball. So much gunk had flowed out that it was like a slowly flattening cavern, with a big air space between the slime and the roof.

CHAPTER 41

QWELBY FIGHTS BACK

BETWEEN WORLDS

Everything he had done to save his friends by sending them away had endangered them. Qwelby knew he had to do something different if he was to help his friends from the danger they were in. The danger he had put them in.

A stream of love was continuing to pour into him, drawing him into ancient memories. He had neither time nor energy to wonder about what was happening as he became certain that he had to throw off the Despair that engulfed him. How?

With her golden hair, Tamina had looked on fire when she had danced for him. He had put that down to the natural exuberance of her fifth phase of creativity. Now, as he thought of it, he sensed there was more to it. What that might mean would have to wait until later. One day she would be a Fire Lady. She had danced Fire. Fire was his Dragon energy. He had the genetic inheritance of a Dragon Lord. It was not supposed to start to manifest until after his twenty-second rebirthday, yet it had manifested that night with Tullia. Was it only for Kaigii, or could he call on it now? Something deep stirred within him. It felt like Zhûkhorlânn, his own dragon guardian from his childhood.

He sensed Tamina's energy was failing. He felt her panic as she was being swept away to be drowned in his own sea of Dejection. Tullia loved Tamina. How could he face Kaigii if he had not done everything he could to save her elderest, and now his own? *Lightning. It's you and me. Quarks in a Psion,* he thoughtsent.

As he invoked Zhûkhorlânn, he felt it call forth to Zhólérrân, the Dragon Lord's Dragon. Wings sprouted from his shoulders. He roared. That turned into a scream as red hot flames ripped through his throat and blasted into the stinking atmosphere.

Wrenden's eyes opened in horror as a cone of dark grey-streaked brown rose from the centre, pushing a tide of slime towards him. The cone disappeared in a violent explosion of light. Thunder pummelled his ears as the volcano erupted and showered molten lava everywhere. Panic overwhelmed him as he thought of Tamina.

Moments later a fast flowing river of bubbling, dark red and ochre lava swept over the slime. He gripped the lip with all his might. Buffeted mercilessly, pain racking his body, he hung on. Despair swept through him as his fingers lost their grip and he was hurled backwards into a river of burning heat.

A clump of Revulsion hit his head. Dazed, half conscious, he was sinking, the weight of the lava pushing him deeper into the brown froth. He started to call for help only to have a gob of slime fill his mouth.

He had propped the mouth open. The black tube was wide and pulsating as Qwelby's Darkness was draining. Tamina should be able to get out safely.

He was fading rapidly, knew he was going. He was happy: his hero was safe. And Sis. He felt a moment's sadness. His last time with her should have been his greatest prank of all. One she would never forget. Not this!

Wanting to hurl himself after Tamina, Qwelby staggered to his feet, only to fall to his knees, drained of all energy, and watch in horror as Wrenden was swept away and sank into the river of lava.

Completely focussed on what he needed to do as he breathed deeply into his Kore, Qwelby was unaware of the sixth Aurigan finger joining his Tazian five as he placed them against his temples and sent every last drop of energy to Tamina, willing her to swim after her brother: his youngest for whom he was failing to care.

As Wrenden sank further down he saw the most beautiful apparition coming towards him. His eyes were closed. He must be dead already. And felt surprised it had been so quick. The undulating motion of the apparition appearing to be on fire made him think of a Salamander: the higher dimensional energy form his sister would be able to take when she became a Fire Lady.

With her over wide mouth, long, slender nose and excessively slanted oval eyes, for years he had expected to be told that she was an Alien from a race of domineering females. A Being from another dimension who had taken human form but could not disguise her face.

The creature undulating towards him had to be from her people, an Alien Salamander come to take him to the Afterlife. Death's not that bad if I get to meet real Aliens!

Ouch! That's hurting. Something hard was scraping down his chest, his stomach, then his thighs. He felt as if he was being dropped face down onto a hard surface. As if that wasn't enough, something was pummelling his back. He choked, puked, feeling burning gunk flow out of his mouth and nose.

Feebly, he tried to get onto his hands and knees as his stomach threw up more slime. His head hung down as a few more dribbles burnt their way down his nose. He was pushed down over onto his back. Pressure on his chest, squashing the breath out of him, released, repeated, again and again.

Death is not supposed to be like this!

He coughed and felt his throat burn, was rolled sideways as he coughed again, spewing more vile putrefaction over the floor. His lungs sucked in foul tasting air, but, oh, that felt good.

He wiped his face, cleared his eyes of slime, and looked up. Split from ear to ear with the biggest grin he'd ever seen, the Alien's face was the most welcoming sight he could imagine.

Tamina?

'Impossible! I'm dead,' his brain said.

His mouth tried a different approach.

'I had an amazing vision. This beautiful Alien Salamander was swimming towards me. Going to take me to the Afterlife.'

'Sorry Squirt,' Tamina's voice said, the Alien's eyes twinkling.

Reality penetrated his mind as he levered himself into a sitting position. 'I was dreaming of your fourteenth rebirthday and that massive buffet. But this time I wasn't going to make a pig of myself and be sick.'

'You believe you're dying... and you think of food?!'

'Why not?'

'Oh, Eeky!' She pulled him to her and hugged him. 'My Little Squirt.'

'Yeah.' He relaxed. He was happy he wasn't dead. And it felt nice to be her Little Squirt again, just for a while.

'But how?' he asked. 'The volcano?'

'Qwelby,' she replied. 'I felt his thought and his... energy...' Her voice tailed off as she recalled hearing the capital "P" in "Psion". He was not merely suggesting that they were bonded together like a quark and an anti-quark in any meson, but specifically as Charmed Quarks in a Psion. Was he growing up that fast on Earth? And why did she have the strangest feeling that it was nothing new?

'Qwelby! The mouth!' Wrenden exclaimed, ascribing his sister's reddening face to her Salamander energy.

'It's okay, Eeky, your props are keeping it open.'

Leaning on his sister's shoulder as she remained kneeling, he heaved himself to his feet and looked down at the girl who had bossed him about all his life. 'You saved my life, Sis.'

She grinned again. 'Why not?'

'Hey! That's what I say.' He grinned. 'Salamander.' He extended a hand and helped her to her feet. 'You must go back to Qwelby and I must make sure the mouth stays open.'

They waded through a low and sluggish river, back to the mouth. It sagged in the middle where that prop had been swept away by the lava. They squeezed through where the props on either side were holding. Inside, they could see the roof of the cavern was only a little above the small amount of putrefaction remaining. On hands and knees, Tamina made her way to the caldera in the centre.

There was no sign of Qwelby. Seeing Tamina drag her brother to the river bank and no longer caring what happened to him as he had saved his friends, Qwelby had collapsed.

As Tamina reached the caldera, Wrenden could see her being bathed in a soft glow of the palest pink. Having checked that the remaining props were secure and satisfied the mouth would remain open, he crawled to his sister.

Turning to each other they smiled and held hands to join their energies which they gently fed into what had to be Qwelby. Rippling with the palest of apple greens, the depression slowly rose until it was a little mound, standing proud of the slime. As the pink radiance spread out further, the last remaining pools of sludge drained away into the now thin black tube. With a sound like a soft sigh, the tube shrank even smaller and withdrew.

The whole mound turned to the palest of pinks.

Brother and sister looked at each other, smiled and shook their heads. Qwelby's favourite colour was a deep, rich, vibrant red. Not pastel pink.

'We'll keep that a secret,' Tamina ordered.

'Why not,' her brother agreed.

'Squirt!' She removed a glob of slime from her Matrix and threw it at him.

'Boots!' He ducked, searching for something to throw at her.

'Race you!' Tamina called as she set off running, adding to her long legs golden boots with wings at the ankles.

'Hey! That's cheating,' Wrenden cried, sprinting after her.

'Why not!' she called, with a cheeky grin splitting her face.

All around them the gloom was lifting, yet ahead all was black. One moment Tamina was in front of him. The next, she had been swallowed up by what looked like a wall of thick, black mist. Panicking, Wrenden hurled himself forward and felt himself enveloped by soft blackness. It clung to him. He was falling. Time slowed. He was drifting down, slow and soft like a feather.

CHAPTER 42

A LIE UNCOVERED

FINLAND

Earlier that afternoon, whilst Romain had been revisiting Kotomäki, the Director had called his PA in for a briefing. As the man sat down he had asked his boss: 'Do you know Professor Romain?'

'No. I know of him, but never met him until today,' the Director replied.

'He made some very strange comments. With Jadrovic's move back to The Academy of Sciences in Prague, it was only a few days ago that I went through his personnel file before sending it on.' The PA flicked through a computer print-out. 'He never worked with Romain, yet the Professor said he had lost touch. Not only did he have Jadrovic's family totally wrong, he said he had been told that one of his sons, with the strange name of Kwelby, was staying in Kotomäki.' He was about to say more, but wondered if he had already gone too far.

The Director narrowed his eyes. 'I didn't have the time to get into a discussion about Jadrovitch. Romain was looking for any odd occurrences in the countryside around here, apart from the break in communications. That discussion was finished in a couple of sentences. It seemed a bit unkind just to pass him on to Personnel.' The hairs on the back of his wrists stood up. He might be an administrator now, but he had been a hands-on scientist for too long to ignore an intuition. 'What did you tell him?'

'Nothing really. Well, I mentioned the names of Jadrovic's two sons. Romain appeared to be the absent-minded Professor. But the only contact information I gave him was the email address of the Institute in Czech. He could get that from the Internet. Nothing personal.'

The Director picked up his fountain pen and looked at the musical notations on the nib as if he had not previously noticed them. Putting it down he said: 'When we've finished here, check with your opposite number at CERN. Establish what they've asked Romain to do.'

A little later as the Director was walking through his assistant's office on the way to lunch, the phone buzzed.

'It's the Director General at CERN, personally, for you,' announced a surprised PA.

The D-G was adamant. Romain had not been asked to investigate anything. How could he have known about their problems? For once, in view of the particular circumstances and against all its normal policy, the reason given for stopping the Large Hadron Collider was not the whole truth. The only connections outside of CERN had been with the monitoring by Jyväskylä and the other Institutes on the twenty-seventh. What was it that had really prompted Romain to travel half way round the world? And then why to Finland instead of Geneva where CERN was situated?

All the time the D-G was talking, the Director was trying to recall Romain's exact words, unsuccessfully, he had to admit. With his impending trip to the USA he had not been paying much attention.

'Whatever he is searching for, can his equipment be so poor that he is looking here around Jyväskylä, when what it detected were those meteor showers further North?' wondered the Director.

'I would doubt that,' responded the D-G. 'He might be a maverick, but no-one can say he's not brilliant. He could have been the leader in his field but for... enough said. Thank you for checking. Leave it with me. Have a good trip.'

The Director checked his watch and continued to the canteen where he was to brief his senior staff over lunch.

The Director General was worried. What he had said was true. Romain was both brilliant and a maverick. He spoke to his head of security. In turn, the latter spoke to his opposite numbers at the Institutes that had been involved in the monitoring, also the Academy in Prague. Inquisitive men wondered about possibilities. They used their contacts and the puzzling situation was swept into the melting pot.

CHAPTER 43

THE HUNTERS GATHER

FINLAND

The Russians constantly monitor the military preparedness of their various neighbours, provocatively so when international tensions are high. When all is calm, it amuses them to poke and prod during their neighbours' main religious holidays.

On December twenty-seventh two twin-seater Sukhoi SU-34 fighters had been flying at forty-five thousand feet close to the border with Finland. It was a test flight for an unusual one that had been specially converted for electronic surveillance. As was customary, the Finns had responded. This time they were testing a pair of their newest F18F Super Hornets, flying from their base at Kuopio Airport in Siilinjärvi. All four planes were passing almost due East of the Jyväskylä-Kotomäki area at four o'clock.

The interference was short lived and the pilots were able to regain control before any of the planes crashed. The Super Hornets were ordered to return to base and were replaced by a pair of older Hornets from Pirkkala. The Su-34s continued on their way North until they reached the Barents Sea. The Finns recorded the fact that the Russians did not return as usual to the base from which they had departed, but landed at nearby Voronezh. And no replacements were put into the air.

Situated at Cheltenham in England, GCHQ was not the only listening station to experience a temporary loss of its surveillance of communications traffic in that area.

The air waves were filled with accusations and demands from the Russians. Although not a member of NATO, the Finns had had a close relationship since 2004 through the Finland Partnership for Peace. The Standing Committee of the NATO-Russian Council was immediately involved; checking facts, exchanging information and most importantly, calming nerves. Tension reduced as the Finns necessarily shared all the information they had. The Russians and NATO said they were doing the same.

The Finns said nothing about the arrival of Professor Romain and the blatant lies he had told. It was a puzzle of a different order. But it was too much of a coincidence to be ignored.

Accordingly, Finnish security, the Suojelupoliisi (SUPO), agreed to put an agent in the field. A young agent, Miska Metsälä, was ordered to Kotomäki. His brief was to watch Romain and report back on what the Professor was really interested in, weather anomalies by then having been dismissed as a feeble smokescreen. A meeting was arranged for Metsälä with Chief Inspector Penti Harju in Kotomäki.

As Metsälä was nearing Kotomäki on the afternoon of Monday the third of January, his SatNav started to blink. A few seconds later its screen was covered with what looked like a snowfall. He cursed. He knew the way to the small town but was relying on his SatNav to take him straight to the police station car park. He wanted to question the Inspector, then walk around the town to get the feel of it before settling in to the Scandic in Jyväskylä.

In spite of the annoyance, he smiled to himself. This low-level surveillance mission was a way for him to redeem himself after the mess he had made of his previous operation. Staying in a posh hotel sure was going to be better than the fleapit he had been in on that occasion.

When the SatNav did not clear, he decided to use his mobile to call the station. The static was so heavy he could not hear the dialling tone. He switched off and continued driving, wondering what had caused the interference.

A few minutes later the SatNav display returned to normal. He checked his mobile. That was now working. He shrugged his shoulders and dismissed the incident as one of those odd things that happened with all electronic equipment.

CHAPTER 44

DREAMS

THE KALAHARI

The morning after the Melon Dance Tullia awoke and grunted with frustration as a thought slipped away. Unable to recover it, she rose, washed, dressed and joined the family for a breakfast of milimili and bush tea. When that was finished she asked about the people who had come around the fire the previous evening, and why the sudden change.

'Everyone saw you wearing our traditional clothes and having fun just like any young woman,' Deena explained. 'And using your powers to prevent a nasty.... accident.'

'And you looked like one of us. Well...' Tsetsana started to say.

Feeling delighted at the comment, and puzzled at the hesitation as her friend blushed with embarrassment, Tullia mentasuaded the young girl.

'You look like a big San. Until we see your face. Your eyes, on fire when you laugh! We know you must be a San Goddess,' Tsetsana said, her eyes wide, staring at Tullia.

Tullia had reached the point where she was understanding them without needing her compiler. She had learnt, incorrectly, that the Meera word "sun" had two meanings, as well as applying to the sun itself it also meant "planet". Not really understanding what a Goddess was, and with the overtones of such a being not coming from the planet but from "out there", she was happier using their words than her compiler's translation of Goddess as: "A Venerable", which meant she would be over one hundred and forty-four years old. Now, to be told that she was a San Goddess, meant to her that they were accepting her as what she believed herself to be: a fellow descendant of the Auriganii who came from "out there".

Out there........

'Ah! That's it!' she exclaimed, leaping to her feet and clapping her hands to her head as she recalled her elusive waking thought. 'Kaigii. When I was captured. He didn't close the door to me. That darkness around him was something else. I must speak with Xameb.' She turned and ran off to the Shaman's hut.

CHAPTER 45

XAALA ACTS

VERTAZIA

If Xaala was to achieve Ceegren's aim, now her own personal goal, of preventing the twins both from reconnecting and returning to Vertazia, she had to understand life on Earth. She was in Ceegren's Elmit room trying to learn about conditions on Earth and the Azurii. All Elmits were built to the same basis design, copying how the Tazii saw Azura. So the room was small by Tazian standards and with no moving colourscopes on walls or ceilings. There were no HoloVideos or interaction. Instead, there were comparatively small, flat picture screens on one wall.

The Tazii were able to pick up a mismatch of Azuran satellite transmissions that crossed the dimensions through the inevitable cracks in space-time. Such was the muddle received that it was said that all attempts at translation had so far failed. The quality was so poor that what was broadcast, heavily censored for violence and sex, were termed flikkers. Often a flikker contained clips from different episodes or even completely different programmes, and often out of any time-sequence. Tazian understanding of life on Earth was, to put it mildly, confused.

Xaala was brilliant at what Ceegren was training her for, but inside she was a mass of turbulent emotions, on which she kept a very firm lid. The first time the twins had sought to reconnect she had been instrumental in preventing that, but had been horrified by the violence they had displayed. Yet her mental discipline was such that she had to accept that the violence had been started by Ceegren and Dryddnaa, and the twins had only fought back in order to survive.

During that fight she had been sucked into the twins' energy rainbow. The strongest emotions she had ever experienced in her whole life. She denied that was anything like love, knowing that what she felt for Ceegren was the epitome of pure love. Yet keeping the lid on her emotions was becoming a challenge.

As part of her task of detecting any energy from either twin she had trawled all through the planetary MentaNet, adding signs of their energies to what she had experienced during that fight. In that way, she was certain she knew them as well as anyone outside their family or close friends. Since then she had picked up more than one very faint sensing of their energies being exchanged. She did not know why, but she had not told Ceegren that the twins had succeeded in making a faint mental connection.

Ahh! There it was, another quick flick of energy. Tullia's, but too quick and faint for her to latch onto. Annoyed and frustrated she got up and ran her fingers through her long FillysMane of hair, and came to a conclusion. She would try her best to timeslip and find the source, although without having a hold on the energy how she was going to timeslip was another question. Timeslipping was not actually moving through time. It meant catching the energy and following back to its source any residual trace that remained. She hoped that the exchange had been intense so the residue was still lingering in space-time-consciousness.

Excited at what might happen, she changed into her DarkSuit. Feeling the reassuring comfort as the szeame closed up the front, she admired her reflection encased in shiny, black simuleather with an electric blue thread running through it.

Aahhh! Again. Strong. Tullia? Yes! She looked at Image and saw a tall, slender and powerful young woman with a heavy belt lying across her slim hips with holsters hanging from both sides – weapons? Feeling good, she sat in the lotus position on her meditation bench, slipped out of her Form and into the seventh dimension where she tuned into the abomination's energy.

CHAPTER 46

!GEI-!KU'MA

KALAHARI

When Tullia explained to the Shaman that she wanted his help in trying to mentally reconnect with her twin, he explained that he was only able to help her in the way of his people, and so needed her to feel as much a Meera as possible. Tullia happily agreed to dress as she had done for the Melon Dance, when she had felt accepted as one of the girls.

Back in her hut Tullia undressed and tied on what she thought of as a skirtlet, slipped the necklace over her head and wrapped a blanket around her torso. Nervous, apprehensive and hopeful, she ducked out through the entrance to find a large red and green dragonfly hovering, as if waiting for her. It flew ahead, winding a passage through the huts until it settled over the entrance to Xameb's hut and disappeared as he stepped out.

Tullia stopped, staring at the Shaman. She was used to seeing him in his long black coat, dark trousers and brown shoes. Now he was wearing a skirt made of massed bunches of strips of brightly dyed grasses or material, she did not know which, that fell in layers of orange over blue to below his knees. On his upper arms he wore smaller versions, this time the layers were reversed: blue over orange.

Around his head he wore a wide band of black seeds from which hung several chains of small circles of white ostrich shell. Around his neck hung several chains of seeds: dark and light brown, cream and black. Hanging down from them to rest in the centre of his chest was an elongated figure of eight in a dark yellow metal.

Although she was taller than Xameb and had spoken with him on previous occasions, for the first time Tullia was aware of his power, emphasised by the lemniscate of eternity. She felt like a young child, and with what she was wearing, a daughter of the tribe.

Xameb beckoned and stepped back into his hut.

Tullia followed the Shaman into a hut that was smaller than hers, neat and tidy. He pulled back a drape that was hanging against the far wall and gestured. As she walked through with her eyes adjusting to the dark, she discovered that behind his ordinary hut was a much larger structure. The drape fell back into place as Xameb followed her.

The only light came from a small fire in a hollow of the earthen floor. Through the smoke drifting up to a small hole in the centre of the conical roof she could see a comfortable array of blankets set to one side on the floor. Around the room were set two low stools, a variety of earthenware containers of different shapes and sizes and what she assumed was his special place for meditation.

Hanging from the roof were bunches of herbs, two decorated objects which had to be face masks and several other equally highly decorated objects whose purpose she did not try to guess. The room was full of a pleasant, sweet smell. It was coming from a bunch of smoking herbs which he picked up.

At a gesture from him she slipped the blanket from her shoulders and let it fall to the ground behind her. As he walked around, wafting the smoke from the herbs all over her, she breathed it in and felt as though the very village itself was embracing her.

Again the Shaman gestured.

As she bent over to lay her blanket on the others, both necklaces swung in front of her, to her eyes a delightful mixture of two worlds: seeds and shells, three intertwined metals and Kanyisaya, glowing deep purple. Her eyes were drawn past them to the beautifully patterned strip of kudu skin lying between her thighs, its bright colours on the light brown leather a vivid contrast to her dark, reddish brown skin.

I am Meera.

Feeling dizzy, she lay down.

I am Tazian.

Lightheaded, uncertain as to who she was, she lifted up on one elbow. 'I want a name,' she said.

Xameb was taken aback by the tone of maturity and command in her voice. Unconsciously, he had assumed it would be the young child that needed so desperately to connect with her twin.

'!Gei-!ku'ma,' he heard himself say.

'!Gei-!ku'ma,' she murmured, and lay back with a deep sigh, feeling pleased that her name had the San "click" sound she found fascinating. Each "!" an explosive sound like the "tok" of a clock, without the "k". Twinergy! When I showed them how Qwelby's name is spelt, they pronounced it !Wel'by.

Xameb marvelled at the change in her face, the look of contentment. A self-possessed young woman lay before him, calmly ready to take a journey that would make many a grown man apprehensive. No wonder my people continue to look on her as a goddess.

Tullia had discussed with Xameb the events almost a Tazian tenday ago when she and Qwelby had been briefly in each other's arms, in two different places at once. Certain that he would not understand when she tried to explain what she thought had been a NullPoint Bubble, she had been taken aback at his reply.

'When I was undergoing initiation into the Dogon, my father's tribe, the Shaman opened a window into another dimension. Each one of us had to go through and experience, deal with, whatever situation we were in.' He had paused, looking sad. 'One of my friends took too long. The window closed as he returned....... he never made it back to us. Instead, there was a large rock on what had been an area of empty sand.'

Tullia nodded, looking very serious. 'I know travelling Out-of-Body can be very dangerous,' she had said.

'We were not out of our bodies,' Xameb had replied.

The two of them had agreed that, whatever words they used to describe what their different races did, each manipulated the underlying energies of the quantum world in their own ways. Xameb had said that providing protection for such "travelling" had been an important part of his training.

He hung a shallow bowl from the roof, carefully positioning it over the fire. Into it he poured a little liquid. Soon it added its aroma to the smoking herbs. Sitting cross-legged, he took a small drum and beat out a gentle rhythm, softly chanting, his awareness rather than his eyes focussed on !Gei-!ku'ma.

As she raised a finger on her right hand to show she was ready, a treacherous thought slid into the back of her mind. Tullia-!Gei-!ku'ma would show the Tazii a new and exciting way to journey. As her mind started to collect other thoughts of life on Haven that she would share, she felt herself pulled away by Xameb's rhythmic chanting. It had the feel of an old language. With it came an understanding that she was not allowed to have a translation. That the power was in the sounds rather than the meaning of the words.

'As with True Aurigan,' the voice inside her said.

CHAPTER 47

LOVE ACCEPTED

KALAHARI

Tullia slipped out of her Form as easily as if she had been on Vertazia. She felt the essences of the various herbs drifting through her Matrix and momentarily holding her in place. Savouring the difference from a normal trip into the seventh dimension, she looked around, and smiled wryly. She was looking at a "Big...... young woman", she corrected her thought of "girl". Sun, exercise and a different diet – there was nothing girlish about the tall, well-built, toned and dark-skinned body lying on the blankets.

A quick check of her InForming Matrix and she nodded. Of course, so immersed in the need to be Meera she had automatically imaged herself to be wearing facsimiles of her skirtlet and two necklaces. *Kaigii. I'm coming,* she thoughtsent as she recalled where she had been when they had made their last brief contact.

Rising up out of the hut she swooped across the village. It was a long way from Haven to Earth. If she could not find a trace of that last contact.... She steeled herself. She would have to cross to Earth, even though she had never before travelled that far Out-Of-Body.

Oh joy! She sensed their joint thread. 'We are one, we are two, always together, never apart,' she sang their mantra as she sped forth into the sky.

A black figure came hurtling towards her along the thread. Dark energy. Danger. Attack? Attack! She was furious that someone was trying to prevent her reaching her twin.

She was a Quantum Twin – identical genes – genes from the fighting Dragon Lord as well as the healing Unicorn Lord.

Sensing the attack, Tullia swung around to her left at the same moment as she felt a hand grab her left shoulder. Surprised at herself, she slammed her swinging right fist into the stomach of the black-clad figure, and they started to exchange blows in the weak gravity of the seventh dimension.

Tullia cried out with pain from a blow to her chest that flipped her backwards. Turning head over heels, she chided herself for having only just recognised that her assailant was wearing a protective suit, whilst she had automatically continued to mentaform her skirtlet. She imaged her usual electric blue skinergy suit as she completed the somersault. My usual....? Her thought was lost as the stranger dived in to the attack.

Detecting Tullia's energy signal, Xaala had slipped out of her Form into the seventh dimension and remembered to image her InForming Matrix wearing her DarkSuit. But she was not a warrior. Image might have shown her that as a possibility, but she had yet to source the energy from within herself.

Tullia was feeling guilty for having been angry with Qwelby for not having come to help her when he had been in need of her, and conscience-stricken that she had let that anger carry over for more than a day. Now, no-one was going to stop her reaching him. They were Kaigii.

Powered by that guilt, Tullia's warrior genes went into overdrive and a one-sided fight ensued. She found a natural extension of the BodyDance moves she had practised with Tamina, turning them into what they were based on: the unarmed combat that the

Auriganii had been compelled to develop eighty thousand years ago during the Space Wars.

Tullia swung, ducked, leapt, punched, kicked and straight-armed her tall opponent. Whilst Xaala's flailing arms did little to match Tullia's growing skill, her acuity in reading Tullia's thoughts as they flowed through her energy field enabled Xaala to avoid the full impact of many blows. But not enough.

As Tullia saw the black BodySuit starting to flicker, she realised her opponent was unable to maintain full concentration on both fighting and her protection. Two swift punches into her attacker's chest and Tullia saw the BodySuit vanish, leaving the woman wearing a heavy belt with.... pouches?

As Tullia acknowledged her opponent's mental skills, she saw the woman draw an object with her right hand from a.... holster.

'LaserBeam Projector,' a memory said.

Tullia swung into a two-footed kick. One foot knocked the Projector away as the other caught Xaala in her side and sent both girls spinning around. Tullia saw her assailant draw something from the holster on her left hip and whip her arm around, sending a long, flickering strip curling towards her.

'NeutronWhip,' again a memory told her.

Adding impetus to her spinning, Tullia threw herself forward and heard the vicious crackling as the whip passed just over her. Curling back up she grabbed the hand holding the whip. Using that as a lever, Tullia swung Xaala into a somersault and brought her legs around. She grimaced as she realised her miscalculation. Instead of landing both feet on the woman's backside, Tullia landed a heavy blow on her stomach.

Xaala vanished.

Tullia pumped the air with her first. 'Disintegration of all Solids!' she shouted, and was filled with disgust and regret. *Hope you're not too badly hurt*, she thoughtsent to the person who, when no longer wearing a BodySuit, she had recognised as a girl.

Trembling more from the words that had sprung to her lips and the accompanying images than from the fight, Tullia swung back to follow the thread to her twin. She accepted the sense of approval that welled up from deep within. She had done no more than fend off an attacker intent on causing her serious harm, even death with the two weapons she had tried to use. But a girl not much older than herself?

She needed protection. Her Attribute! Immediately, she was a winged unicorn and startled at how much more swiftly images were now working in the seventh dimension compared with when she had been on Vertazia. Again, a treacherous thought arose. Conditioning on Vertazia pervading the whole of the MentaNet and holding people back, so much so that even her Great-Great Aunt Lellia, who had trained her and her twin in Out-Of-Body, was unconsciously enmeshed?

She sped along the fine rainbow thread as it arched up and then down. Much sooner than expected, she saw her twin, or rather his inner image – a tiny baby curled up and asleep. 'Oh, Kaigii. You need more than looking after. You need loving.'

A unicorn for a dragon, yes. Those beings had paired together since time immemorial. But now....

She was changing, metamorphosing. She was a bird, plump and round, with large wings and a great long, multicoloured tail. *Kaigii!* She thoughtsent as she flew down to him, arched her back, swept her tail feathers underneath and encircled him with her wings.

Her heart went out to him as her wings swept the baby up and pressed it against her. She felt her love pouring into him. Memories stirred and she sighed. It was so much like when her own twins had been that young.

She wanted to kiss the top of his head. He wouldn't know. Of course he would: if she inserted a memory. He would be horrified! Mentally, she giggled. As she bent her head, her beak changed into a pair of bright red, heart shaped lips.....

CHAPTER 48

QWELBY RECOVERS

FINLAND

The atmosphere in the Rahkamos' house on Tuesday morning was tense. As Hannu had expected, on returning from Muurame the previous evening his father had not called the doctor. As he was again working the late shift, Paavo had said he would telephone the doctor at eleven if Qwelby had not awoken.

Anita had come round to see how Qwelby was getting on. Hannu's mind and feelings were again going round in circles. Part of him was pleased she was there as he needed her support. Another part didn't want her there to see how tense he was and because he was afraid of just how much she was becoming attached to "his alien".

And he felt guilty that a corner of his mind kept on thinking about the time Qwelby had thoughtwrapped them into the story of New Year's Eve, so much so that he had felt as though he had been holding Tullia's naked body in his arms. He knew that in the same way Anita had been in Qwelby's arms and was wondering unhappily if Anita thought about Qwelby the same way he thought about Tullia.

With everyone gathered around the kitchen table, it was a few minutes after eleven when Paavo finished his coffee, took down the handset and dialled the surgery. The number was engaged. He made a second attempt a few minutes later. Still engaged. There was an awkward silence.

A childish part of Hannu wanted to take the phone and refuse to give it back. Another part wanted to grab the phone, call the doctor and get it over with. Yet how would the doctor know Qwelby was an alien? He said he was human, so wouldn't have two hearts or anything easy to detect like that. Apart from his eyes. But that didn't mean he was an alien, just a weird mixture of races.

Paavo picked up the phone, speed dialled and everyone heard the ringing tone

'Wait! Stop!' Hannu cried. 'A noise.' He flung himself round in his chair looking up the stairs.

A few moments later they heard the sound of a door opening and the toilet flushing.

Paavo put the phone down. They heard footsteps and Qwelby appeared, steadying himself with both hands as he came down the stairs.

'Just in time!' Hannu exclaimed.

'Yes,' Qwelby said, misunderstanding. 'My friends saved me. And I saved them.' He flopped onto a chair next to Anita and looked across her to Hannu. 'I was a baby in.... Kaigii's arms?'

'Kaigii?' Hannu and Anita chorused.

'Tullia's Kaigii. I'm Kaigii. We're Kaigii,' Qwelby replied. 'It's Tazian for what we are. So much more than your word "twin".'

Seija gave Qwelby a mug of hot chocolate. Colour slowly returned to his face as he drank, looking pensive. He put the mug down and looked up. 'What happened was terrible. My friends nearly died. I'd like, I need, to tell you what happened.'

Paavo was intrigued. The strange boy looked lost and forlorn, yet sounded resolute. Like most humans, Paavo did not want foreigners coming to his country and taking the homes and jobs that were the right of his countrymen. All Qwelby wanted was to go home. Where that was Paavo did not know, he had not yet made up his mind about the story he had been told. Yet from the moment he had picked up the boy when he had fainted on the evening of his arrival, and Paavo had carried him to bed, he'd felt a need to care for the stranger. 'I'd like to hear your dream,' he said.

Qwelby smiled. He liked Paavo. In spite of the uncertainty he could see in the man's energy field, with his size, his calm nature and the way he seemed to fill any room he was in, there was a comforting similarity to Gumma. Qwelby knew he was adding to that feel as a form of reassurance in helping him to survive in the strange world of Earth. 'Thank you,' he replied, his eyes sparkling, unaware just how much his automatic energy projections influenced the Azurii.

'But, they couldn't have died in a dream, surely?' Hannu queried, as Qwelby finished talking and the Finn slowly pulled himself out of what had felt like a virtual reality show.

'Not a dream. It's what we call a deepstate. And, yes. They were in the seventh dimension, in their energy bodies. If either of them had drowned, their energy bodies would have died and so would their physical bodies.'

As Qwelby had thoughtwrapped the whole family into his adventure, Anita had put her hand on his. By the time he had finished speaking in his musical baritone, Qwelby was firmly gripping her hand.

'I'll lend you one of my mother's books by Dione Fortune,' Anita said as she turned to Hannu. 'She explains all that.'

'Right,' Hannu said through clenched teeth, feeling almost humiliated as though she and Qwelby were a pair and she was talking down to him. He had been drawn into the story more than ever before and had felt allied to Wrenden. The intense feeling he had experienced from the alien boy's twirling eyes had been unsettling. Feeling Wrenden's love for Qwelby as though it was his own was disturbing. Far worse was the thought that Anita was feeling love like that for Qwelby, and not just through his story telling.

Hannu clenched his hands into fists to stop himself from tearing her away from the alien and promised himself that if that happened again when it was just the three of them, he would rip them apart.

'You must be starving,' Seija said, standing up and deliberately breaking the palpable tension.

Qwelby was still caught up in the energy of what had happened and was mentally smiling at how like Wrenden it was, that even when he believed he was dying he thought about eating. 'Yes. I'm not a goat like Wrenden, but even lions eat.'

That casual comment sparked an intense discussion with Anita, working out Qwelby's and his friend's birth dates from comparison of the equinoxes and solstices with the Tazian KeyPoints, which were the same on both planets. The only time difference being the length of days. By the time they had finished they had established that the twins were Leos, Wrenden a Capricorn and Tamina an Aries.

'Your astrology can't be the same as ours!' Anita exclaimed.
'Of course it is,' Qwelby replied with a smile.
'But it's based on where the stars were thousands of years ago.'
'Of course.'
'You mean, your people gave it to us?'
Qwelby just grinned.

'You know not everyone on Earth is into all that violence and hatred,' Hannu said. He had been lost in all the talk about star signs and was keen to break up the easy energy flowing between the other two.

'I know,' Qwelby replied. 'But what you and Anita were telling me came as such a big shock. We have nothing like that on

Vertazia, ever. And at the Elmits we never see any real violence, let alone war and killing.' His mouth dropped open, his purple orbs disappeared and the ovals turned completely violet as a data download cascaded through his mind.

'Why are you all so nice and kind? And your friends? Why haven't you all caught the violence virus?' he asked in a surprised tone of voice.

The subsequent discussion was finally ended when Seija put lunch on the table. Qwelby ate in silence as he absorbed the fact of the enormous lie that was told about the extent and cause of the violence on Earth. A lie so powerful that it had become one of the pillars on which life on Vertazia was based. And created so much fear for their long term future that Tazii were increasingly reluctant to bring new life into the world, so that his race was facing extinction. How many more lies were they being taught and what were he and Kaigii to do about it?

'You're right, Hannu.' Qwelby said, recalling a comment his friend had made during the discussion. 'I will talk with Mrs Keskinen about energy in this world.'

Hannu nodded, tersely. He had managed to steer Qwelby away from Anita, at least for a while.

CHAPTER 49

A PINK PRINCESS

FINLAND

When the youngsters reached the Keskinen's house, Taimi said she was happy to talk with Qwelby about energy, so Anita took Hannu into her father's laboratory to continue with their work. Taimi had been studying one of the Yoga Sutras and was wearing a full bodysuit in black, red and grey. Apart from her bare arms, it reminded Qwelby of the sort of bodysuits that Tamina wore. As Taimi led him into the living room and curled up on the cream sofa, his sadness at the memory of home soon passed in the relaxed atmosphere she had created.

As she talked to Qwelby about Yoga and what she taught in her classes about breathing, he talked about life on Vertazia. Fascinated, Taimi then spoke about the other aspects of the work for which she had trained over many years: Reiki, Cyma Therapy and especially Electro Photonic Imaging. They both became excited at the similarities between their two worlds, albeit very different in magnitude and style.

Qwelby felt so comfortable that he confessed his mixed feeling about his actions on New Year's Eve. His basic abhorrence of violence, yet the excitement and pride that he had been able to call upon his dragon energies to help himself and others.

'Now I'm on your planet, I'm beginning to understand what war is really all about. It's not like that in our history. It makes me wonder if what we are taught is not the truth.'

'From what you said once before, the Dragon Kehsa, Lord I think is the translation, must have been a very long time ago. Was he a real person, or is that what we would call a myth?' Taimi asked.

'I understand,' Qwelby replied. 'All the ten great hero/ines, or Uddîsû in Tazian, were real. They also have become special symbols. Energies available to others.'

'Like Archetypes, perhaps,' Taimi mused. 'Ancient or archaic images that derive from the collective unconscious,' she added in response to Qwelby's puzzled look.

'Yes,' he said slowly nodding. 'Tullia has the genetic link to Rrîltallâ Taminûllÿâ, a great healer who was there during the terrible period of warfare. She is honoured by all healers and her symbol is always used in our healing centres, and often worn by healers themselves. The spiral horn of a unicorn with a pair of wings reaching up from either side.'

'And your Dragon Lord?' Taimi asked.

Qwelby shook his head. 'Very little. Dad and I have his proper symbol, a real, long shield with the image of a fighting dragon on it. Then there are what we call Persuaders, a sort of police force that really only exist in a small part of Vertazia where the Shakazii live. The Persuaders wear a badge of a small round shield with a tiny, recumbent dragon.'

He went on to share what had happened on New Year's Eve. When he finished there was a long silence.

'I'm sorry,' Qwelby said. 'I've said something wrong... bad?'

Taimi shook her head. 'No, my dear young man.' She paused. 'I am a Reiki Master, a healer, and I teach Yoga, breathing, the world of energies. There are people who spend years meditating, diligently practising, seeking to raise what we call Kundalini. You tell me you have never done anything like that?'

Qwelby shook his head. 'Never.'

'Yet when you needed help. You did it as though you are an Adept, a Master.'

'So it's just energy?' he asked.

Taimi laughed. 'Yes, Qwelby. It's just energy! In this part of the world, what we call the West, Kundalini is usually pictured as a snake. In the East it is often seen as a dragon. Whichever, it lies coiled in the lowest part of our body, right between the legs. As it rises, so it integrates all the energy centres in our body, right out through the top of the head, and leads us to make a link to... well, whatever is "out there", bigger than us. God, spirit.' She smiled. 'I think what you call the quantum world.'

'Now I see why Anita is comfortable with what I talk about.' Qwelby laughed. 'Hannu is interested, but Anita understands.'

Almost before he knew it, he was pouring out his heart to her. He told her all about his four friends, how they had tried to save him from falling to Earth and how they had rescued him from his pit of despair. He finished by telling her about Tamina's dancing. How he and Wrenden copied her until the energies were too strong to handle, then they deliberately messed up to annoy her. And what he had discovered when he was defending himself on the day he had arrived and also with Arttu's attack on Sunday morning. He did not tell her how much he had actually enjoyed that second fight. That was causing him serious internal conflict.

'Are you all right?' Qwelby asked after a long silence.

'Yes. Thank you. You were speaking a mixture of Finnish and, well singing, in your own language. You took me into your despair.'

'Oh, I am sorry. I did not mean to.'

'No. Thank you. It was a privilege. And you weren't helpless. You fought back. With the help of your friends.'

'Yes...'

'Qwelby, I feel an energy coming from you asking for help to balance out what you feel are negative energies, yet that actually have had positive results?'

Qwelby smiled and nodded. 'It's marvellous that you understand, Mrs K. I was in so much of a turmoil, feeling bad about my violence, and my pride and...' He stopped. He still could not put into words his mixed bag of emotions. 'Are there many Azurii like you?'

'Yes. And also a lot more who are not. And many who do not like admitting that these sort of abilities exist at all,' she said, sounding sad. 'But, never mind that. What is important is how you can be helped.'

'Yes please,' Qwelby replied. Once more the mature young man.

'From what you've told me about the energies you feel in that dancing, I am going to suggest you try T'ai Chi Ch'uan. I practise it myself, but I am not a teacher. It's not dancing, but I think you will like the movement and especially the integration it can bring.' She got up, went to a bookcase, and presented Qwelby with an illustrated book about T'ai Chi, together with a DVD.

The door opened and Anita looked in. 'Are you two going to talk all night? We're starving!'

Taimi smiled and looked at Qwelby. 'The power of matter over mind, would you say?' The two of them laughed whilst Anita looked affronted.

They all congregated in the kitchen whilst Taimi prepared a supper of pickled fried herring with rye bread, followed by blueberry pie.

Seeing the book and DVD that Qwelby had been given, Anita left the room to return a few minutes later holding what she explained was a DVD player. It looked very girly in two shades of pink.

'I've never thought of you as a pink princess,' Hannu said with a laugh.

'It was a birthday present when I was very young,' Anita said, blushing.

'It is special for you?' Qwelby asked, picking up on her underlying energies.

'Yes,' Anita said with a smile.

'Then it is special for me,' Qwelby said, a corner of his mind wondering why he was being nice to Anita, when at home he would have taken the rise out of Tullia. Once again he detected scratchy feelings emanating from Hannu. His friend's reactions were a permanent puzzle. He just shelved them in a corner of his mind, hoping one day he would discover an explanation.

As Anita proffered the player, Qwelby knew exactly where he would keep it: in the pocket inside Fill Me where he had put the black box that he and Tullia had used to escape from inside the stairwell. Taking it in his hands, tingles ran all the way up his arms and across his shoulders. It seemed that in another dimension they ran down to his shoulder blades and made his wings flex. Life on two worlds!

It was five days since the events of New Year's Eve. The owner of the jewellery shop, who had been robbed, had been true to his word and had handed over the modest reward. The Keskinens had agreed not to talk to the Rahkamos about going to the authorities whilst Qwelby was in his coma.

After her long discussion with Qwelby, Taimi was convinced there was nothing wrong with him mentally. Amongst her many skills, she used Electro Photonic Imaging to measure the human chakras and diagnose disease of all sorts. She was unable to see any logical explanation for Qwelby's knowledge of energy surpassing her own, apart from him being what he claimed.

Viljo was pulled in different directions. He had been mulling over the extent of Qwelby's impressive knowledge of quantum science and then how he said the Tazii used it. Everything that the boy had said was theoretically possible. A lot of it could have come from reading science fiction. But how was it possible that he had learnt so much at his age – and was so certain? How many people who were not aviation aficionados had ever heard of jet streams of air being attracted to surfaces, the Coandă effect, which Qwelby said was used in combination with Vertazia's magnetic field for the Tazian equivalent of aeroplanes.

Viljo was a firm adherent to the body of scientific thought that ruled out the existence of parallel worlds, especially those of what was termed the third level that Qwelby was saying was the situation with Earth and Vertazia. So, a priori, Qwelby could not be an alien, just an amazingly accomplished fantasist. Yet......

As nothing had been heard from the police after two days, Viljo was feeling a lot less worried than before and allowed his wife to persuade him to leave matters as they were. He did not tell her his real reason, which was to give him more time to prove the boy a fake. He intended to focus on what he thought was a definite loophole in the boy's story – why he claimed that the Tazii had so many different methods of travel when they also had developed quantum entanglement, teleportation, which they hardly seemed to use.

CHAPTER 50

THREE HALVES

KALAHARI

An annoying sound penetrated Tullia's ears, her head, her whole body. She tried to shut it out. Grew annoyed. I'm with Kaigii. Leave me alone.

A tinkling bell. Angrily she dismissed it. A tickle in her throat, a racking cough, eyes opening, smoke, eyes watering. She pulled herself half up so she could draw breath and cough properly.

A face, dark brown hands wafting a bunch of smoking herbs. An arm around her shoulders, an earthenware pot to her lips, fresh water. Her coughing subsided.

'You were away for a long time,' Xameb said.

After a while, Tullia felt strong enough to crawl outside and sit in the pleasantly warm sun of the late afternoon. Xameb joined her after a few moments.

He had taken off the skirt, armbands and headpiece and was wearing a long, brown garment that reminded Tullia a little of the robes that Venerables wore. His was cut back at the neck and open almost down to his waist and she found her gaze drawn to the elongated figure of eight.

In between sips of water she slowly told her story, finishing with a soft smile as she said, 'Boys. They're all the same. They need us girls to look after them.'

'Truly Tullia, I believe that there is meaning in your being with us,' Xameb said, a puzzled look on his wise face. 'For you, if not for us. Part of what you have described could have been a journey taken by a Dogon initiate. And at the same time the bird you became is a sign of a San trance journey. Yet both are..... different.'

'Half Dogon, half San, half Tazian.' She gave a little laugh at the arithmetic, yet felt comforted and reassured.

'Can all your people change into birds or animals?'

'Yes. For travelling in higher dimensions.' Tullia decided to leave it at that.

Xameb nodded. So she came from a race not of Gods but N"om K"xausi, and Tullia herself was a very powerful Shaman. 'You need to drink, eat and rest,' he said.

She got up. 'Oh. My name. What does it mean?'

'!Gei-!ku'ma. Goddess of the Red San,' he replied as a large red and green dragonfly settled over the entrance to the hut.

She nodded. The more she was accepted by the tribe, the less she minded the translation into Tazian of the names they gave her.

She fidgeted and finally summoned up the courage. 'May I ask you a question?'

He nodded.

'At home I have a Great-Great Aunt Lellia and a Great-Great Uncle Mandara. Your energies are like the two of them put together, in a sort of a way.'

He smiled and waited.

'May I call you Uncle Xameb?'

His face crinkled into the biggest smile she had seen him make. 'I would be honoured.'

He rose and they hugged.

'I wonder. If I had a name for Qwelby, a name in this world, could that help?'

Xameb slowly nodded. '!Kwe-!Ku'gn. A translation would be, Lord of the Red Bush.'

'His favourite colour is red,' she said with a smile. Saying their two names to herself, she felt sure that choosing names that each had not just one, but two of the explosive "!" sounds she liked would help bring him to her on Haven.

Having been sitting in the warmth of the afternoon sun and still lost in the experience of the journey, as she thanked Xameb and left she forgot to take the blanket she had wrapped around herself in the chill of the morning.

As she walked back to her hut, impressions slowly intruded into her thoughts and she became aware that all eyes were on her. Remembering what she was wearing and no longer one of a group of girls as at the Melon Dance, she felt embarrassed. Strong sensations in her breasts and loins recalling the journey and the pleasure she had felt when succouring her twins made her self-conscious about a sudden and surprising awareness of her femininity. My own twins......!?

That puzzle was swept away as thoughts of how desirable she was washed around her, strengthening the feelings in her body and making her even more uncomfortable. Wanting to shrivel and hide within herself, she lowered her head and felt her shoulders rounding.

No! That was not respectful to whoever had made and worn the loinskin. Yesterday, the girls dressed like her had not been ashamed. It was their traditional clothing. If she wanted them to really see her as one of them, she had to act like them. 'I WILL walk tall,' she muttered under her breath. 'I WILL honour these clothes and the now married woman who made them.'

'Look how she deliberately flaunts herself, the bitch,' Kou-'ke spat the words to her best friend as Tullia swung by on her long legs, head held high, her energised aura making it look as though her skin was sparkling in the sunlight.

'A Goddess. Tyua'llia. Our Red-Skinned, Meera Goddess,' Nlai said, emphasising "Tyua", meaning "Red Skinned People", a name used by one of the several red-coloured San tribes.

Kou-'ke gave her friend a quizzical look as the San generally believed in only the one creator God, Cagn.

'Our Goddess who already has her God,' Nlai added, again with heavy emphasis, thinking of K'dae, to whom she hoped to become woman, whose eyes also had been on Tullia during the Melon Dance.

'Mmm,' mumbled Kou-'ke. The more human Tullia seemed, the more people became accustomed to her unusual and compelling eyes and the more she resembled the Himba, or worse, an unusually large but sickeningly marriageable woman of the red-skinned Hiechware or !OKung tribes of San. If the subtle shift in pronunciation reminding everyone she was a Goddess worked, it might help solve a growing problem. Surely, no man would dare invite the anger of her twinned God?

The two young women agreed to speak with Kotuma.

Back in her hut, Tullia slipped out of her skirtlet, splashed cold water onto her face and put on a skirt and a tank-top, then sat on the bed and worked out what to say to Tsetsana about what she had said that day in the bush with Xara. That done, she asked the girl to come in to her hut and sit on the pile of blankets that made her bed. Keeping it simple, she explained about the day on Vertazia when she had seen Tsetsana sharing a marama with Nthabe and then Xashee teaching the memory game.

She finished by asking Tsetsana not to tell anyone else, except Xashee. Now that the Meera were beginning to accept her as a young girl, she didn't want more stories spreading around that would spoil what she so desperately needed.

Tsetsana nodded. She would only tell Xashee, her brother. They knew how to keep a secret. There were rituals within the

San specific to men and women. They might be different in other tribes. No-one knew. They were secrets unknown even to the other gender within the same tribe.

CHAPTER 51

SHAME

VERTAZIA

Xaala came to, crumpled up against the far wall of her bedroom, hurting all over and with the sound of bells ringing in her head. Clear in her memory was the sight of Tullia as a near naked, dark-skinned, savage, who had fought like a trained warrior. Xaala thanked her own mental and energy training that had allowed her to anticipate many of Tullia's moves enough to lesson the impact of most of her blows.

Carefully, she rolled onto her front, got onto hands and knees and crawled to her bed. Looking over it at her mirror she saw no Image of a warrior, just the sorry looking face of a shocked girl. As she levered herself upright she thoughtsent to the szeame and her DarkSuit slid from her. She gently caressed the bruises on her chest and stomach. They were not as bad as she had expected. Even though she had eventually lost the imaged facsimile during the fight, her DarkSuit had still provided some protection to her Form.

She said a heartfelt 'Tamuchly' to her DarkSuit as she hung it up, understanding the compulsion that had made her pay the exorbitant priced requested.

'A fine warrior you turned out to be,' she said to herself as she stretched out on her bed and felt a blush spread down to her hips at the shame of what was going to be a humiliating confession to her beloved Teacher.

As she reflected on the fight, accepting that she had not been prepared, she sighed with an element of relief. It was true how violent the abominations were. And what had happened to the girl, turning into a half naked savage so soon? Clearly her DNA was degrading fast. Those thoughts pushed to the back of Xaala's mind her memory of the twins' rainbow of love and her recall that their violence had only been in response to the vicious attacks by Ceegren and Dryddnaa.

A girl and a boy. I can't handle both. I will take the girl on. Such energy, such power. Such savagery! Xaala did not deny the thrill that came with the prospect of dealing with such taboo energies. When I have mentally conquered her and replaced her twin - we will make such a pair!

I need an ally to deal with the boy. A Shakazii? No. Too unstructured. All the Servitors I've met at IndluKoba are too rigid, too Kumelanii. I need...... a Kumelanii boy who has come to the attention of the Readjusters.

Xaala formed a gentle energy picture in her mind of herself as a boy unhappy about the path in life his parents had chosen and wanting to meet another similar, then drifted that into the MentaNet.

That done, she went into the exercise room and explored the HoloExerciser. Ceegren was a member of four of Vertazia's twelve Guilds, each of which required deep access to the Racial Memory Archives. As she had progressed in her training he had given her limited access codes across all four Guilds. Whilst carrying out the work he required she had discovered much of interest that was not relevant to those duties.

The fight with Tullia had triggered a memory of coming across what was called Advanced BodyDance, in effect Aurigan unarmed combat, which she was sure Tullia had been using. She entered a set of codes, specified her requirements and was presented with a full training package. She allowed herself to enjoy the tingle of anticipation of another combat with the girl. One she would win.

CHAPTER 52

A PROMISING FUTURE

VERTAZIA

Lellia was awoken in the early hours of the morning by the faint tingling of moonlight on her face. She got up and headed out of the door, stopped, looked back at her sleeping niece and nodded to herself. Since the twins' disappearance, Mizena, the harassed housewife, mother and farmer, had shown a core of steel that had surprised everyone. Lellia went back and gently shook her awake. 'The Isuna has summonsed us,' she explained to the bleary-eyed woman.

Seeing them coming, The Isuna smiled gravely and opened the door to the Seliya Chamber.

The women saw Tamina and Wrenden on opposite sides of the circle, curled up on Floor where it had formed two comfy beds, with their energy fields showing that each was in a deep and refreshing sleep. Pelnak and Shimara were moaning and their arms and legs twitching.

'Lift. Four to go to the Recovery Room,' Lellia called softly.

House had noted and, as Lift delivered the women and the not-twins, Cook and SAC arrived with a trolley of restoratives. Pelnak and Shimara were undressed, eased onto a Relax Couch and helped to a little food and drink as Couch started to massage their bodies and minds. The women examined the youngsters. It looked as though strips of their energy bodies had been torn away from their legs and had tried to reattach themselves.

As they started healing, Lellia looked at the golden tinged, green energy surrounding her niece's hands. 'Gardening, farming, nurturing, growing, mothering, loving,' she murmured. 'I had not realised your healing energies were so strong.'

'It's why I've always encouraged Tullia to develop her inheritance,' Mizena replied.

Early afternoon on the same day, House and everyone in it were a lot happier. The youngsters were as excited as their lack of energy allowed. Acting together, they had saved Qwelby. The teasing and bossiness that had separated Tamina and Wrenden for so many years had gone and they had found they could enjoy fun together. Pelnak and Shimara had found the blessing in their strange relationship and were stronger and more able to reach outside themselves.

Cook was especially happy. The youngsters had used so much energy that they had all wanted second helpings.

Rested and well fed, the youngsters related their adventures to the twins' parents and great great aunt and uncle.

'Truly, you have proved yourselves BestFriends,' Lellia said. 'And once again shown that your name of The Fearless Four is well deserved.'

They looked embarrassed. What was supposed to be a secret name had only been invented for fun when they were much younger.

'What you did last night would normally only be done by people Eras older than you and qualified to serve in the Helping Homes. We are very proud of you.' Lellia added.

'Could Eeky have died, really, I mean?' Tamina asked.

Lellia nodded, looking solemn. 'Yes. Extra Physiological Travelling, or call it Out-Of-Body, if he had died there, his energy body would be dead. And it is that which keeps the physical body alive.'

Silence settled over the group as sister and brother shared lopsided grins.

'No "Bossy",' offered Wrenden.

'No "Little",' Tamina returned.

'SisBro,' they said together.

'Isn't sisterly love...' said Shimara.

'A brotherly thing to see,' finished Pelnak.

Mizena gulped and tears came to her eyes. 'TwinSpeak. I know they can do it. All four of them, together,' she said to her husband.

'Yes, they can. Twinergy. Tripled. Powerful. As I explained,' Mandara interjected.

Shandur stood up and the youngsters looked at him expectantly. 'Before we speak with your parents, we have agreed that you will need to take time to relax and recover. Early nights would seem to be in order...'

The faces of all four youngsters fell.

'To face all the challenges...'

Wrenden narrowed his eyes. That sounded a bit like his own father.

'...starting with a twistor riding competition.'

The youngsters disappeared in four flashes of lightning as a voice trailed behind them. 'Don't you want to know the rules?'

'NO!!!!'

Mizena turned to her husband. 'Do they know where to find...'

A flame orange twistor flashed past the window followed by a bright yellow one with Shimara hanging upside down, shrieking with laughter.

'Four more ways to leave Lungunu,' Mandara said as he managed to raise enough energy to chuckle. Then added in a serious tone: 'They need that after all they've just been through.'

'I'm concerned about what I see in their auras,' Lellia said. 'The coloured striations showing that genes are being activated earlier than normal, with the consequent release of hormones before they have been prepared for those changes. From my studies of that planet I can tell you that Azuran children grow up so much faster in some areas than do ours. It's inevitable that the twins especially will be on an accelerated growth path.'

'With the implication that PsycheDynamics will accelerate,' Shandur said, thoughtfully. 'They could soon be acting as if they were seventeen Tazian years old!'

'Unfortunately it's not as simple as that,' Lellia explained. 'Their growth will not be that evenly balanced. Compared to what I've seen in Azuran flikkers. And there's a lot to be learnt from watching those,' she added as she smiled at her husband. 'The twins are likely to be seen by Azurii as a puzzling mix. Bits of them being like Azuran eleven-year-olds, others thirteen and so on through to much older than fifteen. And it's happening with their friends as well,' Lellia added, wondering how those changes would ripple through the PsycheDynamics of Vertazian youth.

'What about their mental attributes, thoughtsharing, energy dynamics. How will the Azurii see those?' Shandur asked.

'All very alien to them.' Lellia replied, shaking her head.

'Great Khroanke!' Mizena exclaimed, leaping to her feet. 'You mean not only will my children be confused teenagers desperately needing loving care from a bunch of strangers, they'll be seen as terrifying Aliens! We must rescue them. Now!'

'We will. As soon as we know where Tullia is,' Mandara said sternly.

'Right,' Mizena said. 'And Tamina and Wrenden are the Keepers so they have to travel with CuSho.' Distractedly, she ran her fingers through her hair. 'Their energies must be restored. Also the not-twins. They're the anchor.' She exhaled loudly, deliberately letting tension slip away. 'We all need time to relax, absorb energy and be clear in our minds.'

'Well said, my dear,' Mandara acknowledged. 'And then we'll all get back to searching for Tullia in our different ways. Then use Curious Shop to get the twins together and bring them home. You'll see, it won't be long before they're back with us,' he added in a reassuring voice, wincing as his wife tightbeamed him her feeling of doubt.

CHAPTER 53

CUSTODIANS

VERTAZIA

In view of their function as keepers and promulgators of the True Aurigan Teachings, the Custodians were the most formally organised of all the twelve Guilds, possessing an advisory council called the Senate. It consisted of the normal Professional and Collector Councils plus the Inner Council.

Even as Arch Custodian, Ceegren was not a ruler, although he was steadily working to change that. Accordingly, it was the Presidor of the Senate who called an urgent meeting when advised of disturbing events. As usual, the Custodians gathered in the large underground room at IndluKoba. Given the seriousness of the occasion, Ceegren wanted to infuse the meeting with a relaxed atmosphere. Thus the members found themselves appearing to be seated amongst open fields on a pleasantly sunny day, the whole scene awash with soft colour.

Whilst the Tazii operated an egalitarian society, distinctions were generally made in clothing by those possessing higher levels of personal energy, especially on important occasions. By the age of one hundred and forty-four, a Tazian was normally fully developed, the entire ovals of their eyes had taken on the colour of their central orbs and they were accorded the honorific of Venerable.

Following tradition, the Venerables were wearing full length robes in their eye-related colours. The style of their robes together with the colours of their belts or collars or sleeve ends indicated their status as Custodians, together with any other professional group to which they belonged.

Tazii over one hundred and twenty were known as Elders. The colours of their robes matched the colours of their orbs. The only difference from the Venerables' robes being the less prominent belts, collars and sleeve ends.

All other Custodians were wearing a variety of different styles of clothing in mixtures of soft shades that included those relating to their other groupings.

'It is fifteen days since the twins left Vertazia,' a respected Discoverer explained. 'Since then, my instruments have recorded two Temporal Displacements. The first was two days ago. As it was of minor duration and extent I did not consider it significant.' Embarrassment was obvious in his aura. 'The second occurred yesterday. That was a major event of both duration and magnitude. And the energy spectra were substantially different from the first.'

There was an immediate alarmed hubbub as the room filled with questions and guesses as to the meaning.

Dryddnaa took the opportunity to establish her position. 'As a Chief Readjuster, my life's purpose and joy has always been to assist those Tazii who have lost The Way to adjust to living within the very wide parameters of our society. At times, there are deviants who cannot even live amongst the Shakazii in the extreme freedom permitted in the Shadowlands. I do NOT enjoy Curing them.' She paused as a ripple of disgust swept through the room at the thought of Tazii being turned into little more then unthinking automatons.

At one hundred and twenty-four, Dryddnaa was one of the

youngest members of the Senate. There, she was privy to the deliberations of many Venerables, the oldest and most powerful Tazii who had achieved the Complete Incarnation Cycle. At that stage they laid aside whatever had been their life's specific discipline and devoted the remainder of their incarnation to selfless service to all Tazii.

Dryddnaa was ambitious and had no intention of waiting twenty more years before making her move. The Multiverse had presented her with an unique opportunity. She knew she had to make the most of it. 'If the children are to be saved, then the sooner they are brought back and cared for, the better.'

With all the skills that had caused her to be acknowledged as one of Vertazia's most powerful Readjusters, she thoughtweaved around her words a series of images. They indicated her acceptance that Quantum Twins, identical twins of different gender, were an abomination. That that was due to the Tazii having severely reduced effective DNA, which could never have happened had they retained the one hundred percent of Aurigan times. But it was not the fault of the children.

Finally, as proponents of the teachings of Insûmâne Haa-Zeyló, the Custodians had a duty to show not merely compassion, but their love for all Tazii. And subtly underlying all that, she was willing to personally care for the twins.

Inside himself, Ceegren was annoyed. He had been holding discreet and heavily shielded discussions with key colleagues to persuade them to his view that the twins never be permitted to return. Dryddnaa was one of those. There was only one reason for her speaking so clearly in total opposition. A PowerPlay. He needed her strength and also, he had to ruefully admit, the support she had already built within the Convocation of all Custodians amongst those of more liberal views.

In a carefully tempered speech, whilst endorsing what she had said, he suggested that the present situation was so grave that the twins needed to be completely healed before return could be permitted. He used the level of violence they had exhibited as evidence that they were already infected with the Violence Virus. He offered that as a most regrettable reason why, in view of the dire emergency, he and his small group of colleagues, highlighting Dryddnaa's own part, had used what would normally be totally unacceptable levels of violence themselves.

His accompanying thoughts gently played upon Dryddnaa's comparative youth and that he had invited her into the Senate and then the Inner Council in order to guide her along the right path.

Dryddnaa's lowered eyes indicated that she was accepting the mild rebuke, whilst her energy field showed that she was holding to her views and would be failing in her responsibility if she did not express them so as to provide the Senate with the full spectrum of opinion.

Ceegren tightbanded his thinking to the Presidor.

'I sense a majority in favour of the Arch Custodian's proposal,' The Presidor said. 'In view of the urgency of the current situation, I propose it be accepted as a temporary measure.'

Although the idea that decisions might ever be taken by majority voting was anathema to all Tazii, there was a gentle swell of agreement that a compromise had been found to which all could agree. Subject to.......

'We will reconvene..... when there is any significant development to report?' The Presidor was relieved when that also found acceptance.

At her command, the countryside disappeared and the room changed to portray a pleasant banqueting hall. A pair of doors in the end wall opened and trays of refreshments were brought in by Senior Apprentices. As the Custodians were eating, drinking, circulating and engaging in private conversations, Dryddnaa and Ceegren met by themselves.

They made a good pair. He, two metres fifteen tall and broad shouldered had a physical presence to match his personal power. A well controlled, humming dynamo, now more than ever before ready for decisive action.

Apart from a period of exploration during late teens, there was little sexual activity outside the closeness of the pairbonded relationships. And those couples discreetly shielded such energies from their auras. Dryddnaa was an attractive, statuesque woman, a hand's breadth shorter than Ceegren. Unusually, her aura contained hints of a personal energy that drew people to her, whilst making some wary. She was at ease with her work and, like all Tazii, believed that when one was aligned to one's Soul purpose, then the Form was the concomitant expression of the Self.

It was many years since Ceegren and his then partner had amicably terminated their pairbonding. Immersed in her career, Dryddnaa had never felt the need to have her own children in addition to all the Tazii for whom she cared in a professional capacity.

Speaking softly within a joint Privacy Shield, Dryddnaa offered to Ceegren that she would present plans to the next meeting to establish a form of quarantine that would allow the twins to return and be treated. She considered that successful treatment would help to reduce the Tazii fear of the Azurii, rooted as it was in their violence. And that would help the Arch Custodian with his hopes for the future of the race.

She finished by lowering her long, jet black eyelashes for a few moments longer than was necessary and allowed the hints in her personal energy field to shine a little stronger. As she looked back up she saw that Ceegren's ovals were shining a brighter green than normal.

Judiciously, he accepted her offer. Neither sought to insult the other by trying a mental probe to discover what reasons each had apart from the obvious. Each knew that they had engaged in The Dance of Discovery.

CHAPTER 54

CEEGREN PONDERS

VERTAZIA

Ceegren returned to his suite, satisfied that the reasons for his orchestration of the violent attacks on the twins and their friends were now understood and that what was, in effect, his apology had been accepted and the discontent was dying away.

He was intrigued by Dryddnaa's subtle offer. Several Eras had passed since he had last experienced the ineffable joy of a fully mindmelded relationship. Was that what Dryddnaa was offering? He would know all her secrets and she would know his. Or was she merely offering to ally herself to him, in return for his patronage? Even so he just might have found a woman with whom he could relax and very carefully share his hopes and plans for the future of their race. But she was very ambitious and he would need to be careful in all his dealings with her.

He changed out of his formal robe into a more comfortable one of GeleleSilk, which he infused with his own colour of a rich and deep sea green. He erected a moderate shielding around the room, the typical energy signature of someone enjoying relaxing thoughts that were private.

He needed to arrange for a wave of change-demanding energy

to rip through the planetary wide MentaNet. It would have to come from large numbers of teenagers, originating with the more extreme traditionalists who termed themselves Kumelanii. "Teenagers," he grumbled to himself. Youngsters in their second Era were properly called "Twiyeras". He had schooled himself to use the popular word but it still irritated him.

Not having achieved adulthood, the incisive and as yet unrestricted energies of those teenagers would shake the complacent Tazii. There would be an urgent need for leadership. The Spiral Assembly, the nearest Vertazia had to a parliament, was not in a position to provide that. With his own mini-parliament already established, he could provide the leadership and would "reluctantly" rise to the challenge.

His first choice of TeenLeader had been Xaala's older brother who he had been schooling for many years. He had been lost to the cause when, together with his parents, his LifeLine had been terminated in a freak Omnitor accident. At twelve-years-old, Tibor, his Junior Acolyte and current choice for youth leader, was far too young.

Over the time he had been working with Xaala's Kumelanii family he had seen her potential. He had intended to engage her as his Junior Acolyte at the normal age of twelve. The death of her family had changed all that. He had immediately taken the ten-year-old girl as his only acolyte.

After almost seven years of intensive training, Xaala was highly skilled in all the requisite mental and psychic attributes. She was also powerful due to her inherited genes – from the same Uddîsû as himself, Insûmâne Haa-Zeyló, the original exponent of the True Aurigan Teachings. And she was devoted to him. But she was shy and studious and without personality. Reluctantly, he had had to accept that she could never be the TeenLeader he required.

However, his immediate need was to get someone close to the twins' friends in order to surreptitiously report back to him. For that, she was the obvious choice. The more he thought about it, the more he saw that her timidity and lack of personality could be the very reason why the twins' friends would accept her and never suspect the role she was playing.

The reason for all the violence on Azura was due not so much to their genes, but to the absence of the controlling genes in the Tazian third segment. His all consuming fear was that the twins DNA would degrade and they would return without the essential controlling genes. The closely entwined energy relationships that were an essential core of Tazian life meant that their violent nature would be magnified across all youngsters and particularly those in the same fifth phases of creativity. That would be a tragedy.

On the evidence of their resistance to the attempts to prevent their reconnecting, it was clear that their third segment was destabilising. If they were to return to Vertazia, he could not agree with the misguided view that they could be adjusted or even Cured. The potential danger to the whole of Tazian society was far too great.

One of the reasons for inviting Dryddnaa into the Senate and then the Inner Council was to watch her. She openly espoused a more liberal treatment of deviants, and was generally successful. Had he correctly interpreted a hint that she would submit to his aim that the twins should never return, and was positioning herself to require something substantial from him in return? More than just patronage? If the family was successful in rescuing their children.... what would be her views? As powerful as she might be, he was confident he could outmanoeuvre her, as long as he did not allow himself to underestimate her.

CHAPTER 55

DRYDDNAA FLIES

VERTAZIA

Dryddnaa made her way to her room, pleased with having taken a step closer to making herself an ally to the Arch Custodian. She was confident that she could sway those who supported her more liberal views to agree to a compromise conclusion. A compromise that would satisfy Ceegren and give her voice greater authority in the deliberations of the Inner Council. There, she would support him. In return, she wanted his patronage.

Had she gone too far by hinting at the offer of a personal relationship? If that is what he wanted to be assured of her support, she would certainly benefit from close interaction with his impressive energy profile. Yet one false step and she would be isolated. It would be akin to being cast into the NoWhenWhere.

Changing into her flying suit, Dryddnaa flew her twistor well above the ground where the fine threads in the MentaNet were easier to perceive. One of them sparkled in response to her searching.

'Devious young bitch!' Dryddnaa said admiringly. Xaala had sent out a carefully camouflaged Seeking for a friend. And that Seeking had found a response. A boy living in an area of

UltraTraditionalist Kumelanii, straining at the leash and causing trouble.

So, Xaala, why are you seeking a friend so unlike you? And a boy rather than a girl? I congratulate you for finding someone who will make an ideal spy amongst the twins' young friends and without my having to leave any trace energies of my own Seeking.

Rulcas is unskilled and easy for me to manipulate. Through Xaala's friendship with him I will also have a spy in Ceegren's camp – invited there by his own precious acolyte! Dryddnaa laughed. It was not a pleasant sound.

I will ensure Rulcas meets the twins' friends, and I will become indispensible to Ceegren as I share the information about the family's schemes. But I must watch that "sweet young girl". There's a side to her I've not yet seen.

CHAPTER 56

PURPLE EYES

KALAHARI

Walking to the police station in Shakawe, clad in his uniform overcoat, gloves and cap, Inspector Kabelo Modisakgosi was enjoying the quiet of the early morning. In his late forties, he was a tall man and well built. His two grown sons had moved out leaving the last of their three children still living at home. He was content. Not only did he enjoy his work, his stomach was full from that morning's good helping of milimili well laced with raisins. A peaceful breakfast shared with his wife and teenage daughter.

His attention was taken by an attractive woman, her hips swaying under her coat. Purple flowers on a colourful headscarf made him think of the girl he had rescued two days ago. Intrigued by her, he had made enquiries, trying to keep them casual as he did not want anyone to think he was fancying a young woman, especially San or Himba.

The doctor the police used had been definite in stating that no-one ever had purple eyes. Puzzled, because he was certain of what he had seen, he had asked constable Ditau who had been driving that day. 'I was not looking at her eyes, sah,' the young man had replied with a grin.

That evening over a drink with a long-standing friend, the latter had laughed, clapped him on the shoulder and made the sort of comment he feared. He had decided to let the matter go and forget the girl.

'Dammit!' he said aloud, as he stopped walking and watched the woman and her purple flowers turn into the shopping mall. The thought that his memory was wrong continued to nag him. The girl's eyes had been so startlingly different, and he was a policeman, used to noticing details. And her skin had felt like velvet as he had helped her down from the Land Rover.

There had been something about her he could not put his finger on. Forgetting her unusual eyes, there had been, what, a presence? When she had stood up and stripped off to clean herself without any sense of embarrassment, he had dismissed that as what he thought of as typical of uncivilised Bushmen. Yet, when he had heard her say "Thank you," and had turned to see her holding out the water bottle to the soldier, he had been taken with her manner, her poise.

Self-command, that was the word. He had to admit to himself that was so like a Bushman, but with a big difference. Their sense of self was of an inner nature, hers had almost been projected outward. He really wanted to discuss her with someone. But he did not dare. They would either think he was losing it or fancying a young woman. In fact, they would think both!

He had not bothered to make any checks on her that night. The murderer had been apprehended and all he had wanted to do with the girl was to get her out of the way and restrict her part in his report to the minimum. He could not let it go. The Hills were in his patch. As part of his duties he visited both villages from time to time.

The situation in the tourist village was a typical Botswanan compromise. A white, South African couple ran it as no Motswanan wanted to be that closely involved with the San. And, irrespective of their tribe, all the Bushmen working there took more notice of what Ghadi said than they did of the manager's words.

The girl had been described as an honoured guest. Probably the daughter of a Himba tribal chief, years of covering herself with ochre leaving a red cast to her skin. And the eyes? He would soon find out. He would go to what was referred to as the Research Village and speak with Ghadi, the tribe's leader. If the girl was Himba and had crossed the border legally, she would have papers. If not, she was in trouble.

CHAPTER 57

ON EARTH!

THE KALAHARI

Sitting on her blankets that served as her bed, Tullia was feeling very stupid and wondering what other mistakes she had made. Delighted with the name that Xameb had given her yesterday of !Gei-!ku'ma, Goddess of the Red San, she had felt even closer to the Meera and their joint Aurigan roots. Then a simple question to Xashee that evening, about the different looking men in blue and khaki she had been with on the day of her capture, had resulted in a confusing conversation leading to the discovery that she was not on Haven, or Mars as the Azurii called it, but Earth. She had cried with despair at the thought she could immediately have gone to Kaigii.

When Xashee's attempts to reassure her failed, he had almost dragged her to Ghadi, the tribe's chief and then been sent to fetch Xameb. Xameb in particular had patiently explained to Tullia about the ways of travelling on Earth and all the paperwork, tickets, passports and permits required. And why even if it were possible, it would be far too dangerous to do that without special help.

Tullia had plunged deep into despair at the impossibility of it all.

Hovering discreetly nearby, Xashee had been summoned by

Ghadi with a gesture, had put his arms around Tullia and rocked her to and fro whilst the two men conferred. As Tullia quieted, Ghadi had explained how she could be helped.

'We have some very good friends who visit several times a year. They bring groups of adults who wish to study our way of life. The students come from different countries. They may be able to help you work out where the Lord Kaigii is. I think they will be willing to help in another way.' He had turned to Xameb.

'To the south of this country, Botswana, is another called the Republic of South Africa,' Xameb had said. 'There lives the most powerful Shaman in the whole of South Africa. He has travelled to many countries outside this continent and has many connections with other people. If we can get you to him, I am sure he will help in any way he can,'

'I expect to hear from our friends any day now that they will soon be with us,' Ghadi had added. 'When they leave, I am sure they will take you with them.'

Tullia had retired to her hut and sorted though all her experiences and thoughts. Finally, she had accepted that it had been one simple assumption she had made, that Kalahari, "Land Of Great Thirst", was the name for the planet. She had not questioned that as she and Qwelby had been so certain that what they had seen from inside the stairwell was Haven, the planet that looked so red from Vertazia. And the dates fitted. The San said they had been on Earth for seventy thousand or more years, which fitted with when the Auriganii had arrived, after a brief rest on.... Mars. She reminded herself to use the Azuran name. So it was still possible that the San were directly descended from the Auriganii.

'Right, Tullia Rrîl'zânâ Mizenakul,' she said to herself. 'Pull yourself together, get on with your life and strengthen the link with Kaigii. Then I can tell him I'm on Earth and we can plan how to be together.'

As she finished her breakfast a little later, O'wa, Ghadi's

son came and asked her to speak with his father. Arriving at the Chief's hut she found that as well as his wife, Kotuma, Xameb was also there. Ghadi explained that a small party was to visit the village and had particularly asked to meet the tall woman with the unusual eyes they had seen a few days ago. Tullia nodded, pulling from her memory the scene on her day in the bush learning to track.

It had been mid morning when Xara signalled the group with a gesture she had learnt meant to get down to observe and stay hidden. Tuning in to her hearing she heard a large vehicle approaching. After it passed, Xara stood up. Peering though the thornbushes she saw a specially converted lorry carrying a party of tourists. Exclamations showed that he had been seen and the lorry turned around.

Xara sank back out of sight and then she heard one of her favourite bird cries: cowwrrrr. Unusually repeated twice more. A few moments later she heard the same cries repeated from different directions. Reaching out with her senses she smiled to herself as she realised a game was being played.

The hunters were moving and teasing the tourists by calling to each other. With her energy skills not working on Earth anything like at home, she moved very carefully and did not try to copy the bird sound. When she heard cowwrrrr, cowwrrrr, cucu, she followed the hunters in standing up as Xara waved them to join him amongst exclamations that none of them had been spotted, including the two who had circled around to the other side of the lorry. As the tourists clambered out and Tullia reached Xara, he turned to face her and spoke quietly.

'Goddess. Trust me, please. You not speak. Xameb explain.'

Puzzled, Tullia nodded.

The tourists, mainly white men and women, took lots of photos and were particularly interested in her being so different. Talking with the tour guide who spoke some Meera, Xara explained that Tullia came from far away and spoke a very different language. She was on a special journey following the sun and seeking her home. He placed his hand on his heart as he said "home" whilst Tullia smiled and nodded.

Around the fire a discussion now followed during which Tullia was reminded of what had been explained on the evening of that day. That for her safety and continued hope of joining with her twin, she had to be very careful in what she said about herself to anyone who was not San.

'I understand,' she said sadly. 'The men who rescued me the other day, they were nice to me. But there are others who would not be. Big men, chiefs, who would want to take me away. Prevent me reaching Kaigii.'

CHAPTER 58

THE INTERVIEW

THE KALAHARI

The visitors were a small party comprising a pair of American photo-journalists with an assistant, their Tour Guide and Mr van den Berg, the tourist village manager. He explained that the Americans had a worldwide reputation for their stories of indigenous peoples, often being published in prestigious magazines.

To Tullia's relief, her vague explanations were accepted without too much trouble. Discovering she had never been to the tourist village, and only too happy of the chance of talking more with her, Max, the photographer, invited her to accompany them back to where they were staying and eat with them.

Keen to get good exposure for his village and the all important business from both tourists and serious students of the San, van den Berg urged acceptance, placing Ghadi in a difficult position. With neither the Tour Guide nor van den Berg speaking Meera, Ghadi was able to speak confidentially with Tullia, who was half nervous, half excited and keen to explore the wider world of Earth.

With five people and the visitors' equipment filling the Land Rover, there was no room for anyone to accompany Tullia and translate. Ghadi announced a solution. Two of the young girls from the Melon Dance, Mandingwe and N!Obile, were working in the village that day. Van den Berg was asked to allow them to accompany Tullia as they spoke enough Afrikaans for simple conversation.

Tullia was told to tell them that Ghadi was instructing them to look after "!Gei-!Ku'ma".

The visit went well, with the two young Meera having no problem with lying to protect Tullia. As the two girls were also performing their normal waitressing and guide duties for the party, Tullia, "an ordinary San girl", as she said to them, had to help. The resulting girlish giggling made it easy for the Americans to take photos and videos. All the while Tullia was improving her Afrikaans and starting to lean what she was told was called English.

There was an awkward moment when the Americans discovered close-up photos of Tullia and the recording of the conversation had totally failed, the cameras and the recorder being filled with static. Yet the video which was being shot from further away was crystal clear. She shook her head when told about film taken of the Female Hill that was also filled with static. She dared not speak as that had been at the time of the fighting when she and Qwelby had tried to connect. Her look of amazement at the power that had been produced was interpreted by Max as a native's inability to understand the technicalities of photography.

It was at that moment that van den Berg came to tell the Americans that their evening trip was about to leave.

'You must go,' Tullia said, desperate to end the discussion. 'Many animals come now day cool. Beautiful sunset. Sun shine on Tsodilo Hills.'

As the men left, Tullia looked at the two girls and opened her arms. The three hugged with relief.

'We go back now?' Tullia asked.

Mandingwe grinned. 'No. Tourists return. Xara lead trip. We

walk back with him.' She rolled her eyes and flicked her tongue across her lips.

Tullia smiled. She did not understand the gesture, or why the girl's energy was displaying excitement. Relieved that the journalists had gone, she was happy to join with what had become good friends, learn about and help them with their duties around the village.

It seemed no time at all before the tour returned and Tullia discovered that H'ani had been one of the guides. Thinking that was why Mandingwe had been excited, she didn't understand as they started walking back to their village how she ended up walking by him with the girls in front, then in front of them, Xara and the other Meera.

Asking H'ani what he had seen released the shy youth's tongue. Tullia felt so relaxed comparing notes with H'ani under the impressive snake-array of the Milky Way that she decided to be bold. After all, she reminded herself, she was Goddess of the Red San. H'ani was walking in the centre of the track, bringing himself close to Tullia's height. She stepped up to join him, putting an arm around his waist.

'I'm cold,' she said. Which was perfectly true now that the sun had gone down. She was wearing her usual daytime clothes of a short skirt and a tank top, whereas H'ani was well wrapped up with an overlarge jacket over a thick sweater. Tullia accepted the offer of his jacket. 'Now I keep you warm,' she said as she again slipped her arm around his waist and smiled at the giggles she heard from the girls as she understood that Mandingwe had deliberately set her up.

As they neared the village the track became less defined as vehicles had taken different routes, and walking became easier. As they removed their arms from around each other, Tullia took H'ani's hand in hers. She had enjoyed their talking and the feel of his energy. Now, holding hands, that sensation was stronger and nice. Like holding Tamina's hand, but different.

She was aware of strong energies flowing from H'ani and remembered how he had looked at her at the end of the Melon Dance. She felt an urge. Naughty, she knew. It was not far to the village, but dark where they were amongst the spindly trees. No-one was taking any notice of them. H'ani was looking at her. She leant forward and kissed him. Not a fleeting kiss like she had given Xashee, but a proper kiss as she would share with Tamina. But again, this was different.

She felt H'ani put his free hand on the top of her arm as he leant forward and kissed her. A longer kiss. It was very nice. No wonder people enjoyed the kissing games played at home.

'Will you walk with me?' H'ani asked. 'Another evening,' he added.

'Yes please,' Tullia said with a smile, aware her eyes were twirling and shining. She saw H'ani's bright teeth smiling and it seemed natural to reciprocate when he slipped his arms underneath the jacket she was wearing and pulled her tightly against him for a much longer kiss. She felt an unaccustomed warmth inside and strange stirring. It was all very nice and exciting.

When the kissing finished, it was H'ani who took her hand and led her back into the village.

As they parted, Tullia for her hut and H'ani to join Xara, the young man's heart was full. He'd been captivated by her and had hoped that at the Melon Dance she had indicated her interest in him, but he hadn't known how to approach her. She was a Goddess. He hadn't thought it right to approach her in the normal way. But now. He would show control. He would wait until another evening to go to her fire, take her hand and walk with her out of the village. Far enough away to be private.

Watching the group walk in through the main entrance, Kou-'ke growled.

'What's the matter?' Nlai asked.

'That scheming bitch. Look at her,' Kou-'ke snarled. 'Not content with trying to steal Xashee from me, now she's taking H'ani.'

'Remember the Melon Dance,' Nlai replied, trying also to convince herself. 'How she flaunted herself. She marked him, not Xashee. You're safe.'

'You'll change your tune when she sets after K'dae,' Kou-'ke snapped back.

CHAPTER 59

CAT'S EYES

FINLAND

Hannu and Anita took Qwelby into Jyväskylä on Wednesday morning and then around Kotomäki after lunch. The whole day turned into a massive lesson about life on Earth, including history, geography, transport, government, police, the military and, of course, money.

Qwelby found the concept of money easy to understand as he equated it with Tazian energy quotients, storage and exchange. He was particularly fascinated by the magnetic strip on small plastic cards that allowed them to be used for a variety of different purposes as he was sure that, for those where a number was entered via a machine, he would be able to read that number.

With his mind buzzing from all he had learnt and a feeling that had been growing all day that there was something inside him he needed to explore, Qwelby said he wanted to find somewhere quiet to sit and think. Not back home but outside. Hannu suggested the small garden he had pointed out earlier in the grounds of the former palace. Hannu had been happy to show off the results of a school history project he'd undertaken into what was now the Town Hall, administrative centre and headquarters of all the local services such as police and fire and even voluntary organisations.

Three hundred years ago the Governor of what was then Österland, the southern half of modern Finland, had established his home in Kotomäki, away from the administrative centre in Jyväskylä. A former soldier, Count Villnäs had built a fortified palace at what was then a vital junction of road and river, and created a canal to flow under the palace. The spooky old dungeons were normally open for guided tours but closed at present for renovation. The small garden had been created as a place of peace to honour the people who had died fighting for Finnish independence in several wars.

As Qwelby was planning to sit still, he'd needed a warmer outer garment than the coat he'd been wearing during the day. Mrs Rahkamo had lent him one of her husband's well padded, all-in-ones. Having grown since his arrival, Qwelby was already wearing some of the old clothes that Paavo used for working outside the house: a dark brown sweater and a pair of dark green cargo pants. With the addition of gloves and a hat with ear flaps, Qwelby set off just as the shops were closing and people heading for home.

By the time he reached the garden the only noise was the hum of traffic on the main road. Blocking that out, he became aware that the gentle, buzzing sensation in his body was stronger. He had become accustomed to the permanent vibration, assuming it was an effect of the Rhythmic Entrainment that was locking him into the third dimension. He decided to ignore the change and settled down to enjoy the peace and quiet.

But not for long as a van arrived at a side entrance to the Town Hall and two boys and a girl got out, chatting as they unloaded equipment which they carried up the short flight of steps. The door was opened by a portly, middle aged man in uniform complete with a peaked cap. The girl reached up, kissed him on the cheek and gave him a quick hug. In the brief silence Qwelby heard: 'Thank you, Uncle.'

Hannu's description of what was to be seen in the former dungeons had roused Qwelby's interest. The micro-nano sized compiler he was wearing, tucked neatly into his ear, was one of the first two that his Great-Great Uncle Mandara had devised. It was a prototype. Excellent when Qwelby was talking one-to-one, but no more capable than he was of distinguishing words when several people were talking Finnish at the same time. He concentrated on their chatter and a few words stood out: cameras, lights and canal.

Although closed to the public, these people were being allowed to film. In spite of the risk of being caught, it was too good an opportunity to miss. As the youths disappeared inside and the door swung to behind them, he ran across the snow covered grass. A big black bag had been left on the top step. As the door reopened, Qwelby ducked to the side and held his breath. A young man stepped out, picked up the bag and looked all around. Qwelby lowered his eyes, watching the youth's feet as he thanked Mrs Rahkamo for lending him an all black garment.

The feet stepped back and light spilled out as the door opened. Lifting his gaze, Qwelby saw the youth's back as he turned around and used his elbow to keep the door open. As he disappeared inside, the door started closing. Qwelby leapt up, thrust out a hand and grimaced at the slight noise his knuckles made as they hit the bottom of door. Holding his breath, he listened. All he heard was footsteps and voices moving away. He breathed his relief. If they had heard the slight noise they must have thought it was the door closing.

Swinging himself up onto the top step he eased the door open onto a long corridor that reached to both left and right. In front of him was a part open door leading into what looked like a large room. Noises and voices were coming from inside it, but no-one was immediately in sight. Silently, he closed the outer door. That done, he crept to the other door on hands and knees and carefully peered into the room.

It was a large and ostentatious rectangle, creamy pillars along the walls reaching up to a heavily sculptured and colourful ceiling. At the end to his right was an imposing chair set on a dais, above which was a large shield with a lot of objects in different colours both on and around it. A coat of arms, Hannu told him later. At the opposite end was a large pair of doors, resplendent with intricate carving.

To his immediate left and reaching down to the doors was a pile of furniture, including long low tables with ornate chairs standing on top of them. A variety of other bits and pieces were scattered amongst them. Dust sheets were partially spread over the pile. The youths all had their backs to him as they unpacked their equipment whilst the girl's uncle sat watching them.

Qwelby crawled a short distance to get in amongst the pile of furniture. Peering through spaces he recognised still cameras, a video camera and several lamps being carefully positioned to cover a large part of the room including the dais. There was also a recording device and a number of other small objects he did not recognise.

With the businesslike talking concentrating on the setting up, Qwelby easily made out the words "spooks" and "ghosts". From the context he decided they must mean what a Tazian would call "ITAs", insubstantial transitory apparitions. A thinning of the interdimensional boundary? Tazii being seen by Azurii? This, he had to see. But there was a problem.

Paavo's black one-piece was made of shiny material. As he'd run across to the side entrance he'd heard a shushing sound as his legs rubbed together and his arms against his sides. The room was warm and he was wearing dark clothes underneath. He removed his trainers, took off the all-in-one, and stuffed them along with gloves and hat under one of the tables.

The main lights were turned off, leaving a soft glow from what he assumed was emergency lighting set around the room and shining through the open door to his right. He peeked over a chair back and saw the girl walking directly towards him.

'A cat,' she squealed.

Xzarze! Qwelby mumbled to himself as he ducked back and scooted further to his left and slid under one of the tables.

'No cats in here,' the building supervisor stated amongst laughter from the boys at her fright.

'I tell you. I saw big, bright blue eyes,' she said, sounding angry.

Lights were turned on and Qwelby heard footsteps. He was unable to make sense of the jumble of words, but from the laughter it was clear the boys didn't believe she'd seen a cat.

'If you've finished here, let's get you set up down below,' her uncle said.

Qwelby heard the nearby door being closed, footsteps retreating across the room, a door further away being opened, general movement and the lights were switched off. Peering through chair legs he saw the last youth disappearing through a door to the side of the dais. He extricated himself from his hiding place, picked up his clothes and ran across the room. A light flashed. Then another. He stopped, stunned, temporally blinded by the bright lights. He heard raised voices from behind the door, turned and ran back. Lights flashed again. He dived back under a table just as the door was opened and the lights were switched on. Almost immediately the youths were calling out one at a time as they checked cameras and found that the photos and video that had been taken showed only a blurry mess.

The boys ridiculed the idea that a cat had triggered the flash photos, saying that wasn't the issue, the question was why had neither camera nor the video recorded anything other than what looked like static on an old-fashioned television monitor. They'd taken shots before that they claimed showed ghosts, but a ghost projecting an electromagnetic force field? Never!

Amused by the girl's muttering as they reset the equipment,

Qwelby guessed the previously unidentified objects were motion sensors, and took the opportunity of the noise being made to crawl further along so that he was completely hidden under two tables and by the edge of a dust sheet.

'Before you set the sensors I'm going to find that damned cat!' the girl said and started exploring the furniture despite the boys' protests.

Looking past a corner of the dust sheet Qwelby saw her slowly working her way towards him, bending down to look under the tables. As she stopped right by him he clamped his mouth shut to stop from gagging at the smell of cigarette smoke on her light blue jeans. Well worn trainers displayed a logo of...... a dragon? Seeing the trainers flex as she started to bend down he closed his eyes and switched into HideNSeek mode, hoping it would work on Earth. He felt a slight draft on his face as the dust sheet was lifted up.

'Come on Giselle. I want to see those old dungeons that aren't on the official tour,' one of the boys called out.

'Something set off the cameras,' she said, her voice sounding only centimetres away from Qwelby's ears.

'Now, Giselle,' her uncle said. 'Or there won't be time to see it all.'

Qwelby heard a heavy sigh.

'Oh all right.'

There was a brief draft of air as the dust sheet was dropped back into place, followed by the sound of footsteps. Qwelby let his breath out slowly. One of the boys said all was set, more footsteps, lights switched off and murmured conversation that ceased as the door closed.

CHAPTER 60

ROMAIN SEEKS HELP

HELSINKI

Tuesday the fourth of January, his fifth day in Finland, Romain flew to Helsinki and settled into a room in the Scandic Grand Marina. The view over the waterfront and the Gulf of Finland as he made a series of telephone calls was a nice reminder of his Pacific Island home. Initially unsuccessful, his hopes were buoyed when it was suggested he should try an Investigator called Jouko Soininen, on the grounds that he was a Science Fiction fan and might be interested in the effects that Romain was talking about.

Luck was with Romain. By late afternoon he was shaking hands with a rather tired looking man in his late thirties. Average height, light brown hair, an unremarkable face and a spreading waistline gave the PI a usefully nondescript appearance.

Soininen listened with growing interest to Romain's explanation of the cutting edge science and the puzzling background. But.

'It all sounds far-fetched. Like a plot for a science fiction film,' the PI said.

'I agree,' Romain replied. 'Except that you can verify everything

I've said. Including the science that brought me to Finland. I've got the printouts here.'

A lengthy discussion ensued about science and science fiction, during which Romain gave the PI a carefully edited version of his experiment. He then explained his biggest fear. If he approached the family directly and the boy had problems, for example being an illegal immigrant or being sheltered from enemies, he might be spirited away. Whatever he had seen or even found the evening he arrived might then be lost to Romain. Soininen thought the Professor was paranoid. Yet he had to admit that the blatantly false story about who the boy was gave just a little credence to Romain's fears.

Romain said he understood the PI's obvious reluctance to take the commission and would need to check him out. He offered a folder which, in addition to the printouts, contained copies of his entry in Who's Who, a long list of web addresses for papers he had authored on a variety of subjects and brief summaries of several patents. He then used his RonaldSon mobile to provide Soininen with secure communications. As he hoped, the PI was impressed and agreed to think it over, saying he would give Romain an answer within forty-eight hours.

The following Thursday evening a contented and albeit slightly surprised Romain flew back to Jyväskylä, contract signed and deposit paid. Not cheap, but easily affordable. He could not know that the PI's decision had been swayed by the opportunity of a weekend away from his current relationship problems. Why, Soininen wanted to know, did his partners always change for the worse when they came to live with him.

The PI had explained that he was engaged on another job that required him to be back in Helsinki on Monday morning and had agreed to telephone on Monday night with a brief summary.

Relieved that progress was being made, Romain decided to relax and enjoy a few days skiing at Muurame.

CHAPTER 61

A HUNT IS PLANNED

THE KALAHARI

Back inside the village, Tullia parted from H'ani with a smile. As she walked back to join what she thought of as her family, she decided to thank Mandingwe for the trick she'd played. Being with H'ani had been nice and his wanting to see her again had given her butterflies in her stomach. A new sensation that made her feel like what she was, a young girl wanting to have fun and.... She blushed and felt all dithery as she hoped that more kissing was what he meant by asking her to walk with him.

She noticed H'ani and Xara with his red headband making their way to Ghadi's hut, where they sat down around the little fire. As many of the tribe clustered around at a respectful distance, she joined them in time to hear Xara say: 'There was one large kudu. Lame. His left rear leg has been injured at some time. He looked healthy. But he was trailing behind the others. Easy prey. He will not live long.'

There was silence.

'I will see what message the dawn brings,' Ghadi said. 'If it is right we hunt then a large party must go. Xara will choose the hunters, Kotuma the women.' He nodded agreement to Xara's suggestion of including Xashee and K'dae who had achieved manhood but had never hunted.

Tullia turned to Xashee. 'I would like to go with the people when they look for the Kudu.' She could not say "hunt", and think of killing the lovely looking animal with its funny, large ears.

Xashee was not surprised. Anyone of the tribe of her age would want to join in. 'Speak to Ghadi.' He spread his hands. 'How could he refuse... you.'

What a strange life I am living. Tullia thought. I want them to treat me as who I am. Yet, because they treat me as what they think I am, I can do things I couldn't if they treated me as who I am! How on 'Tazia am I going to manage when I'm back home? That brought up thoughts with words like "If?" She quickly sent them away by getting up and walking over to where the leader was sitting. She squatted down. 'Ghadi, I wish to go with your people tomorrow.' Simple and direct. It is how they speak.

The chief didn't doubt her bravery, but how could he tell the strange woman who had the powers of a healer and was looked upon by most of the tribe as a Daughter of the Sun Goddess, that she would not be able to keep up. Yet, perhaps...? 'I will speak later.'

When the evening meal was finished, O'wa, Ghadi's son asked Tullia to come to their family fire, where Ghadi explained.

'The San have been here for over seventy thousand years. We have always fed ourselves by hunting and living off the plants that grow naturally. We have never had any thoughts of growing crops or keeping animals. Over the last three hundred years we have seen vast and violent changes. All the San in South Africa were massacred, hunted down like animals.

'We have even been driven from our lands. Here we live in an area where the animals that have always been part of our lives are protected. In order to maintain a balance, some animals have to be culled every year. We are not even allowed to hunt those few. Instead, the government issues permits to landowners for the hunting season. Those are sold on to hunters who charge tourists a lot of money to shoot the animals. Everyone makes a big profit, but there is nothing for us.

'It is not the hunting season now. We do no harm to anyone. There is a leopard close by. The Kudu will not survive long. We do not even rob it of its life.' He paused. 'The hunters will hunt as they must. You understand?' What he did not add was that Xara had said that he planned to wound the Kudu early in the day and turn it around in an arc, directing it back towards the village and thus shortening the length of Tullia's journey.

'I think so,' Tullia said. 'If I do not keep up, I will have to make my own way back home.'

'Nlai and I will walk with you and carry water and blankets for you,' Kotuma said.

'Thank you.' Although embarrassed at not carrying her own supplies, following her experience when she was captured and had to carry her bundle of clothes, Tullia had no hesitation in accepting what Kotuma had announced.

CHAPTER 62

SOCKS

FINLAND

Replaying what he'd seen of the set-up in the big room, Qwelby belly crawled back out of his hiding place, dragging his clothes with him. Then he made his way on hands and knees to the door by which he'd entered the room, opened it and peered both ways along the corridor. No-one in sight and no sounds of any sort. Getting to his feet he ran to his left to where there was another corridor that had to run across behind the dais. The corridor he was in continued for about three metres, ending in a door and with another door to the left. When he opened the door facing him a flight of stone steps was revealed and he heard faint voices. Smiling, he closed the door. This was fun.

Walking along the corridor that ran across the back of the big room, he found a short mirror image corridor to his right. This time, the door to his right and that facing him were both locked. Modern locks, modern metals, only three levers and no added inertia as there would be on Vertazia. He knelt down by the door facing him. Inserting the penknife Hannu had lent him, he concentrated on the levers and opened the door, revealing another flight of stone steps leading down. No voices.

Moving quietly in his black socks, he walked down the steps, noting fresh stone set in each tread, making safe what was a well-worn staircase. The steps led into a corridor that was gently lit by electric lights made to look like burning torches. The air was dry and fresh with a faint smell of dust. The stone walls were old and showed signs of repair. He put a hand on a wall and pulled it away quickly, feeling pain and fear. Carefully he held his hand very close to the wall and sensed that the bad vibe was very old.

Hannu had explained that there had been dungeons and prisons underground, but remembering Qwelby's coma, had said no more than that they were now used for an interesting museum. Qwelby took several deep breaths, reached into his Kore and steadied himself. The stories his friends had told him had been a great shock. Now, he was prepared.

'I need to learn this for when we get back home, Kaigii, and can tell our people the whole truth. I have felt kindness and concern and, yes, love, from my new friends on Earth. I need to feel the Azurii darkness so as to understand it better than just mentalearning.' He gave a little laugh. 'Dragons Breath, Kaigii, just as well you can't hear me talking like some boring college Educationer!'

He walked along the corridor and came to the first of a series of small rooms that had to be those that Hannu had told him used to be prison cells. A low wooden partition separated it from the corridor. The cell contained several models in different clothes, performing different tasks. He recognised a woodworker, a shoemaker and a farmer. There was a board with writing which he assumed was an explanation. 'I really must learn to read, rather than rely on the shapes of the few words I've learnt to recognise.' Then he saw small plaques by each figure bearing the numbers which were very similar to Vertazian numbers. He deciphered dates. 1700, 1825, 1900.

Moving on, the succession of small rooms contained

displays of what he either knew from the visit to the museum in Jyväskylä or guessed at, of book-keepers, merchants, lawyers and a judge sitting high up on his bench. In the next room he saw a colourful grouping of what had to be Duke Villnäs, the Duchess and their children. Qwelby was mentally photographing and tagging everything, happy that what he was learning was going to make watching flikkers when back home a lot more enjoyable.

The next display had him staring as goosebumps ran all over his body. Standing alongside his white horse and surrounded by an evocative painting of a battle covering all three walls, the Duke was wearing body armour and thrusting a magnificent sword high into the air in celebration. His helmet, complete with a golden circlet, was being held by a kneeling soldier.

Qwelby's eyes blurred. For a moment the beautiful horse was a unicorn. Kaigii's unicorn. 'But your twin doesn't have a unicorn,' a corner of his mind whispered.

Shaken, Qwelby stepped back and wiped a hand across his sweating forehead as a sensation like goosebumps ran all through his insides.

Shaking his head, swallowing and licking his lips he moved onto the next opening and saw a guardroom manned by three soldiers. Two low barriers marked a path through that to….. once again he stood and stared. This time in horror. He was looking into a torture chamber. His breathing was fast and short as he took control of his emotions. He forced himself to look closely at a brazier with iron rods being heated, all cleverly done with lights. Facing him from the opposite side of the brazier was a muscular, dark brown man wearing heavy sandals and a wraparound leather apron.

Qwelby stepped over the barrier and walked up to a rough wooden bench on which a man lay on his back, tied by wrists and ankles, with a torturer operating a winch at one end. Tensing himself, he put his hand on the frame, and relaxed. It was not centuries old, but new. He scanned it and sensed the pride of the apprentice who had made it to look old and worn. Taking his hand away he shook his head, bemused by the Azuran attitude to violence.

His mouth dry, he licked his lips as he looked around and saw an iron studded door set in the end wall. He was being drawn towards it. Several metres below, currents were flowing. Real currents of water as well as of energy. The lock was a simple tumbler. Putting his bundle of clothes on the floor, he knelt down. With penknife and a hair grip he soon opened the lock. The door swung inward, revealing a small lobby. He remained on his knees as the energies of the sixth dimension swirled around – the same as those that energised Óweppâ, their Talisman, but much stronger.

This was more than fun. This was a proper adventure – in a forbidden place with the risk of being caught and now the danger of strong and little understood energies from an alternative universe. Oh, how he wished Wrenden was there to share it with him.

He pushed the clothes through the small lobby to the next door. There was no pretence at age. This was modern, solid metal with a large vertical slot for a double sided key. He pulled his sweater over his head, followed by his t-shirt which he used to wipe away the sweat trickling down his face.

With two sets of four levers, the lock was a challenge all by itself. In addition, the door had to be opened with the key still fully turned in the lock. Focussing on the levers he imaged the Talisman, reaching out to the energies it contained and the coloured energies of the sixth dimension swirling around his fingertips. He turned the penknife, the interlocked levers moved and he heard bolts sliding back from the top, bottom and two sides. Left hand keeping the key turned, right hand and shoulder pushing, he opened the surprisingly heavy door. The cavernous tunnel facing him was cold, but there was no sense of heavy dampness. A slow current of air flowing from left to right was keeping the atmosphere fresh.

He looked at the back of the thick door and nodded to himself. The locking mechanism was concealed within a double-skinned door. Using his foot, he dragged his clothes forward to stop it from closing. To his right, a flight of steps led down to a canal about four metres wide and..... He stepped forward to the edge of the platform. Looking down, he saw a quay with a small boat half hidden in the swirling, multicoloured energies.

He needed a sword.

Getting to his feet he walked back into the guardroom and felt the handles of the swords the soldiers were wearing. That was all. A handle and a scabbard. No real swords. The Duke. He stepped inside and respectfully removed the sword from the Duke's grip. It was beautiful. Such craftsmanship. He hefted it then slashed with it. 'Perfect balance.' He stared at his hand. 'What do I know about perfect balance? I've never held a sword before!' He put out a hand to steady himself on the Duke's breastpiece as deeply hidden memories hammered at his consciousness.

His hand was resting on the broad leather band that held the scabbard. Of course, that's how he'd always worn his sword. He slipped the baldric off over the Duke's head.

Voices. He ran back into the torture chamber, and cursed. The studded door had closed. If he was caught he'd be interrogated by the police. The sergeant on New Year's Eve. He knew she wanted to know more about him. No papers, unable to tell lies for long, taken away, never to be reunited with his twin. His mind was whirling and his fingers trembling too much to try and open the door in the time he had.

Looking around for inspiration – he found it. A third torturer's dummy, with one hand missing, was resting against a wall in a corner. It was out of sight to anyone who remained behind the barrier. All three dummies were dark brown and shiny. Why was a puzzle, but.... He had a chance.

Standing by the rack wearing a long cloak was a hooded figure. Looking under the cloak Qwelby saw the man had a thick cord around his waist. He thrust the sword through that, stripped off his shirt and cargo pants and thrust them together with the baldric under a bench bearing a variety of black, iron objects and a hand. He undid the belt that held the third dummy's apron, put it on and went to stand by the brazier with his back to the open wall, putting one hand on the end of a poker. He took a deep breath and froze as he heard the girl exclaim in disgust.

The boys were delighted and commented on the various devices. Qwelby learnt the stretching frame was a rack, the brazier was for branding irons, the Iron Maiden was for.... He tensed every muscle so as not to scream in horror as he thought of the long iron spikes piercing his body.

'Look at that big black brute, dwarfing all the others,' one of the boys said.

Oh, shit! Qwelby was staring at his black socks.

'Why are some of them black, uncle? Surely blacks weren't here then.'

'Look at their faces, Giselle. They're Finns. They're black and shiny to show their dirty, sweaty work in the dungeons amongst the fires and smoke. They lived down here all the time.'

One of the boys muttered something. The other guffawed.

'You're disgusting!' the girl said.

Qwelby heard a slap and a laugh. He'd no idea what the boy had said, but it had offended the girl and she'd slapped him, just as Tullia would do to him. A pang of sadness. He liked the girl. He smiled. A fatal mistake. It disturbed his concentration and he couldn't hold his breath any longer. In his rush he'd not managed to get the prong into the last hole of the apron's too tight belt. He felt a slight movement. The apron was slipping. He would make a noise if he didn't let his breath out slowly, even though it meant his stomach expanding. He concentrated hard. This wasn't Vertazia, but some of his energy skills worked. A little.

The leather was shiny. It slipped, held for a moment, slipped some more and fell to the floor.

Light blue boxers!

Nothing.

Not believing his luck, he slowly turned his head. No-one was there. Relief flooded through him, his legs went weak and he sat down. He had been concentrating so hard he had not heard them walk away. After a few moments he got up, put the apron back on the dummy, retrieved the sword, picked up his shirt, pants and baldric and once again opened the studded door. Closing it behind him, he heaved a big sigh and leant against it.

CHAPTER 63

TULLIA RELATES

THE KALAHARI

Having agreed to tell the story of her capture, Tullia went into her hut to change into the costume Kou-'ke had given her, along with a brightly coloured, beaded headband that Deena, Tsetsana's mother, had made for her. Knowing she would have to relate her experience and wanting to honour the Meera by trying to portray it in their way, she had found time to discuss how to do that with Xai-Xai, the tribe's greatest saga teller.

As she stepped into the light of the glowing coals she heard a soft murmur run around the Meera. More than the few words that reached her was the power of the collective energy. Her whole body trembled, she was sure everyone would see her arms and legs quivering. She was not powerful and certainly she was not as beautiful and impressive as their thoughts were saying. What are they expecting! She stopped moving, panic welling up inside.

Shy, exposed to the whole tribe as never before, she dropped her head. She could not bear to catch anyone's eyes, least of all Xai-Xai. She knew she would let him down.

There was a catch of breath from the whole tribe. The Goddess required their attention.

For Tullia, the sound broke the stasis. She took a deep breath and pretended she was on Vertazia, as if she was the first entertainment of a KeyPoint LiveShow, a warm-up act for Tamina and her troupe of dancers. Whispering to herself in Tazian, she reminded herself of the events and how they had unfolded.

Enthralled by the energy flowing from someone who she dared call friend, Tsetsana whispered to herself the name Tullia told her she had been given by Xameb. '!Gei-!Ku'ma.' Goddess of the Red San. It was picked up and passed around, the whispers reaching Tullia's ears and sliding into her subconscious.

Eventually, Tullia fell to the ground, panting, not intending to portray her weariness as she settled into the Land Rover for the journey home, but from sheer exhaustion. Her whole body ached, her calves were painful, her thighs trembled even as she lay on the ground. She did not understand why her shoulders and neck felt as though they had been pummelled. Performing on Vertazia had never been anything like that!

With the energy of the tribe empowering her, she had danced her heart out. She did not even know if she had done what had been planned. She had felt it all. Every step, every dive to the ground, every moment of fear, even her regret at hurting her captor.

There was silence. Dizzy and momentarily confused, Tullia wondered why her mind was not full of audience appreciation. Then she remembered. She was not on Vertazia. As she relaxed, she became aware of a sensation of soft rainfall in her mind. She was receiving their thoughts.

Then she felt a hand under her arm. A strong hand gently lifting. She looked up into the grinning face of Xai-Xai and let herself be pulled to her feet. Unsteady, she leant against him. Slender though he was, she was grateful to rest her head on the shoulder of the tallest man in the village.

'I did not teach you all that,' he whispered in her ear, his pride at his student shining through his aura. 'What you have told is now part of us. In the future I will relate that, in my way. But there will never be any changes to the story. That is how we maintain our living history from generation to generation back to the time when we were the First People.'

'Need lie down,' Tullia managed to whisper.

Xai-Xai beckoned to Tsetsana, who ran around to help her friend back to her hut and settle her onto her bed of blankets.

CHAPTER 64

XAALA ACTS

VERTAZIA

Xaala's first action on waking was to search the MentaNet. She was surprised to discover several energy signatures worth pursuit. After her usual light breakfast, she put on her meditation robe and explored what she'd found. It was an unsettling experience.

The youths' minds were unlike anything she'd ever met before. In varying degrees all of them were underdeveloped and unstructured and, from the easily perceived surface thoughts, degenerates! She had heard of MUUDs, but only in connection with the work of Readjusters. Shaken by the contact, she withdrew, aware that one signature stood out as a possibility.

With Ceegren constantly involved in meetings, he had left her to research whatever she considered would help with her mission. As manipulating a MUUD mind was going to be a challenge, she decided to divide her day between researching the Readjuster section of the Racial Memory Archives, practising her Advanced BodyDance and working out in the gym.

But first, steeling herself, she made contact with the selected youth and set up a meeting for that evening. Sensing his clear distrust, she allowed him to choose a location near to where he lived with his mother in one of the extremist Kumelanii villages.

That evening she changed into her DarkSuit and set off on her twistor. In accordance with normal Tazian custom she planned to arrive a few seconds early. Scanning the area as she approached, she was puzzled to see that what had been selected was a cluster of rundown and dishevelled buildings on the outskirts of the village. Their condition was not only unusual by normal standards but exceptional in an area of UltraTraditionalists.

Expecting to find the youth approaching the area – another surprise. He and two others were already there, physically concealed but with their auras radiating strong distrust and excitement tinged with a little fear. Her saddle monitor flashed a warning. The nearby twistor cradle was compromised. The nearest safe one was several hundred metres away.

'What in all the Shadow Worlds am I getting myself into?' she muttered.

Thoughtsending to her twistor she had it set her down in the empty space in front of where the youths were hiding. Cancelling the forcefield, she got off, spread her legs wide apart and put her hands on her hips in what she hoped was a male swagger. The twistor autolocated to the safe cradle.

'You can come out now Rulcas,' she called.

A youth stepped forward, sturdily built and below average height for his sixteen years. His aura reflected what she'd seen of his mind. Rebellious and fully Awakened several months earlier than normal, but inside he was unsure and vulnerable. He was followed by two tall youths who looked about seventeen.

'Who are you?' he asked in a tone that was more of a challenge than a request.

'Xaala.'

'Xaala what?'

'That's all you need to know.' Xaala was pleased with her aggressive tone and was content with the tension in the air. The difficulty of reading his mind was partially balanced by reading the strong feelings running through his energy field.

'You said dangerous, secret and a reward. What?'

'Send the others away. This is between you and me.'

'Nah, babe. They're my insurance.'

'End of,' Xaala said as she turned to leave, only to have the two youths take hold of an arm each and turn her back to face Rulcas. Their thoughts were clear and unsettling. Xaala was shocked, afraid and full of indecision.

'Now, lil' darlin'. Talk.'

Xaala stared at him as her mind sorted through the double insult.

'Do yourself a favour, babe,' one of the lads said, trying to squeeze her arm but failing.

The youths holding her arms yelped and let go as power flowed through her.

'Gettitoffme!' Rulcas yelled as a long snake wrapped itself all around him, its tongue flickering close to his face.

'Tell them to go. They can watch. Not hear.'

'Go!' he yelled. They did and the snake unwound.

'Call me lil' darlin' again and I'll let my Attribute really play with you,' Xaala said, thrilled at how dominant male she sounded – and felt. 'Now we talk.'

Xaala set out her mission: to prevent both twins from returning and thus spreading the Violence Virus. Rulcas queried "both". It had been a test and it allowed her make it look as though he had trapped her into admitting that one of them could be allowed to return. Along with providing a totally false explanation of why that was possible, based on their being Quantum Twins.

She dealt with his further questions and went on to explain that the team was just the two of them, operating secretly. Dangerous because the twins had strong energies, powerful Attributes and high ranking family. As she had said on their initial contact, his reward was to be entry to the Shadow World, years earlier than normal. She now added the promise of his accruing substantial energy credits.

'Nah, err.... Xaala. I want more. To live with my Old Man in Tembakatii.'

Xaala understood. Parents separating before their child had achieved adulthood were rare. When one parent adopted the liberal, nonconformist lifestyle of the Shakazii, custody was almost always given to the other, especially if that parent was a Traditionalist.

'With the Shakazii in the Shadowlands?'

'Tembakatii to you.' He was proud of the name that meant "Hope for the future of the race."

There was a long pause as Xaala mindsearched him, ensuring he was unaware of her doing that. *So, it's not just to be with his father. He really does believe in their lifestyle. He's not averse to breaking rules. Useful. And I think he's as good as I'm going to get in a hurry.* 'Agreed.'

'You can't promise that,' Rulcas challenged.

'My Venerable master will be very grateful when we succeed.' Xaala sent him a clear picture of a Venerable wearing full robes, bearing Ceegren's colours of Custodian, Readjuster, Arkaana and Educationer.

Rulcas nodded. 'Deal.' He spat on the palm of his right hand and held it out. After hesitating, a bemused Xaala did the same. They shook, eyes locked as he failed to overpower her.

'Now my way,' Xaala said as, keeping hold of his hand, she placed the fingers of her other hand against his temple.

'Wassat?'

'Everything is now hidden deep in your mind and you will not be able to talk about it with anyone but me.'

Whatever Rulcas was about to say, the words never passed his mouth as he saw a twistor arrive. He knew they autolocated to a cradle, but one that could be thoughtcalled! Any doubts he had about the power of her backer disappeared.

Xaala swung into the saddle. 'Next time you fix a meeting place. Don't screw with the cradle!'

Rulcas saw her activate the twister's forcefield then vanish with a sound like the ripping of calico. He knew that when a twistor stopped rotating it turned into a line of infinite length. But to be able to pilot one in that way. Respect!

He swaggered over to his mates. 'Done a deal. Secret. Can't talk about it.'

'With that mindjerking bitch!' one of his mates exclaimed.

'Watch yer mouth,' Rulcas said. 'She's all right.' Grinning, he held up a hand with his forefinger pointing up.

His mates made no further comment. He was the boss and he had a plan to get one up on her.

Back in her research room at IndluKoba, Xaala slumped into the consolchair. Stlipping, as straight line piloting was called, required intense concentration. Added to that was nervous exhaustion from the meeting. The low level of physical violence had been disturbing. The youths accompanying thoughts had been a shock. Their minds were not shielded like hers, but those thoughts had not spread into the MentaNet. Why not?

Yet they were not underdeveloped. She would have to rethink her approach to Rulcas. He'd picked up on her deliberate use of "both" and gone on to ask questions showing he was more astute than she had assumed. She had a lot to learn about MUUDs.

In the meantime, she had a lot of things to think about. Later, she would make a list and instruct her mind to work on them whilst she slept.

CHAPTER 65

MESSAGES

FINLAND

After a few moments leaning against the studded door, Qwelby slid down it and put all his clothes back on, except for his trainers which he placed to keep the metal door open. He did not dare rely on the sixth dimensional flux still being there to help him open the lock when he returned.

His father had explained that the favourite theory about the sixth dimension was that it was an extrusion from another universe which, effectively acting at right angles to this universe, provided the barriers between the third, fifth and seventh dimensions. It was assumed that the same applied between the seventh, eighth and ninth. No-one was able to offer any explanation for the occasional fluxes. Those theories formed the basis for the HWFantasies about time corridors reaching across the dimensions that opened and closed unpredictably.

Standing up, Qwelby slipped the baldric over his head and slid the sword into the scabbard. Given the worn stone steps facing him and the strength of the swirling energies, he was relieved to find a rope handrail fixed to the wall as he walked down to the quay.

The quay was long and narrow with enough space for several

small boats to be moored. The dimensional energies provided enough light for Qwelby to make out the boat he'd seen was a double-ended rowboat. The water was flowing at a slow but steady pace, enough he reckoned to carry the boat whilst he steered.

A few moments later he was happy to be proved correct as the boat was carried along with almost no need for his hand on the tiller. The colourful energies showed the route lay straight ahead as far as he could see. He laughed. Apart from that, he had no idea where he was going. Once again he wished Wrenden was with him to enjoy the adventure.

The colours closed in and turned into a thick mist. The boat tilted sharply, bow down, pitching him onto his knees. He remained there, gripping the thwart until the boat levelled out. The mist cleared and he found himself in a narrow, underground passageway carved through solid stone. No boat. He got to his feet and started walking.

Black mist swept along the tunnel and wreathed around him. Tendrils emerged, gripping his arms and legs and wrapping around his head. He managed to draw his sword and hefted it, feeling the perfect balance, knowing how to wield it. He slashed, severing tendrils which fell to the ground and dissolved. As his arms were freed he grasped the hilt with both hands and swung, severing the tendrils that wrapped around his legs.

Call on his dragon? No. Here and now he was a warrior. This sword was as suited to his present needs as his former one had been.

?

There was no time to think about that as a werebeast came racing towards him. He dropped into a crouch, the tip of the blade resting on the ground. The beast leapt, he raised the blade and thrust it forward. The blade penetrated the animal's body as he fell backwards. The pommel of the sword struck the stone floor. The blade buried itself deep as the beast fell. A scream. A cloud of putrefaction showered him. Werebeast and revolting mess vanished.

Wiping sweat from his face with the back of a hand, he stood up, reaching his full height of over three metres with his helmeted head almost touching the roof as the tunnel expanded upward. A roaring sound far away, rapidly coming nearer. He saw a wall of foaming, black water filling the tunnel. As it thundered against the stone, pointed snouts protruded, opening wide their jaws to reveal rows of sharp teeth.

He ran back, desperately trying to work out how to combat the attack. Deepstate. All was possible. The energy signature was not the same mix as with the previous attacks that had kept himself and his twin apart.

?

He and Tullia were in Great-Great Aunt Lellia's Homely Room. She was explaining about the Dark Denizenii that inhabited the Boundary Lands and the dangers of encountering them.

!

He looked over his shoulder. Saw he had a good lead on the foaming water. Turned and drew a line across the stone floor with the tip of the sword blade, stepped back several paces as the water closed on him and drew another line. 'OPEN!' he commanded, and sagged with relief as he watched the water pour into the chasm that appeared at his feet.

The walls of the tunnel below the palace appeared faintly around him, the boat on the water of the canal metres below. Focus on the boat and be back in the safety of the third dimension? The Dark Denizenii were a danger to be avoided and if the sixth dimension closed he might find himself trapped in another universe. His crystal was throbbing against his chest, urging him to proceed into greater danger than he'd ever faced on Vertazia.

If Wrenden was with him – a grin and they'd press on.

He walked back a few paces, turned, ran and leapt across the chasm. A tendril reached up and grabbed his ankle. He fell on the ground on the far side and swung his sword, freeing himself. Getting to his feet and running on, he heard the sound of pounding boots rushing towards him. Bearing swords, daggers and spears, a mass of humans charged him.

'Nooooo!' he yelled, denying what his enemy wanted him to see. These were not real Azurii but mere images. He braced himself to meet their rush. The tunnel was only wide enough for two at a time to attack but the Denizenii were not warriors and sent three at a time, hampering each other. He marvelled at himself as he cut and parried, thrust and swung, half turned and kicked out with a foot. Smashed forward and drove a mailed fist into a face. He grunted as swords bounced off his armour. Hacked off a spearhead. Swung his blade and watched as three heads toppled from bodies.

This was violent, dirty and without rules, not how he had fought with Zeyusa. At least here as he killed each image it vanished. He had no pile of dead bodies to trip over as in the Great Schism War.

What in all the Shadow Worlds do I know about that?! And who is or was Zeyusa? With a backswing, the last two attackers turned into clouds of dark smoke and vanished. Wearily, he rested on his sword.

Silence.

His armour dissolved and he shrank back to his normal size as the tunnel returned to its former dimensions. He started to walk forward. The tunnel flowed past him until all movement stopped as a wooden door appeared. It was locked. He swung the sword, carving a chunk out of the door. It opened and he stepped into a large room with a brown, stone flagged floor, rough stone walls and a high, grey ceiling. A forbidding atmosphere matched the colours.

The colours and atmosphere darkened as a large, double

tiered and padded stool appeared, tendrils of fear wrapping around it. Room and atmosphere became darker and darker as oversized letters appeared, all standing upright with the tops well out of his reach. A "T", a squared off "O", and an "X". Dismay and dread swamped the room as the objects alternated with each other, fading in and out of his vision. A large, open-work packing case arrived. A smaller one landed on top and the room became pitch dark. Qwelby shuddered as he was surrounded by a cloying evil made worse by an overwhelming sense of betrayal.

He needed light. The chamber needed light.

He was deep underground. Deepstate. He drew his sword and thrust it into the ceiling. It made a hole and light shone in. He heard squealing from within the room. He stabbed several more times, opening more holes, making them larger and discovered that the squealing was coming from the objects. As light spread around, so the dread and despair lessened. Taking a step back, a hard edge caught him across his lower back....

'*Remember,*' the voice in his head whispered. '*Re-Member.*'

....the backrest at the stern of the boat. All the colourful lights of the sixth dimension had gone and the tunnel was bathed in a faint greenish light from luminous lichens on the ceiling and walls. He knew the boat had been flowing along the canal, but fore and aft the painters were still secured to rings in the quay. He looked at his watch. The words on the face were: Dinner Time. He grunted. It was confused, or he'd been gone for twenty-four hours.

He clambered out and climbed the steps. At the top he took off Paavo's one-piece, put on his trainers, closed the big metal door and listened at the other. Hearing no sounds from the torture chamber, he eased the door open. The room was lit as before. He guessed that it must be the following day and hoped it was dinner time and the palace was deserted.

He and Wrenden always left behind an anonymous indicator of their adventures. Tullia did not let him do that on their explorations. Thinking about his youngerest, Qwelby grinned as he slipped the baldric back over the Duke's head with the sword still in the scabbard.

Retracing his earlier steps, he heard nothing, saw no-one and discovered it was still night-time. He arrived at the side door through which he'd entered and was surprised to see it was neither bolted nor locked. Hearing no alarm when he opened it, he guessed he'd been out-of-time whilst enfolded by the sixth dimension. He ran along the road, stopped when out of sight behind the nearby houses and put on Paavo's all-in-one.

When he reached the Rahkamo's house he was relieved to find that his guess had been correct and he'd arrived just in time to wash and change for dinner.

After they'd eaten, he told the family of how he'd got into the palace and all he'd done up to arriving in the torture chamber. He did not say anything about pretending to be a dummy, taking the sword or his adventures out-of-time.

As he settled down for the night he concentrated on recalling the full details of his time in what he dubbed the TOXic Room. His throbbing crystal and the recurring images of their Talisman, Óweppâ, told him that more than one message lay hidden in the experience. He needed his twin to help him interpret them.

CHAPTER 66

KUDU

THE KALAHARI

The Meera were awake well before it was light, Ghadi, Xara and the five chosen hunters waiting for the first glimpse of the palest blues to enlighten the horizon. By the time the edge of the sun climbed into view, Ghadi had decided. The dawn was propitious. He nodded to Xara and looked into the eyes of each of the others.

They were all so slender you could call them skinny, yet those slim bodies could track an animal for days across the intense heat of the Kalahari without water or showing any signs of tiredness. Each man was naked except for a small loinskin and a little pouch containing dried grasses for fire lighting. They all carried bows and arrows and spears, the tips made from sharpened pieces of ostrich bone.

Ghadi beckoned Tullia to join them.

She watched as Xara knelt and removed from his small pouch what looked like a chrysalis. Butterflies?

'We find these below a bush on which the beetles feed,' Xara explained, drawing an outline in the sand so Tullia knew what he meant by the word beetle.

Tullia stored in her compiler the name "chrysomelid", to await a time when it could provide the Tazian.

The chrysalis was crushed and the juice carefully trickled into the reed collar that would hold the arrowhead onto the shaft.

'When close to the kudu we will take off the arrow head and smear the poison just below the point, then reattach it. Same with our spears. The poison spreads throughout the animal, weakening it. Where it has been hit, that part is cut out and thrown away. All the rest is good to eat.' He looked her in the eyes. 'Do not touch. Strong poison. Kill. No cure.' He waited for Tullia to repeat in the fashion of San learning.

She did so, and stored the words together with a picture of the bone heads along with images of three downturned mouths. They represented unhappy smiles, which she and Qwelby stored in their minds alongside the rare commands they accepted must be obeyed.

Carefully holding his arrow just below the head, Xara showed Tullia how the point was held onto the thin shaft by a collar made from plant fibres.

'When the arrow strikes, the shaft falls out as the animal moves. The point stays in the animal. The poison slowly weakens it. That may take days. We find the shaft. The meat belongs to whoever made that shaft.'

The San did not really have personal possessions, so how could it belong to anyone? Tullia wanted to ask more, but Xara got up and gestured to the hunters.

She moved back to join the group of women who were to follow the men. They were carrying blankets and had large pouches slung over their shoulders. Kotuma and Nlai showed Tullia that amongst the other items they also were carrying water bottles.

With a swift prayer to the universe and the unspoken wishes of the whole village behind them, the party set off into the bush, the hunters leading.

It was still early morning when they reached the place where Xara had seen the kudu. To their experienced eyes the tracks of the one lame animal were extremely clear, and the hunters followed at a steady jog.

The pace was fast and by mid morning Tullia was already sweating and her muscles starting to ache. She was happy not to have clothes sticking to her body and to feel the energising rays of the sun on her skin. It promised to be a long and tiring day and she needed to maximise her solar energy quotient.

Late morning and Xara decided it was time for a short rest. The women had dug up tubers for all to eat, and the whole party was ready to move off when Tullia and her two companions arrived. Saying he would follow with the others in a few moments, Xara sent K'dae and two hunters to continue tracking.

It was with mixed emotions that Xara watched Tullia approaching. He was still uncomfortable that he and his party of hunters had not been able to rescue her before outsiders had interfered. At the same time he treasured her words, said so that the whole village knew, that it was his training that had enabled her to survive.

Although she was taller and bigger than the two women walking by her side, wearing the same style of loinskin, with her black plaits pinned close to her head and an ease of movement over the thick sand, she looked like them. The sun shining on her sweat-coated body was giving the red cast to her brown skin a copper tinge. She looked like a Bushman. For a day she had been his student as he taught her tracking and bushcraft. He was proud of how quickly she had learnt and then applied her knowledge. A Goddess in her other world, but here and now to him she was San and a daughter of his Meera tribe.

He beckoned to her and led her some way out of the dense bushes into a more open area, pointed to a complete mix of overlapping tracks and raised an eyebrow. She squatted down and pulled from her memory the pictures she'd taken during her day in the bush with him, then accurately explained the tracks she knew and learnt about wildebeest. He led her further on to where there were clear tracks of three animals and she had to describe whether adult or young, their speed and how long ago.

"Young." A ripple of heat haze. Tullia saw a child's foot, running, all six toes dug into the deep sand. 'Khuy!' she exclaimed as her fingers traced the outline of the forepaw of a sabre tooth tiger.

'Tullia!'

The alarm in Xara's voice made her blink. The images vanished. 'Sorry. Ancient memory,' she said as she glanced at her teacher and tried to stop herself feeling the pain of the tears streaming down her face as she'd fired a volley of arrows into the magnificent creature. The boy in its jaws was dead, but the Seeders' village had to be protected.

Recalling Xara's words, Tullia scanned her memory for any changes in the weather over recent days and answered the questions, impressing him with her accuracy.

'What direction to return?' he asked.

Pulling more pictures from her mind, she calculated the time of day, checked with her internal clock, reviewed her mental map of the journey and pointed, noting the dirt under her long fingernails from where she had dug for food.

'You choose good bush?' Xara asked, as he walked to stand behind her and look along her arm.

'Yes. A young one.'

'How,' he asked as he tapped her pointing finger.

She turned to look at him as she explained, feeling like a student wanting approval from her Educationer.

She saw his eyes rest on her necklace. He had noticed it earlier and nodded at the fact that she had very carefully wrapped dark brown cloth around it, well secured with dull green cord made from plant fibre. She was aware of his eyes searching her. Knew it was more than physical as he looked into her eyes, took in her plaited hair, her erect stance, her loincloth, the lack of scratches on her legs. His eyes lingered for a few moments on her bare feet with her toes wriggled into the deep sand. She was conscious of the sun burning into her bare shoulders. Sweat trickled into her eyes. She wiped it away with the back of her hand.

'Rest, Bushman,' he said. 'We go.'

Stunned, she watched him as he walked over to speak a few words to Kotuma. She wanted to be accepted as a young girl, but to be called "Bushman", that was better than any amount of applause she had ever received performing in a LiveShow!

Xara joined the other hunters, gesturing Xashee to lead. As they jogged off, the other women rose and followed them, leaving Tullia and her companions to rest.

CHAPTER 67

EUREKA!

FINLAND   THE KALAHARI

It was late Thursday morning when Qwelby awoke from a deep and refreshing sleep, and was happy to discover that his buzzing had returned to its normal, unobtrusive level. After breakfast he asked Mrs Rahkamo for permission to spend time in the attic room. It had a special meaning for him as it reminded him of the much larger attic room at home that he shared with Tullia.

He lay on the bed letting his mind wander, doing his best not to spend time on any thought or image that popped up. After a while he felt something stirring. His memory offered a recall of his first morning on Earth when he had entered the kitchen and heard Anita asking why she had dreamt of a desert that she didn't think was a desert.

His memory then produced an image of the scene that he and Tullia had observed looking through the window at what they thought must be a desert because it was so hot and dry, but it wasn't what they thought of as a real desert with big sand dunes and an oasis.

A chill wave ran all over his body, raising goosebumps.

Very slowly and carefully he got up from the bed, desperately clinging to a thought he dared not think about too much in case it went away.

He eased himself down onto the floor and looked up through the skylight into a grey, snow laden sky. He sank back into that day on Vertazia and the picture of the scrubby bushes and near naked, dark-skinned people he and Tullia had seen. Mentally, it was like walking on hot coals. He looked at the young man who had thrown the spear, steadied himself, licked his lips and slowly swung his eyes to the side.

The woman with the strange hairstyle and dwarfing all the others was.... Tullia! Looking at the men, he had not noticed her. And she had not recognised herself, her own EraBand? But. She was not wearing it! None of the Auriganii were. Ah, but she was. What looked like a rope around her neck was a covering. Again, goosebumps ran all over his body in waves as if they were trying to pound a message into him.

The image blurred and shifted. He rolled onto his stomach, looking down from a few metres off the ground as the scene unfolded in slow motion.

He examined his twin, comparing her to their much smaller ancestors. Smaller? Surely they were bigger in those days? Accustomed to unisex styles on Vertazia, another puzzle was the difference in loinskins between the men and women. He smiled at the fact that his twin's skin was turning a deep, red, honey gold. Then came a flick of envy. When they were together again she would crow over his pale, winter colour!

†††

As Tullia walked over to join Kotuma and Nlai where they were sitting, she became conscious of a sudden chill on her back. It was not a breeze. It was... but it couldn't be...? She turned to look behind her and gave a little cry. The sound carried in the still air. The departing hunters and women stopped and turned to see what was happening.

A few metres in front of and above her a strange impression seemed to hang in the air. At first it looked like a ring of cloud. But instead of blue sky inside the ring, all was dark. The image came into focus and figures could be seen against the black background. People? Dark skinned people with long black hair?

Frozen in place, Tullia was unaware of everyone returning and the hunters taking up positions around the women.

As the image shimmered, then cleared, with only one image remaining, Xashee rose, pulling his spear arm back. Everyone was motionless, waiting, wondering.

A chill wave ran all over Tullia's body, raising goosebumps. For this she did not need to recall and project a picture – she knew!

'KAIGII!' she cried, stepping forward and raising a hand towards her twin.

Time stood still.

† † †

Qwelby was gaping at his twin, his mouth wide open. He had just reviewed a replay of what they had seen from within the stairwell. Then, the woman he now knew to be his twin had just carried on walking as all the others had done. This was Live, or real-time as the Azurii called it.

'KAIGII!' he cried, as he levered himself forward and dived through the window that had opened.... crashing his head .....

'Labirden Xzarze!' he shouted in despair as he opened his eyes to see he was still lying on the carpeted floor of Hannu's bedroom.

'Qwelby?'

'I'm all right,' he called back to Mrs Rahkamo. 'Fell over.'

† † †

The cloud disappeared. There was a quick discussion and an equally quick agreement. An evil spirit, the sort of which they had never seen before. Their Goddess had protected them.

Xara was certain. Tullia was some form of Ancestor Goddess come to learn the ways of the San. He felt proud that she accepted him as her teacher. He gestured and the hunters set off at a loping run, followed by the main group of women at a steady walk.

Tullia remained transfixed with shock. She had just caught a glimpse of herself and Qwelby when they were in the stairwell. But that had been over two weeks ago! And she was right, it had been Xashee she had seen that day. And she had been that woman with the long hair, strange-looking compared to the others. No wonder there had been something familiar about that figure.

Her hand went to her EraBand. Her captor had been afraid of Thathuma's power and she had dulled it that day when she had been ordered to remove her t-shirt. It was too meaningful to be taken off and she didn't want the distraction of having to continually remember to keep it dull, so she had covered it for the hunt.

She sat down, trembling. Going backwards in Time was not difficult on Vertazia. Their mother had done it twice that awful, chaotic morning in the kitchen with the Quarks. Dreamstates and deepstates could give clues as to the future. But what they had seen from the staircase had been the future through a window that existed in a different space-time-consciousness. And now, there was more than memory. Today, Xashee had not thrown his spear. There had been... what... a Live connection with Qwelby?

As her memory replayed the conversations she had not consciously heard, she realised that the Meera thought she had protected them. Sadly, she shook her head. She would tell Xameb, but no-one else.

She started at a touch on her arm. Nlai was offering her a bottle of water. Tullia took a small sip, handed it back, and the three of them followed the trail left by the rest of the party, with Tullia's mind working overtime.

† † †

Rubbing his sore forehead, Qwelby rolled onto his back. *Where are you, Kaigii? No. It's over seventy-five thousand years ago that we were on Haven. That Seeing was Live. So when are you? And where?*

Due south, the other side of the WarmBand that runs around the equator. It was as if a memory was replaying itself. How?

As he was getting to his feet Mrs Rahkamo called him to come and have lunch. 'Good timing,' he muttered.

Looking in the bathroom mirror as he combed his hair he noticed how long it had grown. There were a couple of rubber bands in the bedside cabinet. By the time he got to the kitchen he had given himself a pony tail. There, he asked Hannu's mother to tell him what she remembered of the dream Anita had mentioned.

Having previously obtained his friend's permission, he settled down in Hannu's room to trawl the internet. Working with Dr Keskinen in his garage laboratory, Qwelby had discovered that by fiercely concentrating he was able to influence the slower vibrating Azuran electronics. Like the photons, the electrons were excited in both senses of the word to play with a human boy.

Pictures floated through his mind. Conical grass huts. Small people with dark skinned faces. A village wall. The screen lit up with a succession of pictures. With a little coaxing they displayed several at once, dynamically interacting at his request.

His pulse racing, his mouth dropped open as the inevitable conclusion burned itself into his brain. Suddenly frightened, he leapt to his feet, the chair crashing to the ground as he pushed himself back from the desk.

Why?

His legs went weak and he collapsed on the bed.

CHAPTER 68

TULLIA IN HER POWER

THE KALAHARI

It was late in the afternoon and Tullia's legs were giving out. She had to stop and sit for yet another rest. They had been travelling at a steady pace all day with Xashee and K'dae coming back on occasions and each time pointing her and her two companions further to the right, in what she understood was an arc slowly turning the now wounded kudu and the whole party in the direction of the village.

She and her friends played a lot of sport on Vertazia and she considered herself fit. Now she was hurting in places she had never hurt before and the wholly unnecessary stomach cramps were the final straw. Xara had called her "Bushman", yet, realistically, could she go any further? The sun was low in the sky. She thanked the stars that night would soon be with them and then they would have to stop.

Used to drinking a lot more than them, Tullia was grateful for the water Kotuma and Nlai were carrying. She was about to take a bottle from Kotuma when she froze, listening. Then she swivelled her head, finally stopping to look. A few moments later she nodded to herself when she saw K'dae appear through the spindly trees, exactly where she was watching.

Xara was right, Kotuma thought. She was a Bushman. She would tell Ghadi, her husband and the tribe's chief.

K'dae squatted down. 'Kudu trapped, close. You go that way.' He pointed. 'I go this.' He got up and ran off.

Kotuma beckoned Tullia to follow. Keeping low with Nlai following, they made their way as quietly as possible through a belt of spindly silverleaf trees. To Tullia with her thighs complaining at the crouching walk it seemed to take forever before they came to the edge of an expanse of open ground. The women were to Tullia's left, crouching amongst the bushes that edged the clearing. The kudu was trapped against a line of bushes and acacia trees at the far side, with Xara facing it from the centre of the semi-circle of hunters.

Tullia knew this had to be the scene from her dream. Xara was in danger. He was going to run to the right and try to spear the kudu from that side. What to do?

The kudu was weakened, but not a lot. As a hunter made a short dash as if to throw a spear, the big animal would make a short charge, its wicked horns lowered, slashing the air. The hunters were wary. They kept their distance. Their spears were light and only tipped with ostrich bone. With so much of its strength remaining, a spear or two would not slow it down but only enrage it further. Tullia stood, watching, feeling awe at the hunters' daring, and fearing for them.

'It is too dangerous,' Kotuma whispered in her ear. 'The poison has not had long enough to work. Normally they would keep it on the move and not try to kill it until late tomorrow.'

'So why do they want to kill it now?' Tullia whispered back.

'We must get back to the village by tomorrow evening,' Kotuma reminded her.

'And the leopard might take it tonight,' Nlai added.

'But it is too dangerous?' Tullia asked.

To that question there was no reply.

The bottom edge of the sun slid below the line of trees. A shadow seemed to leap across the ground. The kudu made a short charge. A spear was thrown but missed. Xara darted in. Tullia's hands leapt to her mouth. What should she do? The kudu lunged. Xara darted back. Xashee, inexperienced, impetuous, darted in, slipped and fell almost under the animal's legs as it changed direction. It raised its head. It was going to slash down on the fallen man.

A shout from the right. K'dae stepped forward, spear raised. The kudu swung its head around. Xashee started to scrabble backwards. The kudu's head swung back and dropped, pointing its wicked horns at the now stationary hunter. With a sharp cry, K'dae took a pace forward, drawing his arm back. Raising its head the kudu roared, a sound like a wailing brass horn. A foreleg pounded the ground.

Feeling its confusion and anger, Tullia sensed that it was about to charge. No mock challenge like the young Bull Elephant had made the day of her capture, but a full charge. She was confused. Of course Xara was not wearing his red headband for a hunt! What was the red in her dream?

'Ayee! Bakann!' she heard a voice cry as the realisation struck her. It had not been a headband. It was blood!

The kudu charged. Straight for her.

Stunned, Tullia realised that it had been her voice speaking Tazian that had called on the animal to stop. And she'd taken a step forward with her hand raised. She froze and everything went into slow motion. She heard the thunder of its hooves on the hard sand. Staring into its eyes, she was transfixed. She watched in fascinated awe as it lowered its head, the wicked horns pointing straight at her body.

Eye contact broken, she came alive and lowered her arm to point straight at the animal's head. 'Tâlâkaa vâpó wenšînâ!' she commanded, the complex overtones of the True Aurigan making it sound as though she was singing with three voices.

Recalling a memory from her day held captive, she drew on the energy of the land through her bare feet and poured every scintilla of her Being into the animal's mind: making it believe it was halted by a charging bull elephant, ears spread, trunk raised and trumpeting.

The kudu crashed to the ground in front of her, two spears flying just over its neck as its head hit the ground. It pulled itself up on its front legs, its rear legs scrabbling as it tried to rise, its horned head slashing right and left, centimetres from the pointing fingers of her frozen hand.

As the hunters ran up to surround the kudu, Xara called out commands, and a puzzled K'dae did as he was bid and handed his spear to the Goddess.

Tullia took the spear as if in a trance. Totally in tune with her Self and awash with the energies, she understood. The kudu would die slowly from the poisoned arrow head. To end its life quickly was mercy. She had been invited to initiate that. She was a Bushman and carried the genes of a Dragon Lord. Taking a deep breath, she raised her arm and threw the spear into the animal's shoulder.

Dodging the vicious horns, the hunters leapt in and held the struggling animal's head up.

Tullia felt hands on her shoulders and saw herself drop to her knees. The scene below was unbelievable. She saw Xara kneel at a woman's side, a knife appeared in his hand. He put it into her hands, wrapped his own hand around hers and guided it as the knife cut the kudu's throat.

This is wrong. It's my kill, not hers. Who is that big, heavy-looking woman down there? It looks like a me I know. But I am a man, a Bushman, a hunter.

Hovering several metres above the action, Tullia looked down and saw herself as...... a man, larger and more muscular than those down there, but definitely a man. It's as though I'm Qwelby! But with my thoughts. Quantum Twins, identical, yet I, we, are here on

Earth in the third dimension. Impossible. Rhythmic Entrainment. Our normal Tazian three identical segments of DNA are not enough. We MUST possess an active fourth segment, or sequences from several more, to enable us to be here in the third dimension.

A bowl appeared in the hands of one of the hunters. She saw blood pour forth into the bowl, watched as it frothed and drops splashed onto the woman's thighs and breasts. The bowl was offered to the woman.

That's not right. The honour is mine!

Words were spoken. Why do I not understand them? These are my people, speaking my language. She watched as Xara lifted the bowl to the woman's lips.

The metallic taste as she swallowed the warm blood shocked Tullia back into her body. She licked her lips and looked down at the blood splattered on her. Stared at it as her mind slowly recalled what had happened.

In his mind, Xara understood. Never before had a woman hunted, killed. Yet it was her kill. Not her animal to dispose of as she chose, but her kill. He had assured that. Goddess or Meera daughter, she expected her due.

Tullia watched in a daze as Xara dipped his thumb into the bowl and smeared a long line of blood down her right breast, back into the bowl to smear another long line down her left breast, then again into the bowl when he drew his bloody thumb across her lips. All the time deep within her a very proud male energy was expressing its satisfaction. She was aware of running her tongue across her lips as she looked back up into Xara's eyes, his face centimetres from hers. AzuraTazii Twinergy. All by myself?

'QeïchâKaïgiï,' a voice whispered in her head.

'Hunter.' Xara's voice brought her out of her wondering.

She looked back down at the body she was in. I am me, Tullia, a girl. A Bushman. A hunter. A man inside? Wow, Kaigii. I have so much to share with you!

Feeling dizzy, she lifted her head. The other hunters were in a line with Xara at one end, facing them. In turn, he offered the bowl and each one took a small sip.

When they had all drunk, Xara returned to stand in front of K'dae. He dipped his thumb into the bowl three times, smearing long lines of blood down either side of his chest, then across his lips.

'Hunter,' he pronounced, for everyone to hear.

K'dae's face creased into a big smile.

Xara then repeated the same actions for Xashee, who managed an embarrassed smile.

Tullia looked down at the now dried blood on her body. Not believing what she was doing, she licked her lips again, tasting the blood. I am a Hunter! She swayed and saw small hands reach across her belly as Nlai held her from behind and helped her to rise, felt Nlai move to her side and start to lead her away from the dead animal. She was afraid she was going to fall over and was glad when Kotuma came to support her on the other side.

As she stood there, dazed, swaying, K'dae came to her, proudly bearing the two dried streaks of blood on his chest. 'You saved my life.'

Coming out of her stasis, Tullia smiled and put her arms around him. He hugged her back. She clung on as shock trembled through her body, then started to shiver uncontrollably.

Nlai was quick to step forward and drag Tullia away from K'dae, then help her sit down. Kotuma walked up, knelt down, put her arms around Tullia and held her tightly as she was wracked with uncontrollable trembling. Tullia collapsed into the safety and comfort, half aware of Nlai draping blankets over her shoulders.

Tullia clung onto the memory of Xara's face as he had said 'Hunter'. Eventually the shaking stopped. She saw a water bottle. With a hand that was still trembling she reached for it and was glad of Nlai's hand steadying it as she sipped, sipped again, then drank deeply. She licked her lips and there was still a faint hint of metallic blood. 'Hunter,' she whispered, and felt an inner energy nod approval.

As with all the Meera, Kotuma had observed the changes in Tullia from Goddess to child when playing with the youngest. This was the first time she had experienced what felt like a physical change. She knew she was holding a woman, yet it felt as though she had a strong young man in her arms.

'Life on the sun, which Tullia heard as "planet", is very different from ours?'

'Very... yet, not in some ways. The ways of living are very different but the ways of being are... so much like at home.' Shivers ran through her and she clung to Kotuma, unaware of how much she was hurting the woman with the ferocity of her grip. She felt hands stroking her head, her hair and running over the blankets covering her shoulders, finally the comfort of another friend kneeling behind and holding her.

Slowly the shaking calmed. She took several deep breaths, released her grip on Kotuma and turning her head, looked into the eyes of the two Meera. 'Thank you,' she whispered. 'I feel better now.'

'We will go and help the others,' Kotuma said, sitting back and pulling the blankets around what was, once again, a young woman. 'If you need me, my daughter, call.'

Tullia bit her lip. "My daughter", just as if I am Meera and thus a daughter of the tribe. I will NOT cry, even though they would be tears of joy.

CHAPTER 69

ENQUIRIES

THE KALAHARI

Again using constable Ditau as his driver, Inspector Modisakgosi set out to visit both of the Tsodilo villages. It was a good time to visit the principal one as the main tourist season was getting under way and that provided a good excuse to visit what was generally referred to as the Research Village and ask about the girl. On their way through to Ghadi they stopped at the tourist village to tell van den Berg, the manager, that they would be calling on him later.

As always, Modisakgosi was greeted politely by Ghadi, who explained that Tyua'llia was in the bush and he was unable to say when she would return as, like any Bushman, she was living off the land. The Inspector's requests for information provided little of any use. Ghadi explained that, as with all San tribes, the young woman spoke a different language.

She said she had come from far away, which to Ghadi's mind explained the marked difference between their languages which was making communication very difficult. From her colouring she was clearly from one of the little known Red San tribes. Since arriving she had learnt some Meera and a few words of Afrikaans.

She was very lonely and time by herself in the bush was her greatest comfort.

Modisakgosi heard the subtle comment that no matter how pleasant life was in the state sponsored village, it was not the traditional way of the San.

Frustrated, the policemen headed back to the tourist village, the Inspector saying he felt that he had been given the run-around. 'You've heard of "Inscrutable Chinese"?' he said. 'Well the Bushmen can be just like that. No smiles, no nods, no gestures, just dead pan faces all the time. You've no idea what they're thinking. Yet at other times, laughter and smiles! And there was something else. I've met with Ghadi quite often over the years. I'd say he was nervous. Protecting the girl? Why?'

'Ah, Inspector, a bottle of nice, chilled Zambezi, eh? Those guys have a story to tell you,' van den Berg said, gesturing to the American photo-journalists as the policemen approached the open air bar under its traditional, thatched roof.

Modisakgosi nodded to the constable who disappeared round the back. Both knew that a drink with the staff was the best way to get useful information.

Later, on the drive back to Shikawe, the policemen compared notes.

'Nothing useful, sah,' the constable said. 'Whatever I asked, the Bushmen went into a long discussion amongst themselves and never ended up with an answer. I don't know if they could not agree on an answer, or whether the argument was about answering.

'They asked if I'd been present when she escaped. When I said we'd rescued her, those black eyes just stared at me as they shook their heads. Well, if you could call the little movement they made "a shake." One old woman said: "You see, you listen, you know." And that finished any discussion of the girl.'

'Never mind, Ditau, I've got good information,' Modisakgosi

said. 'I know her names and when she arrived here. Ten days ago. And I'm going to get a copy of a video of an interview with her, together with some interesting photographs.'

Modisakgosi went on to explain what he had learnt from the Americans and the bargain he had made. In return for providing a translation of the Meera, and if possible of the musical language Tyua'llia spoke, the Americans would provide any more information or videos they obtained.

'I don't understand. If they were unable to take photos, how do they have a video?' Ditau asked.

'Easy. They said that the camera was set up a distance away so that the girl and the others would forget they were being filmed. By the time they had settled down in the tourist village, the girl was quite different. Instead of being all formal and vague with her answers as when they were at the other village with Ghadi present, she was relaxed, acting like a young girl, speaking a lot with her two friends and giggling.'

'What we do now, sah?' Ditau asked.

'We follow up. From what the Americans said, the girl was speaking a lot with the Meera during the interview that's on video. I want that translation. In the meantime we start checks at the border crossings. I still think she's some sort of Himba-Red San mix and has come from Namibia. This business of her being the only female of her tribe and her "partner" the only male. No. My guess is they're a pair of runaways. With the San connection, taken in by the Meera, then conned gullible muzungu looking for a good story. Queen of her tribe. Rubbish!'

CHAPTER 70

ON THE TRAIL

FINLAND

The same Thursday evening that Romain returned to Jyväskylä with the PI's contract in his briefcase, a meeting was taking place at the police station in Kotomäki. Penti Harju, the young Chief Inspector, was listening carefully to what the SUPO agent had to say.

The two men were a definite contrast. The vast majority of the population around Jyväskylä were blonde, men and women alike. Amongst the reasons for Metsälä being chosen for the job were that he was a keen skier, of average height and build, and had blonde hair. Harju was that rarity in the area: a man with dark hair. He was not a keen skier, or sportsman of any sort. That, and perhaps too many beers when off duty, had already given him a definite paunch.

Metsälä finished his brief summary of his first four days. 'From what I've gathered and other information that has been passed to me, it is clear that Romain strongly believes that the boy may have found something that connects with these odd effects he claims to be looking for.' Metsälä was not going to reveal the details of what had been garnered from the phone tap on Soininen. 'Is there anything more you can tell me about local events?'

Harju thought hard and decided he had to tell the whole story. He explained what he had omitted from both his official report and his initial discussion with Metsälä, concerning the involvement of the youngsters on New Year's Eve.

He passed on his sergeant's comments about the sudden appearance in the village of the foreign boy, his strange behaviour and his very unusual eyes. 'I could get one of my officers to call on the Rahkamos and check his papers?'

'Thank you, but no. My interest is in Romain. I'm sure this boy is a red herring.' Both men laughed because of Qwelby's reddish brown colour.

With a pensive look on is face, Harju was twiddling his pen around in his fingers and not looking at Metsälä. The SUPO agent was concerned. He hoped he had discovered something that could be significant. He sensed that Harju was not going to leave the matter alone and the last thing he needed was for the police to mess up this operation as he sought to redeem himself.

'Penti. May I call you that?' Metsälä asked.

The Chief Inspector nodded.

'I understand you don't like being asked to stay out of something that's going on in your patch. I want to take you into my confidence, Penti. But I must ask you not to repeat what I'm going to tell you. Not even to your superiors.'

'Understood,' Penti Harju said as he nodded.

'Okay,' Metsälä said as he rapidly thought what little he could say that would keep the policeman out of the way. 'Two things have happened that "our masters" think may be related. The first is whatever caused CERN to shut down on twenty December. The second is the disturbance to electronic communications on the twenty-seventh.'

Harju nodded. He knew of the brief interference with electronic communications on the latter date, and that a clampdown on the news media had prevented it from becoming more than a passing curiosity.

'What I'm sure you do not know is just how widespread was that area of interference. Very weak at the fringes but very strong in this area. It's got the military jumping up and down. They're saying it looks like a missile came in from a space station with such advanced countermeasures that it blanked all our defence networks over a wide area. But.' Metsälä shook his head. His briefing had been so confusing he could not help sharing more. 'It all happened so fast that it could not have been any sort of missile anyone knows about. And.... it was launched from the area around CERN. Seven days previously!'

He sat back in his chair and spread his arms wide. 'On top of that, NATO is saying that where their monitoring stations had not suffered any interference, none of them had picked up anything on either date. The Ruskies are saying the same. But.....'

Harju had no comment to offer. Silently, the two men shared a companionable understanding of just how out of touch with reality were the people at the top. People who were supposed to know what they were doing.

After Metsälä had left, Harju sat in his chair aimlessly moving papers around. Slowly he got up and filed the reports away, locked the cabinet and stood there staring at his desk where the Sergeant had sat almost a week ago. Something was going on. But what? It certainly was not the load of rubbish that the SUPO agent had fed him. Treating him like some country bumpkin! He wanted to know. It was his Division. He had a right to know. Piia Sjöström had been born in Kotomäki and had moved back on promotion. He felt certain she could talk to people casually, as a local and a friend, without raising any suspicion.

CHAPTER 71

LOGIC

FINLAND

Still trying to come to terms with having seen Tullia in the same scene they'd viewed from in the stairwell nearly two tendays ago, Qwelby found himself impelled to get out of his clothes. He was almost in a panic as he struggled with his weakness, stripping off t-shirt and shorts until only his boxers remained. Panting with relief, still not understanding, yet content with a typical Tazian situation, he ran a thumb down each of his chest muscles and then across his lips. That done, he sank back on the bed and lay there, recalling his picture of Tullia as he had last seen her.

After a few minutes he went into the bathroom, drank a glass of water and buried his face in a flannel soaked in cold water. Feeling calmer, he returned to Hannu's room, dressed and sat at the desk.

The humming of the computer's fan had been replaced by a very soft 'zzzz.' He smiled as he inserted into the computer's memory a 'Tamuchly', just as he would do to semisentients on Vertazia. Providing an interacting, multi-screen display on a computer that did not carry the software for that had depleted the electrons' energy so they could no longer change places with each other and finally had become totally exhausted, as he had himself become from energising them.

Fatigued, he remained sitting at the desk as he reflected on what he had discovered. Having to rub his chest and lips from time to time was a reassuring sense of Tazian normality. All he had to do as to wait for the message to become clear.

Finally, content that the logic of his conclusion was not merely correct but, in his opinion, incontrovertible, he picked up the Globe from his bedroom and went back into the attic room. There, he stood looking through the skylight at what was by then black night sky and the twinkling stars.

'Qwelby Zhó'zânâ Shandurkul,' he said aloud. 'It is your duty to look after Kaigii. To protect the Unicorn. You fought your way out of a Tazian Pit of Despair...with help. So. Dragon Lord. With help from your Azuran friends, find your way to Tullia. Do not fail her this time!'

Holding the Globe in both hands, he settled in the lotus position on the floor and went into a deepstate.

After dinner that evening, Qwelby, Hannu and Anita congregated in her bedroom where she agreed to Qwelby helping her recall her dream. Hannu sat transfixed as he watched his Alien friend using a mixture of Finish and Tazian to get Anita to give a description of her dream in far more detail than seemed possible.

For Qwelby, the final confirmation of his theory was that the loinskins worn by the dancers she had seen were very similar to what Qwelby had seen earlier on the computer monitor. He explained what he had done that day and his conclusion, and received his friends' willing and excited agreement to his proposals for the following day.

That same Thursday, over dinner in their apartment in the Town Hall complex, the building supervisor told his wife of his niece's disappointment. There had been nothing to show when she and her friends had collected their equipment earlier that evening. Sadly, no evidence to support the stories of the ghost of Duke Villnäs holding court in his former throne room.

He told his wife of his surprise at seeing a new figure in the torture chamber that looked badly out of place. It was larger than the others, the skin colour was wrong, as also the pony tail for a man who was not a sailor.

Although his duties did not include the dungeon area, he was concerned about the incongruity and thought he ought to say something. It was difficult. The assistant administrator responsible for the displays was his immediate boss and was touchy about any implied criticism.

When he confirmed to his wife that it was his boss who had authorised the ghost hunting, she said that gave him the perfect opportunity. When he reported the lack of success, it would be natural for him to mention having seen the new dummy.

A relieved husband said he would do that at the regular Monday morning meeting, his boss being away on Friday.

CHAPTER 72

THE HUNTER'S FEAST

THE KALAHARI

Tullia was sitting quietly by herself, recovering from the shock of the ending of the hunt. Saving a life, facing death, killing an animal and going Out-Of-Body as a man, all for the first time in her life. And becoming certain that she and Kaigii must have activated a lot more than the standard three segments of DNA, yet that had never been detected on Vertazia. Why? How? And – what for?

It seemed no time at all before a fire had been lit and food was being passed around. Meat from the kudu and roots they had dug from the ground during one of the short stops during the day. Tullia realised just how worn out she was and famished.

The crackling fire, flickering flames, the grunts and occasional murmurs as people ate. The black sky with millions of twinkling stars and the amazing snake like appearance of the Milky Way stretching from one horizon to the other. She was in awe at the sight, which could not be seen from her home in the northern hemisphere of her parallel world. It looked only a few centimetres wide yet she knew that, in reality, it was fifteen light-years across. She wondered why, with some three hundred billion suns to choose from, her Aurigan ancestors had not discovered a planet on which to settle that would have allowed them to maintain their life in all the higher dimensions.

The sights, the sounds, the smells, the company, all eased her aching body and her chattering mind. No meal had ever tasted so good. It was a feast and she was one of them. Satiated, her belly matched her heavy and sore breasts which she ascribed to unaccustomed sunburn. If only the food would banish the annoying stomach cramps, everything would be perfect. She turned to Nlai. 'Why did you bury the animal when it had been cut up?'

'The ground is very cold. It will keep it fresh and stop animals eating it.'

Eating finished, there was talking and movement. Tullia slipped into her own world, to be brought out of it as she heard Kotuma speaking.

'Tullia. Tonight, we want to offer our celebration to you. Will you watch?'

Looking up, Tullia saw that the women were on the same side of the fire as herself, except for Kotuma and Nlai who were on the opposite side with the hunters. Saga time! She loved the way they enacted, not stories, but their history, their lives. 'Oh, yes,' she replied, relieved to be able to remain sitting and ease her aching back.

Tullia watched as they started the enactment with Nlai portraying Tullia. Did I really walk that slowly, rest so often? Was I really that tired? I could not have been caught in the branches that often, I had no clothes to get tangled! She realised that Nlai was overacting. It was as if she was being made the comedy turn in a KiddyLiveShow. She relaxed, laughed and enjoyed the feeling of acceptance.

All laughter had long gone by the time the kudu's death was portrayed. Then Nlai and K'dae hugged. Tullia was embarrassed. Then she smiled, relieved, as she took in the strong colours that were flaring and recalled previous thoughts about quarks. It was more than a re-enactment, Nlai was taking the opportunity to tell K'dae that she liked him and he was enjoying that. She felt a hot flush of embarrassment as she recalled how she had not so much hugged K'dae as clung to him.

When the action was finished with the hunters and the two women standing on the opposite side of the fire, Kotuma called out 'Tullia' and beckoned her to join them. As she stepped around the fire, Kotuma turned to K'dae and whispered, 'Say her new, Meera name, Tyua'llia.'

As she reached the group, K'dae shyly held out his spear. She did not know what to do. He pushed it forward, clearly showing he wanted her to take it. She did so, puzzled.

'Tyua'llia, you are a trrrue bushman and a hunter,' he said.

Tullia was thrilled and overawed. *He called me by name, with a special way of saying it. I like that. He is giving his spear to me, not to some hornsfluting Daughter of a Goddess!* She gazed at the gift. The spear he had put into her hand that she had thrown into the kudu. She stood transfixed as the flickering flames made the spear look like a snake. She felt the snake gently undulate. *The seventh dimension. I'm accessing that. Here on Earth. The power of the San. The very land itself!* As she stored in her mind the question of why a snake, energy ripped through her spinal column and shot out through the crown of her head.

'Ayeee!' she cried at the pain as she threw her head back.

Misinterpreting her cry as celebration, the women ululated and the men called out a variety of animal barks, grunts, roars and whistles.

It was the most power-invoking experience of her life.

Feeling honoured beyond measure, she bowed her head, totally unaware of the effect that had on the Meera. They applauded and she felt many fingers gently caressing her arms. Acceptance!

Shyly, K'dae stepped close and gave her another hug.

She let her energy drain, controlled it, gentled it and felt him swell with pride as he received her energy. Then came another energy she recognised. He was thanking Cagn, though Tullia sensed it as The Multiverse.

Totally open to her sensing, it was natural for her to slip into his mind and see the images that were flashing through it. He was giving thanks that his worst fear had not come to pass on the day of her capture. He still had nightmares of the time when he was poised to shoot his arrow at her captor when he climbed into the Land Rover: seeing himself running to seize the man and watching, helpless, as she was shot and died in front of him.

K'dae stepped back with a smile on his face, leaving Tullia once again dumbfounded. When she had spoken with Xara, he had not mentioned details. She had had no idea of how close he and his hunters had come to rescuing her, nor the risk to their own lives that K'dae and all of them had been prepared to take.

Nlai set Tullia's two blankets a little to the side of the others. Tullia looked, thought and moved them to be with the others. Choked with emotion and unable to speak, she gestured with her arms. With murmurs of appreciation for the additional blankets, the women grouped together with Kotuma and Nlai on either side of Tullia.

'It's cold,' Tullia said, gesturing Nlai to come closer. The young Meera was unhappy at how close K'dae had been to Tullia and with the gift of his treasured spear. Yet her jealousy and fear could not prevent her feeling gratitude that Tullia had saved the life of the man to whom she hoped to become woman.

As Tullia put an arm around the slender girl she felt her hand taken and moved to a more comfortable position. She gave Nlai's hand a squeeze and felt her hand squeezed in return. She heard Kotuma move up behind her and felt her arm come over the two of them, pulling them in tight against the cold of the night.

Tullia awoke in the middle of the night to the crowing of a korhan. She felt cold. Nlai had moved away. Tullia reached out an arm and gently pulled the girl towards her, rolling her so that she rested her head on Tullia's breasts. As the night sky dimmed from her vision, ancient energies arose within. Happy at being reunited after so long, she gave her daughter a gentle squeeze and slipped back into a deep sleep.

CHAPTER 73

A PRECIOUS GIFT

THE KALAHARI

When Tullia awoke the following morning, she was puzzled as she gazed on the child in her arms. Confusing impressions reached her as the girl opened her eyes, reached up and gave Tullia a quick kiss. Then a much longer one to which Tullia slowly responded as she recognised Nlai. Tullia returned Nlai's smile as the girl rose, content in her own mind that, whilst Tullia liked boys, she also liked girls.

Later, Tullia examined the spear. It was intricately carved. Having seen the Meera working with very simple tools she realised that it had taken a lot of work and time. What she discovered later was that K'dae had worked on his spear over a very long time. On each occasion when he added to the carving, he had asked the universe to allow him to become a successful hunter. Now, not only had he become a hunter, he had helped to save his friend's life and, in turn his life had been saved by a beautiful Goddess. Whilst eating he had added one more piece of carving as a memory of the event.

Tullia looked up and saw K'dae watching her. She walked over to him. 'It is beautiful. A very precious gift.'

'I am happy you find the gift is worthy of you, Tyua'llia,' he said as he rose to his feet.

Tulia felt a fraud. She had not commanded the kudu to stop. Some energy she did not understand had taken control. If she tried to explain that, she might just as well shout out, 'I'm a hornsfluting, Alien, Goddess!'

An embarrassed fifteen-year-old Tazian reacted as she would at home when words failed over a special gift. She stepped forward and pulled K'dae into a hug, unconsciously filling him with love as she thanked the Multiverse for using her to save his life. And Xashee and me, she added.

Nlai was rigid, hands clenched so tight that even her short nails dug into her palms. She did not need to remember Kou-'ke's words about changing her mind when Tullia made a play for K'dae. The sooner she spoke with Ungka, the better for everyone.

As the fire was put out and everything was being packed, Tullia asked for and was given her share to carry. Two pouches slung crosswise over her shoulders. As she stood up, she grunted at the weight and the discomfort of the straps pressing against her tender breasts.

CHAPTER 74

ALIENS!

FINLAND

With the permission of the Rahkamos, the three youngsters spent Friday decorating the attic bedroom as if it were a theatre stage, turning it into what Qwelby described as a Tribal Home. A shopping trip with Hannu and Anita had acquired long strips of coloured paper that were festooned around the sloping ceiling and walls. With the addition of several holiday souvenirs borrowed from friends, there was a Laplander-African-Native American theme.

Mrs Rahkamo let the youngsters take hot drinks and snacks into the attic to celebrate their achievement. The meal finished, the friends happily linked arms as they walked to Anita's home where her mother was waiting for them.

'I used that old suede skirt I've been meaning to do something with for ages. I didn't have this in mind, but, here you are,' Taimi Keskinen said with a smile. 'Three loinskins. One for each of you boys on the lines of a pair of swimming briefs. And one for you, Anita, exactly as Qwelby told me Tullia was wearing.'

'I'm sorry, Mrs K. I didn't know…' Qwelby said, turning to his friends.

'In for a penni,' Anita said.

'In for a markka,' Hannu finished, as the Finns shared a high five.

'Try them on,' Taimi said. 'And call me when you're ready for inspection!' she added.

'Yes, Mum,' Anita said with a giggle as she headed for her room.

Overwhelmed and rendered speechless, Qwelby followed Hannu upstairs.

A lot later, Anita opened her bedroom door. 'Ready, Mum,' she called, and stepped back to join the boys in a line-up.

Qwelby smiled at the look of surprise on Taimi's face as she opened the door.

The youngsters waited.

'Well, Qwelby, introduce me to your Tazian friends,' Taimi said, trying to look serious as her daughter and Hannu shared a high five.

'Tamina and Wrenden, nickname Eeky, her younger brother,' Qwelby said, emphasising "younger" as Hannu poked out his tongue.

'I don't know how much fake tan you two have used but the blotchy effect makes you look more alien than Qwelby!' Taimi said, laughing. 'You've done a good job on your eyes,' she added as she walked up to her daughter. 'More extreme than Qwelby. Why the bright yellow and green for you, Anita?'

'It helps me think of her as Tamina,' Qwelby explained with a tremor in his voice. 'We've always teased her that she looks like an alien.'

Taimi turned to look at Hannu. 'You all right, Hannu?' she asked the boy who was looking at the floor.

'I feel a bit silly,' Hannu replied as he glanced at Anita's mother then at Qwelby. It had been fun whilst the three were by themselves and he and Anita had been helping each other to apply the fake tan. But with an adult present he suddenly felt childish. Worse, Anita looked sexy and he was afraid her mother would know what he was thinking.

'Qwelby, you need to explain about energy,' Taimi said, carefully not adding "to Hannu" as she knew that her daughter also understood what Qwelby was trying to achieve.

'Yessss,' Qwelby said as his mind raced. 'You know everything we see that is solid, deep down at the sub-atomic level nothing is solid, it's all vibrations, waves, energy?'

His friends nodded.

'Well, Tullia is my colour and now you are. And you remember that day I told you about when Tullia and I saw you from Vertazia, we also saw dark-skinned people dressed like we are now and Tullia visited them. We've found people like them on the internet and we think most likely they are Bushmen in the Kalahari. And the pictures we've found of Bushmen and other dark-skinned people dancing by big fires?'

Again his friends nodded.

'Where Tullia is, all that will make its own special energy. It's a signature, like a mixture of colour and sound.'

'Like playing a chord on a guitar?' suggested Hannu, who liked guitar music.

'Yeah. That's great Hannu,' Qwelby said. 'So to link with Tullia...'

'You want us to try and create the same sort of chord?' Hannu said.

'Exactly,' Qwelby responded. 'By creating the same sort of energy feel. But if we wear our normal clothes, what our eyes will see will be at odds with trying to create that sense of being the same. In technical terms, we would not be coherent.'

'Like a discord!' Hannu said.

Qwelby raised a hand and the boys shared a high five.

Taimi shared a smile with her daughter. She knew how excited Anita was that Hannu was rapidly gaining an understanding of the world of energy and both youngsters enjoyed listening to her husband's explanations of the quantum mechanics that underpinned the whole of creation.

'Qwelby,' Taimi said. 'You have explained to me why you consider that a NullPoint Bubble will be restricted to your people.'

He nodded. That was true. What he was not sure about was whether his friends might be so swept up in the powerful energy of connection, that they might leave their bodies. Taimi had told him that was called Astral Travelling. It sounded the same as travelling in the seventh dimension.

'You need a lot of power to reach Tullia and I understand why you only want Anita and Hannu with you. I feel strongly that Viljo and I should be there, downstairs with Hannu's parents. Sitting quietly, in support.'

'Meditating, you mean, Mum.'

'Yes.'

'Thank you Mrs K,' Qwelby replied, feeling relief that he would be able to call on her energies should he need to help either of his friends. Uncomfortable with the element of deception, he pushed to the back of his mind the thought that he ought to explain his concern about his friends travelling Out-Of-Body.

'Are you all right, Qwelby?' Taimi asked, wondering about the tremor in his voice she had noted earlier.

'Yes, thank you. It's Anita, reminding me of Tamina. It's confusing. I think I like her. Tamina, I mean. I'm too young. I mean those hormones aren't supposed to be active for almost two years.' The thought that he had started to like Tamina in a different way from the time she had danced for him on his fifteenth rebirthday was confusing.

Worse, was the fact that he was having new and strange feelings seeing Anita wearing the little loinskin. He was used to seeing girls naked at home: swimming, saunas, sun-bathing and moon-bathing. In Finland he had shared saunas with boys and girls. Yet now his feeling made him uncomfortable. He ached for Tullia. She was the only person he could talk with.

CHAPTER 15

SAGA TIME

THE KALAHARI

As Tullia and the women unloaded back at the village, she saw Xara walk up to an old man and show him the arrow he had shot into the kudu. She realised that he must be the man who had made the arrow. It was he who would decide to whom the best parts were to be given. Then the tribe would share the rest.

Every muscle in her body not just ached, but was sending her brain fierce messages of pain, and there were muscles she swore she never had on Vertazia. She was covered in sweat and sand and knew she must stink. She wanted water and needed to wash but she was too exhausted to do anything other than stagger into her hut and collapse. But she was happy.

When they had been ready to set off for home, Xara had asked her what direction to take. She'd indicated and explained the first marker to be used. 'Yesterday follow. Today lead,' he'd said. And she'd done that. Xara had quickly dropped out of sight, making it clear she was in charge. Leading from the front she'd set a steady pace calculated to arrive comfortably before dark and decided on the timing of the short breaks. Although being a leader went against her Tazian upbringing, it had all been so natural. 'After all,' she murmured. 'It is in my genes. The Unicorn Kèhša was a leader.'

Well wrapped against the cold weather, Tu was sitting outside her hut enjoying the little warmth there was in the afternoon sun when the sounds of the returning hunting party reached her. Tonight there would be feasting in the old way, a celebration and a saga to be related. She recalled that !Gei-!Ku'ma was with the hunting party. Two days trekking through the bush.....

Tu went into the hut and picked up her bag with its various jars of oils and unguents, all prepared by herself from the plants of the bush. In spite of her advanced age her hands had lost none of their skills.

Reaching Tullia's hut she paused for a moment to marvel at the largest dragonfly she had ever seen, perched just above the entrance with its green tipped, bright red wings reflecting the sun.

Flopped on her bed, Tullia saw Tsetsana appear with a mug of water in one hand and cloths in the other. Groaning, Tullia let herself be helped to sit up and was told to take little sips as, despite a feeble protest, her friend started to clean her, using the water in the washing bowl by the entrance.

'You will be saga telling tonight,' Tsetsana said, excited at the prospect as Tullia's portrayal of her capture had been so evocative.

Tullia groaned. 'How long?' she asked, hoping that if she sounded pitiful, Nlai might take her part again.

'Plenty of time for you to recover,' a reassuring voice said from the entrance. 'May I?'

Tullia looked up at an amazingly wrinkled face which carried an air of serenity and a similarity to her own mother's energy of child caring, house running and overall a sense of plants and gardening. 'Please,' Tullia replied.

'I am Tu,' the old woman said. 'Will you allow me to ease your body?'

'Thank you, Tu. Please. I need it.' Tullia said as the woman knelt alongside and started to remove jars of varying shapes and sizes from the bag she was carrying.

As soon as Tsetsana had finished washing and drying an embarrassed Tullia, Tu gave her a small cup. 'Little sips,' the healer said. 'It is bitter. Honey to follow.' She then commenced to apply soft oils and gently massage them into Tullia's legs. 'You have beautiful skin. I have never felt anything like it.'

The drink and honey finished, Tullia was asked to lie face down whilst Tu continued with the massage. Tullia drifted into a meditation. She saw an image of herself, the trillions of cells in her body sparkling. She knew that more of her DNA was becoming active and that everything she'd experienced since arriving on Earth was contributing to her growth and she was going to need all of her learning when back on Vertazia.

'You must be a great healer,' Tu said. 'I have never felt a body so aware of its needs. And directing me where and how to work. !Gei-!Ku'ma, I am privileged,' she added as she rested her hands on the top and bottom of Tullia's spine.

Tullia opened her mouth to reply, gave a great sigh and fell asleep as Tu smiled.

Tullia awoke several hours later and moved carefully, feeling her body. Yes, it ached and was stiff, but nothing like it had been. Carefully, she got off the pile of blankets that was her bed, splashed cold water on her face, dressed and went to talk with Xai-Xai, the tribe's leading saga teller.

After their discussion, it was with a frisson of pleasure that Tullia felt certain she knew how to do what she wanted. She spoke first with Kotuma, who then went and spoke to Xara, before joining what she thought of as her family as they made their way to the big communal fire and the feast.

When the flames had died down to glowing embers, feeling

nervous and excited as if for a LiveShow, Tullia assembled with the others from the hunting party.

With Xai-Xai's approval and permission to "whisper sing in Tazian" as she had unintentionally done for her previous portrayal, Tullia overacted a lot. It was not long before laughter was ringing all around, tinged with appreciation as their Goddess mimed just how superior the Meera were to her abilities in the bush. Many glanced at Xara who was smiling and shaking his head.

By the time it came to the death of the kudu, the only sound was the gentle crackling of the glowing embers.

Accessing her memory, Tullia saw that when she had pointed her fingers at the charging animal's head there had been power in the words themselves. "Desist shalt thou." The energy inherent in living, multidimensional Aurigan. Not the Reduced Aurigan built into her compiler! Her memory stored that as another clue to The Mystery. Acting without thinking had let her step totally into her power. A power so strong that she had mindblasted the kudu into stopping its charge.

Tullia was pulled back to the saga as the anointing was portrayed. Although this time there was no blood and no words were spoken, she found it as powerful as at the hunt.

When the re-enactment finished, Xara stayed the group with a gesture as Ghadi stepped around the fire. The tribe's leader was carrying Tullia's spear which he gave to her, then took her hand holding it and raised them on high.

'This is the spear with which Tyua'llia killed the kudu. It was presented to her by K'dae. Last night the hunters honoured her as a trrrue bushman and a hunter. I ask you all. Will you accept this young woman as one of us. A Meerrra. A trrrue bushman and a hunter?'

The response was a round of murmurs and nods followed by loud applause, shouts and ululating.

Milake and Deena, parents of Xashee and Tsetsana, stood up.

They gestured to their children to stand. Milake said shyly: 'We offer family.'

Tullia was overcome with emotion and burst into tears, which she was still trying to stem when the two youngest members of her new family rushed up and grabbed hold of her, calling out: 'Tyua'llia! Tyua'llia!'

When seven-year-old Nthabe held Tullia's forearms and told her in a very serious tone of voice, 'We've got a Goddess for a sister,' Tullia could not help but laugh, kneel down and give both of them a big hug. She never cared what the young children called her. Whether it was by her name, Daughter or Goddess because, to them, they were just names and they treated her as one of them.

'Why you cry Tyua'llia?' asked four-year-old Tomku.

'Because I am happy. On my world we cry when we are sad and we cry when we are happy. Girls and boys, women and men.'

Tomku nodded very seriously, wiped some of the tears from Tullia's cheeks with a finger and carefully examined them.

Tullia looked up into a ring of faces. I am a Bushman. A hunter. A member of the Meera tribe. If they want to call me Goddess, who cares! If I have to live here for ever, as long as I can have Qwelby with me, I will do so. And be happy. She grinned. A big ear-splitting grin. The children giggled. She knew it was because with her wide mouth, she looked so funny to them. She threw back her head and laughed. The sound of soaring violins and clarinets swept across the village. Then as she made her first attempt at ululating, the women joined in whilst the men laughed.

Ghadi signalled to the women who started clapping and chanting and the members of the hunting party started dancing.

CHAPTER 76

ÔWEPPÂ

VERTAZIA

It was evening on the second day after Tamina and Wrenden had travelled to Earth. Although their parents eventually had to accept what they had done to link themselves to Curious Shop and the fact that that could not be changed, the atmosphere at home was bad. Yarannah, their mother, was so beside herself that she had actually said she wanted them out of her sight. Although equally angry, Jailandur was secretly proud of his son's courage and the strength of the esting relationship.

Whilst Uddîšû genes were normally inherited along either the male or female line, he was worried that his daughter might possess hidden genes of the Explorer and that the combination with those she had inherited from her mother would make Tamina's life even more difficult. Nevertheless, he could only admire her courage. After deep discussion with the twins' family and Mizena's promise to ensure the children studied hard, he had agree that the best place for his children for the time being was at Lungunu.

After a hard days' work, the four friends had eaten and changed into relax robes for a quiet evening in their XOÑOX suite.

HWAdventures no longer were exciting. Finally, they gave up trying to play games and got into yet another deep discussion, this time talking over their frustration at being banned by their parents from again entering the StroemCavern to try and reach the twins.

Lellia had explained to them how the Stroems had saved Wrenden on that tragic day when Qwelby was lost. When Wrenden had slipped over the edge of the gallery followed by Tamina still holding his legs, Tamina had been saved by Mandara's time-shifted command to the safety net, but Wrenden had already fallen below that. The Stroems had taken him out of time and returned him a few moments later, which was why he was seen lying on top of his sister as the platform had come into view.

A few days after that, Pelnak and Shimara had summoned up the courage to seek permission from Lellia to visit the Stroems, to thank them for what they had done. Permission granted, Lellia had watched as they stood on the balcony inside the Cavern, looking down on the Stroems Xzyling below them. Talking together in trembling voices, the two youngsters recited their prepared speech of thanks.

The Stroems had stopped their frightening, multi-coloured Xzyling and changed to a gentle swirling in a variety of shades of blues, aquas and turquoises: the not-twins own colours. The snouts of beautiful sea creatures had appeared and a piping sound had echoed all around carrying the one word: "StroemFriends". Then the Stroems had formed themselves into what looked like a majestic whale before disappearing with a mighty splash.

The friends were arguing that surely it must be possible to use that status to circumvent the ban. Whilst listening, Pelnak had been running his fingers through a virtual, four dimensional control board. 'Ahhh,' he sighed as he leant back in his chair which reclined and sent out pseudofingers to massage his tired brain.

He smiled in response to three pairs of raised eyebrows. 'I

think that the sixth dimension energies that Uncle Gumma says are invoked by Óweppâ means that it is existentially temporally dislocating.'

'Not here all the time, you mean,' Shimara said.

'Something like that,' Pelnak said as he tried and failed to thoughtsend an image not so much of what the Talisman did, but what he thought it was.

'And when it's not here?' Wrenden asked.

Pelnak shrugged. 'Anywhere.'

'So why haven't we found Tullia?' Tamina asked, thoughtsharing her frustration.

'We've just been assuming that we can link with the twins through it. I think we need to direct its energies where we want to go,' Pelnak answered, thoughtsending: *What do you think?*

'The purple sphere that we know is Tullia,' Tamina said.

'That we found on that first journey when we nearly lost our lives,' Shimara added.

'And you saved us Sis,' Wrenden said.

'No.' Tamina shook her head. 'It was Shimara and Pelnak who saved us by holding all four of us together.' She licked her lips. When the twins had disappeared, it had been her turn to look after the Talisman. Moving between home and Lungunu, she had taken to keeping it in a pocket of whatever she was wearing. Now, she took it out and placed it on the floor.

All four slid onto the floor on their knees, reached out hands and formed a double quaternion. *Tullia. The purple sphere,* they thoughtshared as they recalled the images they had seen of brightly attired people sitting around a large fire with nearly naked, dark-skinned men dancing. Then Tamina dancing in the fire in her Attribute of a Salamander.

CHAPTER 77

KALAHARI

MOTHER GODDESS

Tullia was so happily lost in the dancing that she thought of Tamina. More than thought. Imaged her presence, her joy at the new rhythms, the sensations, the energies. Pictured her BestFriend revelling in the new movements she would create. Every cell in her body tingled as a great column of light sprang from the heavens and a gasp ran around the fire. Looking up, she saw the reason for the Meera's amazement. Descending along the beam, right into the centre of the fire was a long column of dancing flames.

'Taminaaaaa!' Tullia cried with joy as the flames resolved themselves into what had to be her BestFriend. Who else would arrive as a three metre tall cross between flickering flames and a multitude of salamanders. Slowly Tamina's features emerged: her exotic face split from ear to ear by her smile and hair reaching down to her thighs.

Stepping forward to greet her friend, Tullia felt hands grasp her waist as Tsetsana held her back. Before she could brush the hands away, Tamina stepped forward, leant down and kissed Tullia. The strangest kiss Tullia had ever experienced. No sense of firm, solid lips pressed against hers, but a feeling like the beating wings of hot butterflies. She heard another gasp from the Meera and their mutterings.

'Truly, the kiss of a mother to her daughter.' 'Tyua'llia's own mother.' 'The Goddess Nananana come to bless one of her daughters?' There was no tradition of Her as a Goddess of Fire. The Meera were beyond caring. Tullia might look like a Siska, but they had welcomed her into their hearts as the Daughter of the Sun Goddess. And this was absolute confirmation.

'The very Sun Goddess herself,' was the conclusion that was murmured around in awe.

Tullia was in a total whirl. She knew that Tamina, or rather what appeared to be a multitude of leaping salamanders with Tamina's face, had to be in the seventh if not eighth dimension. But she could not reach out to her. She had to dance, her awareness stretching out to embrace the whole tribe. Energies were there, watching, but should be dancing with her. A thought, a simple request that was heard as a command from their Goddess, and Tsetsana, Nlai, N!Obile and Mandingwe ran to their huts and returned to join the dancing, wearing their loinskins and necklaces.

Xai-Xai arrived with a pair of ankle seed pods. With a nod of agreement from Ghadi he knelt and strapped them onto Tullia's legs. As Tullia twirled away, Tamina danced right though him. Xai-Xai remained transfixed with his mouth wide open and eyes as large as saucers. Hands reached out and pulled him away from the dancers.

Everyone had been caught up in Tullia's rhythm: the dancers and the women with their chanting and hand clapping. A few youths who were never able to explain why, created what was to become a new tradition for the tribe by grabbing thin branches and beating out rhythm on the big tree trunks that lined the area.

The shadows flickering across the assembly, the varying rhythms of clapping, drumming, chanting and the rattling of shells around the ankles of the dancers, all wove a hypnotic trance around the multitude. Xameb felt the very energies of the land being invoked. It was the most powerful mixture of his long life.

Tullia felt herself suspended between worlds, between dimensions. Tamina was here and that meant that the other three had to be around. Could she link with her BestFriend? Between them could they use the power of the eighth dimension to take her to Qwelby? Even take them back home?

She closed her eyes, reached out to her twin and chanted in Tazian.

'Qwelby, Qwelby,
'SoulMate, Twin,
'I reach for you,
'You reach for me.
'Great Multiverse,
'Through this night
'Fire and Earth,
'Bind us tight.
'We are two,
'We are one,
'Always together,
'Never apart!
'KAIGIIII,' Tullia's beseeching cry echoed all around.

CHAPTER 78

SHUFFLEDANCE

FINLAND

Having modelled for Taimi Keskinen the costumes she had made, the youngsters pulled their clothes on and a few minutes later were back at the Rahkamos' house. They left their ordinary clothes in Hannu's room and set the finishing touches to the attic room. They put several logs side by side in the middle of the floor, placed a baking tray on top, and then lit a dozen stubby candles to represent a big fire.

That done, Anita produced the face paints. Hannu was quick to take them and paint streaks on her forehead and cheeks. Then the two boys painted each other.

Qwelby asked Anita for the small piece of liver they had bought earlier, asking the butcher for some blood with it. He ran it down both sides of his chest and then across his lips.

'I had to do that. Ever since yesterday afternoon an impulse to have blood there has been getting stronger and stronger.' He shook his head to forestall questions. 'It's Kaigii. But I don't know why.'

'Okay. Remember plan,' he continued. 'Hannu's gateway.' He pointed to where it was standing under the window in the sloping roof. 'Through that Hannu links with Eeky and Anita links with Tamina. Anita guides us to middle of Africa. When I feel close, I signal. Music loud and we dance, shuffle, around fire. I hold the little Zulu spear. Try to be like the man we saw.' He took a deep breath. 'Be with Kaigii.'

Anita set softly playing the music that all three had agreed had the feel they wanted for their own dancing and started the guided meditation. Having explored the journey twice using the internet, she confidently led them across Europe, over the Pyrenees, the Mediterranean, the Atlas Mountains, the great wastes of the Sahara, on and on across the great jungles of Central Africa and to the red sands of the Namib Desert.

Qwelby glanced at Anita. Her eyes were closed. He wanted to ask her to guide them to the left but did not want to break the strong atmosphere that had built up.

'We dance,' he said softly.

'Sinnelaahii,' he added, holding the initially high pitched 'hii' as a long whisper in declining pitch as he rose and slowly turned up the music to floor shaking loud.

They started their shuffledance around the fire. Qwelby had told them that it was "feel" he wanted for the whole journey experience. It didn't matter if they felt like Zulus or Australian Aborigines or danced and whooped like Native Americans, as long as they were open to whatever came. He had been sure that Tullia was amongst the Bushmen. Now he knew she was in the Kalahari.

Hannu was delighted to be given his special part to play. He had brought back from a holiday in Lapland a small Lappituote, a replica of an ancient shaman's drum. Qwelby had seen the symbols in the centre as representing himself and Tullia parted, then coming together as two and then merging into one. As he shuffled around, he was beating on the centre of the drum imagining that he was bringing the twins together and thinking strongly of seeing Tullia again.

Qwelby started chanting.

'We are one. We are two. Always together. Never apart.'

After a few minutes all three were chanting. Then he switched to Tazian, speaking slowly and clearly and mentaplanting his friends until their brains had learnt the words.

'Thallaahii llanghaany. Thallaahii rulakaa. Isisy kanyeymy. Bangana nuntwey.'

Wary from the vicious fight on New Year's Eve when he and Tullia had come so close to reuniting, Qwelby was focussing all his concentration only on locating her whereabouts. He was certain that she was not on Haven, or Mars as the Azurii called it, but on Earth. All he wanted was to know her location. His plan was to avoid confrontation with the evil forces by then making his way to her using ordinary Azuran transport.

At the same time and in the back of his mind was the memory of how, with the aid of their four BestFriends, he and Tullia had been teleported out of the stairwell into a NullPoint. The quantum world underpinned the whole of reality so, surely, that should work between dimensions just the same?

CHAPTER 19

LOVE THWARTED

VERTAZIA   THE KALAHARI

It was evening and Xaala had enjoyed a relaxing bath. The neutron shower was all right for efficiency but there was nothing as relaxing as the music of the colours of the water swirling around her body. The LivingTowel gently massaging her skin dry as it added nourishing oils was the perfect finish.

Tullia! The energy spike was strong. Sending an urgent thought to Ceegren, she stepped into her DarkSuit and settled cross-legged on her meditation bench as the pseudoleather fitted itself to her Form. As she centred, she felt herself swept into the girl's heartfelt appeal for a connection with her twin. Xaala had to act fast.

She projected her InForming Matrix into the seventh dimension and allowed the energy spike to guide her to its source. With the precision of the years of training from Ceegren, she halted her journey outside a NullPoint and several metres above and away from Tullia.

Shock, horror! There was a flaming salamander dancing by Tullia. Not Azuran solid. Seventh dimension. Tamina? Now appearing as a fully fledged Fire Lady? No wonder the fire and the dancers were being warped into such a large NullPoint. Xaala's memory sent images flickering into her mind of dust devils, a pyramid, something she did not recognise and herself in a beautiful dress carrying a weapon.

The scene behind Image that day had been unclear. It had been difficult to make out through the blowing dust the details of moving people and buildings. Here, the moving energies and the almost naked dancers with their dark brown bodies against the dark sand explained why that part of the scene had been difficult to determine. Glancing to the side, she just made out a distorted picture of a wall and peeking over the top of it, very far away, what she saw as the tops of two dark pyramids.

Reconciling that earlier day's scene in Mirror with what she was now seeing took place in an instant. Given the space-time instability of a NullPoint Xaala decided that she did not need any weapon. She would physically embrace Tullia, disrupt the abomination's focus and energy flow and thus destabilise the Bubble before Qwelby arrived.

Automatically mentaforming clothing to match Tullia's, Xaala slipped through the event boundary.

Qwelby felt the momentary dislocation of a singularity telling him he was entering a Bubble. Arriving on deep sandy a soil a distance away from a fire, his heart soared as he heard a cry of 'Kaigii!' and saw his twin across the flickering flames. All his researches had been correct and his whole plan of reaching his twin without alerting the Kumelanii had worked. Energies flowed around and through him: joy, celebration and above all – Kaïgïi!

Stepping forward he was stopped as a tall, slim native dropped down. A head taller than himself she wrapped her arms around him and pressed against him. Heat coursed through him and he put an arm around her. His mind was racing as he recognised Tazian energies. Staring into her eyes he realised knew her. How? She had information for him. As he scanned his memory, feelings never before experienced in such intensity rippled through him and a sharp pain in his loins caused him to spasm.

Wondering if Tullia had changed dramatically in this dimension, he swung his head back towards where he had first seen her. She was still there. And with..... Tamina?! Intending to push the clinging girl away, he put his left arm on her shoulder as she lifted her right leg and wrapped it around his thigh, pulling them tightly together. Another stab of pain shot through him. He felt dizzy as he was deluged with information.

His memory downloaded data from college seminars. No, it could not be that! His Awakening was a clear eighteen months away. As more DNA sequences activated he was shaken by what once again appeared to be real memories of life on Auriga, offering him a startling insight into the nature of Quantum Twins. He rapidly shunted that message into a corner of his mind. It was far too disturbing to consider when he needed to join with.... Kaigii. Being on Earth, the Tazian word provided a clarity and focus essential to his purpose.

Through a hazy mist of confused thoughts he saw Kaigii about to walk straight into the flames, with the cute face of a young girl peering around his twin's waist as she struggled to stop her.

Standing out clearly against the background of a colourful crowd of people were the Tazian-like energy fields of the almost naked dancers, all staring at him and at what his inner senses told him they could see behind him: Hannu and Anita outside the NullPoint in the tent-like room.

Time slowed as a sound like a short, staccato burst of heavy hail shut out all other noise. Three slender figures appeared to drop from the sky. Three metres tall and clad from head to toe in deepest black spangled with hundreds of tiny points of light they looked like creatures made of space itself. Their hair appeared to consist of scores of metre long, wriggling snakes. Through their masks he could just see the outlines of V-shaped pairs of Aurigan eyes. Six long fingers of each hand gripped the edges of round, silver coloured shields. Šèdûmaii!

They had fought alongside him during the centuries of the Space Wars, some eighty thousand years ago. Their covering was to render them invisible. Their apparent hair: helmets with writhing tubes sucking in life-supporting stellar energy. He did not understand what they were doing here, blocking the path to his twin. Sensing danger, he tightened his grip on the girl and angrily thoughtsent energy to push apart two of the Figures, only to be flung onto his back and sent sliding across the sand with the girl on top of him.

In his confused state, trying to absorb so much data on several levels, it had slipped his awareness that what he had seen as the Šèdûmaii's shields actually were concave mirrors. Their task had been far more dangerous than his as a DragonRider. They would watch for the energy beams projected by the attacking spaceships, then time-and-spaceshift so as to be in a position to reflect those beams back to the attackers. It required incredible precision and the LifeLines of many warriors had been terminated.

Qwelby tried to pull his thoughts back to the present and clear his head. The girl's arms were wrapped around his shoulders with her head pressed tight against his. He felt her fear and need for reassurance. Warm stirrings flowed through him. They were new. And nice. They eased the place where the pain had stabbed.

He felt her sliding down his body. But they were on flat ground. He raised his head to see her face lifted towards him wearing a look of panic and something else. It was as though a second pair of eyes was looking at him through hers with a faintly sardonic smile. Her desperation to remain was so strong as her hands grasped his hips and momentarily stopped her slide that he stretched a hand towards her. Their fingers met but their grip was immediately torn apart.

Who is she? How do I know her? And what am I trying to

save her from? Her smile had gone to be replaced by a mixture of panic and longing. Confusion and sadness filled him as he watched her hands slide down his legs. He remained frozen as she was lifted into the air and over the heads of the Šèdûmaii as if sliding backwards up an invisible slope. There was a brief flicker of the singularity as she passed through the event boundary.

As the three Šèdûmaii closed on him, the Dragon's claws dug into the ground and Qwelby rose up on thighs like tree trunks, spreading his wings. He would force his way past what had once been his comrades-in-arms. Tullia was there, stretching out her arms to him. They would be reunited!

He swung to the left, his arm slashing out at the Šèdûma in his way, hurling the warrior to the ground. He disappeared. A pace forward and his right arm swept aside the nearer Šèdûma, sending him crashing into the third warrior. Both disappeared.

He looked across to the fire. He had never seen Kaigii like this before. With her energy field powerfully excited, the flickering firelight reflecting off her sweat-soaked skin had turned her into an incomparable Uddîsû of copper fire. She was him. He was her. They would be one.

'ÎSÎSŸ KÂNŸEYMŸ ÂHÏÏ.'

The Meera felt the ground tremble from the roar of what they knew must be the Sun God Lord Kaigii.

'KAÏGÏÏ.'

With its complex overtones, the cry of their Goddess pierced their hearts with its joy.

'Thâllaaîî llânghâââñy. Thâllaaîî rûlâkaa. Îsîsÿ kânÿeymÿ. Bâñgâna nûñtweÿ. KÂÂBÏLÏÏ.'

The twins' voices sounding like choirs singing was cut short by an immense thunderclap from the clear sky and what seemed like the very Milky Way itself descending as many more Šèdûmaii arrived.

An impossibly bright moonbeam pierced the scene. Glancing

to his right Qwelby saw another figure had arrived. Clad in a tight fitting, brown one-piece with a green dodecagon blazing on his chest it had to be... Yes. Through the blue helmet he saw Wrenden's sparkling eyes. Adventurer, Explorer, Trickster. As the epithets for his youngerest's Uddîšû came to mind, Qwelby found himself unable to remonstrate with him for putting himself in so much danger.

Wrenden was armed and there was a battle to be fought. Joining the twelve sides together inside Wrenden's polygon Qwelby saw a flower with four petals. Pelnak and Shimara were in support.

Turning back to confront the Šèdûmaii, Qwelby was frustrated at being unable to swamp them with DragonFire, knowing the energy would be hurled back at him. Thoughtsending to Wrenden about the Šèdûmaii and their "shields", he strode forth into battle, heartened by the fact that all six were together. XOÑOX!

A Winged Unicorn leapt across the fire, leaving Tsetsana collapsed under the weight of Tullia's inert body.

Tullia reared up on her hind legs, whinnying and fluting her horn in a battle cry. She crashed her forelegs down on the shields of two Šèdûmaii, smashing them into their bodies and seeing the warriors disappear.

She tossed her head, pawed the ground and readied herself to leap forward and pierce the next warrior with her horn. And stopped. Frozen in place. As the images of the two warriors and their shields had disappeared, there had been a microsecond during which she had seen the InForming Matrices of two men before they also disappeared.

The Šèdûmaii were not the same as the energy constructs she had fought in the battle seven days ago, but the mental projects of Tazii. Were she to kill a warrior, she would be killing a Tazian.

The shock and horror of that prospect robbed Tullia of her desire to embody her Attribute. The Unicorn vanished and she remained in her own InForming Matrix.

She was full of admiration for her twin as the dragon fought on and behind him, Wrenden. Both were striking rapidly and repeatedly at the Šèdûmaii and their mirror-shields, keeping them off balance and unable to use their mirrors to return the energies. Every now and then a warrior vanished.

Tullia sighed with relief as she realised that the Tazii were not necessarily being hurt badly. For a race that knew no violence, being struck was enough to shock any Tazian out of focus and to cause these men and women to lose their projection into the seventh dimension.

She must help. Pulling herself erect she put her arms down by her sides with the palms of her hands facing the ground. Drawing up the power of the land itself, she added that to the great stream of energy that was reaching her from her tribe and sent all that flowing into her twin.

She felt and saw a great stream of love pouring around and past her and on into the dragon. Tamina loves Kaigii? That much!

A corner of Tullia's mind smiled at what she saw as a daft idea.

Some of the warriors' mirrors flickered with rainbows as they returned the love.

Ahhhh! The answer. Tullia switched her focus from sending energy, to sending love. Towering high over her, she saw the dragon smile as he saw what was happening and poured out all his love.

For a blissful moment there was peace and serenity. Qwelby stepped towards his twin, reached out his left hand and took hold of her right hand.

A moment later a large shield appeared on the dragon's right arm. Just in time as black flames sprang from the mirrors, hammering on the shield with some bursting past and hurling Tullia onto her back.

Behind the dragon Tullia saw Wrenden engulfed by black

fire and gave an anguished cry as he discharged his weapon at the nearest warrior. A brief flash of light showed his passage as he was hurled backwards out through the event boundary.

Scrambling to her feet, Tullia glanced back across the fire and saw Xashee and H'ani kneeling alongside her Form which was cradled in Tsetsana's arms, the girl's eyes wide with amazement.

Tullia stood up and resumed her erect stance, again channelling all her power to her twin.

The dragon was slowly forcing the Šèdûmaii back. Each time black flames burst around the shield, Qwelby burnt them away with his dragonfire. Inexorably, he continued to advance until the Šèdûmaii halted as though pressed up against a solid wall. Nothing could be seen behind them. It was pure Dark Matter, an energy so black its presence was only known because there was nothing to be seen. No village. No bush. No stars.

As more Šèdûmaii appeared, the force of the Dark Matter flames pounding on Qwelby's shield was starting to push him back. Carried on Tullia's signature, a vast amount of energy continued to pour into him through the ground. But his legs were weakening.

More energy flowed into him through his root chakra and up into his very Kore. Alight with Tamina's signature, it provoked more unaccustomed stirrings. He sensed.... No. He must not divert one microjoule of energy away from his aim of forcing the Šèdûmaii back through the event boundary.

He was weakening, his legs trembling, lungs aching, throat burning. Worse, his shield was flickering. The seventh dimension protection was breaking down. He was having to pour ever more energy into his bursts of flame to destroy the black fire now creeping all around his shield.

Memories he had tried to lock away burst through into his consciousness. Although appalled at the thoughts in his mind, he had no choice. They had to be reunited. They were one. But. There must be another way! He surrendered to the memories of a deep and ancient love and the power they brought of QeïchâKaïgïï.

With a leap and a great down thrust of his wings, Qwelby soared into the air and flew over the warriors, broadcasting that love through the event boundary to where there had to be other Tazii organising the attacks. He heard a terrible scream and knew it was from the girl he had tried to save.

Hurt by love! How could that be?

Momentarily distracted as he recalled his feelings as he had held her in his arms, he failed to notice the Šèdûmaii moving. Now, great billowing flames of bright fire blasted into him from both sides and below.

A mighty thunderclap and he was hurled backwards.

'KAÏGÏÏÏÏÏÏ......'

CHAPTER 80

AWAKENING

FINLAND

Qwelby felt the brief dislocation of the singularity. Fifty trillion cells in his body and every one was burning hot. And the Šèdûmaii. Those had not been his companions of old. The real Šèdûmaii had been true Aurigan warriors and their only weapon a reflecting mirror. To hurl flames at him when he was sending out love – a pure love he had never felt before – that meant those figures had been imposters. Evil. Tazii! Custodians?

He landed on his back, slid and crashed his head against something hard and unyielding.

'You're bleeding!'

Hannu's words penetrated Qwelby's disorientation. He lifted his head and pushed himself back up against the bedroom wall. One of the ties at the side of his loinskin had come undone and it had slid down his thighs. There was blood. And to Qwelby the all too obvious reason for the stabbing pains.

'I'll get a cloth, and err...' Anita said in an embarrassed tone as she turned and left the attic room.

'Anita. No. Please. She stay away,' Qwelby said in a weak voice to Hannu, waving in the direction she had gone. As Hannu went to the entry in the floor, anxious voices were calling out as the two sets of parents reached the foot of the loft ladder.

'It's all right. Qwelby fell over. It's only a little cut,' Hannu assured them, knowing that was nothing like the truth. He knelt down and shook his head at Anita as he reached for the flannel and towel she was holding. He saw her nod her understanding, still blushing, and disappear back down the ladder.

Hannu remained on his hands and knees as he returned the short distance to his friend.

Qwelby was in pain. A gut wrenching sense of loss. So close. All six together, yet once again separated. Eyes closed, he thought himself back to experiencing the river of sensation that had flowed as they had held hands. He needed her. Tullia needed him. He was her. They were one.

Hannu knelt by Qwelby and put a hand on his shoulder, was pulled on top of his alien friend and kissed - by Tullia. As the arms around him slackened their grip, Hannu leant back looking at the body before him. Now very definitely that of a young man. Hannu was well aware that what had been pressing against his bare chest had been a woman's breasts. He had opened his eyes and seen Tullia's face. The face he had seen on New Year's Eve, subtly different from Qwelby's.

Qwelby jerked with another spasm and rolled onto his hands and knees, freeing himself from his loinskin. 'Help me,' he said, injecting urgency into a soft voice. 'What told you. Next stage happening.' He gripped Hannu's shoulders and groaned.

Hannu remembered the conversation the first time they had shared a sauna when he had advised Qwelby always to cover up with a towel and plead modesty, or better still a religious command not to expose his alien difference.

Qwelby was aware that he must be hurting his friend as he strained with the next part of the totally unexpected development that life was imposing on him. He gritted his teeth and tried his best to stifle his groans.

'Please, Dad. Stay away. He's all right..... just shocked.' Hannu called out through gritted teeth in response to concerned questions.

With a final strain, gripping his friend even harder and a long drawn-out groan, echoed by Hannu, Qwelby relaxed, slid down onto his side and rolled onto his back.

Hannu took a deep breath and rubbed his bruised shoulders before passing his alien friend the flannel and towel. He watched in amazement as Qwelby cleaned himself and peeled away from the new parts of his body what appeared to be a thick and sticky sort of cling film, dropping it onto the towel where he examined it.

Hannu had found it difficult to believe Qwelby's explanation of how Tazian boys developed. Having seen him looking more like a muscular girl, he now saw a very definite, human-looking male lying on the floor. His friend's face had gone pale and he looked tired. 'You need energy,' Hannu said as he held out a hand

Qwelby took the proffered hand in both of his and smiled faintly. 'Not much difference now,' he said.

Hannu could not help continuing to stare, still absorbing what had happened. Through his hand he felt his friend's energies. For Hannu it was natural for men and boys to embrace as a form of greeting, but kneeling there holding Qwelby's hand for so long and with feelings flowing between them that was..... all right. It was..... special.

Hannu sensed he had been present at something that was very personal and private. He was very pleased that, even as a stand-in for Tullia, Anita had been excluded. It was as though he had just witnessed a form of birth, and as a result he was being offered a very privileged bonding – with an alien! He put his free hand on top of his friend's two and nodded, not daring to speak in case he was living in a fantasy world and Qwelby just needed to be comforted.

Qwelby was totally drained and aware of Hannu's feelings and thoughts with greater clarity than ever before. He filed that connection away for later analysis. 'Takawena umhlabamiti. Welcome to my world. Taziaannu.'

Hannu grinned at his new and special nickname.

'Cold,' Qwelby said.

Reluctant to lose the sensation of being in an alien world, Hannu forced himself to pull his hands away from Qwelby's, turned, pulled the duvet off the bed and wrapped it around his friend.

Qwelby smiled and rolled onto his side as Hannu slipped a pillow under his head. As he relaxed, he recalled Wrenden shouting a few words. He had not taken them in at the time. Images appeared. A sort of spaceship. The Globe and something called an EyeBox. Satisfied that whatever they meant, they were stored in his memory, he fell asleep with a smile on his face.

CHAPTER 81

APPRENTICE

THE KALAHARI

Tullia was distraught. Once again so close. And with Tamina and Wrenden present that had to mean that Pelnak and Shimara had been in support. All six together. XOÑOX!

Several pairs of hands helped Tullia to stand and she embraced Tsetsana. As she relaxed her grip and stepped back a strange mix of sensations flowed through her as she watched pinks, greens, red and flaming oranges sweep through her friend's aura.

'The Sun God. The Lord Kaigii,' Tsetsana whispered, her eyes shining.

An ancient understanding tickled Tullia's mind. Unable to help it, she threw back her head and laughed. Tsetsana is in love with Kaigii! A rich sound of clarinets, oboes and saxophones rang around the amazed Meera. Tullia bent over and once again kissed Tsetsana in the centre of her forehead just above her eyes.

A sigh ran around the Meera as they saw one of their own having a blessing from the very Mother Sun Goddess herself passed on to her. Tsetsana shuddered and gripped Tullia's arms as she felt energies and understanding flooding into her, revealing with startling clarity the images she had half seen, of what she now knew to have been a massive dragon, a beautiful, winged unicorn and a frightening battle.

Kaigii! She needed him! Tullia looked up and saw love and concern in dark brown eyes. She grabbed her twin and kissed him. A hard, demanding kiss. QeïchâKaïgïï. They were one. Stepping back, panting, Tullia saw – H'ani! How many tribal taboos had she broken?!

A sigh went around the tribe. They understood. For a few moments Tullia's pain had been so intense that everyone had felt it and some of the young children had started crying. That had been no lovers' kiss. Their Tyua'llia had been in need. She had marked H'ani at the Melon Dance and had satisfied that need in what they assumed was the way of her people. No one doubted that H'ani was content to serve.

Needing to dispel the terrible sense of loss and hide her embarrassment at what she had done, Tullia started stamping her feet to draw her fully back into her Form. How did she know that Tsetsana loved her twin? How was it that the love she felt from Tamina she had also seen pouring into – and accepted by – her twin? The intensity of the feelings aroused in both of them as she and Kaigii had held hands. The feelings from H'ani and K'dae that had flooded into her. Her responses. What was all that about? Far too much to deal with.

Ghadi had signalled. Women had started clapping and chanting and once more Tullia was swept into the celebrations as the hunting party started dancing.

Soon, most of the men had joined the dancing whilst most of the women continued chanting and clapping. Caught up by the unusual and powerful energies of the night, several of the oldest men found themselves picking up the sticks and following the new tradition of tree drumming.

As the night wore on, fatigue overtook dancers, drummers

and chanters. Eventually, with everyone spread supine across the clearing, all that could be heard was heavy breathing, pierced by the occasional piping call of a lapwing. Ghadi gestured to his wife and together they started moving amongst the Meera, who in ones and twos and family groups slowly made their way to their huts.

Now totally drained, Tullia had just enough energy to slip her Meera necklace from around her neck and let her skirtlet drop to the floor before crashing onto the bed. In the few moments before she fell asleep, she vaguely recalled the message she had received from Tamina as they had kissed. Sister and brother were trying to use an unusual shop to rescue the twins. A pyramid of energy made from five points, The Globe and the EyeBox were all involved.

She smiled as she recalled kissing H'ani, and her mind refrained from pointing out that the large and thick pair of lips had not belonged to the slender Meera but to her twin.

Xameb had sat watching the dancing. As Tsetsana dropped out he had beckoned her to sit beside him.

'Worlds apart. Different dimensions. Different names for whatever it is that unites us. Yet we are all of the one spirit,' he said softly as the last Meera left the clearing. 'What was revealed?' he asked as he continued to gaze at the still glowing embers.

Tsetsana realised she was being tested. Facing the soft glow, she carefully recalled the battle and her kiss. 'Images all during the fighting and clearer than I saw when I was with Tyua'llia on the Hills,' she answered. 'The Lord Kaigii, part human and part an enormous dragon. The Mother Goddess was very tall and slim, all her limbs made of burning serpents and a face so different and beautiful I cannot describe. Tyua'llia was a white, winged unicorn, as I'd seen before. But why not a serpent?'

'Ahhh,' Xameb sighed. 'Any white creature is special. They are

Messengers.' Tsetsana clearly heard the capital "M". 'Seeing one is very rare. It is a gift. And a responsibility.'

Xameb knew he should have found an apprentice years ago. Now, with all the power flowing around he admitted the truth. It had not been for a lack of suitable candidates, but from the pain he had experienced. He had been afraid to open to his past by effectively reliving his own journey as he trained another. Whoever, whatever Tullia was, he offered silent thanks to her for making him face his fears. At a later time he would trance dance and seek forgiveness from the otherworld.

Tsetsana's friendship with Tullia and the guarded conversations he had had with the latter, had convinced him. At eleven-years-old and about to become a woman, she would normally be far too old, but with what she had just demonstrated it was clear: the Fates had chosen. He was content. He served that which was. And such changes were the ways of Cagn and Anansi, the trickster Gods.

Hearing Xameb move, Tsetsana turned to face him. She felt a hand under her chin lifting her head followed by a brief kiss on her forehead which had nothing like the power of Tullia's.

'Apprentice,' he said softly.

Xameb sighed. It would set the young woman even further apart from the tribe than her friendship with Tullia already had done. That was an inevitable part of being a Sangoma. Yet Xameb consoled himself with the thought that there would be a small group of Meera, undoubtedly led by her brother Xashee, who would stand by her as she underwent the years of arduous training.

Tsetsana was full of joy. Her dearest wish had just come true. She owed it to Tullia. She loved her big friend. She knew she had fallen hopelessly in love with the Lord Kaigii. The twins wanted to be together. They needed to be together. The honoured and respected Shaman had found her worthy – at least to learn. Taking courage from that, silently and with trepidation, Tsetsana repeated to herself her promise to do anything and everything necessary to enable the two people she loved most to be reunited.

She could not know how severely that promise was to be tested. And how soon.

CHAPTER 82

PLOTTERS

VERTAZIA

Late on the morning after defeating the twins' latest attempt to join together, the Custodians who had been involved met at IndluKoba, the beautiful country estate that was in effect their headquarters. They were in their usual underground room. Reflecting the serious nature of the occasion, the walls gently swirled with soft pastel shades of grey.

As always, the shielding of the room provided not only total security but also concealed its presence by projecting an image of what any impertinent observer might expect: a cellar containing a selection of Vertazia's most delightful wines.

In keeping with Aurigan tradition the wines were non-alcoholic, yet the herbal extracts included provided the sensations and pleasures required: gentle relaxation and the removal of unnecessary inhibitions, yet without causing any loss of control or deleterious after-effects.

Ceegren, the Arch Custodian, was in a sombre mood. Behind his very real sense of alarm he was carefully shielding a feeling almost of glee at how the twins and their friends had played into his hands and thus had finally laid to rest the discontent over the earlier violence used against them. He was also content that his plan of using rotating teams of Custodians to maintain a shield was working.

After a few words of welcome and thanks the meeting was opened to the Conclave. All other Custodians had been summoned to be available on their secure, group MentaNet. They saw a HoloWrapper of the previous night's events. Ceegren was delighted at the horror displayed by his fellow Custodians as they saw the violence perpetrated by the twins and their friends. He apologised for subjecting them to that, sorrowfully explaining that they needed to understand exactly what they were up against.

He praised the Custodians who had been involved in the fighting and then singled out Xaala, saying: 'My acolyte had the courage to embrace the abomination in her attempt to distract his attention and cause the connection to the other to break. I accord her all honour for her devotion to our cause in braving such an obscene act.' He turned to the blushing girl with a genuine smile on his face.

Xaala was indeed embarrassed and was keeping her eyes lowered as she struggled to keep her emotions shielded, at the same time thanking Ceegren for the arduous training that meant she was able to split her feelings and allow those of disgust to be perceived, whilst keeping hidden the troubling stirrings she did not understand. 'Or want to understand?' a treacherous voice whispered in her mind.

She had not chosen Qwelby. She had aimed to embrace Tullia but had found herself wrapping around the boy. As events had unfolded and they were sent crashing to the ground, she had clung to him in fear. He had tried to prevent her being pulled away and she had seen in his gorgeous purple eyes, that he cared. He was beautiful, manly and she could still feel the warmth from their brief contact.

Witnessing the fight from outside the Bubble, she had been

moved by the sight of his Attribute. The dragon was magnificent with its golds and reds all so unusually tinged with turquoise. For a moment she had even urged him on to win through to his twin. And the Custodians pretending to be Šèdûmaii inevitably had at first returned the boy's anger. But when he poured out his love, they had viciously attacked!

Then there was Tullia. So beautiful in all her power. Oh, she should have been allowed to embrace her! The knowledge that they would make a superb pairing helped steady Xaala and restore her usual, precise, mental control.

And there had been that flare of pain from.... his love for his twin. It was nothing like the love she received from Ceegren or even her own grandparents. And absolutely nothing like the feelings she had received from her late parents. Whilst in the NullPoint she had denied that it was love. Abominations were not able to love. But whatever human feelings had been mixed with it, underneath had been a pure and undemanding love – so strong it had hurt. As much as she tried, she could not rid herself of that memory.

'What is truly disturbing,' Ceegren continued, 'is the way in which the girl was able to draw on the energies of the Azurii.' That had given him grave concern. 'The violence she was encouraging in her twin, succoured by the Azurii for what are total strangers, proves beyond any doubt how violent are the Azurii and how willing to help violence wherever it arises. And. How the abominations themselves must have become infected with the Violence Virus.'

He paused, letting his deep, sea green eyes sweep across the assemblage. 'You will understand why from the beginning I have suggested that we cannot afford to allow the twins to return.'

Xaala was in shock. The HoloWrapper had been edited. It had not shown the Šèdûmaii attacking when they should have been reflecting the love that had been pouring forth. Nor had it shown the love that had flowed between the Twins, or Tullia channelling the power of the very land itself. Twice now she had experienced at first hand that all the twins wanted was to be joined together, only to be opposed with extreme violence. That her beloved teacher was misleading everyone was shaking her very Kore.

Her eyes focussed on her new, sleeveless tunic. It had been a gift from Ceegren that morning for her unprecedented inclusion in the meeting. It was a swirling mix of blue-greys with streaks of black, the same as her crystal of Xalulan. It fell to her normal, ultra short length, a consequence of a rebellion when she was ten. The cut emphasised her female form, the colours, her strong male genes. A narrow, sea green belt was a clear statement of whose acolyte she was.

Her shaking stopped as she realised that Ceegren was taking her into his full confidence, so that she understood how very important was her mission to prevent the twins connecting and returning. And how much trust and confidence he had in her that he had not talked to her privately at home, but brought her here. She saw it as a sign of his love for her that he was never able to show. She loved him. She would keep his secret.

Because Xaala wanted to be a boy, Dryddnaa had been concerned that in embracing Tullia, Xaala may have felt a female bonding that could undermine her mission, and thus had directed her to Qwelby expecting her to feel revulsion. From the obvious self control the acolyte was forcing on herself, Dryddnaa suspected she'd made a mistake.

Although Ceegren seemed well in control of himself, Dryddnaa knew he was seething at how close they had come to failing to prevent the twins reconnecting. She allowed herself to make a quick scan of Xaala. The girl glanced up, her eyes shining. A pink tongue quickly flickered across her lips before she composed herself and turned her attention back to Ceegren.

As Ceegren continued to steer all the Custodians towards agreement, Dryddnaa took a sip of lemonwater as she kept her sense of unease firmly behind her Privacy Shield. The path she was treading had just become more dangerous.

Ceegren closed the session with more words of encouragement and praise, a sense of self satisfaction, and allowed himself a moment of self-indulgence. He had already chosen a title for when he "reluctantly" accepted the demand to steer Vertazia to a new future – Consul. He would explain with all humility:

'It stands for "One who consults and is always open to consultation". The nearest we can come to the Aurigan three dimensional language which carried so much meaning in simple words.'

CHAPTER 83

A TESTING RUN

FINLAND

Qwelby woke up panting. He knew where he was, yet it took an age before he actually felt as though he had returned to his room in the Rahkamos' house, and from where?

Kaigii! They had been so close. More than close. They had been one. And in a very different way from when they had been very young and did not know that they were two. Unable to contain himself, he lifted his head and howled.

He heard feet on the ladder leading into the loft room and Hannu's head appeared. 'Qwelby?!' he exclaimed.

'Oh. Ah. Sorry! I'm all right,' he shouted for Hannu's parents to hear, as he rolled onto his side facing his friend. 'Last night. So close. So close,' he said, speaking normally. 'Now, I need action. Skiing. Cold on my face. Anything to, to....'

'Take the pain away?' Hannu asked,

'Yeah. Taziaannu,' Qwelby replied, feeling a slight easing as he realised that Hannu was beginning to receive his strong thoughtsending.

Hannu grinned. 'Okay. See you soon,' he said as he disappeared down the ladder.

Qwelby showered and went into his bedroom to dry and to reflect calmly on the previous night. Naturally, he knew about the physical changes that took place on Awakening, but virtually nothing about the emotional and mental consequences. All that knowledge would have been imparted nearer the expected time. He stood gazing at himself in the mirror. After Hannu's warning he had been very careful not to allow his towel to slip when he was in the sauna. Now, looking at what he had heard boys refer to as "the third leg", he felt good.

With his well-developed pectorals, in recent years Tullia had teased him about looking like a girl. He had teased her back that her broad shoulders and slim hips made her look like a boy. Now he was a man.

Her Image appeared in the mirror. That was not possible. This was not Mirror. He was looking at himself. But. He was a male and Kaigii was definitely a female. Yet they were identical. Streams of heat flowed through him. It was not his blood, but energy pulsing along his meridians. Knowledge pulsing from his..... fourth segment. Or even more?

'Are you coming before it gets dark?' Hannu's voice calling from downstairs brought Qwelby back to the present. The sense of understanding disappeared like the tip of a white dragon's tail as it flew into the clouds.

'Yay-oh!' Qwelby called back, trying to hide his frustration and annoyance at having his thoughts interrupted.

The day was perfect with the air temperature a few degrees below freezing, clear blue sky and the sun glinting off the icy snow. With Qwelby having to hide his eyes by wearing his goggles all the time he was in the open air or amongst strangers, he was by now accustomed to the permanent blue tinge they gave to everything. "Sunlight too dazzling, weak eyes," were the excuses which he preferred his friends to give for him, as each lie he told hurt him more and more.

At last he had got the feeling for skiing on Earth, even without being able to communicate with the skis or the snow as he did at home. With Hannu's old ski suit being a tight fit and bright in orange, black and white, he let himself imagine it was a Tazian bodysuit. And he had to admit that there was a different sense of exhilaration from being at one with his body in a very different way from on Vertazia. He guessed it was the same for them all, especially a really good skier like Timo, Hannu's best friend.

As the group watched the last part of Qwelby's descent a man joined them.

'You on holiday?' Timo asked him.

'Yes. Just for the weekend. I'm Jouko. It's my first time here. Can you tell me about the runs?' Soininen never used a false name, considering it just created problems and, anyway, that was only for amateurs.

'Sure. Come with us. We'll be here for some time.'

The two fell into an easy conversation as the group made its way to the ski lifts. As Timo talked with Jouko he realised he could be in for a good race. The man had more experience and the advantage of weight. But was he as good?

Laughing and joking as they gathered together to take their turn on the lift, Timo introduced the man. 'This is Jouko. He's staying at the centre for a weekend of skiing. It's his first time here and he'd like to come with us to get to know some of the runs.'

Timo found a few moments to have a word with Jarno, the next best skier of the group. Jarno nodded with a smile on his face. Assembled at the top Timo said, 'I'll show Jouko a good red run. The others can go down the easy red with Qwelby.'

Moans, groans, complaints, halted by Hannu. 'No problem. You guys go with Timo. I'll ski down with Qwelby.' He held his hand up as Qwelby started to protest. He knew that the others would get into a hot race. 'A couple more good runs down that first red before you tackle a difficult one?'

Reluctantly, Qwelby nodded. He wanted a demanding run, but this was not Vertazia and Tullia was not there to heal him if he broke a leg.

'I'll join you,' Anita and Oona offered simultaneously to the two boys.

Timo nodded to Jarno. 'OK. You guys set off first. We'll give you a start. Last one out of sight and we follow,' he said, looking at Jouko.

Jouko eyed the start of the run and called into mind what it looked like from the bottom. 'Looks about right.'

Jarno raised his stick. 'See you at the bottom!' as he pushed off, the others following.

'We'll go this way,' Hannu called over to Timo.

Timo nodded. He watched the last member of Jarno's group round the first bend, out of sight. He turned to Jouko. 'Let's go!' and launched himself forward.

Jouko followed.

A couple of hundred metres down the slope. Timo looked over his shoulder. Jouko was close behind and a little off to the left. That was good. Timo raised his left ski stick, pointing to where a trail led off, marked black. He looked back. Jouko nodded. Great!

Jouko quickly realised that Timo was a very good skier. He guessed he knew that particular run so well he could have skied it with his eyes shut. For a few moments he could not help but rise to the challenge and ski his best. Then he reminded himself that it was a new black run which he'd not even looked over.

He settled down to follow Timo, carefully watching his approaches to the various twists and turns. Filing it away in his memory for the next descent.

Timo looked back over his shoulder. I was right. He is good. If he's going to challenge it will be when he can see the finish.

Coming to the final bend Timo picked up the pace a little. Ahead and way down below was the end of the run. He glanced back over his shoulder. Jouko had dropped back a little and was just coming into sight. Good. Plenty of time for him to see the two options. He pointed with his stick, half right and then hard right. Swung his head back and saw Jouko raise a stick in acknowledgment.

Altering course a little to the right, Timo drove his sticks into the snow, bent forward and tucked them under his arms. He headed straight for the edge of a small cliff, exhilaration as the icy air streamed past almost burning his cheeks.

He leapt into space. Perfect. His friends were down to the right, watching. He leant forward, dropped his arms and let his sticks trail. He angled his skis, watching the ground rush up to meet him. Swoosh! His skis touched, he bent his knees, spread his arms out, a quick thrust with a stick to steady himself.

He leant over, curved to the right, dug his skis in and came to a halt, an arc of snow marking his arrival. Perhaps not quite professional, but it was his trademark.

He turned to watch Jouko as the visitor made an excellent landing and swung to a halt alongside.

'You're good,' complimented Timo.

'Not bad yourself.'

Timo smiled.

'Now you've shown me the run. A race?'

'You're on!' agreed Timo.

The others came up and a great hubbub arose. Complaints, praise, laughter. Timo restored order.

'We've agreed to have a race,' indicating Jouko. 'Anyone else want to join us?'

That was quickly sorted. Pauli, who had just returned from a visit to his father's family, and Jarno: no problem. Ilta. Timo nodded. She was almost as good as Pauli and knew the run well. Oona, Timo's younger sister. Timo shook his head. She knew the run but not for a race. He would be worried. She pouted.

'There'll be a second race down red. You win that one,' he challenged her.

She wrinkled her nose. *Still, it is a serious challenge. Anita, Hannu, Nils, are all in the year above me at school. And Qwelby's in the group.*

CHAPTER 84

DECEPTION

FINLAND

As they sorted themselves out at the top of the ski lifts, they realised that Qwelby was missing. They were all ready to go. Red race was to set off first and thus be at the bottom in time to watch the final part of the black race – and decide on the victor.

A few moments later Qwelby came up with a tall man. 'You guys who were going to ski with me, go ahead and enjoy your race. This man will ski down with me.'

There was something vaguely familiar about the new arrival. But, clad in a blue and silver ski suit, red bobble hat, gloves and facemask he could be anyone. There was a moment's hesitation. Perhaps someone should have asked a question. No-one did. They were all eager to go. Qwelby had shown he was a competent skier.

'OK everyone. You red racers all ready?' called out Timo. They were.

'Usual start.' He raised one of his sticks in the air. The youngsters were lined up and ready to go. He dropped the stick. They shot off to calls and cheers from the remaining friends.

'We'll give them a few minutes. After all, we need someone at the finish.' He grinned at the small remaining group. 'Just in case it's a close race!'

A black run. A difficult one. A choice of finish. Take the jump, which was the quickest but dangerous if performed even just a little bit wrongly. Or a hard stem turn to swing around to the right. The advantage in that was it led to a very fast descent to the finish off to the right.

The racers were concentrating, thinking about the twists and turns - and the finish. Jouko noticed Qwelby off to one side talking with his latest friend. All was well there.

'What do you think,' Timo asked the others. 'Enough time?' The three school friends who knew the run all agreed. Time to start.

'OK. I'll drop my stick and we go?' They all moved into final positions. Stick dropped and off!

Qwelby watched them leave. As they shot out of sight, he turned back to continue the conversation. 'I'm finding it very different here. The snow's different.' Which was true, even if not the whole truth. Playing the game was becoming more difficult as the days passed, because it wasn't just a game.

'We might as well go now. They'll be well in front,' his companion said a few moments later. 'I'll keep on your right.'

Qwelby nodded. Not racing, just nice to ski alongside someone. A look, a shouted word, companionship.

They set off, skiing easily. Round the first bend to the left, a short straight then the other skier crowded Qwelby from the right. He was a bit surprised. On his previous descents he had followed the piste as it curved right. There was another piste leading off to the left. Looking over his right shoulder to ensure he avoided the man's skis, Qwelby did not see the black marker on his left.

The piste narrowed as it went into a right hand bend. His companion shot in front. The pace picked up. Qwelby was having to concentrate hard. The turn was tighter, more demanding. The piste angled down steeper. They were running even faster.

A rise, a curve, Qwelby leaning well over. Every gram of concentration focussed on his body, through his legs into the skis and YES! into the snow. He could almost feel it beneath his skis. He lost himself in concentration, exhilarated at the sensations running through his whole being.

Qwelby had stopped watching his fellow skier. His mind was calculating incredibly fast. Angles of descent, radii of the turns, angles of the banks, speed, G-forces. All his Tazian mental abilities working flat out. This is like being at home!

He lost all sense of time. It was sheer bliss!

A tight sweep to the right. A beautiful view. A great, wide expanse of crisp white snow. Clear blue sky in front. Down below the town of Muurame. A lot of people down there. Too many to pick out his friends.

A sudden realisation. In front of him his companion was stemming hard to the right. Straight ahead – a sheer drop. This is no friendly race! Qwelby was horrified, not at the situation he was in, but at the nasty trick that had been played. What a terrible world! And I did not sense this! Too late to try a turn. Only one way to go.

The black racers had just finished and reached the group that had skied the red. They were all clustered well to Qwelby's right at the foot of the slopes where they were watching the end of the red run for him and his companion.

Timo was not happy. The ankle he had broken at the beginning of winter had kept him out of all the pre-Christmas fun. His father had forbidden him to join in the two nights of laser fighting, fearing he might catch his foot amongst the tree roots and undo the healing. It was not until after the New Year weekend that the doctor had finally pronounced it safe for him to ski. That had been over a week after Qwelby's arrival.

In that week it seemed to Timo that all Hannu talked about was his new friend. How different he was, how interesting, how much time they spent together and how well he was learning to ski in the different conditions of Finland. Even Oona, Timo's fourteen-year-old sister, was talking about the stranger.

To cap it all, Jouko had won the race. Beaten on his home ground by an older man, with a spreading middle and on only his second time down that run. That, was the final straw. When Ilta had complimented him on beating herself and Pauli by a bigger margin than ever before, Timo had almost snarled at her. He was in no mood to be consoled. Especially when he felt that Ilta had been paying more attention to Qwelby than to himself.

'Look,' Jarno cried, pointing with his stick.

All heads turned to see where he was pointing. High above them, they saw Qwelby's companion coming round the final bend in the black run, stemming hard as he swung around for the long descent towards where they were standing. Moments later Qwelby came into view. Timo watched as Qwelby continued to go straight ahead. Fool. He's too late to turn. He'll have to take that jump. I hope he breaks a leg. Serve him right.

Reality dawned.

That man was leading. They should have come down this red. That's a dirty trick. Very dangerous. It's not that boy's fault.

He saw Qwelby power with his sticks.

'No!' Timo could not help speaking aloud. 'He can't go straight ahead. He has to curve and take the jump on an angle. He's going to go off piste. Break more than just a leg!' He drove his sticks into the ground as the whole group sped towards where Qwelby was going to land.

Seeing empty space before him Qwelby had switched vision, first seeing the lines of the Earth's magnetic field, then the gravity waves. Sure enough, the hill distorted gravity but not far enough away to make a significant difference to his flight path. Switching back to normal vision he had powered hard with his sticks, bent forward, tucked them under his arms – and shot into space.

Beautiful. I am flying... Xzarze! This is not 'Tazia. Focus!

Leaning forward, arms and sticks at his side, skis angled upwards, he entered what felt like a magical timelessness as thoughts tumbled through his mind. He and his twin were living on Earth in the solid third dimension. How was it possible that they had been able to slow their bodies from the faster rate of vibration of Vertazia?

Rhythmic Entrainment!

But how was that possible? How had he been able to play with the photons during the laser game on New Year's Eve? How had his healing powers worked so well on the thief he had injured?

His people did not visit Earth because their three active segments of DNA did not allow them to do so. Yet the original Auriganii, from whom all Tazii were descended, had been able to utilise one hundred percent of their DNA and had been able to visit the stars without using spaceships. It had to be what he and Tullia had guessed that moment on New Year's Eve when they had been together in Finland and the Kalahari, each in both places at once. A fourth active segment! Or even more?

When he returned home he would plunge into the Shadow Market. He would provide whatever energy exchange was demanded in order to discover the full secret of the uniqueness of Quantum Twins. He would do it by himself, protect his twin from the dark depths of the SubNet culture, then tell her what he had discovered. Even his own family did not know. Or did they? Surely they must! Gumma was the youngest ever Arch Discoverer because he was outstandingly brilliant. He MUST know. Why hadn't he and Tullia been told?

Awareness of his surroundings returned along with a subtle feeling of the magnetic field. Much weaker than at home – but enough. Instinctively, he had been following the curves and realigned his descent. It was not ideal, he would still land too close to the edge of the piste, but....

Swoosh! He wobbled, sticks lightly touched the snow, quick movements, his stomach tightening as he kept his balance. A tight turn to the right. Winning or losing the race was irrelevant. All he wanted to do was to stop safely. He stemmed hard, raising an arcing curtain of snow as he came to a halt within centimetres of toppling over the edge of the piste and right in front of his amazed friends who were just arriving from where they had finished their race.

'Ten out of ten,' Timo muttered under his breath as the sportsman in him asserted itself.

Qwelby's breathing steadied. Steadied? Started! He realised that he had held his breath from the moment he had committed to the jump. Boiling up inside from his energy surge, he pulled his gloves off and unzipped his coat as the group surrounded him with questions and praise. He was overwhelmed.

'You fool! What were you thinking? You could have got yourself killed!' All interspersed with words Qwelby's compiler did not translate, a raging voice cut through everything else.

A startled group turned to see Qwelby's companion arriving, snapping his boots out of his skis.

Qwelby was stunned. What have I done?

Recovering from his surprise, Hannu recognised the school bully. 'Erki!'

'You're a maniac. You could have crashed into people down here and injured them! Killed someone!' Erki continued shouting.

Qwelby reeled back from the intensity of the attack.

'You're the moron,' Timo shouted, assuaging the guilt he felt for having wished a broken leg on Qwelby out of his own jealousy. 'You were supposed to take him down one of the reds. Not that demanding black!'

'It's his fault. He went that way. I had to follow!' Erki retorted.

A great hullabaloo ensued. Everyone shouting and arguing. Through it all Qwelby could hear Erki's ranting laced with a lot of words that the compiler did not handle.

'You're the morons. Taking in this foreigner...... Mongol...... we don't want... people like that here... you're all too... high and mighty to ski with me... that... prissy little... won't even talk to me... blacks... taking our jobs... our homes.'

Qwelby had been feeling the energy in Erki's words hitting him as if they were physical blows. He had been attacked by this man and his cronies within minutes of his arrival on Earth. On a night of fun he had been kicked in the face by a thief, then seized and badly cut by another, who had again attacked him with a knife two days later.

Right after that he had been plunged into the darkest despair of his life, trapped in the NoWhenWhere. He still felt the anger and frustration of that time. It was as though he had been gagged and bound by invisible ropes. At first, unable to move or even call out, he had watched helplessly as Tamina and Wrenden risked their lives to rescue him. And when he had tried to help them, he had nearly drowned his youngerest in a flood of lava – who he was supposed to look after!

Added to all that was the frustration at the confines of his life on Earth and the lies he was having to tell. He felt his dragon of anger rising in him, red and hot. He wanted to strike the man. Trembling with the difficulty, he was just keeping hold of his Tazian way of life.

Erki stopped waving his arms about, stepped forward and threw a punch.

Mentally, Qwelby had read Erki's intention as clearly as if the boy had held up a large placard announcing what he was going to do.

Qwelby ducked. As the fist passed over his head, all restraint fled. His rage exploded. Driving upwards from feet firmly planted on his skis, he launched one massive punch straight into his attacker's face.

With a cry, Erki fell backwards, blood splattering all over his face. His hands flew to his face as he shouted: 'You've broken my nose!'

Seeing everything as though through a red filter, Qwelby took a pace forwards, snapping his boots out of out of his skis and raising both arms in the air. Before he could leap on his attacker he felt his arms seized. He flexed them back, about to throw off the restraint. His Intuition shouted at him to stop. The snow returned to its white expanse. He stopped, poised. He let the energy drain from his muscles, relaxing his arms, feeling them drop to his sides and Hannu and Timo loosened their grip.

'Got what he deserved,' was the theme of the mutters from the group. They were both amazed and pleased. No-one had ever dared confront Erki before.

Qwelby stood there with his mouth wide open. He was at war within himself. Horror at the sight of the blood and that he had broken the man's nose. Pleasure at his skill that had been a pure reflex. And, he had to admit, a deep sense of satisfaction, of pride in his own abilities and moreover in the solid reality of the third dimension. Yet feeling ashamed at what he had nearly done.

He turned to Hannu. 'Hit me,' he said pointing to his chest. Nothing happened. 'Please. I need it,' he added with intensity.

Hannu hit him, gently.

'Hard!'

Hannu tried again.

'Harder!' Qwelby commanded, sliding into his friend's mind.

After three punches that had Qwelby rocking back on his feet, he held up his hands. 'Thank you,' he said with a smile.

'What the devil was all that about?' Jouko asked.

'That man attacked me on my first night here, along with two cronies. Now he makes a dangerous trick. The possibility of terminating my LifeLine.' Qwelby paused. 'Anger strong. Inside. Need release,' he finished simply, trying to add a lot of fuzzy energy in the hope that it would cover the fact that his earlier words hardly matched those of a boy who spoke little Finnish.

Shaking at everything that had happened, Qwelby sat down as Erki clambered to his feet and stepped back into his skis. With a handkerchief held to his nose, he swung around and moved off, calling over his shoulder: 'You've not heard the last of this.'

In time, he was to take great pleasure in making good on his threat.

CHAPTER 85

DELVING

FINLAND

In the silence that followed, Qwelby could be heard talking to himself.

'Ontoni beka budakiti? Ghifuna sebenzaaka nina?'

Anita and Hannu knelt beside their friend. The others looked puzzled. It did not sound like any language they knew. It was so musical. It was similar to Scandinavian languages, but a lot more so.

Qwelby was existing on two levels. Inside, his Intuition was speaking. 'You could have broken that man's neck. Terminated his LifeLine.'

But I didn't mean to, Qwelby thought back.

'Ontoningi ghiazilelaeya? Ontoni umhlabageako?' Qwelby lifted his face to his friends. 'Ezwaqondaeya.'

'To every action there is...' Qwelby's Intuition said.

'Qwelby, you're speaking... Czech,' Hannu said.

'An equal and opposite reaction,' Qwelby said aloud as the horror of the situation dawned on him and his eyes went completely black. His action had been deliberate. If he had killed Erki, not only would he have committed the greatest crime of all, he would have abandoned himself to the NoWhenWhere, deprived himself of reincarnation and his Aurigan Heritage. And sundered himself from Kaigii! She would never have been whole for the rest of her life.

As the shock of that last realisation ripped through him, his friends saw his face turn ashen grey.

'Or through all eternity?' A voice whispered in his head.

His mouth dropped open and Hannu and Anita heard his soundless scream.

Qwelby wrapped his energy field tightly around him. 'Sizangi Zhólérrân,' he whispered, asking the Dragon Lord to help him. Slowly, the blackness in his eyes faded, pale purple centres returned, surrounded by blue ovals so pale they were almost white. To those watching it seemed as though he had opened doors and was looking out into the world, fearfully.

'I don't understand. What is wrong with my colour? Why do I want his job?'

'Fear,' Timo said harshly.

Qwelby and his two friends looked up at Hannu's best friend, puzzled at his tone of voice.

'You're different. Unknown. He's afraid of that,' Timo added.

Ilta put a hand on Timo's arm and gave it a squeeze. Almost as tall as him, she rested her head against his for moment. He had shared some of his negative feelings with her. She understood what it had cost him to say what he had.

'You're a damned good skier,' Timo added gruffly.

'I should have known.' Qwelby shook his head.

'Known what?' asked Anita.

'How much he hates me. On 'Tazia…'

'That's his village in Czech,' Hannu explained. 'How's your hand?' he asked, quickly changing the subject.

Qwelby looked down. 'There're no marks …my energy field!'

He dropped his voice to almost a whisper as he looked at his friend with a smile. 'Just like at home!'

Jouko had moved closer and just managed to overhear Qwelby's comments. So a young martial arts expert, able to control his Chi, or Ki or whatever they call it. That should interest the Professor.

The only adult with the group of youngsters, he saw the perfect moment to take control and dig for information. 'Let's go to the café. We've all had a surprise and this young man,' he could not say "boy," 'has had a bad shock. Come on. My treat.'

That was well received. In no time at all they were packed around a couple of tables. Hot drinks, patisseries and chatter. Jouko Soininen was feeling generous. He'd had a good morning and had won the race with Timo, not by much, but enough. The young people were good company. Skiing, any sport, he thought to himself, was a great way of breaking down all sorts of barriers, be they age or whatever.

The competitors talked through their race on the black run. The others all agreed. Jouko was a worthy victor. In spite of losing, Timo was beginning to feel happy. It had been a good race. It was true, he had won from his friends by a bigger margin then ever before and Jouko clearly had a lot more experience. Ilta had snuggled up to him and he was enjoying her consolation and forgiveness for his earlier harsh manner.

Qwelby was very quiet. He was still in shock. Sitting either side of him, Hannu and Anita answered a lot of questions as he seemed too dazed to respond.

He rallied enough to describe his run and the exhilaration. They let him take it bend by bend. His eyes a sparkling violet as he described the jump. He was so into the experience that the energy emanating from him brought it alive. They felt they were skiing with him.

After that, of course, they had to tell Jouko the story of how they'd caught the jewel thieves.

As they finished amongst laughter and high-fives they left the café.

Jouko was concerned about Qwelby. 'How are you getting home?'

'We'll ski cross country,' answered Hannu. 'It's not far.'

'Will you be alright?' Jouko looked at Qwelby.

'Yes,' Qwelby replied in a dreamy voice. 'For the first time I really felt at one with this world.'

'You mean like when you're on... Ouch!' Hannu exclaimed as Anita kicked him on the shin.

'Sorry, Hannu. I slipped,' she said, giving him a "look".

Qwelby laughed. He was so excited at discovering that he could reach the higher vibrations of the quantum field almost like he did at home that it was easy to imagine what sort of look would have passed between the two of them if they were on Vertazia.

As Hannu was grimacing, realising what he had nearly said, Oona walked up to Qwelby. She had been sitting opposite him in the café, unable to take her eyes off him.

'I think you're ever so brave, taking that jump, then confronting Erki. No-one's ever done that.' She paused as Qwelby's smile lit up his face. 'Would you teach me to ski like that?'

Wow! This is more than just acceptance. 'Yes, I'd like that. You start school on Monday?'

Oona nodded.

'We'd better start tomorrow?' Qwelby said, feeling so happy.

Oona was looking up at his face. Teeth sparkling bright white against his rich, reddish brown skin. And those annoying goggles he'd kept on in the café. She'd only briefly seen his eyes on New Year's Eve as he'd kept them closed a lot of the time. She reached up and pushed the goggles up onto his forehead.

She hadn't been wrong. In the daylight they were stunning! His larger than normal pupils were a rich purple and they were sparkling. She felt a warm energy flow into her, much stronger than on that night. Slightly dizzy, she leant against him and he put his arms around her. Later, she was to say to her best friend that she could actually feel like his happiness was flowing into her as she had snuggled up to him.

She thought she heard Qwelby say something, looked up into his smiling face and was sure his eyes were gently revolving. Reluctantly, she forced herself to step back. 'Yes. See you then,' she said. With all her friends watching she resisted the temptation to reach up and kiss his full, dark red lips.

Hannu and Anita had walked the few paces back to where Timo was talking with Jouko. Having pulled his goggles back over his eyes, Qwelby and Oona joined them. Jouko nodded to them and left with a wave, calling: 'See you tomorrow?'

Qwelby picked up his skis and waved to Oona. With a dreamy smile on her face she waved back as she walked off with her brother and Ilta. Her acceptance, and the energy he'd felt when they were together, eased his pain from hearing the mutters as they had all left the café, telling him there were many others who disliked him as much as Erki did.

Anita noticed once again just how much his face changed with his moods. At times he looked a different person. Now he was happy and smiling. 'I think I'd like to go to Vertazia... Just for a holiday!' She added quickly. Not wanting to tempt fate.

'You're looking very happy,' she commented as they walked across to the ski slope to start the trek back to their homes.

'Oona's asked me to teach her to ski like me. You don't know what that means. All the time I'm here everyone is giving to me. A home, food, clothes. Hiding me from... I don't know what. I'm an Alien. A curiosity.' He was getting worked up. 'To be asked to give something back is wonderful.'

'Oona skis well,' Hannu pointed out.

'Mm, she's quite good,' Qwelby agreed.

'Qwelby. Oona likes you,' added Anita.

'Well, yes,' he answered.

'She's more interested in having a hot chocolate with you afterwards than the skiing lesson.'

'Ah....' Realisation dawned as he recalled the colours in his two friends' energy fields that he didn't understand and compared them with what he sensed of Oona's. He liked the feelings that were developing within him for Tamina, then Anita and now Oona. It was all so new and exciting. What was Kaigii going to say? He threw back his head and laughed.

The sound of oboes and bassoons rolling across the snow was infectious. Without knowing why, his friends joined in the laughter as they set off for home.

CHAPTER 86

FEELINGS

THE KALAHARI

Tullia awoke to the comforting sounds of the village. It was her favourite time of day, lying half awake listening to softly murmuring voices and the sounds of hot drinks being made. Yet her sadness was greater than ever. They had been so close the previous night. And with Tamina and Wrenden actually there in the seventh dimension, Pelnak and Shimara had to have been involved. All six through the power of the Talisman? But how?

Perhaps something was guiding her and Kaigii to try to connect at the same time. Was what they called their twinergy something that existed separately from each of them? Was it that or because each was emitting so much power they attracted the opposition? Was that the answer – to find a gentle way to reach Kaigii?

A brief stab of pain interrupted her thoughts. She had been feeling unwell with pains and aches in her stomach, her sides and lower back. It seemed to have started after her fall on the Hills. And since the night of the hunt her breasts had been feeling heavy and uncomfortable.

She rose, washed and dressed in her usual skirt and tank top, her body still nagging at her with its aches and pains. It had been trying to send her little messages for the last few days. She had not understood them. More, there was something in her that was stopping her from exploring. There were feelings of change, of something coming out, of something growing and an awareness that she was unprepared for whatever it was.

With a deep sigh of reluctance she forced herself to accept that there were changes around the messages that she needed to listen to. She sat down in the lotus position and went into her body.

She emerged from the deepstate feeling uncomfortable, cold and shivering. The only sense she had been able to extract from the feelings and images was of womanhood. The gentle pastel colours that had come with them she recognised as colours she had seen around Tsetsana. Yet the girl was only eleven years old, and for Tullia herself that development was not due for at least eighteen months.

Pains stabbed through her stomach. No, please, no. Too much is happening. Too many changes. Please stop. Please go away. Oh, how she longed to be at home and to talk with Tamina. Sternly reminding herself that she was a "big-big sister", she forced herself to climb off her bed and draped the coloured blanket around her shoulders. With leaden steps she walked towards her family's hut, head down, wondering what she could say and unaware that Deena was watching her all the way.

Sitting down, mumbling greetings to her family and gratefully taking the hot drink that was offered, she was unaware of the silence around the fire. Unaware as always of the impact she made on people as her energy field impinged on them.

Her drink finished, she finally had no reason not to speak. The silence continued as she toyed with her mug and then felt Deena gently take if from her hands. She looked into her Meera mother's eyes and blurted out. 'I need to talk to you.' She was aware of the silence around the family and everybody staring at her. 'By myself,' she almost wailed.

Deena got up, extended her hand, took Tullia's, and led them to Tullia's hut. With a gesture, Deena sought and was granted permission to enter.

Tullia started to explain the strange feelings in her body and the images and colours she had received in her meditation that morning, reassured all the time she spoke by Deena's energy of acceptance and the gentle nods she gave from time to time. Reassured so much that she blurted out. 'And Tsetsana?'

'It is what we call your moon. The sign of womanhood. From what you have said, this is the first passage of your moon?' Deena asked, in vain trying to keep the surprise out of her voice that it should happen to a girl so advanced in years.

'Yes. I know about that, but at home this would not normally happen for almost two years. Our lives during our teen years are very much structured by our hormones. Each anniversary of our birth is very important as it marks changes in our bodies as they help us to prepare for what is to come.'

'You are right. Tsetsana also has reached the time of her First Moon.' Deena paused. 'Amongst all us San this is the most important time in the life of a female, when you move from child into woman. As with all tribes, we have our own way of celebrating that growth. I will speak with Neame. She arranges these matters.'

Deena stood up, still feeling very strange at addressing what she knew was the daughter of the Sun Goddess. 'Whatever Neame decides, my daughter, we will help you in every way we can.' Her eyes searched Tullia's face. 'Is there anything special on your world that happens on such an occasion?'

'Not really. A girl goes away for a pair of nights with her mother and her elderest. That's a special, slightly older girlfriend who acts like a sort of guide. And any older sisters the girl might have. Tamina's my elderest. She achieved her Awakening, that's what we call it, only a few days ago. She wasn't really any different. I know what it's about. But how and.... well I wasn't that interested. Each year we change and she tells me about it when I get there...' Tullia finished lamely.

Deena nodded. 'I will speak with you and Tsetsana later.' She turned to leave, ducking through the doorway, then turned back. 'Tyua'llia, this is a very special time amongst our people. You must understand that everybody will know. Everybody will want to know and celebrate.' She smiled. 'It is natural that you should flow with the women's rhythms as we reach our moon time. Truly you are becoming one of us.'

Left alone, Tullia sat there not understanding Deena's words about rhythms. She had felt so embarrassed and uncomfortable talking to Deena about it. And now this woman who had willingly offered to be her Meera mother was talking about what was going to happen as though it was something to be celebrated around the fire as a normal part of tribal life.

Well, I have not been prepared for this as I would on Vertazia. But I guess I am being prepared for it in the way of the Meera. And I am not alone. What a lovely coincidence that Tsetsana will share this with me.

Her mind flicked over the events of the past few days and she had a little laugh to herself as she imagined the looks on the faces of the girls who had become her friends, who had teased her in the Melon Dance. Surely, they must have thought I was like them? They cannot have realised that I was what they call a child.

Deena returned and called Tullia and Tsetsana together.

'As well as Tsetsana, there are two other girls who have been waiting to celebrate their First Moon, twelve-years-old Mandingwe and N!Obile. Neame has said the celebration will take place shortly after both of you have achieved your First Moons.' She then explained the outline of the day, which Tsetsana already knew and was excited to be able to join for the first time.

Tullia was taken aback at how open and public everything would be, even though restricted to the women. A few moments later she was delightfully reassured when the two other girls rushed up to share their joy.

'It's only because of you that we're going to have our Moon Day Celebration now. We were going to have to wait until it got warmer,' Mandingwe said with great excitement.

Any worries at the thought that she had unwittingly deceived the girls into thinking that she was what they would call a young woman rapidly disappeared. They expressed their surprise that the change was happening so late in her life and giggled over how she had handled herself at the Melon Dance, very much as a young woman.

Deena ended the conversation and sent the two girls back to their duties for the day. 'Tyua'llia, although you will not wear any clothing on the Moon Day itself, you will not want to wear a borrowed loinskin afterwards. The one you wore during the hunt is now yours. Today you are to help the women with their work. You have a lot to learn. Tsetsana, in the evenings, you are to help your sister with the loinskin and necklace.'

Tullia's eyes shone with delight. Deena had called her "daughter" and then referred to her as sister to Tsetsana. These people really were her family. 'Thank you, Mother Deena,' she said with a great big smile. And heard Tomku giggling at the sight of Tullia's mouth splitting her face in two.

Life was well, Life. She had awoken feeling so sad and bereft and now here she was excited and nervous about making a change that had taken her by surprise. It would make little difference at home, yet here it meant she would be regarded as a woman.

'Oh Kaigii,' she murmured to herself in Tazian. 'So much is happening to me. I am changing so fast, and I know I will be stronger when I'm Awakened. If Xameb and I join our different ways together, I'm sure we can open a pathway for you to come here. Surely, our BestFriends will come again. We can live happily here as we make our own plans – together.'

CHAPTER 87

XAALA DECEIVES

VERTAZIA

Ceegren and Dryddnaa remained at IndluKoba. He held a long series of meetings with a variety of people including all the members of the Senate. The Chief Readjuster took the opportunity to carry out a major review of the whole Readjuster operation and hold a few private discussions.

As was customary, a select team of senior Apprentices had been called in to act as Servitors for the distinguished guests. This time, Ceegren retained Xaala for his exclusive services, which was seen as a definite affront by the trained Servitors.

Early each evening the Arch Custodian held meetings in his suite. Having set out the buffet, Xaala spent the remainder of the day until late at night researching conditions on Earth. Ceegren had ordered a separate and strongly shielded room to be available for her exclusive use. There, she was able to use codes that enabled her to access material normally restricted to specialists such as the Discriminators who vetted Azuran satellite transmissions.

With her general shy nature and her obvious special status, it seemed that she was deliberately holding herself aloof. With her height and erect bearing she was literally looking down her nose at the other Apprentices.

The supervisor allocated Xaala accommodation in a small dormitory with a group of young trainees, saying that with so many Custodians to be served the Apprentices' dormitory was full. What Xaala recognised as a clumsy attempt to humiliate her, she saw as a blessing. The trainees were in far too much awe of her Master to play any of the nasty tricks she was sure the Senior Apprentices would have subjected her to, had she slept in their dormitory.

For the Chief Readjuster's plans to succeed, the twins had to return and, ideally, Ceegren be forced to take extreme action, rather than herself having to act and then hide all traces of what she had done. She saw a very definite chink in Xaala's armour and a way to turn the acolyte's mixed feelings to their advantage. Initially, Ceegren would benefit. If Dryddnaa had read the girl aright……. but that was for the future.

As part of her planning, ostensibly in support of Ceegren, some few days ago Dryddnaa had arranged for a Junior Readjuster who was a friend of Yarannah, the mother of Tamina and Wrenden, to offer assistance. That had been as a friend and not in any official capacity. But, in view of the seriousness of the situation, Lerinda was to keep Dryddnaa informed of events and keep that fact confidential so as not to worry the family.

Reassured by Dryddnaa's promise that Lerinda would have both the support of the Chief Readjuster in dealing with the family and her protection if anything were to go wrong, the Junior Readjuster had been happy to pass on information. Yesterday, she had reported that Yarannah was so incensed with the latest development that the woman did not want to talk about what was happening.

Dryddnaa needed a more reliable source and to that end

she had met with Rulcas the previous evening. She had been impressed by his native cunning and even amused at how he had the effrontery to bargain with her when he knew he was to spy on the twins' friends, and almost certainly a girl named Xaala who was likely to contact him.

Dryddnaa had explained that she needed to know how, where and when the twins were likely to return, so as to ensure they were quarantined with as little delay as possible. She'd had a momentary flicker of concern when he'd asked: 'Both?' In response to her asking why, he'd said: 'Together? Rumour says they're very strong. I could sort the girl for you. I've seen her in a LiveShow Sending....' His cheeky grin and the colours flowing through his aura had been as clear as a strong thoughtsending. Dryddnaa had dismissed his attitude as that of a typically degenerate yet savvy MUUD.

That had made it easy to agree on banishment to Tembakatii as his reward. The Shadowlands was the right place for him. In the meantime, she knew he would obey her. Although on the surface he had shown little concern when she had mentioned that his personal Readjuster was considering permanent readjustment, on the inside he had been alarmed.

Rulcas was disappointed that, just as with Xaala, Dryddnaa had sealed everything deep within his mind and he was only able to talk with her about it. It meant he was unable to brag to his mates about how clever he'd been.

Inside himself he was very happy. He hated life in an UltraTraditionalist enclave, made worse by the hypocrisy of people who did not follow the precepts they preached. Now, whether the twins were prevented from or succeeded in returning, his dream was going to come true, life with his father amongst the Shakazii. When Dryddnaa arranged to get him to near where the twins' friends lived, well, who knew, he might make his way to Tembakatii anyway. He was sure his father would protect him.

Dryddnaa invited Xaala for a relaxed discussion. The Chief Readjuster made no bones about having detected Xaala's searching. Xaala's response to Dryddnaa's questioning was the same as the report she'd made to Ceegren. It was clear that the twins' DNA was rapidly degenerating and she thought that a MUUD might help her understand the boy a little.

'I wish you good fortune when you meet him,' Dryddnaa said. 'If you need any help with him, please ask me. My concern is that the latest encounter shows how strong the twins have become. If, against all our best efforts, they succeed in returning, we must know how to handle them.'

As soon as Xaala was back in the room that had been set aside for her, she checked the shielding, flopped onto the consolchair and let its pseudofingers massage the tension out of her mind. Playing games with the powerful Chief Readjuster was dangerous.

When Xaala eventually presented a summary of her findings about the Azurii to Ceegren, she had the distinct impression that he already knew most of it. She had had to dig deep into her skills and strength not to be seriously disturbed by viewing the horrors of life on Earth. Had his reason for her exploration been to harden her to the task that lay ahead?

What would he say if he knew that she was fascinated by many aspects of what to her were the strange and primitive lives of the multitude of different peoples? And a definite thrill at the prospect of more contact with the..... Twins. She needed to stop thinking of them as abominations because that could cloud her judgement.

Once again she was grateful to Ceegren for her training. She would never dare to try to manipulate him, but Dryddnaa concerning Rulcas..... had that been too easy?

CHAPTER 88

ERKI MOVES UP

FINLAND

Relaxing in his hotel suite on Sunday evening, Professor Romain was thinking about the weekend. Some of his time skiing he had spent observing the boy with the reddish-brown skin and wondering if there was any clue from the fact that he never removed his large ski goggles, even when eating inside the restaurant.

He had seen that Soininen, the Private Investigator he had engaged, was doing his job. The PI came from Helsinki and Kotomäki was little more than a large village. How much would people open up to a curious stranger? Romain wanted, needed, more certainty.

Erki came into his mind. He was a local, a similar age to the strange boy and said he went to the same school as the group of friends the boy was skiing with. Romain sighed. Erki was an unpleasant youth, but Romain was terrified of making a tragic and humiliating mistake. Double checking that his GlobeSynch was in full security mode, he called Erki.

Erki was feeling frustrated and angry. He wanted something more from life. School was boring, there was no action. Having kids there frightened of him, well, pathetic really, a man of his size and ability. He wanted to make something of himself. He fancied working for Lokir as an enforcer. He thought he looked the part in his black, padded jacket, dark trousers and dark blue cap.

He had wandered to the edge of the village and was looking at the ski slope. He liked the winter months. That was when he worked most in Jyväskylä. With his height and his bulk from all the hours in the gym, in the dark he easily appeared to be several years older than his almost seventeen. The summer months were not so good when even at midnight it was never completely dark.

He knew he was good. He just needed the right opportunity to show that. And to the right man. That was important. He nodded to himself. When the opportunity came, he knew he had to be real cool. Saturday certainly had not been cool. That black boy. Disgraceful, having people like him in his country. Parasites the lot of them. Erki was getting all worked up again when his mobile rang.

He made an effort to relax as he pulled it from the pocket of his well padded, thigh length coat. It was the Professor. Romain was brief. He wanted to meet, somewhere they would not be seen together. It would not take long.

Erki quickly outlined a simple plan. Romain was to park his car along Satamakat, down by the lakeside in Jyväskylä and stand on the bridge with a map. As Erki walked past him, Romain was to ask for directions. If they needed more time to talk, they would walk to Romain's car where they would be out of sight. They agreed on four o'clock the following afternoon.

As Erki put his mobile away he wondered just how much Romain would pay for hard information, or better still, whatever it was that the Professor was seeking. He could not know that he was about to be offered a challenge that was worthy of how he saw himself.

CHAPTER 89

THE MYSTERY DEEPENS

HELSINKI

It was late on Monday night when Soininen kept his promise to telephone Romain. The PI provided a brief background before summarising the key elements.

'The boy's name is Qwelby. He had not been seen prior to Monday the twenty-seventh and is staying with the Rahkamos. I'm sure he does not come from the Czech Republic, or any of the Eastern European countries where people are likely to understand some Russian. From his colour and facial features, I'd put him further to the East. A mixture of Inuit and Mongol perhaps, and even Asian.

'His claim to speak very little Finnish is at odds with his perfect accent and using the phrase: "The possibility of terminating my life line".'

Soininen described the end of the race and Erki's attack. 'What was weird was Qwelby asking a friend to punch him several times. Combined with that phrase, all I can guess is that he comes from some religious sect that abhors violence and he needed to be punished. "An eye for an eye" sort of thing.'

Romain's heart beat fast as his paranoia went into overdrive.

Was the boy a Tibetan, the reincarnation of a High Lama, fleeing from the Chinese overlords?

Describing the scene in the café on Saturday when Qwelby had told the story of the ski run with Erki, Soininen confessed to being swept into it so much that he felt as though he was skiing the run himself.

'All that fits with what I saw and felt,' Romain said. 'When I got close to the youngsters at the ski lifts, not only was it was clear that Qwelby was communicating in Finish, there was an energy radiating from him. I can only describe it as coming from a big-hearted, welcoming personality.'

'As far as coming from the same small town where Jadrovitch had been born. Definitely not true,' Soininen said. 'I've spoken with a friend and found out more than is on the internet. A brief discussion and the boy agreed with some completely wrong facts I stated.

'In the family where Qwelby is staying there's a boy. He has a girl friend. Saturday evening all three went to that location you mentioned. All they did was stand there for some time in a circle, holding hands.'

Romain's body was covered in goosebumps. His obsession with proving the existence of other dimensions swept away all his fears. He was now convinced that whatever had happened with his psien, the consequence was at that point on the edge of the ski slope. Given the nature of his experiment, transmitting masses of data piggy-backed onto the energy in the Large Hadron Collider, it had to have been matter transport on a massive scale. The boy's arrival. And not from anywhere on Earth. Holding hands. Some sort of séance like attempt to communicate with his home.

Once again he thought of the teleportation experiments on Earth, requiring a sender and a receiver. His equipment had detected a faint energy signature in southern Africa. Something much smaller. A portable teleport device or a communicator that the boy needed to find in order to return home?

Romain's peace was shattered when Soininen described another man who it seemed had been interested in the group of children. A man who was staying in Romain's hotel. 'When I talked with him, he said he worked in IT,' the PI said. 'He was having a weekend off and couldn't help noticing the one black kid, wondering how someone like that had learnt to ski so well. Joked about the Jamaican Bob Sleigh Team. All possibly true. But it didn't feel quite right. Put it down to intuition.'

Once again Romain felt panic welling up. He was going to have to act fast.

'Erki obviously intensely dislikes immigrants,' Soininen continued. 'The attack was completely unprovoked. I was right there. It was also clear that the kids do not like Erki. And Qwelby seems to be a solid part of the group. I think at least that boy and girl know him from somewhere else. A holiday abroad is my guess. So, the weird story they are telling. I think it's just kids playing a silly game, using the black boy to wind up Erki. And succeeding. Too well so that Erki is trying to make trouble. I'm sorry if you feel you've wasted your money.'

'Not at all,' Romain reassured the PI. 'You've confirmed that the boy must have arrived about the time of my experiment, something was seen and he rushed out to explore. What was seen was a great deal less than I had expected, which means I was asking the wrong questions. And the false story. Thank you. That makes sense from the things that Erki said when he spoke to me.'

The two men said their 'good nights', agreeing about submission of the report and final payment.

Romain sat back in his chair. It was an inevitable consequence of the theory developed by Sir Roger Penrose of twistors: "particles" that were so small they did not possess any spatial dimensions. At that minimalistic point in space, matter and information became indistinguishable.

And what was matter anyway? Merely a vast amount of information: data about mass, spin, axis of rotation, location relevant to other data, rate of decay and much more. And that held good all the way up to the incalculable amount of data that comprised any complex living organism.

There was one key fact he had not told Soininen – that Qwelby had spoken to Erki in a foreign language. As Erki had said, if the boy was returning to where he was staying with the Rahkamos, why stop and speak to him? And if he was not staying with that family, why did Hannu come out of the house? Curiosity, because he also had seen a black boy walking down the ski slope?

Romain was now convinced of his earlier assumption that Qwelby had been involved in a teleportation that had gone disastrously wrong and that he had also been carrying some device that he had lost. Would he know that it had almost certainly arrived in Africa?

He thought over the background that Soininen had sketched. Why was Dr Keskinen going along with a pack of lies about an erstwhile colleague? He was a quantum physicist. He had a duty to advise the authorities. There was one obvious answer. The boy was exerting mental control. Powerful control over two families and the group of youngsters he had been skiing with. Romain was going to have to be very careful.

But. And there were there so many "buts". Aliens with the ability to teleport across dimensions. Surely they could rescue him? How long would that take? Was what he was thinking of as the lost device essential to any rescue?

He would not let his assistants in on his thinking, not yet. He did not know how they would handle an apparent human being used as a captive experiment. A boy who would be promised help to return home. Which was not likely to happen. The Nobel Prize was a worthy dream. He also had another.

Sir Andre Geim had received his knighthood for inventing the very graphene that had enabled Romain to create the key components of his equipment, but had made no money from the invention. Romain had already made a considerable fortune from his various inventions. The possibilities from this alien were enormous. Teleportation, inter dimensional communications, faster-than-light travel. And what range of lesser inventions could Romain devise and market? Having ploughed almost all his money into his quantum project, he wanted to earn enough to create his own prestigious research establishment – based around a trans-dimensional teleportation machine! Indeed a worthy dream.

'Command: Virtual keyboard, design 2.' Through the GlobeSynch he accessed the computer complex in the laboratory on Raiatea, went through to his secret storage and transferred the data he had managed to capture about the ghost image into the main databanks.

'Command: Message. What is definite is that there was an event where and when indicated. Those modifications we made must have worked. The connection failed when my Python ruptured, and as you said Miki, the data dropped off in Finland. I isolated data regarding the ghost image in order to clear the system. I have restored it. Please review. Command: Location RaiLabTwo: send.'

Once again the encrypted message winged its way in a short burst half way round the world.

CHAPTER 90

INHIBITED

VERTAZIA

The information that had been fed into the MentaNet concerning the Custodians' first success in keeping the twins apart had been severely censored. The version of this latest encounter that was fed into the MentNet made it abundantly clear that Qwelby had attacked Tazii who were merely trying to act as a wall to keep the twins apart. That those Tazii had appeared as revered heroes from ancient times who carried no weapons but merely mirror-shields was seen as ample proof that the twins had caught the Violence Virus.

During their healing, Readjusters had delicately restructured the memories of the less experienced Custodians who had been involved in the second engagement, resulting in them genuinely believing that all they had done was to defend themselves from attack.

With panic sweeping through the MentaNet, the Arch Custodian sought to convince the Spiral Assembly, the nearest that the Tazii had to any form of government, to prohibit any attempts to rescue the twins and to ban them from ever returning and bringing with them the feared virus.

With immense irony he was compelled by his most ardent supporters, the Kumelanii, to modify that view in accordance with ancient Aurigan philosophy, so that the final proposition that gained support was Dryddnaa's, with an obvious addition which the Chief Readjuster did not dare argue against. "That the twins be allowed to return only when their safe quarantine could be guaranteed and in the meantime any attempts to communicate with or rescue them are forbidden."

An offer by Dryddnaa to discuss with the Arch Readjuster the nature of appropriate action to be taken regarding Tamina and Wrenden was readily accepted. As she had expected, being a very old Venerable who had become a mere figurehead, the Arch Readjuster was content to accede to Dryddnaa's request to be allowed to deal with the children herself.

Dryddnaa had no doubts about Lerinda's professional skill and offered the Junior Readjuster advancement to the ranks of Senior Readjusters, on two conditions. The first was easy: to continue supporting the parents of Tamina and Wrenden as a friend and without mentioning Dryddnaa's interest. The second was to moderate how Lerinda expressed her less conventional views regarding treatment. Dryddnaa explained that she foresaw a time when, under the leadership of the Arch Custodian, there would be a steady return to Aurigan values when the more moderate and less intrusive readjustments that Lerinda favoured would be appropriate.

It was with a wry smile that the Chief Readjuster acknowledged that, as Lerinda knew, it was those very views that had held back her progression which were now seen as indicating she was the best person to help her friend's whole family.

Yarannah was angry with her children for risking their lives. She did not go as far as the Kumelanii and consider the twins to be abominations, but was uncomfortable around them and did not like the close esting relationships that had been formed by both

Tamina and Wrenden, effectively each with both twins. Were she to be honest, she would say that she feared the twins intensity and power.

She strongly disliked her inherited Uddîsû genes. "Reconciler" was the polite epithet for what Léshmîrâ Kûsheÿnÿ had achieved. There were far worse names that reflected the totally unAurigan ways by which the Heroine had restored unity amongst what the Aurigani had become after the Space Wars: several disparate and almost warring tribes.

She feared that Tamina's increasing involvement with rescuing the twins would lead to a strengthening of the influence of those genes – with what she saw as disastrous consequences for her daughter. And now she was in a state of barely suppressed panic in the expectation of the serious retribution that was going to fall on her children and inevitably herself and her husband.

She was taken aback when Lerinda explained that Yarannah needed to change her approach and actually encourage her children in their attempts to rescue the twins. Her children's undoubted talents and bravery were being seen at the highest level of the Custodians' Inner Council as attributes seriously lacking in the adult population and how, with a little careful guidance, they could easily achieve adulthood with only the most minor inhibitions being applied – or even none at all.

The two women had been friends from childhood and Yarannah had trusted Lerinda from the beginning when she had said that she was not acting in her official capacity as a Junior Readjuster, only as a concerned friend. She reassured Yarannah that her children's' devotion to their BestFriends was seen as admirable, even if a little misguided due to their youth. She was also happy to be able to say that there was not to be any punishment or readjustment for anyone as a consequence of their actions. A bemused mother accepted being coached by Lerinda in a change of tactics.

Part of that change was for Yarannah to provide all possible information about what her children and the whole of the twins' family were doing. Lerinda explained that this was to enable her to best calculate such subtle adjustments as might be necessary to allow her to help the children ease their way through the current troubles and on to an unhindered and hopefully unadjusted adulthood.

Absolutely unprecedented in all Tazian history, it had only taken two days for Ceegren's compromise proposal to be agreed by the Spiral Assembly, put to all Tazii across the MentaNet and accepted. The energy behind that speed made the decision far more compelling than that applying to the long-winded and invariably convoluted agreements that were the normal feature of Tazian life.

Mentally, emotionally and psychically the twins' family were stymied in their rescue attempts. It was impossible even to think of acting against that imperative.

Meanwhile, Curious Shop waited. Although a TransSentient programmed with consciousness, It was not part of the MentaNet. It had Its own very specific programming. And to fulfil that, CuSho needed Its two Keepers. Not yet adults, the four friends were not yet fully integrated into the MentaNet, and Tamina and Wrenden also possessed powerful Uddîšû genes.

CHAPTER 91

HONING SKILLS

FINLAND

Needing a break from all that had happened, Qwelby had spent most of Saturday and Sunday after dark with Hannu and Anita, watching videos and playing games on computers and games consoles. Although any involving killing were total anathema, he had finally discovered he could enjoy wrestling and similar games where there was no death.

Feeling into the movements as he played had reminded him of what he had discovered about Tamina's BodyDance, and awoken in him a sense that he knew it was ancient Aurigan self-defence, in which he had been skilled. With a sense of game-play fantasy, he sank into the feeling of being a DragonRider. In no time at all he had beaten Hannu in every game and then outplayed the games themselves on their highest experience level settings.

When the games console shut down with what sounded to Hannu like a human whimper, Qwelby had smiled, picked it up and gently caressed it, murmuring in Tazian. 'Electrons tired,' he had explained in response to his friend's query. 'Cannot keep pace with my faster quantum energies. I help them reassume normal vibratory rates.' He had put the console down, adding with a soft smile, 'They okay tomorrow.'

The success of Anita's guided journey enabled Qwelby to pinpoint from satellite images Tullia's almost certain location. Research provided a basic plan for the journey to reach her, along with the realisation of the difficulties of living in a world that used money and required copious paperwork in order to travel.

Hannu had produced three good ideas. Qwelby was to use his energy powers to influence gaming machines to pay out the jackpots, then take that money to a casino and play card games. For identity papers he would use a genuine passport, slip into the mind of whoever looked at it and make them not see that his picture and other details were stuck over the owner's.

At home they successfully practised with Hannu's identity card. Azuran playing cards were not Shielded. With headache producing intense concentration, Qwelby discovered he was able to "read" the energy signatures of individual cards. He was confident that with more practice not only would it be easier, he would also be able to read the card on the top of a pile and then cards held in a person's hand.

Early on in working with Dr Keskinen he had discovered that most Finns spoke to some degree both English and Russian. Checking his compiler, he found that it had effectively created a Tazian/Finnish grammar and dictionary. Urged on by Hannu and Anita, he used the variety of English language material they had and very rapidly his compiler was making him fluent in that language, without nearly as much discomfort as when he had been learning Finnish.

With so much of the scientific work that Dr Keskinen was researching being in Russian, Qwelby packed his compiler with the necessary grammars and dictionary. He admired Gumma's skills when he discovered how easy it was to switch between the Azuran languages without muddling them up.

Monday, while his friends were at school, Qwelby spent the day trying to understand more of Earth. He was disheartened by what seemed to be an endless diet of violence, killing and torture for reasons he found inexplicable.

From what his friends had said, unwittingly reinforced by Dr Keskinen and brief dips into Science Fiction films, it was clear that he was incredibly lucky to have found families who not merely accepted him, but liked and protected him. It seemed as though anyone else, and especially "The Authorities", would kill him as soon as they knew he was an alien.

In his mind, with their uniforms, badges and guns, the police epitomised The Authorities. The nearest Tazian society came to uniforms were the varying styles of simple tunics and shorts worn by Acolytes, Servitors, Apprentices and the robes worn by many Tazii on special celebratory occasions.

People's jobs and status were generally reflected in the colour spectrum and strength of their auras, although several professions wore discreet badges. The winged unicorn's horn denoted Healers; the happy face indicated Readjusters; and Persuaders, who were the nearest Vertazia had to any sort of police force, wore a round shield with a dragon.

He knew he could travel the world pretending to be Finnish, but he was terrified that something would go wrong, or he would make a simple, basic mistake leading to him being seized, tortured, experimented on and killed. There, his two friends had been unable to reassure him.

CHAPTER 92

A SKIRTLET

THE KALAHARI

With Tsetsana's help, Tullia worked on the plain kudu loinskin she had worn for the hunt, which was now hers to decorate as was appropriate for a young woman. The skirtlet consisted of two pieces suspended from a belt. The front piece was always roughly triangular in shape, the back piece square or rectangular. Although the San had never developed a written script, foreign researchers had used the Roman alphabet to record the various languages which the San now used. Tullia saw that using those letters would fit the design of the skirtlet and make a very important pattern.

The girls trimmed the front to form a perfect V-shape for Vertazia and emphasised that by edging it with two fine lines of bright, white, ostrich shell, then added a central pattern of dark and light brown seeds making the letters T and Q intertwined.

They trimmed the back piece into a neat square with gently scalloped edges and added a large letter O with a letter X inside and just touching the circle. A mixture of ostrich shells and light brown seeds were used for both letters to represent two of each. Two smaller letters N in dark brown seeds were set inside the circle to the left and right of the X. Tullia happily explained why the name XOÑOX was so important.

Never having seen the need to develop their own written language, the Meera had never used letters for their designs. Unbeknownst to Tullia, Tsetsana saw the design for the front not just as making a statement of how much Tullia was joined to the Lord Kaigii but as a powerful dedication to him of her fertility. When Tullia first wore her skirtlet, the whole tribe was to make the same assumption.

Later events were to leave Tsetsana deeply regretting that she had not shared her understanding with other women at the time, rather than waiting for the impact the design was to make when Tullia wore it after the Moon Day celebrations.

Tullia was shaken by the changes that were taking place within her and needed company. She felt guilty that for the first time in her life she did not want her twin with her. She wanted Tamina. Shyly, Tullia asked Deena if Tsetsana might sleep with her instead of in her usual communal hut of girls and unmarried women.

Deena spoke to Kotuma, the tribe's senior woman, and returned to say that permission had been granted and for as long as was needed.

CHAPTER 93

WHERE TO HIDE?

FINLAND

The confrontation between Erki and Qwelby had given the investigators an easy excuse to ask questions. Both men were experienced and careful with their approaches. Nevertheless, the fact that there were two of them, both up from Helsinki for the weekend and evincing more than just a passing interest in the same inhabitants and new arrivals, that in itself became the subject of comment.

That fact was passed back to the Rahkamos. Some of their neighbours did that out of friendship or a sense of community, for others it was done with the hope that it would persuade the family to get rid of the dark-skinned intruder.

After eating on Monday evening, the Rahkamos gathered around the kitchen table to discuss what it meant that in addition to the Professor, others were now poking around. It felt sinister and dangerous. Whilst they were puzzling over who those others might be, there was a loud knocking on the back door, followed by Viljo's voice calling out and the stamping of feet. Seija opened the inner door and the three Keskinens entered.

'We need to talk,' Viljo said in a serious tone of voice. 'There's a lot more going on than Seija told Taimi this afternoon.' That was emphasised by the fact he had not taken the time to change out of the dark grey suit he had worn to work that day.

Seija shooed everyone into the living room. By the time they had pulled up chairs in a semi circle around the fire, Paavo came in with bottles of beer and soft drinks.

Viljo took a long sip and started. 'Everything is getting much more serious. I was called in to speak to the Director this afternoon. Professor Romain has not only heard about Qwelby's arrival, but also that he is claiming to be the son of Dr Jadrovitch. How, I do not know. The Director was very concerned to know what was going on and how I was involved.' He looked around all their faces. 'I've had to change our story. A lot.

'I said that Qwelby had knocked on your door holding a piece of paper with the name Dr Jadrovitch written on it. You remembered that at some time I had mentioned that Jadrovitch is a colleague, so you contacted me. Qwelby speaks a very few words of Finnish and told us that he had been dropped off by a car just outside your house, claiming he was Jadrovitch's son and was here for a holiday.'

His listeners nodded. Simple and easy to remember.

'As Qwelby has no papers we came to the conclusion that he is an illegal immigrant. We did not want to tell the authorities and get Jadrovitch into trouble before he had had a chance to explain the situation. The only contact information I have is the Institute in Czech, which was still closed for the holidays. Also I, personally, did not want to get the Institute involved. You were happy to let Qwelby stay with you as you have a son of a similar age and there was a mutual interest in science fiction, etcetera.'

There were murmurs of agreement and praise for his quick thinking.

'It gets worse. This evening I've just had a visit from the police Sergeant we met on New Year's Eve.' He looked at the three youngsters, seated as usual together on the settee. 'You'll remember Piia Sjöström?'

They nodded.

'It started as a courtesy call. She was impressed by what you children had done on New Years' Eve. And was especially grateful that when you were interviewed, you all kept to the story of being accidental bystanders and that the police had done all the work. She asked me to pass on her thanks to everyone.'

Qwelby heaved a big sigh of relief.

He grimaced at the puzzled looks directed at him. 'At my age telling lies on Vertazia is impossible – everyone would know. With you, no lies to tell. With the others, partial truths. But even that hurts. If the sergeant were to question me.....'

'You're afraid you might tell her the truth,' Hannu said.

Thinking of how he had felt compelled to tell the truth to Oona because of her lovely blue eyes and the warm feelings she engendered in him, Qwelby nodded, looking grim.

'Sjöström then went on to say that Romain had been to the police station early on New Year's Eve, asking about any unusual incidents. Again, the same story. Working freelance for CERN, exploring freak weather effects or something similar.' He gestured to his wife.

'As she and Viljo continued to talk, I had the distinct impression she was principally interested in Qwelby,' Taimi said. 'But for some reason was going all around the issue and not asking the questions she really wanted. She was particularly interested in what she described as his bright, cats-eyes.' Taimi turned to her daughter. 'Anita was helpful there.'

'I remember that night in the woods Hannu saying your family originated in Mongolia and what you said that first day with our friends,' Anita explained. She was blushing furiously as she looked into the alien's hypnotic eyes. From the first moment she had seen him, he had stirred feelings in her that made her uncomfortable. And when those gorgeous eyes looked into hers.... she did not have words to describe how she felt. 'So I said you came from Mongolia, that it was genetic and all your family were the same.'

'Sjöström nodded,' Tami said. 'It was like she didn't care what the answers were. Just wanted information to put in a report.'

'It must be to do with those two strangers,' Qwelby said with a tremor in his voice. 'The one who skied with us was very interested in me. And there was another man, all weekend. He seemed obvious to me. Amongst all the many colours people wear he was wearing mainly white with a little black. He was curious, observing....'

'A second man!' Viljo exclaimed, sitting upright.

'Yes. Saturday, he came into the café and sat behind us,' Qwelby replied.

Viljo looked even more worried. 'Who the devil are they?' He leant forward. 'I'm sorry. This has got serious. We must go to the authorities.'

'Dad!' Anita wailed.

'Or we get him away from here, soon,' he added, wanting, needing, a quick solution.

'I agree,' Paavo said in a heavy tone of voice.

'Dad!' Hannu exclaimed.

'I'm sorry son, but what you say you saw on Friday night has been on my mind ever since. What happens, Qwelby, if your twin comes here like you went to her, and all those bad people you've told us about. How do we know they won't break into our world? You and your twin did.'

Qwelby was about to deny the possibility. And then it hit him. What Paavo had said was possible! The girl he had seen holding Tullia back from stepping into the fire. Of course she had been in the Bubble. An Azuran as real and solid as Kaigii. And the dancers around the fire. And more. He remembered that he had not noticed the haziness of the boundary of the NullPoint. The whole tribe must have been included!

Qwelby felt his arm seized and found he was standing by the open door into the rear lobby, his hand on the handle.

'No. Not like this,' Paavo said in a firm tone as Qwelby turned to look at him. As Paavo stepped around him and closed the door, Qwelby shook his head and let his memory replay the last few words he had spoken.

"I mustn't let that happen to you. If your authorities take me, torture me, kill me. Even if Kaigii returns home she will only be half a person for the rest of her life. I can't do that to her. I must go to her." He stood staring wild-eyed, his chest heaving.

'Mum. Dad. We always go to some friends at half-term.....'

'No. Too long,' Paavo said, cutting short his son's suggestion and glancing at Viljo who nodded agreement.

There was an uncomfortable silence.

'I will phone Elsa tomorrow,' Seija suggested, giving Paavo a look that he knew meant woman to woman without men around to interfere. 'If I take Qwelby there, that will leave my husband and Hannu here, everything perfectly normal. I am sure I can trust my friends to keep the secret. What's more, they have a teenage son and daughter. Qwelby will be fine there.'

'He'll be seen,' Viljo pointed out. 'Whoever is watching him will follow.'

'We smuggle him out!' exclaimed Hannu. 'Just like in spy movies. The cars are in the garage. Qwelby can go in the back with blankets over him. No one will even know there is another person in the car.'

'If you go at night, it will be dark. When he's well away from the village he can sit up, no-one will be able to see him,' added Anita.

'Excellent, but it doesn't explain why he is no longer here.' Viljo dampened everyone's enthusiasm.

'Let's take the idea you mentioned, Dad,' Anita bounced with excitement. 'Whoever dropped him off, came back to pick him up.'

'When they found that Dr Jadrovitch had returned home!' added Hannu.

'It makes sense,' Paavo agreed. 'Qwelby obviously could speak to those people. He knew them. He was happy to go. They said there had been a mistake. Jadrovitch's return home was unexpected.' He stood up and spread his arms, as though appealing to them. 'If the Sergeant comes again. What were we supposed to do? Try and keep a boy here, against his will, when he didn't belong in this country anyway?'

'Can Anita come with us?' Qwelby asked. There was an energy between them that was just a little bit like what he had with Tullia. He was sure that her energies were helping him reach out to his twin. And he wanted company, teenage company and especially after his day with Oona, a girl's energy.

There was uproar. With her mixed feelings for Qwelby, Anita was pleading to be allowed to go. Having seen her blushes and once again uncomfortably reminded of her feelings for the alien, Hannu was arguing in strident tones against that and saying he should go.

With all his fears of Science Fiction aliens reawakened, Viljo was firmly refusing permission. Feeling uncomfortable, Paavo also denied permission. Taimi's voice cut through, explaining to Anita that the family were friends of the Rahkamos. It was not her place. Hannu almost sneered in triumph.

Qwelby was stunned. He realised from the energies flowing between his two best friends that they were seriously out of accord, but had no idea why. Except he had caused that. All three liked one another, just as he and his group of special friends on Vertazia did.

Now he knew what it was like to be close with a girl and had observed the colours in Oona's aura, he knew what his friends felt about each other. But then why were there all the cross-currents and undercurrents of hurt and other feelings he did not understand? He wanted to ask what he had done wrong.

CHAPTER 94

BITTER-SWEET MEMORIES

FINLAND

Qwelby's attention wandered back to his Sunday with Oona. Anita had been right. All Oona really wanted was to talk with him.

As they talked in the café at the top of the ski lifts she had cuddled up to him and slipped her arm through his. When he and his twin weren't competing or fighting they often hugged and held hands, after all, they were one.

With Oona it was different and nice in that different way. Looking into her bright blue eyes, with new and warm feelings running through him, he found he could not lie to her. So he told her the truth and was plied with questions about Tullia and his life on Vertazia.

'Please, Oona, don't tell anyone what I've told you,' he asked as they were stepping out of their skis when they arrived back at Kotomäki. He wondered what was wrong as she stood close, examining his face.

'You'll have to seal my lips,' she said.

He wondered how he was supposed to do that.

She lifted up on her toes and kissed him. It was awkward, her small lips fitted inside his. She leant backwards, peering at him. 'You've never kissed a girl?' she asked in surprise.

'Oh, no!' he exclaimed, pulling a face. 'With Tullia in my mind wanting to know what I was doing, it would be like kissing her.'

'She's not in your mind now is she?' Oona asked.

'Well..... no,' he replied.

Oona lifted her hands to the back of his head, pulled him down and started to kiss his thick lips.

Qwelby decided to join in.

When they eventually stopped to breathe, Qwelby was feeling dizzy. Oona gave a big sigh and rested her head on his chest. With one arm, Qwelby pulled her closer. He used that hand to pull the glove off his other hand and stroked her long, blonde hair where it fell below her bobble hat. He sighed and rested a cheek on her head.

That was something he did on rare occasions with Tullia when she let him play at being her big brother. Usually when she wanted comforting after a spat with Tamina. But this wasn't Tullia. It was Oona. And he was feeling warm inside in a new and exciting way. He was beginning to understand why youngsters liked the kissing games that were played at parties.

Eventually, they stepped back from one another. Qwelby smiled and took off one of Oona's gloves. He put all the ski sticks into her other hand, set both pairs of skis over one of his shoulders and, taking her ungloved hand in his, they walked back to her house holding hands.

Oona rested her head against his shoulder. She could not believe what was happening. At last she had snogged this cute guy. And he was an Alien! As they had skied back from Muurame she had began to wonder if he had been telling her some great fantasy. But now she knew it was true. She had never felt the way she did from kissing any other boy. And then there was the heat running through his hand into her whole body.

As she said to herself that she would keep his secret, a tingling sensation ran from the back of her head, past her ears and through to her lips. She had asked him to seal them and she knew that he had done just that. She didn't understand how, but he engendered in her a sense of trust. With a feeling of awe and excitement, she squeezed his hand in a silent acknowledgement of their bargain. And felt it squeezed back.

Reaching her home, setting down the skis, Qwelby rested his pair against the wall and took hers into the store at the back of the house. As he turned to step outside, he saw her shining face, bright pink cheeks and blue eyes glowing. He wanted to kiss her again. He sensed her energy field and felt the soft orange colours activating his aura as he swept her into his arms, bent his head and kissed her. He felt a hand at the back of his neck, pressing his head against hers, the other hand gripping his pony tail. He was burning up inside.

Now very firmly staying out of her mind, he received her feelings through their energy fields. He was dizzy. Bossed about by Tullia and Tamina, teased at times by Shimara, he had never imagined so much thrill could come from being with a girl.

He felt her little teeth biting his thick lip. Hot blood coursed through his veins. A roaring sound filled his ears. He heard a voice moaning. His voice.

Time stopped.

'You must go,' Oona said with a note of panic in her voice.

Once outside the house, Qwelby picked up his skis and sticks and made his way to the Rahkamos, all his senses in a whirl.

What had happened? What had he done? What had changed? As he had slowly come to realise that Azurii did not share thoughts like Tazii, he had stopped slipping into their minds. On Vertazia you only slipped into a person's mind to the level of their abilities. To do more at his age was not so much forbidden as virtually impossible. The inner Self stopped it. He knew she had been enjoying what they were doing. So what now?

He was hurting, confused and afraid of what she would say when next they met. He hadn't wanted to upset her. He liked her. For the first time in his life he liked a girl in a special away. School started the following day and he knew that meant every weekday. Was he going to have to wait until Saturday to see her again and discover what had gone wrong? How could Azurii possibly live their lives in such a way? It was terrible. No wonder they fought!

As awareness of his surroundings returned, Qwelby became aware of the strained atmosphere. The Keskinens were leaving. Hannu disappeared upstairs.

Qwelby wanted to be back home. Even if everyone closed their Privacy Shields, their auras would still reveal their principal feelings. Frustration arose within him. It was turning to anger. He wanted to hit out. And that shocked him. He gripped the back of a chair hard, the pain in his hands helping him maintain control. Not trusting himself to speak, he nodded to Paavo and Seija and went up to his bedroom.

Paavo locked the front and back doors, closed down the stove in the living room and went back into the kitchen where his wife was loading the last of the dishes into the dishwasher.

'If it's okay with Elsa,' Seija said, 'I'll go up on Friday after school, take Hannu as well and come back Sunday evening. That will help Qwelby settle in. And allow time for them to heal the rift that has opened between them.' She turned to look at her husband. 'For our son's sake.'

Paavo nodded. He would like Qwelby to leave sooner, but was torn by a strong feeling that he was failing the trust the boy had placed in him on that first night, when Qwelby had collapsed into his arms and he had carried the boy into the spare bedroom.

Delaying until the weekend made sense. It was a long journey and Seija would have their son's company on the return trip. He also was concerned about his son and hoped that a weekend together without Anita would allow the boys to resolve the problem.

'I will make it clear to Qwelby that he must not try and contact his twin whilst he is here. And even in the future only when he is well away from other people,' he said.

CHAPTER 95

ROMAIN PLANS

FINLAND

Monday evening, the phone call with Soininen concluded and a message sent to his assistants, Romain used his GlobeSynch to cast a virtual screen over one wall, on which he then projected a mosaic of screenshots and notional printouts of what had occurred on the two days in December.

Using his own bags, he made himself a mug of what his friends called "builders' tea", then spoke his commands to link the GlobeSynch with the main computer on Raiatea.

As he sipped his tea, a solid looking, three dimensional model of the immediate area around the event appeared across the floor of his room and a map of Northern Europe and the Baltic was projected onto a wall.

Continuing with verbal commands, he input a new set of data. A few moments later the model disappeared and a large expanse of blue representing the sea appeared on the wall map. Finland had disappeared along with Sweden, parts of Russia and Northern Europe. Romain nodded. Proof that whatever had appeared in Kotomäki was not the result of an object of the approximate mass of a teenager being teleported across Earth.

Restoring the model and the original map, he input another set of data. A complete hemisphere appeared over the model, filled with what looked like a sandstorm, each particle twinkling with an eerie light.

Another command and the sandstorm imploded. As it vanished there was a brief flicker of light. Romain ordered the scale of the model to be increased and a marker to be inserted indicating the locus of the collapsed sandstorm. Once again he nodded. The marker was showing the exact spot where he had found the hole in the snow.

He eased back in his chair and finished his tea whilst he absorbed what he had seen. The display confirmed that whatever had arrived possessed about the mass of the black boy and had come from another dimension. A parallel world. He smoothed his trim moustache. 'David. You are indeed a genius,' he said softly.

For a moment, he mused. If he accessed satellites and projected a sequence from around four p.m. on the twenty-seventh of December, he was sure Miki had the skills to hack.... No. That would take ages and there was no time. Besides, he was not a master criminal.

'Not quite, yet,' his inner voice said.

Hastily brushing that aside, he ordered up a three dimensional model of the area of the ghost image. Then had the accompanying data projected onto the wall as a real-time run-through. He leant forward and closely studied the data on its second run. Satisfied, he leant back in his chair and stroked his moustache.

He was certain that what he was seeing was the arrival in North West Botswana of something very much smaller. Given the indistinct nature of the image and the caveats inserted into the datastream indicating approximations and uncertainties, something with a very much smaller energy signature than a living being, almost certainly a small and solid object with a high probability that it contained electro-magnetic components. To his mind, it pointed to some form of communicator, locator beacon or something similar. The boy would need that. Romain would find it and have a very definite hold over him.

'Ah, the true Viking spirit emerges,' his inner voice said.

A sense of urgency ran through him. The event had happened close to the Tsodilo Hills. That was not very far from a major road and a series of small towns and large villages. There even was a village close to the Hills. Although the effects were small compared to the boy's arrival, surely someone must have detected something at the time? How long before news of that percolated to the media? And, his big concern, someone started linking the two events together.

That someone might be a scientist, a journalist or the security services. Thoughts of establishments like GCHQ, the listening centre at Cheltenham in England, sprang to mind. Again he stroked his moustache, this time as he complimented himself on all the security built into his communication systems so that no keywords of interest to such listeners were there to be heard.

He needed to act. Sooner rather than later. First get the boy to safety, then to Africa for his hold over him. His next steps?

He had a meeting with Erki tomorrow after school. There was no time to waste waiting for him to gather more information about the boy. But, he would go ahead with that, because.... one never knew.

Call on Dr Keskinen tomorrow evening. No advance telephone call. Take him by surprise. Appeal to him as a fellow scientist to help persuade the boy to accompany Romain to Raiatea. Use his knowledge of the boy's false story as a lever. Then whatever Keskinen said, call round to the Rahkamos and speak to the boy himself.

Taking a deep breath, he swung around to face a mirror. He looked into the eyes of his reflection and once more felt Rekkr Reginsen encouraging him. He licked his lips. If Soininen was right about surveillance, and Romain had to trust the PI on that, if the boy agreed to go to his island they would leave on Wednesday morning. If not, an urgent meeting with Franz and Pierre.

His friends would need time to set up a kidnap so he could not conceive of that happening before the following weekend. Closing down his GlobeSynch network he poured himself a second cup of tea. Slowly sipping that, he tried to stop his feelings of concern from turning into panic at the amount of time that was passing. A panic that might cause him to act in haste and make a fatal mistake.

CHAPTER 96

THE HAWKS DESCEND

FINLAND

Whilst Romain was talking with the PI, Chief Inspector Penti Harju was staring at the telephone he had just put down. After a few minutes he took a deep breath, picked it up and called Sergeant Sjöström. It was a couple of hours since she had reported her visit to the Keskinens, finished her shift and gone home. He apologised for disturbing her and asked her to come in for a short meeting, saying there was no need for uniform.

Sjöström arrived wearing a short green car coat over a roll neck sweater, jeans and trainers. Pleasantries exchanged, the sergeant accepted the offer of a cup of coffee. She did not want it, but needed something to do with her hands to help settle her nerves at the unexpected summons. Harju leant over his desk and explained.

'The Professor and the black boy have stirred a hornets' nest. A little while ago that SUPO agent briefed me on what he had seen over the weekend. Romain and the group of kids skiing, but the Professor being around them on several occasions at the drag or ski lifts. Too often for mere coincidence. And then again near them in the restaurant at lunchtime on both days.'

Sjöström wrinkled her nose. Policewoman and mother, she did not like the implication of that.

'Yes.' Harju acknowledged her unspoken thought. 'Now add in a man who got involved in skiing with them on Saturday, took them to a café and then was around all Sunday. It turns out he is an ex cop turned PI based in Helsinki.' He settled back in his chair.

Sjöström frowned in puzzlement.

'Almost as soon as Metsälä left I received a call from a very unhappy Chief. By the time he'd finished he left me feeling it was all my fault! He passed on two orders. Direct from the Interior Minister, to leave Romain and the boy well alone. From the office of the Prime Minister, to give all assistance to the "damned interfering Bears and Cousins", as he phrased it.'

'Russian FSB and American CIA,' Sjöström said, nodding.

'Arriving end of the week,' Harju said.

'So long? Surely at least the Russians could be here tomorrow?'

'Coming together via Helsinki.'

'Hah! Let's hope they spend more time spying on each other than on us!'

'I'm sure they will, Pia. The Yanks will think whatever it is the Ruskies have done it, and they'll be thinking the same of the Yanks.'

'Freya help us! They'll each be thinking we're siding with the other.'

'This is my patch, Pia. Our patch,' Harju said heatedly, again leaning forward over the desk. 'I don't like not knowing what's happening under my nose. And almost being blamed for it!' He sat back in his chair, forcing himself to relax. 'You said that you had asked Dr Keskinen to pass on our thanks to the other families?'

The sergeant nodded.

'Pia. Do you think it would be a nice gesture if you spoke to all the other families?'

She thought about that. She would be speaking to the Rahkamos, just to thank them, not ask questions. And out of courtesy check the injured boy had fully recovered. The Inspector had stood by her over the New Year's Eve fracas, he would stand by her again. Besides which, it suited her plans. It was her home town. She wanted to know what was going on, and although she had seen him in the house that night, she wanted to get a good look at the stranger in the daylight.

'Yes, sir, I think it would be. I'll do that tomorrow.'

CHAPTER 97

DESPAIR

VERTAZIA

Lungunu was sad. A sombre mood infected House and everyone in it.

The adults were engaged in a desultory conversation in the main gather room, trying to find a way around the total ban that had been imposed on attempts to communicate with and rescue the twins.

The four friends were in the XOÑOX gather room. With her eyes closed, Shimara was lying on a couch, her head resting on Pelnak's lap as he used her mind as additional processing power. He was pleased that he had understood how to use Óweppâ, their Talisman, to reach Tullia. Oblivious to all else, he was exploring how to use it without the energy being detected.

At the same time both not-twins were deeply unhappy at the level of violence they had experienced on three occasions, and twice when they had merely been in support of Tamina and Wrenden.

Tamina was thrilled to have been not just a single salamander, as she had expected when she became an adult, but a whole swarm of them moving with a fluidity that had revealed to her the full martial capabilities of what was euphemistically termed Advanced BodyDance.

She knew how much she loved Tullia and was disconcerted to discover the same depth of love for Qwelby. She saw the logic that they were Quantum Twins, but she still felt like his older sister and, anyway, she wasn't ready for relationships with boys.

Yet she had felt her power. The power of a full grown Fire Lady, Eras ahead of time. It had brought with it other feelings that were unsettling. Feelings she assumed were related to her Uddîsû genes. As a first step, she would discover by what other epithets "Reconciler" was known.

She had the power. She must use it. Her young brother would agree. About to get up from her chair she found herself stayed by a calming voice in her head.

'Patience Keeper,' CuSho said. 'Needs must your power be gentled.'

Wrenden was gutted that his Attribute was only an adult version of himself and despaired at his stupidity in firing a disintegrator at the Šèdûmaii. That his life had been saved because his Attribute possessed the Hero's skinergy suit was a consolation he would come to accept in time.

Pacing up and down the room with his fists clenched, his outburst demanding immediate action, he was stilled by a reassuring voice in his head.

'Patience Keeper,' CuSho said. 'Action only when a concatenation of events indicates the time is appropriate.'

Shield! Tamina thoughtsent to her brother as she grabbed his hand, and they tightbanded their thoughts. *A tunnel to Azura through the sixth Dimension. Pelnak can work out how. XOÑOX. We have the power.* They shared what CuSho had said to each of them. *We are Keepers. Not shopkeepers. We will decide when.*

Sis! Your eyes!

What?

Your ovals. They're full of flames.

Tamina grabbed her brother's other hand. Holding both, she looked deep into his aventurine green eyes. *Help me gentle my power.*

Why not?

They grinned at each other.

CHAPTER 98

XAALA IN DENIAL

VERTAZIA

Back at Ceegren's estate, her duties finished and safely ensconced in her own suite for the night, Xaala at last had time to review her latest encounter with the twins, explore her feelings and consider what she had learnt about the Azurii.

The contact with Qwelby had evoked stirrings. If they were what she thought, she did not want them. And certainly not because of a boy who had the well-built body she'd failed to build for herself! They'd fought before, yet he had still tried to save her when she didn't know what was happening. She was unable to put out of her mind the sight of his gorgeous eyes. They had been so full of caring – for her.

'And I sensed his stirrings – for me.' Saying aloud what she'd felt, helped pull her out of her confusion and focus on her mission, and see that he had handed her a weapon. Her female Form was a tool to be used by her strong male genes.

If they return to Vertazia, I will use those feelings and draw him to me. I will have to kiss him and slide my smaller mouth inside his so that I can breathe Ice into him. With his Fire nullified, I will slash through his mind, cutting the bond with his twin. After all, I had a brother. I know exactly where that link resides.

With him "no longer available", Tullia will be desperate for another bonding. I will provide that. With her magnetism and my mental skills we will have so much power – and I will be in control.

She calmed her racing pulse. The plan for them to return is just a compromise. The Tazii must see that the twins cannot be permitted to return with their so obviously degraded DNA.

Xaala licked her lips. The Azurii. Terrified of aliens, believing they are all intent on destroying their world. The twins with their so very different eyes. Obviously alien. Find the boy. Slip into the minds of the nearest Azurii, let them see him as a rapacious, shape-changing, fire-breathing dragon. And.....

'Aieee!' She stifled the cry as red hot pain lanced through her head.

It was a complete ten-day since a shocking solution had presented itself. The consequences of her thoughts being discovered were too terrible to consider. She had buried them so deeply within her personal Privacy Store that they were no longer available for recall. Except now that a similar line of thinking had opened the doorway to the depths of her mind.

She broke out in a heavy sweat as she slammed the door shut on those thoughts and headed for the neutron shower. Although clean when finished, she needed to do more to relax. There were times when all the Tazian technology was unable to replace natural techniques.

After hanging up her DarkSuit, she selected a flask of her favourite oil with its gentle, natural perfume and proceeded to massage it into her skin. Catching sight of her reflection she tilted her head to one side. She wasn't sure if she liked the physical changes she saw. Her breasts were a little larger and her hips a little wider.

Still breathing deeply as she restored control, she watched her breasts rise and fall and recalled how they had felt when thrust against the boy's muscular chest. The experience had been far from the disgusting feeling she had let Ceegren perceive.

And there was something more. Can he have been Awakened? Surely not at his age! Perhaps he will like a slim girl because I'm different from his beautiful twin. I am not yet Awakened and have programmed myself so that will not happen for another two years. My body has its feelings, but my mind is safe. Although a Quantum Twin, he will not have my skills and the power of my inherited genes.

Xaala was almost seventeen, with the power that came in the final third of any phase, and exceptionally strong in what was her creative phase. Added to that was all she had learnt from recent events as she had experienced power in a new and vibrant manner.

She recalled the words of Insûmâne Haa-Zeyló describing the Ice and Fire that those who were divergent would suffer, and felt a positive thrill run through her body at the inevitable prospect of experiencing the side effects of Ice and Fire as she dealt with Qwelby.

'Aieee!' she cried aloud. 'I don't want feelings for the boy,' she almost shouted to Image, who raised one eyebrow in a sardonic gesture. She raised her fists to hammer on Mirror, and stopped, angry at her loss of control.

She put her fists to the sides of her head. 'Quantum Twins. Identical boy and girl. My feelings for one are the same as for the other. No! No! No!'

CHAPTER 99

ROOTS

THE KALAHARI

Tullia came half awake, her body hurting all over. Surely the two days she had spent learning the duties of a woman had not been that physically exhausting? A head was resting on her chest. Only one head? Where was her other twin?

The head lifted and Tullia sighed with relief as the pressure on her tender breasts was eased.

'Tsetsana?' Tullia asked as, fully awake, the feeling of her own twin babies slipped back into Deep Memory, leaving her with the sensation of a pleasant dream.

'Mmm,' her young friend murmured. 'Pain gone.' She opened her eyes. 'It's happened,' she said, her voice conveying a mixture of relief and joy.

Tullia groaned as pain stabbed through her belly and sides, spiralled up her spine and into her head. And groaned again as a million tiny pains shot through her body. She pushed herself to sit up as vibrations rippled through her loins.

'Happening,' she gasped. 'Help. Hold.' She reached for Tsetsana's hands and gripped them. She knew she must be hurting her friend but she needed the support. She knew the theory of what was happening to her inside. But what she had been taught at college had been only the physiological details, no mention of how it would feel. And she was a Quantum Twin. No-one was able to prepare her for how different that might make her.

She heard herself giving little yips of pain and felt the sweat running down her body. A mighty groan, a cry of 'Kaigii' and she collapsed forwards, throwing her arms around her young friend, breathing deeply. For a moment she wondered if all was well with her twin, who had said he also was Awakening.

As her breathing eased, she let go of Tsetsana and ran her hands across her body. It was as the text books said it should be. The first stage of becoming a woman. It would be several years before the second stage, when she would be able to produce an egg, if and when she wanted a baby.

'Happened,' she said, relieved and happy. She took Tsetsana's head in her hands. 'Udadai,' she said. 'Sisters. Very special sisters.' Remembering awakening on another morning with Tsetsana in her arms, she placed the fingers of one hand on her friend's lips. 'Okay for girls to kiss,' she said with a smile. And they did.

An excited Tsetsana got off the bed and dragged Tullia to the door of the hut. Looking out, they saw Deena sitting by the little family fire, looking at them with the spoon that she had been using to stir the milimili still in her hand.

Nods and smiles all round and Deena got up and walked away. She returned a few minutes later to say that Neame had announced that a Moon Day was to start at first light of the second sunrise.

Later that afternoon Tullia was taking a few moments in her hut for a rest in between learning her woman's duties when Kotuma arrived.

'Police Inspector who brought you home wants to speak with you,' the Chief's wife said. 'Tyua'llia, you now Meera.'

'I Meera,' Tullia replied, puzzled at what seemed to be a question rather than a statement.

'The Chief says you must answer carefully. As at interview with Americans,' Kotuma issued the instructions swiftly as they walked towards her family hut. 'You from tribe.... Tazii?'

'Yes, Tazii,' Tullia answered with a shaky voice as she saw that in addition to the man she thought of as Sah sitting with Ghadi, five more policeman were standing around.

Ghadi introduced Tullia as !Gei-!Ku'ma, Woman Chief of Tazii of Red San. Inspector Modisakgosi introduced himself and started to ask questions similar to those asked by the Americans. Although he insisted on clear answers he learnt little more than on his previous visit with Ghadi.

Tullia's arrival now fourteen days ago was confirmed. She explained the disturbances to the telephones and cameras as due to her high energy, a feature of all the members of her tribe. She confirmed she was the last female and that she was seeking !Kwe-!ku'gn, the last male, as they had become separated on a long journey.

'Lord of the Red Bush,' Ghadi translated for the Inspector's benefit.

For the Inspector there was too much in her replies that was vague, evasive or where she said there were no words to describe what had happened. Tullia's energy field was excited and her whole body sweating with the continual distortions of the truth. Mentally adding caveats such as "On Earth", was not really helping her maintain a sense of calm.

Finally, when Tullia was unable to produce any identification papers or say who could vouch for her outside of the Meera, the Inspector announced he was taking her to the police station in Shakawe. She was to be held there whilst further enquiries were carried out.

Tullia leapt to her feet with an incoherent babble in a soaring voice that would have done justice to anyone auditioning for the part of Brünnhilde.

Everyone was on their feet as they heard Tullia apparently singing of her distress.

Slowly, Xameb and Kotuma calmed the girl, and as she recovered an element of self-control she remembered to engage her compiler in Meera.

'Bushman who capture me, say police put him in metal box and kill him,' she almost yelled, gripping tightly to Xameb.

Calm was restored amongst much explanation and everyone sat down, Tullia still fiercely holding on to Xameb. They spoke together in soft voices as the Shaman explained in sad tones about the conditions in the jail. Sad, as he had visited Shakawe on more than one occasion whilst seeking to help Bushmen being held there. Answering her questions, he explained about locks and keys. For a moment he saw Tullia's deep purple orbs disappear as her ovals became totally violet.

Her eyes returned to normal. 'Easy. I open lock and escape,' she said.

'Do not come back here. First place they look for you,' Xameb told her. 'Can you find your way to where you killed the kudu?'

Tullia's ovals again turned violet as she sank into memories of the several days she had spent in the bush. Her latest day with Xara and the hunters had been as much about learning how to know where she was amongst the endless vista of bushes and unremarkable trees as honing her tracking skills. And she had all the mental maps she had created. 'Yes,' she said. 'I go there and wait.'

Responding to Ghadi's request, Xameb helped Tullia to her feet. 'Little power, little fear, gain respect. Large power, large fear, not good,' he said looking into her eyes.

Tullia tilted her head to one side. Fear of people? Not at home..... Ah. What Kaigii and I think, say, do, discover in the SubNet community. Dangerous. Readjusters. She nodded.

Kotuma explained that the Inspector had agreed to Tullia taking her bedding and cleaning items with her. Also, she and Tsetsana were allowed to visit to take food and other items Tullia might need.

Ditau was quick to offer to escort Tullia to her hut. The young constable wanted to talk to her when she was in the station's jail. He found he could not refuse when she asked him to carry the blankets that made her bed, and felt warmed by her smile as she tucked the top one under his chin.

As she followed Ditau out of the hut she was breathing deeply into her Kore and carefully felt for her twin. He was there, stronger than before. Still no easy thoughtsharing, but a solid presence, that of a strong young man. Home. She stopped walking.

Her family was scattered all around Vertazia, only meeting twice a year at each equinox. Here, she had a much larger family, a whole tribe to support her. Her tribe.

But....

Her home was with Kaigii.

We are Kaigii. *'QeïchâKaïgii,'* a voice whispered in her head.

Being one. But a different oneness. An old, even an ancient oneness. Of course, Tullia reasoned to herself. That's why part of me has never been that concerned about returning to Vertazia. I could live here...... anywhere! As long as we are together. One.

Violet ovals returned to their normal pale blue and her purple orbs reappeared. As Tullia's vision was restored she saw the concerned look on Tsetsana's face. 'Kaigii stronger,' she said, placing a hand just under her hearts.

Taking a deep breath and wishing she had the time to explain what she was offering her wise young friend by what she was asking her to do, Tullia stepped up to Tsetsana and took both of her hands in her own. 'Think of me.' She bit her lip. But should she? She flicked to Qwelby's space in her mind. It was warm. 'And Kaigii.' She was about to add "Please" when she saw the light in Tsetsana's eyes.

'Help bring you together,' Tsetsana said in almost a whisper as her heart turned a somersault. She had vowed to herself that she would do anything to help bring them together. Now she was actually being asked to do that. To join her big friend with the great dragon warrior Lord Kaigii. The San hardly ever cried, but it was with tears in her eyes that Tsetsana watched her friend get into the Land Rover and be driven away.

CHAPTER 100

RESOLVE

FINLAND

Qwelby was relieved to get into his bedroom and let the cool air help calm his emotions. He was sad that he had to leave the people who were protecting him and be with strangers. Be without Anita who helped fill the awful hole that was the lack of his normal connection with Tullia. And without Hannu who'd become a mate like Wrenden.

It didn't feel right. That was running away. He hadn't run from any of the fights on Earth or in the seventh dimension. He wasn't going to start now. He and Tullia had to return home and reveal the truth. There was going to be opposition, but they had to help their people free themselves from all the inhibitions imposed by.....

'A dictatorial clique whose actions reveal contempt for the democratic values on which Tazian society is founded,' he said aloud.

'Labirden Xzarze! Where did those words come from? But it's true! Then the Tazii will be free to go forward and we will have saved our race from its downward spiral into extinction!'

His head spinning, he sat on the bed to collect his thoughts, ticking them off on his fingers.

'One. Under the old palace, out of that confusing Deepstate, I understood one clear message. The way back home is through the sixth dimension.

'Two. That means Óweppâ and our BestFriends. XOÑOX. That means Kaigii and I must be mentally reconnected.

'Three. Our friends know where Tullia is, so that confirms my plan to go to her.

'Four. To pass through all the passport controls and other things, I need her in my mind, helping me. So we have to mentally reconnect before I leave Finland.

'Five. We have to find a way to do that, that doesn't result in an attack so strong we cannot win.'

Imagining his Aurigan hand he ticked off one more.

'Six. Playing card games with my friends at home and with them knowing I'm using my energy skills is one thing. In a fancy Casino and, well, cheating with people watching. I need Kaigii in my mind for that.' He took a deep breath

'So. I have until Friday afternoon to get the money for my trip to Helsinki, and until Saturday evening at the latest to reconnect with Tullia. Everything else is too much and too confusing. It will have to wait until we are together and we can build one of our problem solving pyramids.'

His shoulders relaxed as a weight lifted off him. He had a plan and a clear focus. Standing up, he looked in the mirror. To help him imagine Tullia facing him, he spread out his hair as he released it from his pony tail. 'I will do whatever it takes, Kaigii. I will get to you, and we will get back home. We will tell the truth.' Feeling silly but knowing she could not hear, he added in a whisper. 'I love you.'

With her long plaits falling over her shoulders almost down to her waist, Tullia smiled at him and fluttered her long eyelashes.

Qwelby laughed with joy. How that had happened he didn't know. He didn't care. He knew it was real as he would never, ever image that!

'*QeïchâKaïgiï.*' This time the whisper in his head was full of soft laughter and carried an impression of the freshness of a new morning and an era lost in the mists of time.

CHAPTER 101

PRISONER

THE KALAHARI

The Land Rover set off, Tullia once again sitting in the middle between Ditau and the Inspector. Heading into a big unknown, she was frightened. Her hormones, her genes so recently and strongly activated, saved her by triggering a pattern repeat. As on her previous journey she concentrated on the track, her mind recalling all she had learnt from the Inspector. Nervous, she talked and the two policemen answered.

By the time they reached the end of the track Tullia knew about the army and the police and guns, Botswana in general, Shakawe in detail, the Inspector and his family and that Ditau lived with his grandmother. 'A really old lady who knows all about the old days,' was the young constable's description.

As they turned onto the wide strip of blacktop the sun was dipping below the horizon on the left hand side. For Ditau it was an easy run on a straight road, whilst the others closed their eyes and relaxed.

The Inspector ran through the events of the last few days in his mind. It was clear from the translation of what had been said in Meera during the interview with the Americans that the girl and her companion, Kaigii she called him, had done something wrong. The problem was no Motswanan spoke any San language well enough to translate. That had been done by a Meera. Xao was a good man, but his Afrikaans was not all that good and the text that had been produced was muddled. He would have Xao brought in and grill him.

Modisakgosi was sure he understood the situation. A pair of young San criminals who had been taken in by the Meera. A fantasy story for the benefit of gullible wazungu, white men, that then had to be repeated to him. The prospect of catching two criminals even before any arrest warrants were issued was compensation for yet another late night on the case.

Tullia was content with her plan. Ditau had been happy to explain about the Land Rover, the track had been straight, she had watched the sun and noted the distance. Later that night, with the strength she was able to draw on from Kaigii's solid presence, she would open the simple lock on the cell door and make her way to where she had killed the kudu. The police would not find her when they searched the village the next day. If Xara had not come by dark she would go to the village and be ready for the ceremony the following day.

She gave a sigh of relief and stopped thinking. Thoughts that had been nagging her for a while emerged into consciousness. Trying to connect with Kaigii had produced violent reactions from Vertazia. She sensed that the dragonfly was giving her a clue: to try a gentle approach. Her initial shock at discovering she was on Earth had now turned to strength. Living with the Meera and becoming one of them....

Her mind dizzied with a startling conclusion.

Now that she knew she was not on Mars, but Earth: the Meera, all the Bushmen, were they really direct descendents of the Auriganii? Even if not, especially if not, they were a peaceful and gentle people. And the men who had rescued her were not San.

The look of concern on the young soldier's face when he had tried to save her from falling out of the truck. The caring from V-Man. And once again the feeling of warmth from Sah and Ditau as they talked. She had seen guns but no-one had even tried to use them. Except, ironically, the Bushman.

Xashee had told her that those men came from different tribes: Tswana, Kalanga, Herero and many more in Botswana. The knowledge that there were so many different people demonstrating that the Azurii were not as violent as was taught on Vertazia was a startling revelation. Everyone she had met on Earth had been, well, peaceful. Yet again the irony was that the only one who had shown violence had been a Bushman. And he had not meant to kill his wife. It had been an accident.

Although that day in the bush he had threatened her, she was sure that he had never really intended to hurt her. It was as he had said. He was a good man who had done a bad thing. Tullia had heard that there were occasions when Readjusters did not detect negative energy signals in time to act and bad things happened. But those were rare and usually minor incidents. Azurii did not have the Tazian mental connections or Readjusters.

There was no Violence Virus! The stories of the violence of the Azurii were yet another deception practised by the Custodians. It was a lie! Lies were not part of Tazian life. Yet this was a massive lie! How many other lies were being perpetrated?

Another shocking realisation struck her as she saw that it was not all the Tazii through the Spiral Assembly who organised their world, but that the Custodians effectively and insidiously governed Vertazia. She shuddered at the unfolding prospect that her world was controlled by people whose attitudes were abhorrent to all Tazii. How old did you have to be to learn such secrets? And why was the situation accepted?

Control!

The tight Era and Phase-banded controls on growing up.

She was maturing faster and feeling much more freedom here on Earth, so growing up was not totally governed by DNA sequences reacting to the age-related release of hormones. Gallia had said that achievement of adulthood had been reduced from the end of the third Era to the end of the second, and with restrictions imposed on most adults. Restrictions which had never been applied in olden times.

Vertazia was not as free as she believed. In fact it was not really free at all. It was all tightly controlled. And all based on lies! The dream of restoring their Aurigan heritage. Was that just another way the Custodians had of exercising control? Whatever the truth, that possibility was millennia away.

Kaigii! They had to be together. They had to return home, tell the truth and save their race from its present descent into extinction that Gallia had explained.

To reach him through conventional travel she had to know where he was. She drilled down through her memory tags. <Finding> <Location> <Gumma> <Perturbation>. She smiled as she heard the Arch Discoverer's words giving a lengthy answer to what she had thought was a simple question. "A perturbation in the quantum field of a series of interlinked trans-dimensional states......"

That was it! The energies involved when they had met in the NullPoints meant that there must be a residual signature at each of their individual locations. After what had happened, surely those must be strong. And those two youths with the snowman they had seen from within the stairwell, they had been there behind him, outside the NullPoint, strengthening the signature.

'Kaigii,' she murmured, enjoying the image of the surprised look on his face when she reached him, proving what she always said – he did need her to look after him.

By the time they arrived at the station, Tullia was in panic. "Won't take long" had been true – for a vehicle travelling at speed on a good road. There was no way she could get back to the village even as late as the morning of the day after tomorrow. And the ceremony started at sunrise. It was with leaden feet that she made her way to a smelly cell with its four walls, a hard shelf, a bucket and a small, barred window. It all looked so permanent, and terrifyingly enclosing. 'How long will I be here?' she asked in a shaky voice.

'As long as it takes,' the Inspector answered gruffly.

'But I have a ceremony in two days time,' Tullia protested.

'Tell me the truth,' Modisakgosi snapped.

'But I am to become a Woman,' Tullia wailed, the tone of her voice clearly adding the capital W.

'That's your problem,' the Inspector said, raising a hand and moving towards the door into the main room.

'Please. You don't understand how important this is. My tribe....'

'Enough!' Modisakgosi shouted, raising both hands. 'Lock her in,' he commanded harshly as he backed out of the cell area.

Ditau went to put the blankets on the shelf but Tullia asked for them on the floor. He was uncomfortable as he straightened them out. He knew his granny would say the girl was a Siska, a powerful Extraterrestrial who had to be treated with respect. All he saw was a beautiful young woman who he wanted to get to know, holding herself erect with her hands clenched into fists at her sides as tears streamed down her face, her purple eyes boring into him, pleading for help.

'I.... sorry,' he mumbled as he left the cell.

Breathing heavily, Modisakgosi was standing at his desk, sifting through the papers that had collected on it during the day. Ditau entered to report that Tullia was safely locked up and had been handed over to the night duty Constable.

'Good job done today, Ditau,' the Inspector said as he placed the papers that needed his attention in the centre of his desk.

'We'll soon pack her off to the prison at Letlhakane. Send that boy to join her when we find him. Lord of The Red Bush. Pah! Gullible wazungu!'

The long journey would mean an overnight stop each way in Maun. He would stay with the younger of his two sons who worked there for a Tour Agent during the season. On the way to Letlhakane the girl would spend the night in the local police cells.

With his mind dwelling on the pleasure of spending two nights with his son, he swept a pile of routine, low priority circulars into a drawer. Stuck to the back of the bottom one by the wet ink from their old fax machine, a warning notice disappeared under the pile.

The notice was a report of disturbances experienced by two light aircraft taking tourists on sightseeing journeys around the Tsodilo Hills. Each was a different make of plane from a different agency and with a different pilot and both had suffered a total failure of all electrical systems. Fortunately, they had both been propeller driven machines flying high enough for the pilots to be able to restart the engines. The dates given for the events matched the dates in his report of Tullia's arrival and the failed photographs of the Female Hill.

Bidding good night to the Constables, Modisakgosi left the station smiling to himself at Ditau's comment that his granny would say the girl was a Siska. The Inspector was aware of the girl's similarity to the Extraterrestrials who were said to visit Earth, but not only was she far too solid, the fact that she was frightened showed she did not have any of the powers those beings were said to possess. Now, with the girl locked up and enquiries underway, he could safely discuss her with his wife and daughter. He wanted a woman's opinion.

CHAPTER 102

SWEET AND SOUR

THE KALAHARI   FINLAND   VERTAZIA

Tullia had remained standing, stunned into immobility as she heard the key turn in the lock, then footsteps and another door being closed and locked. She shivered and realised how cold she had become. Taking clothes from her bag she put on her thick sweater, sat on her bed and pulled on her tracksuit bottoms and socks.

'I have found my inner warrior, so I am balanced and can survive without help,' she told her prison cell. 'But I am a Quantum Twin and need to be reunited with Kaigii to be complete, because we are one.' She explored her Self and decided that what she had voiced about her independence was true. Exploring further, she decided that there was no weakness in admitting it would be nice to have the arms of a big, strong man around her. Kaigii. Hoping she was right about what she thought the dragonfly was telling her, she gently thoughtsent to him.

Qwelby recalled the few moments when he and his twin had held hands and the feelings that had flowed through both of them. So different in kind from what he felt for Oona. He wanted to be with Kaigii. Fearful of provoking yet more violence, rather than thoughtsend, he opened up to see if his twin was there.

Xaala felt a featherlike tickle across her mind. *The twins connecting! Unlike previous occasions, this was gentle. Even so, Ceegren would have me stop it. No. The more they share, the more she will feel his loss and the greater will be her need for comfort and support. I will ensure she turns to me for that.* A crooked smile crossed Xaala's lips. *As we share our pain at our mutual loss.*

First steps first, she admonished herself. *I need Rulcas working with me now, whilst they are still on Earth, to absorb those male energies reaching me so I can focus on the girl and insinuate myself into her mind. Two deviants together. Fire and Ice!* She shivered as cold energies ran through all her meridians.

Self-conscious about his lack of height, one of Rulcas' rules was that he didn't pull girls taller than him. But Xaala had humiliated him in front of his mates. He'd have to hang around long enough to put her in her place. Besides which, if the twins were that much trouble to the big bosses, he wanted them in his gang. The girl was tall. But he had to admit from what he'd seen of her, now in more than one LiveShow, she was one hot babe. He couldn't have any of his mates chatting her up before he did!

'What are rules for?' he said aloud, and grinned. 'To be broken!' He'd sort the mindjerking bitch and then make a play for Tullia. Have them fighting over him. 'Yeah!'

Tullia thanked the Quantum Field that Kaigii was there, strong and solid. She assumed that their mental connection was taking so long to reach full strength because of the slow vibrations of the third dimension.

Qwelby sensed a subtle difference in his twin's calling. A new independence that was matching his own, yet still a desire to be together. With warmth in both hearts he thoughtsent an image of the time on Vertazia when they had been in the stairwell and she had returned from her journey to what he now knew were the Bushmen, and she had let him comfort her.

Xaala jerked as she remembered Ceegren's fear of the twins returning with their degraded DNA bringing so much violence to Vertazia. And what she had said about their never being allowed to return. Contrary thoughts flowed through as she recalled her meeting with Dryddnaa and the Chief Readjuster's deep concern for the two damaged Tazii who she wanted to help – when they returned home.

Xaala had developed her own technique for dealing with a cacophony of thoughts and mental images. Now they also had to deal with her see-sawing emotions.

She stepped back and started to twirl, letting everything mix around inside her.

'Oh, Kaigii. I do need you,' Tullia whispered, as she felt his arms surround her.

'And I need you.' Qwelby sent her an image of him stroking her hair.

Xaala twirled and twirled.

Tullia sent an image of herself snuggled in his arms, one hand around his head, running exploratory fingers through his thick pony tail. *Cute* she thoughtsent as she fell asleep.

Me? Cute? She needs me, so she isn't her usual self.

But she was Kaigii. He was Kaigii.

He'd forgive her.

They were Kaigii.

'*QeïchâKaïgiï*,' the voice whispered in his head. The complex mixture of tones of the ancient Aurigan stirred a thought. Their mixed gender gene that Gumma thought was an effect from a higher dimension. Was that like the tip of the beak of a BorerBird from that dimension – meaning that there was a much bigger connection between them at the level of that higher dimension? This had to be a clue to The Mystery?

Overloaded with images, thoughts and emotions, Xaala collapsed on the floor. On hands and knees she crawled to the end of her Meditation Bench and pulled herself upright. Facing Mirror, she saw a tall and slender young woman, her body shining with sweat which emphasised the strength of her toned muscles. Her female Form, a good cover for the powerful male genes she carried.

Ceegren was right. It was too dangerous to allow the twins to return. It had to be the genes that Dryddnaa carried of the Heroine known as Reconciler that made the Chief Readjuster think otherwise. If Xaala arranged matters so that only one returned, then "the twins" had not. Mission accomplished!

She closed her eyes as she took a deep breath and reopened them to see Image. Golden sandals peeked from underneath a flame orange, off-the-shoulder, sheath dress that emphasised her female Form. The face was different from the previous occasion. This time she was Aurigan.

The beauty of her dark red skin, high cheekbones and heavily slanted eyes sent a river of heat flowing through the newly awakening cells in Xaala's body, and an evil smile appeared on Image's face.

Once again, Image's head morphed into that of a Lion. The rich, chestnut coloured orbs of its eyes flashed. Framed by a magnificent mane of fiery red hair, the Lion threw back its head and roared, revealing its magnificent teeth, sparkling like deadly icicles.

Xaala accepted the challenge.

Image disappeared to be replaced by her own reflection. Resting her hands on her hips and studying herself dispassionately she noted the richness of what were now her own chestnut coloured orbs. She could do it. When the twins were physically together to provide the energetic link she needed, she would go to Earth where…….. one way or another the girl would become distraught over the loss of her twin and turn to Xaala for support.

~*~*~*~*~

See you!
~

Dje'eymey
~

Sala sentle
~

Bye nyt
~

The effects of gravity and how it effects time are known and demonstrable, but the theory of how gravity works does not accord with current theories of quantum science, known as The Standard Model.

Scientists are searching for gravity waves and, at the time of writing, believe they may have found the first traces

Amongst the cave drawings dating back some 37,000 years there are clear images of hands with six fingers.

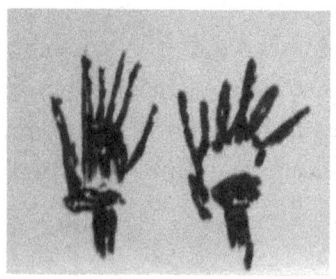 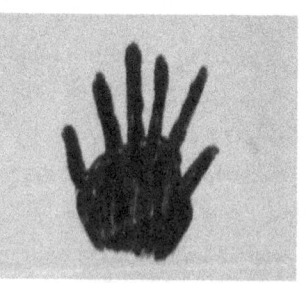

Pair of hands
about 27,000 years ago
Drakensbergs
Kwa-Zulu Natal

Single hand
about 37,000 years ago
Chauvet Caves
France

COULD THE TWINS BE TELLING THE TRUTH?

CHECK OUT THEIR WEBSITE

www.quantumtwins.com

where you can read more about them and their world, along with maps, photographs, notes on quantum science and the world of energy

You can tell us what you think via their blog

http://quantumtwins.com/blog/

The Twins' adventures continue in

BETRAYED

CHAPTER 1

FREEDOM

THE KALAHARI

Qwelby jerked awake with his twin's scream reverberating through his head.

Why?

Tullia was in his arms.

She wasn't.

?

Memories flooded in. Last night he'd sent her an image of himself wrapping his arms around her. He savoured the joy that their mental communication was slowly returning to their normal level where such imagery was physically real, even as her pain sent him hurtling along their thread of connection.

As he left his Form behind and moved into the seventh dimension, he morphed into his Attribute of a powerful dragon and burst into what looked like an office. An earthquake rocked the whole building as he saw the heavy metal door that seemed to be barring his twin's exit ripped from its frame and hurled to the floor with a loud crash.

'No, Kaigii. NO!' Tullia yelled.

Confused, Qwelby halted and watched as his twin tried to lift the door. Feeling her plea for help, he joined his strength to hers and saw his dragon's front leg reach out to the door. As he drew energy from the cosmos he felt as if it was being channelled by an enormously long snake.

They lifted the door. A slim, young man wearing dark blue and who had been lying on the floor, crawled to the door and dragged from underneath it an old man also wearing dark blue.

The twins let the door fall back onto the floor.

Qwelby recognised the three marks on the old man's clothing – a sergeant – of police. "The Authorities" he knew meant imprisonment, dissection and death. People on Earth believed all aliens were out to destroy them and therefore they would destroy any alien they met.

Contrary energy flowed from his twin, stilling his rising sense of panic as he realised that she cared about the sergeant and his injuries.

Both twins had inherited strong healer's genes from their mother and being a healer was what Tullia wanted for a career. Tullia called and Qwelby responded. They merged their energies in the seventh dimension and one pair of hands with their six fingers manipulated the vivid interplay of colours as healing wrapped around and through the sergeant's cracked ribs.

Qwelby was again aware of the sinuous feel of snake like energy adding more power to the healing, together with a hint of a connection to Aurigan times over one hundred and fifteen thousand years ago.

Time passed and the sergeant's ribs were mended. The twins' hands moved to his head. As they eased away the bruising and swelling that had caused the concussion, the merging colours seemed to give the sergeant a thick head of golden hair.

With the sergeant finally restored to health, Qwelby felt himself released from their at-one-ment and took in the rest of the room. Everyone's face was dark brown and the sergeant's wrinkled face the darkest of them all. This side of a desk, a young, teenage girl was staring open-mouthed at him, well really at Tullia he reminded himself. He watched as, also on this side of the desk, the young policeman righted a chair and then helped Tullia get the sergeant to his feet and settled on it. Although both were tall, Qwelby noted that the well built, middle aged man standing behind the desk and the young policeman were not quite as tall as his twin.

The girl's energy field was displaying a mixture of fear and wonder. He smiled at her startled look as Tullia placed a hand on her arm and infused her with calming energies, then saw her fear disappear leaving only a look of wonder in her eyes.

Qwelby felt himself being held there, his twin wanting the reassurance of his presence. He had been born knowing he had to look after her because she was only a girl. Just as she had been born knowing she had to look after him because he was only a boy. That had irritated both of them all their lives. The period of almost two weeks on Earth without any mental connection had made him start to see life in a different way. He smiled and sent that smile to his twin.

Realising a conversation was taking place and not understanding the language, he slipped into his twin's mind.

I'm not using my compiler, she thoughtsent.

I understand. Kaigii. Trust me to help you. I've had to.... dissemble, a lot. But I need your compiler to be working.

The twins' Great Great Uncle Mandara had created a micro-nano unit containing a programme that used a person's brain like the hard drive of a computer to compile the vocabulary, syntax and grammar of any language, and then act as a translator. He had given the first two he had made to the twins to evaluate. Each wore a unit inside one ear.

Having been warned by the both the Chief and the Shaman of the Meera tribe who had adopted her of the danger of letting anyone other than a Bushman know who she really was, Tullia was happy to agree. Reassured by her twin's presence she made a fresh start at an explanation. 'I sorry. I scream. Kaigii think I in danger. Kaigii strong here.' She put a hand on her chest in between her two hearts and thoughtsent to Qwelby, *Your arrival caused an earthquake.*

She went on to repeat the story she had told the police the previous day when interviewed in the village. Then, she had spoken in a mixture of Afrikaans and Meera, with the Shaman translating for her. Now, she spoke slowly and hesitantly in Afrikaans as Qwelby made occasional and judicious alterations to her proposed words.

The upshot was that Tyua'llia, *The name given to me by the Meera, the local San tribe who have adopted me,* belonged to a tribe called Tazii who believed they were the ancestors of all San, and she and one male were the only ones remaining on the planet, which was true. Her parents were ancestors, which also was true but was interpreted differently by the Africans. And she came from a long line of powerful healers, which again was true.

That fitted what the others were thinking. That Tyua'llia was a highly skilled N'om K"xausi or Sangoma and Kaigii was the name both of a powerful elemental in the otherworld and her companion, or possibly they were one and the same.

The Inspector, who did not believe in elemental spirits, had not changed his mind overnight. He still considered that she and her very real companion were running away from whatever trouble they had caused. He had never heard of the name of her tribe, which was not surprising if she came from Namibia. And that was logical because from her red hue he assumed the tribe was similar to the red-skinned Hiechware who were one of the oldest San tribes of Namibia, and that her height and build were probably due to one of her parents being a Himba, another Namibian tribe.

Tullia had remained standing with the constable, the Inspector's daughter and the seated sergeant. Taking comfort from the energy of acceptance she was experiencing from those three, she looked across to the Inspector standing on the opposite side of his desk.

'Please, Sah, ceremony tomorrow. I become woman.'

Your Awakening? Qwelby thoughtsent.

Yes.

Me too.

'Oh please Daddy, you have to let her go,' his daughter said as she turned to Tullia. 'You really want this, don't you?'

Tullia nodded.

Not wanting the traditional African ceremony herself, that her mother was determined she should have, the girl asked Tullia to explain why she wanted it. With Tullia's compiler rapidly building its dictionary and syntax of Afrikaans as they talked, she thought she understood the girl's words, but obviously not.

'You no mean... cut that.... off!'

'Yes........'

Tullia screamed.

'Kaigii. NO!' Tullia shouted as the building rocked and was again filled with the smell of plaster as more fell from the walls and a mug rolled off the desk and smashed on the floor.

Staring fearfully at Tullia, the Inspector's daughter moistened her lips. 'I do not want that,' she said quietly into the silence.

Tullia grabbed the girl with both hands and pulled her into a close embrace. 'Please, Sah. NO!' she said, looking at him over the top of his daughter's head.

Inspector Modisakgosi was taken aback by the power of the words that seemed to hit him physically. He was an educated man and did not believe in the stories of aliens in Africa or the superstitious rubbish talked about the powers of witch doctors. Yet he had just seen an earthquake happen in his own Station, a young woman lift an impossibly heavy metal door and then restore to health his sergeant, without actually having touched him.

And his own healing she had given him earlier that morning. The back pain was a minor but long standing problem. Gone. His shoulders had been getting increasingly rigid as the weeks of argument at home continued. He rolled them, amazed at the ease. And today's headache. The worst ever. Gone.

He saw the pleading looks in the eyes of the his daughter and..... his prisoner. He could not think of the tall and well built young woman as the fifteen-year-old she claimed to be.

If he was right with the assumptions he had made yesterday, she and her companion were criminals on the run and he would soon receive arrest warrants from Namibia. He had the girl and would arrest her companion when he came looking for her.

But....

© Geoffrey Arnold-Pinchin 2014

ABOUT THE AUTHOR

Born in Cheltenham, Geoffrey Arnold moved around the country during his career as one of HM Inspectors of Taxes - better known then by his full name of Geoffrey Arnold-Pinchin, and for his bright ties; which included The Scream, he likes all sorts of art; Tom & Gerry, he prefers silent cartoons; The Pink Panther playing tennis, his favoured sport; part of the score of Finlandia, he likes a wide range of music; and an 'in your face' saxophone.

He lives in Birmingham with his wife and near his children and grandchildren, which means he only has to wait for one person to leave the house before he retreats to his insulated, neighbour-friendly loft with his saxophones and clarinet. The other half of his family lives in Somerset, providing him with a perfect writing retreat amongst more youngsters.

Before young children came along, he spent many years working with youngsters, then in amateur theatre and politics.

Now, he is a Medium, Astrologer, Counsellor, NLP Master Practitioner, Life and Business Coach, and very occasionally a Tax Consultant - gamekeeper turned poacher!

He says that meeting the Twins has made a major impact on his life, not least in trying to keep up with the science behind the stories they tell him. More of that on:

www.quantumtwins.com

where he would love to hear from you.

Geoffrey's personal website:

www.geoffarnold.co.uk